Praise for Thom Madley's
Marco's Pendulum

'...a gripping read: a thriller-cum-detective story peopled with ultimately convincing characters and leavened with plenty of unforced humour.'

Books for Keeps

'The author blends local history and folklore together with a fast-paced plot to make magic and fantasy believable.'

Carousel

'Complex and enticing... It is compulsive reading, a very exciting and fascinating narrative... It could appeal to fans of such books as those of Robin Jarvis or Garth Nix and to boys and girls equally.'

School Librarian Journal

'A page-turning read.'

The Book Pl@ce

MARCO
AND THE
BLADE OF
NIGHT

THOM MADLEY

USBORNE

Thanks to Rick and Claire Kleffel of Santa Cruz, and to
John Moss of the British Society of Dowsers, Malvern.
Thanks to Megan Larkin, Rebecca Hill and The Cat,
as ever, for working it all out.

First published in the UK in 2007 by Usborne Publishing Ltd.,
Usborne House, 83-85 Saffron Hill, London EC1N 8RT, England.
www.usborne.com

A CIP catalogue record for this book is available from the
British Library.

JFM MJJASOND/07
ISBN 9780746076989
Printed in Great Britain.

Part One

'When I went to live at Glastonbury, I heard
that the place was "sleepy" and even "dead".
That has not been my experience.'
GEOFFREY ASHE
Avalonian Quest

That Hill

GLASTONBURY

Sometimes, life could be seriously unfair.

For about as long as he could remember, Marco had wanted to see an Unidentified Flying Object. Didn't matter what kind: glowing orb, shiny spinning disc, cigar-shaped shadowy thing on the horizon.

Any kind of object, basically, as long as it was flying and, like, unidentified.

So *why*, when something seriously weird had appeared in the big, wide, luminous sky over Glastonbury, did it have to happen not to Marco, who'd spent hours at his bedroom window checking out coloured stars and night planes, but to someone like *this* guy.

The evening air was getting thick and Glastonbury Tor was growing dark. Mr. Cotton, the solicitor, glanced at it over his shoulder as if it was about to mug him from behind.

'Bit alarming,' he said. 'Never seen one before, as you might imagine. Indeed, wouldn't normally come anywhere near here...*that hill.*'

Which, with that suit and that tie, really didn't need saying at all. There were two kinds of people in this town: the Avalonians, who loved the Tor, and the Glasties, who wished it was on the edge of some other town. Preferably hundreds of kilometres away or, better still, abroad.

Generally speaking, the Avalonians looked like Woolly and the Glasties looked like Mr. Cotton.

'Go on then,' Woolly said. 'Tell us.'

'Hmm... Well...'

Marco sighed. His dad was a lawyer, too. It always took them for ever to get to the point. Mum said this was because they were usually buying time to think of a convincing lie, but maybe that was just about Dad lying to Mum.

Eventually, Mr. Cotton told them how he'd had to visit this client at one of the farms and, unfortunately, his car was being serviced.

'Pleasant evening, however. Walk across the fields seemed in order. Set off along one of the paths from Wellhouse Lane, about 6.30 p.m. Sky began to go dark. Very sudden. *Very* sudden.'

It was odd. Blokes who spoke all the time in this professional sort of mumble never seemed to get wound up.

So Marco was quite shocked when he saw something that could only be fear breaking out like a cold light over Mr. Cotton's smooth face.

* * *

The guy had phoned Woolly about an hour ago, asking if they could have a private talk.

Not in the town, though. Apparently, Mr. Cotton didn't want to advertise the fact that he was meeting Woolly. Some people didn't.

'Sounds like a dowsing job,' Woolly had said to Marco. 'Which case, you wanner come along too, dude? Only way you're gonner learn all the techniques is by watching.'

He didn't need asking twice.

A few weeks ago, if you'd asked Marco what a dowser was, he'd have been like, *duh*... Even those walking-dictionary guys, like his London mate, Josh, thought it was just another name for water-divining: some old country thing that went with morris dancing and cheese-rolling.

But no, listen, dowsing was cool. Okay, it was ancient – no Pentium chips required. And not *exactly* magic. But, for an expert such as Woolly, it nearly always worked. He'd show up with his bent rods and his pendulums, and it wouldn't take him long to discover, well, yeah, underground water. But also anything that was missing. Some valuable ring. A lottery ticket. And *other things*.

Woolly was an awesome person for a granddad. A granddad who, until a few weeks ago, Marco hadn't met in all his thirteen years because his mum hated this town, and he still didn't know why.

Anyway...he'd pocketed the pendulum that Woolly had given him, and he and Woolly had set off from the cottage and met Mr. Cotton by a stile at the entrance to a footpath leading to the Tor.

That hill.

Odd how it scared some people. Not Marco, though. The closer Marco got to the Tor, the more excited he felt. As if he was approaching something he'd seen in weird dreams.

The Tor was like a steep, green pyramid, with an old church tower growing out of the point like a stone stalk. Just a tower, no church. The tower was hollow, like a big chimney. You could wind your way to the summit of the Tor and then stand inside the tower and look up, as if you were looking up a lift shaft into the sky.

There were, of course, stories about the Tor. According to Celtic legends, it was the entrance to the Land of the Dead.

Anyway, not just a hill, that was the point. People who thought it was just a hill were people who thought Woolly was just another tubby little guy with a white ponytail, a droopy moustache, an earring, a yellow T-shirt with LET'S LEGALIZE LOVE on the front, and a pair of quaint dowsing rods.

Which, as it turned out, they didn't even need this evening.

'Reason I wanted to talk to *you*, Mr. Woolaston,' Mr. Cotton said, 'is that you're a *local* man. We all know the town's full of people who go around claiming to have had strange experiences...but they tend to be people who've moved in. Usually because they're the sort of people who *want* to have strange experiences. Can't bring oneself to talk to those...those...'

'"Loonies" be the word you're after?' Woolly said.

'Solicitor, Mr. Woolaston. Tend to choose one's words with care. However...'

'So you wanner talk to me 'cause I'm a *local* loony.'

Mr. Cotton looked uncomfortable.

'Look,' he said. 'Just need to know if anyone *else* is seeing these things. I'm afraid...afraid I...'

'Afraid you're becoming a loony, too?' Woolly beamed and went to stand between two gorse bushes. 'So where exactly was you standing when you seen it, Mr. Cotton?'

Another thing that marked Mr. Cotton out as a Glastie was the fact that Woolly called him Mr. Cotton and Mr. Cotton called Woolly Mr. Woolaston. Avalonians, like Woolly, seemed to have only one name: Woolly, Orf, Eleri, Sam...

'Well...' Mr. Cotton took a few timid steps in the direction of the Tor. 'It was about here, I suppose. That was when I noticed that the sky had suddenly gone terribly dark, even though it was not yet seven o'clock. But when I looked back towards the town, it was in full sunlight down there.'

Woolly nodded. 'This happens.'

'Difference was very alarming. Suddenly, everything felt so utterly strange and full of...full of foreboding. Admit to feeling rather nervous.'

'I bet you was. What happened then?'

'It...' Mr. Cotton suddenly put his hands to his head as if he was in terrible pain. 'It's no good, I...I just can't. Have some very important clients, and if they thought I'd become the sort of person who saw—'

'Look,' Woolly said. 'Relax, man. Ain't nobody gonner know. Not from me. And not from Marco. Guarantee it.'

Mr. Cotton looked over his glasses at Woolly and Marco and took a long breath.

'Came from the East. At first, all I could see was the

lights...red, orange and blue...a line of them. Very bright against this dark sky. And then I could see a kind of shadow behind the lights. Showed me they were part of the same...craft.' Mr. Cotton swallowed. 'It was like a long flying cross, and it passed over from left to right and then disappeared.'

'You're sure it wasn't a plane in trouble?'

'I'm not an idiot, Mr. Woolaston. Anyway, next thing that happened...saw it directly ahead of me...over the tower on the Tor. Sky was almost black now, like a night fog, but the lights...very clear.'

'Did it make a noise?' Marco asked.

'No...absolutely silent. Air was silent, too. Not a bird sang. Great hush all around. As if the air itself was *waiting*. And then...' Mr. Cotton reeled away, throwing up his hands in definite terror at the memory. '...suddenly it was coming *straight at me*, this enormous shadowy thing with lights... and awfully low, as if...as if it...was going to take my head off.'

Mr. Cotton's head shrank into his shoulders, and Marco knew he was seeing it again, really clearly, in his head and feeling what he must have felt at the time.

Marco found that he'd also ducked.

'Thought I was going to die...' Mr. Cotton shook his head. 'Think I cried out. And then it suddenly went straight up...and vanished again.'

'Nobody else there?' Woolly said.

'No, I was absolutely alone. At least, I thought I... Oh dear God, can't believe I'm saying this.'

'Go on...don't stop now.'

'It was as though there were many people all around me.

Not people I knew. Dark, shadowy people. A silent army of them. All looking up into the sky, watching where it had been. But you see *they weren't really there at all...*'

Marco felt little creepy shivers in his back.

He meant like...ghosts?

He heard a kind of chattering behind him and spun round, as if all those dim figures might be forming amongst them at that moment. But there was only the hedge and the gorse bushes, rattling in a sudden thin breeze.

'Ridiculous, isn't it?' Mr. Cotton stared at Woolly. 'Please assure me that's ridiculous, Mr. Woolaston!'

'Only thing sounds ridiculous to me,' Woolly said, 'is somebody like you coming out with it. Whole lot of folks had some weird experiences in Glasto over the years, no doubt about that. But normally it's fellers like you who're the first to say they're one star sign short of a full zodiac.'

'How do you think this feels for *me*?' Mr. Cotton howled. 'Having to come to a notorious crackpot like you and admit to having seen something one simply can't explain.'

'That's gotter be tough,' Woolly said, as if being called a notorious crackpot was some kind of compliment.

'So...' Mr. Cotton mopped his forehead with the white handkerchief from his top pocket. 'Has anyone else seen anything like that?'

'Not as I know of,' Woolly said. 'But I'll ask around at The Cosmic Carrot.'

'Won't mention me, will you?' Mr. Cotton said nervously.

'Course not. And if I finds anybody else seen it, I'll drop by the office, let you know.'

'No...don't come into the office! Not looking like... I mean, be simpler just to call me on the phone.'

'All right,' Woolly said.

'Thank you.' Mr. Cotton stumbled away, his face red and sweating. 'Thank you, Mr. Woolaston.'

Woolly and Marco stood watching him walk back to Wellhouse Lane and his car.

'Either he's a real good actor,' Woolly said, 'or he really seen it.'

'So what do you think it was?'

'It was a UFO.'

'Well, yeah, but does that mean it was like...aliens?'

'Dunno,' Woolly said. 'It *is* a fact that places like the Tor attract what could be visitors from other worlds. Likely extraterrestrials can detect powers we don't fully understand.'

'So what are you going to do about it?'

'Only one thing we can do,' Woolly said. 'Bring it to the attention of the Watchers.'

'Oh.'

He meant the Watchers of Avalon. The secret guardians of the alternative side of Glastonbury. Of which Marco – because of what he knew and what he was learning about the art of dowsing – was now the youngest member.

'Er...does that mean we'll all have to...meditate on it?'

His heart was sinking like a stone dropped into a deep well.

'Could be,' Woolly said.

'Oh,' Marco said.

After all the UFO excitement, he now felt like he was losing the will to live.

Sanity at Stake

LONDON

No point in covering it up. It was too serious. Josh just came straight out with it.

'He's very sick, Father.'

It was a dull evening in the capital. The sun had already sunk below the tops of the tower blocks across the river.

'Joshua...' Dr. Goldman switched on his desk lamp and took off his glasses. He was looking a little wary. 'If I could just—'

'There is no doubt in my mind that he's becoming seriously mentally disturbed. In fact he may soon need to be sectioned. Look at this...'

Josh spread out the e-mails on the ebony surface of his

father's desk. There were four of them, and Josh had been over some sentences with his yellow highlighter pen. His father didn't look at them. He just looked at his son, sort of sadly.

'Josh...'

'Huh?'

'Why don't you call me Dad any more?'

Josh stared at him.

'You've always called me Dad. And now suddenly it's Father. Why is that?'

'Why? Well...'

Josh thought about this. His father sat back in his chair and waited, polishing his glasses on the sleeve of his pale blue corduroy jacket. *Pale blue corduroy!* Why wasn't he wearing a black jacket, like the great Sigmund Freud? Why weren't his glasses rimless? He was supposed to be a *top London psychiatrist*, for heaven's sake.

'Well, I'm thirteen now,' Josh said.

'Yes, I realize that.'

'Therefore, it's necessary for our relationship to be on more of an adult footing. Of course, if you prefer it, I could simply call you Simon. Or, as a professional colleague, what about just *Goldman*?'

'No, no!' His father seemed to shudder and then slump into his chair. 'Father will...Father will be fine.'

Josh shrugged. Obviously a difficult Rites of Passage situation for his father: losing a child, gaining a colleague. He'd get over it.

'Anyway,' Josh said, 'to get back to Marco's condition.'

Father's expression distinctly said, *If we must*, but Josh pressed on. This was important. Marco had been away for over three weeks now and the situation was becoming urgent. As Marco's psychoanalyst, Josh could probably work the whole thing out for himself but, in the sphere of mental health, a second opinion was always helpful.

He opened the file containing his case notes.

'You know some of the background,' he said, 'but I'll recap briefly. Marco's mother had to go and work in America and his father was too busy to look after him and so arranged for him to go and stay with his grandparents – that is, his mother's parents, in Glastonbury, Somerset. Now, incredibly, these were people Marco had never met before... *in his entire life.* Can you believe that?'

'Some family problem?'

'Dead right, Da— I mean, well-deduced, Father. There is indeed a long-standing rift between Marco's mother and her parents, although we don't yet know the root cause of this. It's pretty clear to me, though, that Marco's mother would be absolutely furious with his dad if she knew where Marco was spending his summer holiday. But, as they're separated, Marco's father isn't too fussed about that. In fact he's probably quite happy to stir it all up again.'

'Stir it up?'

Father's expression suggested this was somewhere he really didn't want to go. Sometimes Josh wondered if Dr. Goldman had been doing this job for too long. He seemed to be losing his professional acumen.

'Ah!' Josh leaned across the desk, narrowing his eyes. 'Well, you see, Marco's mother has always told him her parents are, you know...*weird.*'

Dr. Goldman blinked. 'In what way?'

'A good question, Father. And the answer is in these e-mails which Marco sent to me from Glastonbury.'

His father still didn't look at them. 'Aren't they private? Between you and him?'

'It's got beyond that. With Marco's sanity at stake, I feel I can no longer sit on this.'

His father sighed, put on his glasses and picked up the nearest e-mail gingerly, as if it was coated with something nasty. Josh smiled and nodded. He'd analysed the contents of this one so many times that he could remember exactly what it said.

It works! It finally works! That's amazing!!!!

My laptop had just completely packed in. Like, as soon as I arrived in Glasto???? And Woolly (that's my granddad, only he doesn't like being called Granddad) said not to worry because technology often goes haywire due to the powerful vibes around here. Because this is a Place of Ancient Sanctity, steeped in Earth Mysteries and Arthurian Lore.

And you can take that look off your fat face right now. I didn't believe a word of it either when I first arrived. In fact it seemed totally clear to me that Glasto was just this clapped-out old town full of people who were like totally barking.

But I can't tell you how wrong I was!

Well, I CAN tell you, and I will. Only right now I've got my dowsing lesson with Woolly. Wow! It's just so cool that the laptop's started working again – on its own! What does THAT mean?

'It means that Marco's losing his mind,' Josh said. 'That's what it means.'

His father peered at him over his glasses.

'And on what do you base *that* diagnosis?'

'Stands out a mile. He's been brainwashed. See, what you need to understand about Marco is that he's seriously impressionable. I've had him under analysis for nearly a year now, and he pretends to be cool and cynical but, in my experience, he'll believe anything you tell him. Anyway, after he promised to e-mail me again that night but didn't, I went on the net and downloaded everything I could find on Glastonbury.'

'Because you were lonely?' his father said. 'Because you missed having Marco around?'

'What?'

Unbelievable! His father actually seemed to be suggesting he was at a loose end just because of the absence of the best friend he'd ever— That is, his most like-minded associate. Possibly. *Outrageous.*

'*Absolutely not!*' Josh almost shouted. 'I just felt responsible for him – especially when I discovered that what he says here is absolutely right: Glastonbury *is* full of people who are completely barking! It goes back centuries. There are actually idiots who think King Arthur was buried there, as well as the Holy Grail – which everybody knows doesn't exist any more than King Arthur did. And there's this pointed hill where the ancient Druids were supposed to have done magic rituals, and loonies go up there thinking they're going to enter a different state of consciousness. Can you believe that?'

'It's interesting,' his father said. 'I expect someone's made a study of it.'

'Probably. But you're missing the point. Marco says here that he *used* to think everybody in Glastonbury was barking.'

'But doesn't any more?'

'*Exactly*. Because he's been brainwashed! After just over one week he's been totally got at by his evil granddad and his bonkers friends. *His mind has been warped.*'

'Erm...' His father didn't look entirely convinced. '...that's quite a sizeable assumption to make from one e-mail. Anyway, he promises here to explain everything. Did he?'

Josh nodded grimly. 'Oh yes. A week later.'

Listen. I mean, like, REALLY LISTEN!!!

Because your mind is about to be blown, as Woolly would say. Blown big time.

Listen, EVERYBODY should have a granddad like Woolly. He's got this big, white, droopy moustache and he wears T-shirts with the names of Jurassic rock bands like The Grateful Dead on the front. And, okay, Nancy, my gran, has tattoos and body piercing. But, in spite of all that, they're brilliant! It's totally beyond me why my mum hasn't spoken to them for years.

Like, the dowsing...

A townie like you probably doesn't know what that's about. It means Woolly can track things down with the rods and the pendulum – like, not only underground water and missing items, but weird things like the Dark Chalice, which is something so bad that I refuse to talk about it on an e-mail which anybody can get at. But take it from me...it's bad. Like, DON'T GO THERE.

'Now, this *is* interesting,' Josh said. 'Because, as I understand it, in psychiatry, the chalice or cup is a female symbol. In fact, it's often seen to symbolize the womb.'

'Well, sometimes, yes, but that's not necessarily—'

'We know that Marco's parents are living apart, so his family background is unstable, right?'

'Well, that's true, but, Joshua—'

'And we know that there's a long-standing rift between his mother and his grandparents.'

'Yes, but I don't see—'

'And Marco talks here about a *dark chalice*, which he says is something so bad he doesn't even want to deal with it in an e-mail. Which means he doesn't want to talk about it, *period*. Because it's too painful, right?'

It was his father who looked pained. Sometimes he seemed to have forgotten the basic tenets of psychiatry.

'Josh,' he said, 'in psychiatry...' He sat back, obviously trying to regain some professional credibility. '...one of the things we learn in psychiatry is that it's unwise to make a snap diagnosis.'

'*This* isn't...' Josh was insulted. 'This isn't a *snap diagnosis*. I've been observing this kid closely. I've studied his *behavioural patterns*. And I can tell you, he's been got at. It all fits. Work it out: his grandparents hate his mother and they're determined to turn Marco against her, too. And it looks like they've succeeded. Because he now sees the womb as a *dark* chalice. *Don't go there*, he says. Which means *he* mustn't go back to his *mother*, because he's been brainwashed into thinking she's evil and his bonkers grandparents are the good guys!'

There was a silence. The sun had almost gone down. Lights were coming on in the tower blocks. Josh's father sighed deeply.

'There are times – and this is one of them – when I wish

I'd become a shopkeeper,' he said. 'Or perhaps a chartered accountant.'

Josh hardly heard him. He was thinking of Marco's last e-mail, in which the guy's mind seemed to be totally on the blink, as he rambled on about – get *this* – storm clouds gathering over Glastonbury and the Lord of the Dead racing down from the pointed hill with his pack of black hounds. This was another psychiatric signpost.

Black dogs: a well-known symbol for clinical depression.

Case closed.

'Father, we've got to get him out of there before he becomes permanently damaged,' Josh said.

Glasties Two, Avalonians Nil

GLASTONBURY

'Something,' Eleri said that night at Bowermead Hall, 'is starting to happen.'

Tiny flames glowed in the jewelled eyes of the snake that curled around her head, making it look as if it was about to strike. The candles flickered and the shadows rose and swooped.

Marco looked around the circle of silent, grown-up people sitting in their stiff-backed chairs with their hands on their knees...and now *they* were looking around, too, into the corners of the vast room, as the shadows danced up and down the walls like dark ghosts.

'I didn't mean *here*!' Eleri rose up, gathering her robe

around her. 'I meant in the town. It's very clear that something *is* beginning to happen! Something that we, as the Watchers of Avalon, should be aware of.'

'Only we aren't, are we?' big, posh Diane said dolefully. 'Because it just isn't happening to us.'

'No,' Eleri said. 'It isn't.'

She sounded bewildered – almost hurt. Eleri was a Priestess of Isis and Glastonbury's most renowned seer. And hearer. And feeler. Anything happening in this town that wasn't happening to Eleri was...well, it just *didn't*, did it? It *always* happened first to Eleri, who had dreams of death and dark foreboding, usually involving weeping women accompanying the dying King Arthur on his last journey on a black barge to the Isle of Avalon.

Well, dreams were one thing, but *actual experiences...*

'Oh, come on, Eleri...' Diane's husband, Sam said. 'People've always seen UFOs over the Tor. What's new?'

'You *know* what's new,' Eleri said. 'This time, for the first time ever, they are being seen by *all the wrong people.'*

It was true. As he'd promised Mr. Cotton, Woolly had asked around in The Cosmic Carrot café, where all Glasto's leading psychics went for their vegetarian lunches. Not one of them had seen anything that might have been a UFO in months.

But Woolly had learned that a rumour was going round that Mr. Cresswell, the tight-fisted bank manager who'd refused to give Woolly's friend, Orf, a loan to replace his thirty-year-old minivan, had heard the chanting of monks in the abbey ruins.

Weird. Scary.

And these phenomena seen and heard by *the wrong people*. By people in suits who lived in big houses and drove BMWs. The kind of people who looked down their noses at the likes of Eleri and Woolly...the very people, in fact, who normally insisted that these things *didn't happen*.

Eleri took her seat – the ornate one with the carved, pointed backrest, against which she straightened her back. She placed her hands on her knees.

'Let us meditate upon this,' she said, and Marco tried not to moan aloud.

When the room went quiet, he was sure they must all be able to hear his stomach rumbling away like a JCB on a building site. How long was he going to be able to hold out?

This room was huge. It used to be the banqueting hall in the days when the Glastonbury gentry used to gather at Bowermead Hall to eat massive dinners. There were long windows and a high ceiling with miserable-looking angels and sour-faced cherubs carved around it.

But the banqueting table – tragically, in Marco's view – had gone long ago. Now it looked like all six of them were sitting around in the candlelight waiting for someone to bring them TV dinners on trays.

Huh. *No* chance. No chance at all, unfortunately, because...

...*because* it was a rule, apparently, that when the Watchers of Avalon were meeting at night, to meditate on some problem, they had to fast all day. *Fast.*

As in NOT EAT!

Who could *possibly* invent a rule as *TOTALLY INSANE*

as *that*? Marco's money was on Eleri herself, who was so thin and old she probably existed on a couple of sticks of celery a week. But, whoever it was, alive or dead, it was doing his head in. Having done his stomach in hours ago.

This morning, Nancy had said that, as he was a growing boy, it would probably be okay to bend the rule a bit and give him some breakfast...as long as he didn't have any lunch.

Or tea. Or a mid-morning snack. Or a mid-afternoon ice-cream.

Marco shuffled in his chair. This was *total agony*.

It seemed, however, that you had to make sacrifices if you were one of the Watchers of Avalon.

There were twelve people altogether in the Watchers, although only half of them had been able to come to tonight's emergency meeting. Marco was by far the youngest. His friend Rosa had been invited to join, but her dad, the curate at St John's Church, had refused to allow it. So Marco, as Woolly's grandson and the natural heir to his dowsing skills, was the only kid, and at first this had seemed seriously cool.

Before the downside had started to show itself.

You see, it wasn't only the fasting. There was also the meditation itself. *Meditation* was a complete and total definition of the word *boring*. Except that boring was shorter and meditation went on for ever.

You were supposed to close your eyes and become aware of the rhythm of your breathing and let everyday thoughts drift away so that your mind was like a blank tablecloth. Not eating all day was supposed to lighten your body and open up your Inner Space.

It did that, all right. As soon as Marco pictured the blank tablecloth it started to fill up with plates of veggieburger and chips from The Cosmic Carrot and he had to open his eyes to take it away.

Diane must have opened hers at the same time. She was probably starving, too. To have put on so much weight, she must have a fairly healthy attitude towards food.

She sighed.

'It's no good, Eleri. We're not going to get anywhere tonight. The atmosphere's completely dead.'

She was actually *Lady* Diane, or something like that, and she *owned* this vast, stately home, Bowermead Hall, which she'd inherited from her father, Lord Pennard. Actually, it was not so stately any more. It looked gloomy and faded and needed hundreds of thousands of pounds spending on repairs. Woolly had said he didn't think Diane and Sam could afford to keep it much longer.

'We can't give up,' Eleri said. 'We can't let everyone down. What about you, Nancy?'

'Sorry, lovey, not a thing.'

Nancy looked like Queen Guinevere's auntie, or something, in a medieval-looking red velvet frock. Except Guinevere's auntie probably didn't wear a ruby-red nose-stud. Marco had to keep reminding himself that this was actually his grandmother.

Eleri looked at Nancy as if she was trying not to scream.

'What about you, Woolly?'

'Well...' Marco's granddad shook his white ponytail and pulled his T-shirt (bright orange, with WISHBONE ASH printed on the front) down over his little pot belly.

'Thing is...I'm a dowser, Eleri. Means I gotter have something specific to dowse *for*. I ain't much good at this all-in-the-air stuff. Sorry.'

Eleri scowled. Marco was next, but she'd obviously decided not to ask what he'd experienced; as a retired university professor as well as a Priestess of Isis, Eleri didn't have much time for kids. Which was lucky, because no way did Marco want to tell her about the succulent cashewburger with sundried-tomato relish that the meditation had arranged on his inner dish.

Looking all hollow-eyed and desperate now, Eleri turned instead to Sam Daniel, who was sitting on Marco's other side with his legs stretched out and his hands linked through the back of his long hair.

'Er, to be honest, Eleri,' Sam said. 'I think I fell asleep, look.'

'*What?*'

'Well, I been out all day, trying to untangle the old vineyard and stuff and I was a bit knackered.'

Marco tried not to laugh. Eleri leaned forward, the head of the brass snake pointing at Sam's third eye. Not that Sam had three actual eyes; the third eye was something invisible in the centre of your forehead that could tune into psychic vibrations.

Just one of the crucial things Marco had learned in the past couple of weeks.

'And did you *dream*?' Eleri demanded.

'If I did have a dream, I must've forgotten it.' Sam sat up. 'Look, Eleri, maybe this is not *such* a bad development. The Glasties've been slagging us off for years. Now we can call *them* loonies, for a change. Can't wait to see the old man's face when he finds out the family solicitor's seen a UFO over the Tor.'

Sam's old man, Griff Daniel, was a local builder and the mayor of Glastonbury – king of the Glasties, basically. Naturally, they didn't get on, although the mayor apparently had been a lot nicer to his son since Sam had married the mistress of Bowermead.

Woolly looked up.

'Who told you about Cotton?'

As he'd promised, he'd kept quiet about what Mr. Cotton had seen. Woolly always kept his word.

'Ah, it's all over town,' Sam said. 'Cotton went into Juanita's bookshop and spent three hundred quid on books on UFOs, Glastonbury Tor, King Arthur, the lot...'

'Holy Joseph!'

'Yeah, him, too. Joseph of Arimathea, the Holy Grail... Cotton goes out of the shop with three carrier bags full.'

'My Goddess!' Eleri sprang to her feet, which couldn't have been easy in that long black robe with all the mystical jewellery weighing her down. 'Something really *is* happening!'

'Just that this time it ain't happening to us,' Sam said. 'Glasties two, Avalonians nil. And before you make anything of that eerie howling, that's the hounds telling me it's time for their evening walk. You wanner come, Marco?'

Marco just about restrained himself from leaping up and shooting to the door before anybody could object.

Instead, he glanced politely at his grandparents.

'I could do with a bit of a walk meself,' Woolly said. He winked at Marco and stood up.

'Cool.'

Marco jumped gratefully out of his chair and followed Sam Daniel out into the passage.

'Be vigilant!' Eleri called after them. 'Be aware of *the darkness on the threshold*!'

'Er...right,' Sam said.

Some Kind of Cage

Rosa was watching the expensive new plasma TV in her room. Some old film about ancient Romans with American accents; she wasn't really seeing any of it.

Problem was, she felt bad if she didn't watch TV in her room, or at least appear to be watching it, because she knew it must have cost a lot of money – the kind of money Mum and Dad didn't have.

Of course, it wasn't *her* fault that they'd spent all that money. Well, not exactly. That is, she'd never asked for her own TV, nor particularly wanted one.

But she knew, of course, why they'd bought it. They wanted something to make her bedroom seem modern and normal, in the hope that *she* would be normal. They wanted the pictures on the screen to capture her attention so she didn't start seeing pictures in the wall again.

Well, they needn't have worried. There were no pictures in the wall any more. No need for Richard to hide any more. They had an understanding, now, her and Richard.

The door opened and Mum's head came round.

'All right, Rosie?'

'Sure.'

'Don't watch *too* late. Even though it's the holidays, you need your sleep. You're still a growing girl.'

Oh yes, Rosa thought. *Growing in all kinds of ways.*

'It's not very good,' she said. 'The film. I was going to switch it off.'

'Oh,' Mum said. 'In that case...'

She came in, shut the door behind her, started tidying things on the dresser that she'd painted bright blue to cheer the room up.

'Shall I draw the curtains, Rosie?'

'It's okay.' Rosa switched off the TV with the remote. 'I like to lie here and imagine the abbey on the other side of the...'

Oops. Mum frowned.

'...and if you can see a bit of the sky,' Rosa said quickly, 'it doesn't seem quite as closed in.'

After moving down from a village in the North, both she and Mum had found it hard to get used to living in a flat in the centre of a town, with all the traffic and noise. And a huge ruined abbey hidden in the trees on the other side of the little backyard.

'It's just until we can find somewhere else,' Mum said.

'You know that. Maybe a house on the outskirts.'

Oh yeah. Like if they won the Lotto, which Dad refused to enter because it was gambling.

Mum came and sat on the edge of the bed and switched on the reading lamp on the bedside table.

'Why don't you bring your friend home for tea tomorrow.'

'What?'

'We'd like to meet her.'

'She can't.'

'Oh?'

'Because...' Rosa thought frantically. 'Because her mum works late and she has to look after her, um, little sister.'

'Well, they could both—'

'No, best not. Honestly. Little sisters are a pain.'

Mum said, 'It would just be nice to know—'

'You mean...' Rosa sat up in bed and folded her arms. '...whether I'm hanging out with the right kind of people.'

Mum looked uncomfortable. 'Well, you know what your dad's like. After that...that eccentric lady said...what she said...'

'That I was developing OCD because I was repressing my natural psychic instincts.'

Mum blinked, a familiar sign of anxiety.

'Because of Dad being a priest,' Rosa said.

Mum winced. They'd never talked about this. Not once, since that night, over two weeks ago, when Rosa and Marco had listened behind the door as the rather creepy woman called Eleri had laid it on the line for Dad: *Your daughter is a sensitive. It's clear that she has some of the same problems I had at her age.*

Eleri said this explained why Rosa had developed certain habits, like having to do things four times or something terrible would happen. The technical term for this was Obsessive Compulsive Disorder – OCD – and, of course, smart-mouth Marco had been the first to diagnose it. He had a mate called Josh whose dad was a psychiatrist, and Josh apparently knew all about this stuff.

Naturally she'd told Marco to get lost but, unfortunately, he'd proved to be dead right. Even Dad accepted this now. What he didn't accept was Eleri saying she was having all these nervous reactions because she was afraid to let her psychic side come out.

And the reason she was afraid was Dad. He used to be a policeman and was now a hard-line Church of England priest who thought all psychic stuff was Evil.

Because she's been brought up with the belief that anything psychic is wicked, Eleri had said, *her mind has set up its own screening mechanism. As soon as she begins to experience something other-worldly, it kicks in and forces her to go back and repeat the action she was doing when the feeling came over her… Do you understand what I'm talking about? OCD, Mr. Wilcox. Obsessive Compulsive Disorder is her subconscious defence mechanism against becoming someone she's afraid her own father would not want anywhere near him.*

Dad had obviously been deeply shocked by this, and neither he nor Mum had mentioned it since, not realizing that Rosa had overheard every word. Dad had been, on the surface, very friendly and considerate towards Rosa over the past couple of weeks and, at every opportunity, he'd taken her to the church with him and kept suggesting they should pray together.

Rosa didn't think it would be a good thing to tell him that she was finding help with her problems in a far older church, with...another priest.

She looked into Mum's worried face and saw that she was looking for some kind of reassurance that Rosa was not doing anything that would upset Dad.

'It's all right,' she said. 'My new friend...it isn't Marco, if that's what you're worried about. I wouldn't...I mean, I wouldn't deliberately go against something you felt so strongly about.'

And I sincerely hope, Dad had said sternly, *that you'll now keep well away from that boy and his troublemaker of a grandfather.*

'I know you wouldn't.' Mum stroked Rosa's hair. 'And we really don't want to keep you in some kind of cage or tell you where to go or who to mix with. It's just that Glastonbury is not...'

'Not a normal town,' Rosa said wearily. Like, how many more times did she have to hear that?

'It's full of people with all kinds of warped ideas,' Mum said. 'And, as a minister at the church, it's your dad's job to...stand up for what's right against, er, what is...not right.'

Rosa said nothing. She'd realized that sorting out what was right and what was not right was not all that easy in a place like Glastonbury. Dad's answer seemed to be to put up a big wall and insist that everything outside it was evil, and Rosa was expected to stay inside Dad's wall and be grateful.

And it just wasn't that simple.

It really wasn't.

Bit Early for Poachers

It was almost dark now and a moon was rising mistily over the Tor as Sam released the hounds from the kennels.

They came out in a rush. There was something about them that was *elemental*.

Marco liked that word. A shiver passed through him as he remembered the legend of Gwyn ap Nudd, the Celtic Lord of the Dead, who was supposed to live under the Tor and cruise the night sky with his hounds of hell. On the former Isle of Avalon, legends were so *close*.

Sam's dogs used to be hunting hounds – the Pennard pack, owned by the late Lord Pennard, the big landowner in these parts. Sam Daniel and Lord Pennard had not exactly been best mates in those days, on account of Sam being opposed to blood sports and pulling all kinds of stunts to disrupt the hunt.

It was probably just as well that Lord Pennard had not lived to see Sam marry his daughter and take over Bowermead Hall and the hounds. Because Sam was seriously anti-blood sports and so, from that day to this, these hounds had never been sent after a fox. They were all really friendly, in fact, and Marco and Woolly and Sam were struggling to stay on their feet under this pulsing furry avalanche.

'All right...all right, fellers...' Sam was grinning and his long hair was all over his face, already glued down by dog-drool. 'Go on...off you go.'

The dogs tumbled away down the field, under the red-streaked, darkening sky. Looking down the hill at the golden lights of Glastonbury, Marco was half-expecting – okay, hoping – to see strange balls of light forming and dancing around the Tor. But the Tor stayed black and the sky was still.

'There you go, Marco,' Sam said.

'Huh?'

'Managed to grab these on the way out, look.'

Marco looked down. Sam was holding out three big bars of chunky chocolate.

Magic!

'Got three more in my pockets,' Sam said, 'so you don't have to make it last.'

'You're a good boy, Sammy.' Woolly ripped open his chocolate. 'I was gonner suggest leaping into the truck and whizzing down the chippy, but these'll see us right meanwhile.'

Marco bit deep, as if this was the last food left in the

world, and the three of them stood watching the dogs and munching and looking down over the lights of Avalon.

All was cool. Fasting over, meditation over, and he was gazing out over what he was beginning to think of as *his place.*

From here, you could even tell where the sea had been in the days when what was now Glastonbury had been the Isle of Avalon. The land was flat and often waterlogged until you came to Glastonbury town, which was built around its ancient abbey, now in ruins. The abbey where King Arthur was said to have been buried.

Behind the town – and you could just see it now, like the back of a big fish – sat long, low Wearyall Hill, where the seagoing trader Joseph of Arimathea, uncle of Jesus, was said to have planted his staff, which had grown into a thorn bush. And a thorn bush still grew there! Not the original one, of course, but it was supposed to be a descendant of Joe 'Mathea's actual staff, and it flowered, appropriately, at Christmas. Or so it was said.

And then there was Chalice Hill, where Joe was supposed to have hidden the Holy Grail, the sacred cup from the Last Supper, which also caught drops of Jesus' blood as he hung from the cross. The holy blood was supposed to account for the red water in the Chalice Well at the bottom of the hill – Woolly said it was actually the iron that made it red but it didn't matter; it was symbolic, right?

King Arthur's knights had gone in search of the Holy Grail but had seen it only in visions. The actual Grail had never been found.

Unlike the *anti*-Grail, the satanic cup made of bones, known as the Dark Chalice, which Roger Cromwell, who used to run Glastonbury's black magic shop, had gone after – Cromwell and the big business consortium, Wilde-Hunt, who wanted to open the out-of-town theme park, Avalon World, to capture all the tourists and put out of business all the little shops on the High Street that sold mystical crystals and scented candles.

If Cromwell had succeeded, the Dark Chalice would have been the secret symbol of the new Glastonbury, ruled by the god of money who never smiled or looked up at the changing sky.

But Marco and Rosa and Woolly had managed to stop it. Cromwell had left town and Woolly had secretly reburied the Dark Chalice where he hoped nobody would ever find it.

Marco's sweeping gaze arrived back at Glastonbury Tor, which sprang up, black now, with the church tower like a rigid finger pointing at the stars.

'Quentin Cotton, eh?' Sam said. 'And a big dark UFO over the Tor. Wouldn't credit it, would you? A solicitor.'

Like Marco's dad. Who, it turned out, had actually been secretly working as legal adviser to Wilde-Hunt. Discovering this had been so totally shattering that Marco could still hardly bear to think about it. Since learning the truth, he hadn't seen his dad, who had gone back to London and rarely phoned.

'And Roland Cresswell, the bank manager?' Sam said. 'He's not interested in anything he can't turn into money. Dunno about hearing ghostly monks in the abbey, he'd be happy to bring in bulldozers to dismantle what's left of it.'

'He wouldn't really, would he?' Marco said.

'Like a shot, Marco, if it wasn't all protected. Think about it: the abbey ruins take up a big chunk of the town. Think what a great shopping precinct you could put there – B&Q, Asda, PC World.'

'But you can get those *anywhere*.'

'But you ain't got 'em *here*, and that's what rankles with the Glasties. Woh! Far enough, fellers! We better get back.' Sam stopped near a stile, where the dogs had gathered. *Come on!*' He patted his thigh. 'You seen Rosa lately, Marco?'

'Er...no. Not really.'

Another sore point. Despite everything being more or less brilliant, there were quite a few sore points.

'What's that mean?' Sam put his head on one side. 'Not *really*?'

'Well, I've *seen* her, but I'm not sure she saw me. Or if she did, she pretended not to.'

Marco thought that maybe Rosa had seen a bit too much of him when they'd been trapped together in the forgotten labyrinth under the town. He hadn't exactly been much of a hero down there, although people seemed to think he'd become one afterwards, which was all a bit embarrassing.

'Likely she's got things to work out,' Sam said. 'And with her old man being curate at St John's...well, you can understand why he don't want his daughter hanging round with a mad old pagan like Eleri.'

Sam turned back towards Bowermead Hall. Although the big house was crumbling a bit, across the darkening fields, with the banqueting hall lit up, it looked like a palace. Amazing to have mates who owned a place like that, Marco thought, even if they couldn't afford to maintain it. Josh was never going to believe it.

Just one of the things Josh was never going to believe, but he'd deal with that when he got home.

Home. He felt a strange kind of throb in his chest because London somehow didn't feel like home any more. *You're an Avalonian now, dude,* Woolly had said to him, more than once.

'You lot...come *on*,' Sam shouted over his shoulder to the dogs.

But the dogs were ignoring him. They were getting excited, some of them snuffling and scuffling around the base of the stile, others jumping up at it, barking.

'Looks like they found something, Sam,' Woolly said.

'Oh hell!' Sam set off back towards the stile, which was submerged, now, beneath this heaving mound of hounds. 'It better not be a fox or a badger, that's all. Lancelot! Gawaine! Bors! *Leave it!*'

As Glastonbury was supposed to be the last resting place of King Arthur, Sam had named the reformed hounds after various Knights of the Round Table, until he'd run out of knights' names, after which he'd called them...

'Towser! Fido! Come *here!*'

And there was another one called Rover somewhere in the pack.

'*Aaargh!*' A ragged voice rose up into the cooling night air. '*Nooooo! Gerroff!*'

Marco jumped.

'Hmm.' Sam brought out a small but powerful torch and focused its thin, white beam on the stile. 'I'd've thought it was a bit early for poachers, but you never can tell.'

'*Sam? That you, boy? Get these beggars off me!*'

'Oh, no...' Sam stopped. 'Think I'd've preferred the poachers.' He switched off his torch. 'This is *all* we need.'

'*You want me to get ripped apart, is it, boy?*'

'They're harmless!' Sam turned to Marco. 'Unfortunately.'

'Who is it?' Marco *thought* he'd recognized the voice but...

'Sounds like Griff Daniel,' Woolly said. 'Sam's old man. What's *he* doing up here this time of night?'

'The mayor?'

'Sam! You there, son?'

The voice came quavering over the stile, all frayed and feeble. The one time Marco had met Griff Daniel, the mayor had been loud, full of himself...and full of contempt for Woolly. Griff Daniel: King of the Glasties.

'You gotter help me, Sammy! I'm outer my mind, look!'

'So what's new?' Sam said to Marco, then he shouted. *'Dad, they're harmless!* Got to be careful,' he told Woolly and Marco out of the side of his mouth, 'or he'll find a council by-law that says you can't exercise your own dogs on your own land during the hours of darkness.'

'Ain't just them, boy.' Griff Daniel came wading through the dogs, breath hissing fiercely out of him like the air brakes on a big lorry. 'I've had a terrible experience, look. Terrible! God almighty, Sammy, am I going crazy or what? I tell you, boy, I ain't never gonner sleep again, after this. *Never!*'

'What – not even during council meetings?'

'Don't you go mocking me, boy! Don't you ever—'

The mayor started to cough. Sam looked at Marco, grinned and switched the torch back on. Marco thought Sam was being a bit heartless, frankly. The old guy might be grasping and dishonest, but he *was* his dad, and it looked like he was genuinely upset as he came labouring up the field towards them in his heavy tweed suit, his spiky-bearded face shiny with sweat in the torchlight.

When he reached Sam, he nearly collapsed. Sam sighed, handed Marco the torch and took his dad's arm, the way you'd pick up a spade which had fallen into a cowpat.

'Thank God.' Griff Daniel put his other hand to his chest, as if his heart was about to fail. 'I never believed it. Oh God, I never believed any of it, and now... *What's happening to me?*'

'What *are* you on about, Dad?'

'Never believed any of it, boy. But I...I seen it, no question. *I flaming seen it!*'

'What?'

'Gh— *Gh*—' Griff Daniel looked at Sam in anguish. 'Look at me – I can't even say it.'

A thin chill began to ripple up Marco's spine. Sam put his head on one side. 'Looks like you seen a ghost, Dad.'

Griff Daniel made this choking noise that turned into a strangled sob.

Sam took a step back. 'What?'

'It was horrific, boy. *Horrific.*'

'Dad, are you telling me you...?'

A night breeze rattled across the stile and then died, as if something had followed the mayor...and even Marco backed away.

Black, Smoky, Ghosty

The moon was rising, spreading a grey-green light over the field and Griff Daniel's face, which was the colour of curdled milk. Marco could see his hands were still shaking as he held them out in front of him as if he was having difficulty keeping his balance.

But Sam was still unsympathetic and getting impatient.

'Dad, you gonner tell us what you saw, or not?'

'I don't feel well, boy.'

Sam sighed through his teeth.

'All right, we'll get you back to the house.'

'Glass of brandy might help,' the mayor said.

'Yeah, it usually does,' Sam said. 'Specially if it's

somebody else's. *Home!*' he shouted at the dogs, and they all started barking and headed back up the track in a bunch, white tails waving in the dusk.

Marco was glad they were going back. Whatever Griff Daniel had encountered down there, he wasn't sure he wanted to hear about it in the spooky moonlight.

'What's *they* doing here?'

The mayor seemed to notice Marco and Woolly for the first time.

'Mates of mine,' Sam said.

'*Gah*,' Griff muttered. He hated Woolly. He'd called him a traitor who wanted to keep the town in the Dark Ages, just because Woolly had refused to sell some of his land to Wilde-Hunt for Avalon World.

At the time, Marco had thought Avalon World had sounded like a cool idea: this huge Las Vegas-style theme park, where you could pay five pounds or whatever to go in search of the *virtual* Holy Grail – computer-generated. But he could see now how it would have totally dominated the landscape, making even the majestic Tor seem insignificant – the modern world bulldozing in, the ancient mystery seeping away. The real mystery replaced by something phoney that didn't *change* anybody, deep down. Just gave them a day out, and that was it.

Marco had learned since, from Sam, that the mayor, who was in the building trade, would have made a whole pile of money out of Avalon World.

Bent as a nine pound note, my old man, Sam had said bitterly.

But right now, bent or not, Griff Daniel looked as scared as any adult Marco had ever seen.

The kitchen, like everywhere else in Bowermead Hall, was vast, with three sinks and a table you could have parked a van on. Sam sat his old man down at one end of it, and brought him a glass of brandy.

'Just *one*, Dad, all right?'

Griff Daniel drank the lot in one long gulp and shivered, and then just sat there with the glass in his hand, and he *still* looked pale.

And then he blinked.

'Oh no,' he said. 'Not with *them* here.'

Marco, leaning against the fridge, which was as big as a bus shelter, saw that they'd all come in – Woolly and Nancy and Diane...and Eleri with her snake headband. The Watchers of Avalon, all keenly watching Griff Daniel.

'Forget it,' the mayor said. 'I ain't saying nothing in front of these loonies.'

'Better call Dick the Taxi, then,' Sam said. 'Get you home.'

'*Dick the Taxi*?' Griff Daniel glared at his son like he was insane. 'You think a man in my position would be seen dead getting out of a clapped-out black cab with pink stars all over it and a big grinning moon on the bonnet?'

'Well, *I* ain't gonner drive you home,' Sam said. 'Not if you don't wanner talk in front of my mates.'

'Fine son *you* are.' The mayor ran his hand over his ratty beard, peered at the Watchers of Avalon and shuddered.

'Aw, come on, just spit it out, Dad,' Sam said. 'It won't go further than this kitchen, look.'

The mayor hung onto his glass and clamped his mouth shut.

'Mr. Daniel...' Diane came and sat down next to him. 'You haven't been...mugged or anything?'

Griff reared up. 'Of course I ain't been mugged, girl!'

'On account of everybody knows he never takes his wallet with him,' Woolly said. 'Specially down the pub.'

The mayor's eyes narrowed. 'Don't you push it, Woolaston.'

'Or what?' Woolly stepped out in front of the mayor and rose up all the way to the mayor's chest. He was wearing two-tone flared velvet jeans, frayed at the bottom over the holes in his trainers.

'*Gah!*' said Griff Daniel.

Except for the sludgy rumble of the fridge, there was an uneasy silence in the huge, echoey kitchen, and Marco thought how ridiculous adults were, never knowing how to deal with one another.

Just as well there was a kid around.

'He must've seen something *seriously* scary,' Marco said. 'He's terrified! His eyes are all over the place.'

The mayor turned to face Marco, his eyes no longer all over the place and his fingers going into strangling mode.

'Only he thinks if he tells you about it you'll all think he's gone as loopy as he thinks you are,' Marco said.

Was that right? It *sounded* right.

Woolly caught Marco's eye and gave him a little smile, which nobody else would know was a smile unless they could interpret the various twitchings of Woolly's big, white, droopy moustache.

'Right,' Griff Daniel said. 'That kid leaves now, or I'm saying nothing.'

'Okay...' Marco put up both hands. 'I'm out of here.'

It was hard to imagine what it must be like to live in a house the size of a block of flats. Marco had been to Bowermead Hall three or four times now, and he was only just starting to find his way around.

It was actually a bit creepy. No wonder wealthy families used to have loads of kids and loads of servants. Otherwise, the house was boss.

Marco padded softly down the passage, lit by feeble, low-watt bulbs, from the kitchen to a door that had been painted green about a century ago. The paint was flaking off it now and the lock was broken, so he had no difficulty at all getting into the servants' quarters.

Sam had taken him down here once, pointing out that, as he and Diane could only afford two cleaning ladies who came in twice a week, this part of the house wasn't used any more.

Marco pushed the door shut behind him and stumbled down three steps into almost total darkness. It was grim enough in here by daylight. In the dark it reminded him uncomfortably of Roger Cromwell's old black magic shop below Rosa's flat on High Street.

He saw a strip of grey light indicating another door, ajar. On the other side of it he found himself in what Sam had told him had been the servants' dining room. It was like a big stone warehouse, with a damp, greasy smell and meagre light filtered through spiders' webs across windows set high up in the far wall.

But he knew there was another short flight of steps, leading to another door, and this one came out in what was now a larder, accessed from the kitchen. So, if you didn't mind sitting on the cold flagged floor you could ease this door open a couple of centimetres and...hear everything said in the kitchen, no problem.

'...so, I'm leaving The Pilgrims,' Griff Daniel was saying. 'Just coming up to sundown. Business meeting, look. *Council* business! Don't you look at me like that, Woolaston, you sarky little hippy! Some of us got civic responsibilities!'

'Let him talk, Woolly,' Eleri said softly.

'Thank you, madam. So I'm walking back to the car, up Magdalene Street.'

Marco closed his eyes, and *he* was in Magdalene Street. He could see everything in his head: the wide road with the tall memorial at the crossroads and the abbey gatehouse, everything glowing sunset red.

'There was traffic,' the mayor said, 'but the sound of it was...it was suddenly far away. Like it was on telly and I'd turned down the sound. And I couldn't smell the traffic fumes no more. All I could smell was the hay in the fields and the scents of the orchard...all fresh.'

Marco opened his eyes. This was *really* weird. According to Woolly, Griff Daniel thought the countryside was just a waste of good building land.

'It was like I was dreaming, look. Suddenly, I was alone on the street, and then the street went all funny. All the buildings was going *fuzzy*. And then they fades slowly away, and I'm walking along a track...footpath kind of thing. Through the apple trees, full of green apples.'

Big, rusting hooks hung from a beam above Marco. He supposed dead pigs and things had hung there once but, with Sam and Diane being vegetarian, it was just sprigs of herbs now, filling the air with a peppery aroma. He shut his eyes again, and he was with the mayor in the apple orchard.

'And through the trees,' Griff Daniel said, breathing hard. 'I can see water...a lot of water. The sea!'

Like the Isle of Avalon, as it used to be? Marco put his ear closer to the crack in the door.

'And then I hears...the sound of a *trumpet*. Well, a horn, anyway. A long blast, low and hollow. And I sees that the sky's gone a deep, dark red, like blood. And then...'

For a while, all you could hear was Griff Daniel's harsh breathing, like he'd been running.

'...*tramp, tramp, tramp*...the sound of marching feet, moving towards me. *Tramp, tramp, tramp*...only it's a hollow kind of sound, as if them feet's a-tramping in my head...'

'Likely all the customers you ripped off, come for their money back,' Woolly said.

'*Shut up!* Don't you mock me!'

'Yes, stop it, Woolly,' Eleri hissed. 'Carry on, Mr. Daniel.'

'Well...it's too dark to see any distance but I can feel them coming towards me, *tramp, tramp, tramp*, only there's more of 'em now. Could be hundreds, and I want to run. I want to run like hell, but *I can't move*. I'm *paralysed*! Can't move my arms or my legs. I'm rooted to the ground, look! And they keeps coming, on and on...closer and closer...and they ain't gonner stop. Crunching through the trees, heavy as a JCB. *Tramp, tramp, tramp*...'

Marco could hear this rhythmic, creaking sound as if Griff Daniel was rocking backwards and forwards in his chair, remembering. Only this was more than remembering. It was like part of him was still out there.

'And now...now I can see the glint of burnished steel in

the last of the deep, red sun, and I can see them now, with the red light glinting off their helmets...but their faces...their faces are all smoky...black, smoky, ghosty faces!'

Marco felt cold and looked over his shoulder into the greyness and the hulking shapes of things.

'And I can't move...and then I hears a voice whisper in my ears...*that* close...and it whispers, *"Kneel!"* And, at that moment, my knees just...give way, and I'm kneeling there with my head hanging down...'

The mayor's breath was coming in a long rush now, like a train in the night.

'...and my eyes was squeezed tight shut and I hears this... like a wafting sound...and I knew it was a great heavy sword being raised high in the air...and it was gonner...come down on my neck! I thought they was *gonner chop my head off*!'

Woolly must have been about to say something funny, because Eleri hissed at him again, and then there was a long, long silence.

'But it didn't happen. I looked up and saw this huge sword held high, all golden in the last rays of the sun. And the next thing...I must've blacked out, and the next thing I knows I'm up on the hill and your flaming dogs is all over me. Oh, I—'

There was the sound of a chair scraping on the flagged floor and then this hollow snuffling.

Then Sam said, 'He...he's crying...'

The atmosphere in the big kitchen was hushed and sober when they let Marco back in.

Griff Daniel had gone. They'd given him another brandy and then Diane, who was known all over town as a really kind person, had agreed to drive him home.

Outside, it was fully dark now and big moths were beating themselves against the windows. Sam was looking pale and shocked.

'Normally I'd've said the old beggar was lying as usual, but I always *know* when he's lying – his face goes all stiff and upright and honest-looking. Woolly, *he wasn't making it up.*'

'No,' Woolly said. 'I don't reckon he was. But what's it mean, Sammy?'

Eleri stood up. She'd taken off the snake headband when the mayor first came in, and now she looked a few centimetres shorter and more like an ordinary elderly lady than a Priestess of Isis.

'I'm afraid this is a lesson for all of us,' she said. 'People like me...we come to Glastonbury, as pilgrims, thinking we understand the mystical forces that the local people have turned their backs on. But *their* roots are deeper than ours.'

'Now, just a minute, Eleri, man.' Woolly looked annoyed. '*You* might be an immigrant from Wales, but no way Griff Daniel's roots go back further in this town than the roots of the Woolastons!'

'Look at it this way,' Eleri said. 'For years we've been struggling to convince the ordinary townsfolk – the Glasties – that they live in a sacred place, and they kept telling us we were all mad or on drugs. And now all our efforts are finally paying off.'

'*What?*' Woolly said.

'Now they all *know*. The solid citizens of Glastonbury – Quentin Cotton, Roland Cresswell, and now even Griff

52

Daniel – have had visionary experiences. It might be disappointing, at first, for those of us who didn't see these things, but think of what it means for the future of our community! No longer will we be dismissed as idiots with our heads in the clouds. We'll all be able to live together in peace and love and harmony!'

Marco stared at Eleri. Peace, love and harmony? This was the woman who dreamed of death and destruction and hooded women in a black barge with a dead body!

On the way home, bumping along in the truck, he said to Woolly, 'Do you think she's right?'

'Dunno, dude,' Woolly said. 'Griff definitely wasn't inventing it. But he's still a crooked builder and a bent councillor. In my experience, fellers like that don't change. And they don't suddenly become psychic.'

'Perhaps he's repented of his evil ways.' In the back seat, Nancy was bundling up her green and purple hair with a big rubber band. 'We're always saying what a spiritual place this is and how it can change your life. Perhaps now Griff'll stop doing dirty deals and ripping people off. Perhaps he'll become...saintly.'

Woolly gripped the wheel, going, 'Grrrrrrr.'

'And perhaps, like Eleri says, it's a test for us,' Nancy said. 'Folks we thought we didn't like...suddenly they're just like us, after all. We should embrace them!'

'Embrace Griff Daniel? You gone mad?'

'I never said it was going to be easy,' Nancy said. 'That's not what life's about.'

'Nance...' Both hands tight on the wheel, Woolly glared

grimly through the windscreen. 'I can't handle this. It ain't the Glasto I know and love.'

Marco nodded. He hated being confused about who were the good guys and who were the bad guys.

And it was about to get even *more* confusing...

A Pure White Hand

They must have been following him.

He was practising his dowsing, the next morning, in one of the fields next to Wellhouse Lane, but on the opposite side to the Tor – you discovered it was not a good idea to experiment too close to it because all the energy coming off it could seriously affect your results.

So he'd tossed a fifty pence piece out into the field and he was now trying to find it, using the rods.

The rods weren't as easy to use as the pendulum – not to Marco, anyway – but Woolly said he needed to master them if he was going to be a real dowser.

They were thin lengths of dull brass, with the ends bent

into an L-shape to provide handles, and you held them out in front of you like antennae.

Which was what they were. You visualized what you were looking for, and the rods would tell you which way to go by the way they moved. If they didn't move at all you were cold, but if they opened out or suddenly crossed over, you'd cracked it.

There was nothing magic about this. The rods were just responding to some deep-down part of you that knew where the fifty pence piece was lying.

So Marco was walking up and down the field in the bright sunshine, holding the image of the coin in his head, with the rods held out in front of him when a foot hooked itself around one of his ankles, and the dewy grass came up in his face.

'Uuuurgh.'

Marco was eating mud and feeling what could only be a knee, as hard as a cricket ball, in the back of his neck. His face was pushed into the ground, and a voice was rasping in his ear.

'You're coming with us, hippy trash.'

Oh no...

Marco really thought he'd seen the last of Shane on the day they'd reburied the Dark Chalice.

He didn't say anything because he couldn't with a mouthful of grass, and also because he was pretty sure Shane wouldn't be on his own.

This was confirmed when he was dragged to his feet and had his arms twisted behind his back. Shane had two mates with him that Marco had never seen before, but they were both bigger than him, and that was all you really needed to know.

Shane was red haired and had a face like a relief map of the Amazon Basin. He smiled.

'Look,' Marco said. 'If we're going somewhere, why don't I just walk along with you? Why do we have to go through the old prisoner routine.'

Shane punched him in the stomach.

Marco doubled up in agony.

''Cause it's more fun,' Shane said.

Through his watering eyes, Marco saw, to his horror, that one of Shane's mates was holding up the two dowsing rods. The new rods Woolly had given him the night before last.

'Duh...what's these?' the kid said.

'Giss 'em here,' Shane said.

Oh no.

Shane held up one of the rods and grinned and bent it in half.

'Oh dear,' Shane said.

'Sorry, didn't I tell you?' Marco said, furious. 'There's a curse on those rods, and both your arms will have rotted away by lunchtime.'

He was briefly pleased to see Shane looking worried before hooking his trainer around one of Marco's ankles and slamming him back into the grass. The two other kids held him down this time and his hands were dragged behind his back, he felt something cold and hard against his skin.

Now he began to feel scared, realizing, as the metal bit into his wrists, that Shane was turning his dowsing rods into manacles.

* * *

Jasper Coombes was waiting for them under a horse-chestnut tree.

'On your knees, scumbag,' Shane snarled, and Marco thought of Griff Daniel's vision.

But Jasper didn't have a sword.

He had an air rifle.

Terrific.

With the rods binding his hands behind his back and Shane kicking peevishly at the sides of his trainers, Marco had no choice.

He went down on his knees in the grass.

Jasper Coombes was probably a couple of years older than Marco. He had a thin, tanned face and tight curls. Girls apparently fancied him, even though his dad was an estate agent.

He prodded Marco with the rifle.

'Got some questions for you, hippy trash.'

Marco tried to look all around the field without moving his head. Like, where were all the hikers when you needed them?

'Nobody comes in this field,' Jasper said. 'You can't see the Tor, and that's all the scumbag tourists are bothered about. I could shoot you dead and bury you, and nobody would know.'

'It's an air rifle.'

'Just means nobody would hear the bang. And you can kill somebody with an air rifle quite easily if you know what you're doing.'

Marco bit his lip. If there was a time for smart remarks this was probably not it. Jasper went to a private school and had quite a posh accent, but he wasn't even pretending to be civilized any more. It was like the further they got into the summer holiday and the deeper his tan grew, the darker he became as a person.

'Okay, trash, you know the Glastonbury Tribunal?'

Marco nodded. It was in High Street, one of the oldest buildings in the town, used as a tourist information centre now.

'You know in the garden at the back there's this old well?'

'Sure.'

You could look down the well, but there was a protective grating across so nobody could fall in. Not a bad idea, as the well probably led into the Glastonbury labyrinth...into which Marco never wanted to go again ever, ever, *ever*...

'Any legends about it?' Jasper said, kind of nonchalant. 'The well.'

'What kind of legends?'

'About, say, something...down there.'

'Never heard of anything. Why are you asking me? I've only been here a few weeks, and you were born here.'

'I've never had time for that crap,' Jasper said. 'I have a life. It's just...a mate of mine thought he...thought he saw something. Down there.'

'Oh.'

'And I should point out that this mate is a real hard guy, and if he ever heard that you'd breathed a word about this, he'd kill you.'

'With his air rifle,' Marco said, putting two and two together.

'He wouldn't need an air rifle. He'd snap your spine.' Jasper made a breaking-twigs-type gesture. 'Like *that*.'

'He must be nearly as charming as y— *urrrrgh*!'

When he'd picked himself up, Marco took a serious vow of silence.

'What I want,' Jasper said, 'is for you to find out.'

'What?'

'If there's a legend about the well. My mate doesn't usually go in places like that, obviously, but there's a hot girl doing a holiday job in the Tourist Office, and he...anyway he was there. And he thought he saw something.'

'But you can't just...' Marco would have thrown up his arms if they hadn't been manacled behind his back. 'There could be loads of legends. You know what it's like in this town. You've got to tell me a bit more about...whatever your mate saw.'

Jasper thought about it.

'You want me to hit him again, Jas?' Shane said.

'Why, what's he done?'

'Nothing. I just like it.'

Marco clenched his aching stomach. This kid was a total psycho.

'All right,' Jasper said. 'Say if there was a...a hand coming out.'

'Out of the well?'

'And say it was...holding a sword. A hand thrusting a sword out of the well.'

'Wow. You saw—' Marco saw Shane's fist retracting like a piston and backed away. 'I mean, your mate saw...a sword?'

'Clasped by a white hand. On the end of a pure white arm. Or that's what he said it looked like. So I want you to find out...if there's any legends...about that well.'

'And what do I do when I've found out?'

'You do nothing. You talk to nobody. Shane will come and fetch you again.'

Shane grinned and rubbed his right fist with his left hand like he was polishing it.

'Can't wait,' he said.

Evil Everywhere

Rosa liked it better when her dad had been a police detective. Even though he hadn't been there most of the time, when he *was* there he was more fun.

Also he didn't have this big black beard and he didn't walk around in a dress.

Okay, it was actually a cassock and it was what all vicars and curates wore. But not all the time, surely? When he was a cop, Dad used to wear jeans at weekends, glad to get out of his working suit. Not any more.

'Being a priest is a 24-7 situation,' he'd say sternly. 'I am always on duty.'

Even when he was out for a walk with his daughter, by the river?

Unfortunately, yes. As they walked along the riverside path, Dad's eyes kept scanning the fields in this penetrating way – the way she guessed they used to scan tough housing estates in the North for possible drug dealers.

There was nobody about, only the Tor in the distance, all pastel-coloured and innocent-looking. It didn't fool Dad, though. In his eyes, it would be black and dripping with poisonous pagan evil.

To Dad, everything was either black or white.

And this wasn't just a pleasant walk on a hot August morning, was it? You didn't have to be a former detective's daughter to recognize a set-up.

Dad's head suddenly swivelled, following a bend in the river, which was placid and edged with reeds, not at all like the rushing, stony rivers in the North.

'Did you see that?'

'No. What?'

'A movement. I'm sure somebody was down there.'

'So what?' Rosa said. 'You're not a policeman any more, and anyway—'

'I'm God's policeman now,' Dad said, and Rosa groaned.

'So what exactly does Mum want you to talk to me about?'

'What makes you think your mum wants me to—?'

'Because it's obvious,' Rosa said miserably. 'We never just go for walks. Only when you want to talk about something heavy.'

They came to a damp bit and Dad lifted up his cassock like one of those *ladies* in *Little Britain*. Rosa felt distinctly embarrassed and hoped there actually wasn't anybody around who might see them.

'All right,' Dad said. 'We feel – both of us – that you're becoming rather secretive.'

'Me?'

'You go off on your own and don't tell us where you're going and when you come home you don't tell us where you've been.'

'You wouldn't be interested.'

'Of course we're interested, Rosa. We're your parents!'

'I go to different places.'

'It's who you go *with* we're more concerned about.'

'Well, you know...different people.'

'You haven't been near that Marco again, I hope. Or his grandfather.'

'No.'

'What about Teddy in the Crystal Shop?'

'I just go in now and then to see if he needs any help,' Rosa said defiantly. 'In line with my Christian duty. He *has* only just come out of hospital, after being badly beaten up.'

'I don't like you going in that sort of shop.'

'Dad, he just sells glittery rocks!'

'Which some people claim they can use for healing. Which is absolute nonsense.'

'Healing people is nonsense?'

'Doctors are for healing people. In Church we pray to God to help *the doctors* to heal people.'

'Well, the doctors don't have all the answers,' Rosa said, feeling stubborn, now, because Dad thought *he* had all the answers, too, but his mind was so closed it was like a bank vault.

Which made it impossible to tell him that the friend she spent time with had died over four hundred years ago.

'Rosa, you haven't been seeing any more...odd shapes on your bedroom wall?'

'No.'

On the wall which backed on to the Abbey grounds, she used to see the shape of a monk. Not any more. Not now she understood what that had been about.

'And what about your...habits? Your need to keep doing the same thing over and over again.'

'It's a lot better,' Rosa said truthfully. But didn't, of course, tell him why she thought that was.

'Good,' Dad said. 'I'm very glad.'

As he'd been about to take her to a child psychiatrist, Rosa was fairly glad, too. But she knew she had occasional lapses and the OCD could come back anytime, rushing and foaming like a northern river in winter, and she'd be back to walking over the same bit of pavement *four times* and licking an ice lolly *four times* before she was allowed to bite the top off...to make sure something horrible didn't happen.

In the old days, the only time she stopped doing things four times was when something horrible was actually happening.

'Er...what I was going to ask you, Rosa,' Dad said, 'was whether you'd like to get away from here for a while.'

'What?'

'Perhaps go back up North for the rest of the holidays, to stay with Auntie Michelle and Uncle Andy and your cousins.'

'What for?'

'Oh, just to give us...give you a break.'

'Hang on.' Rosa stopped walking. 'When we lived up there, you totally hated me going there because you said all they did was watch videos and play computer games.'

'Oh, I don't think I *did*—'

'It's a sin to tell a lie,' Rosa said. 'You'll get three points on your prayer card.'

Dad glared at her. He didn't like religious humour.

'Now look, Rosa—'

'I don't want to go anywhere.' Rosa kicked at the ground, hating herself for being childish and petulant and hating herself even more for kicking the ground again and again...*two...three...f*—

On the fourth kick, her foot became trapped under what felt like a root that had grown over the path. When she tried to pull it out, her foot came out without the trainer.

Damn. Now she'd look really stupid hopping around; she could already see the pitying look forming on Dad's face as she bent down.

The trainer was totally trapped, and the root was so hard it was probably fossilized or something.

'Can I help?' Dad said.

'I can do it.' Rosa pulled at the root. Only to find that it wasn't a root. 'Oh...it's metal.'

'In that case, get away at once,' Dad said. 'It might be a gin trap set by poachers.'

'Oh Dad, do you have to see evil *everywhere*?'

Rosa got down on her knees and tugged. Just hoping to God it *wasn't* some kind of nasty trap.

It came up suddenly in her hands.

'Just an old gate hinge,' Dad said, relieved.

'No, it isn't...'

It was too long for that, unless it was off a really big gate, and there were these two short bits coming out of the sides and lumpy bits further along. But it was far too rusty to—

66

'Good heavens.'

Dad was on his knees, now, getting mud all over his black cassock.

'What's wrong?'

He took the thing from her, very gently, and rubbed it with a forefinger.

'You know what you've found, don't you?'

Rosa shook her head. She didn't really care as long as it had taken his mind off Auntie Michelle and Uncle Andy.

'I'm not entirely sure,' Dad said, 'and we'll need to take it to an expert...but I think...I think this is something very old. I mean very old. Possibly over a thousand years old.'

'Huh?'

Rosa peered at the scabby bar of rusty metal.

'I think what you've found,' Dad said, 'is an ancient sword.'

Part Two

'Two legends are wound
about Avalon –
the legend of the Cup and
the legend of the Sword.'
DION FORTUNE
Avalon of the Heart

The Boundaries of Psychiatry

LONDON

Josh reread the e-mail.

It was actually worse than he'd thought.

Now it's getting really weird, man. Really heavy.

Man. Marco was calling him *man*!

I mean, I could just about handle it that Mr. Cotton had seen a UFO and the mayor had had this timeslip kind of experience with these ghostly armed men.

But JASPER COOMBES...

Jasper Coombes seeing a sword coming out of a well in a snow-white hand?

I am so totally hacked off, I just can't tell you. It's doing my head in! Jasper Coombes does not deserve to see <u>a rusty penknife in a gardening glove!</u> It's like something has gone seriously, seriously wrong here...like the Antichrist has taken over or something.

<u>WHY ARE ALL THE WRONG PEOPLE SEEING THE *COOL VISIONS?*</u>

I don't know why I'm asking you really, except to kind of sound off about it. There's obviously no way you can explain it, on account of it's definitely outside the known boundaries of psychiatry.

Huh. Josh smiled. *That's what* he *thinks.*

He went to his psychiatry bookshelf, pulled out one of his psychiatry textbooks and looked up...

Persecution Complex.

Hmm. Close. Marco was certainly convinced he was getting a raw deal.

But it didn't go quite far enough. Marco was actually offended because people in this crazy town who he didn't like were having hallucinations.

Josh looked up *Paranoid Schizophrenia.*

This was closer.

A person thus afflicted will often seek to split his ego into good and bad parts, thus projecting his destructive impulses onto the person by whom he or she feels persecuted.

Yes, this was definitely a possibility. Marco was clearly jealous of this Jasper.

Why? Because Jasper was having the kind of hallucinations

that *Marco* wanted to have.

He was jealous of this Jasper's mental illness.

He wanted to be just as mentally ill as Jasper, if not even more mentally ill. He wanted to live in a weird fantasy world of his own, surrounded by total figments of his imagination.

He actually *wanted* to become insane!

Wow.

Josh rocked back in his executive chair in the office portion of his bedroom, which was also his consulting room.

He was pretty sure his father had never had a case this complex.

In fact, it was probably totally unique in the history of psychiatry.

And when he – Joshua Goldman – had researched it fully and written a learned paper on it for the *Journal of Psychiatry*, his analytical skills would be recognized the world over.

In fact they'd almost certainly name the condition after him.

Goldman's Syndrome.

Marco would also be famous – well, in a way – as the first recorded case of *Goldman's Syndrome*.

So he couldn't complain.

Josh thought long and hard about the situation.

This was definitely too important to be dealt with by an e-mail consultation.

Somehow – no matter how distasteful he was going to find it – Josh would have to get himself to Glastonbury.

The Abbot

GLASTONBURY

The Summer Blight had come, big time.

It didn't come every year, but it was well-known in Glastonbury.

What happened... Well, *nothing* happened, that was the point. Everybody was too sapped for anything to happen.

It was like all the life had been drained out of the air. The sky was often heavy with sour-lemony clouds. The days were hot and tiring and the nights were hot and sleepless, and if you did manage to get to sleep you'd have these murky half-dreams that never worked out but seemed to hang over you like a dirty veil for most of the following day.

And everybody was in a bad mood, particularly Woolly's

donkey, Merlin, who prowled the orchard glowering at people and then retreated to his stable and glowered at people from its doorway.

The nights were probably the best times, just about. Marco would stand at one of the two windows on either side of his attic bedroom in Woolly and Nancy's cottage. One window overlooked the lights of the town and the other looked up at the Tor. Marco used to think the Tor was his friend, but he wasn't sure now. He still hadn't seen a UFO.

But, on the plus side, he hadn't seen Jasper, either.

That was another good thing about the night-time – not only was it *slightly* cooler, but you didn't have to go out. Therefore, you didn't have to walk around looking over your shoulder or approaching corners with trepidation in case Shane and his mates were waiting to snatch you.

Marco had genuinely tried to find out if there *was* a legend connected to the old well in the garden behind the Glastonbury Tribunal, but Woolly hadn't heard of one and neither had any of the friendly mystics who hung out at The Cosmic Carrot.

'Why you wanner know, dude?' Woolly had asked.

'Oh, just, you know, wondered. It looked kind of...you know...'

He hadn't told Woolly about Jasper and Shane. When you were thirteen you were supposed to be able to look after yourself.

So a whole weekend had passed, with Marco mainly hanging around the cottage, practising his dowsing while trying to hide his rods from Woolly...having spent hours and hours, after Shane had de-manacled him, trying to straighten them out.

It hadn't really worked. One of the rods still looked like it was trying to dowse round corners.

On Monday morning, he gave up, raided what was left of the twenty-five pounds his dad had given him before he was dumped on Woolly and Nancy, and sneaked into town to buy a new pair.

The idea was to find a shop that sold rods and pendulums made by Woolly and get some identical rods. But the only dowsing dealer he could think of was in a fairly crowded part of High Street, which meant he'd be very visible.

And if Jasper or Shane were around...

Wearing his dark glasses and his baseball cap, pulled well down, Marco came in from Wellhouse Lane, keeping close to the shops so he could dodge into doorways, if necessary. And tensing up, ready to make a dash for it whenever he came to the entrance of an alley or a side street.

Luckily, everybody was slumping around looking miserable because of the Blight, and he was sure he was going to reach the shop without being spotted when...

'Oh no! It's Alex Rider's little brother on a secret mission for the government.'

Marco spun round.

The girl with long, dark hair laughed.

'Rosa!'

'You're not supposed to recognize me,' Rosa said. 'You're on a secret mission.'

'Yeah, yeah, very smart.' Embarrassed now, Marco pulled off his dark glasses. 'I thought you were avoiding me.'

'I was.'

'Oh.'

They walked into the Glastonbury Experience arcade,

where you could get your aura dry-cleaned and stuff like that.

'My dad still thinks you're bad news. He thinks you're carrying...' Rosa giggled. '...the stain of paganism.'

'Damn.' Marco looked down at his dark green T-shirt. 'I thought it had come off.'

'But we're safe this morning,' Rosa said. 'Dad's at the museum meeting some experts who've come to look at this piece of rusty metal we found. He thinks it's an ancient sword.'

Marco stared at her.

'What's up?' Rosa said.

'You didn't find it down a well, did you?'

'No, we found it down near the river. Dad reckoned it had been underwater for years until the hot weather and global warming and all that dried everything up. Look, what's wrong? Why *were* you wearing dark glasses?'

'It's sunny.'

'No it's not.'

Marco sighed and dumped the glasses in one of the pockets of his cargo trousers.

'Jasper's after me. And Shane. Probably.'

'Oh. *Those* psychos.'

'It's weird,' Marco said. 'Jasper's seen this vision of a sword held in a pure white hand...like coming out of the water?'

'Like in King Arthur? When the sword Excalibur is handed over by the Lady of the Lake and they just saw her hand?'

'Exactly.'

'Well, there you are,' Rosa said. 'He's read the story – or

more likely, in his case, seen the DVD – and he's made up his own version.'

'I don't think so. Jasper hates all that kind of stuff, doesn't he? And anyway, the sword Excalibur comes out of a lake, not a well.'

'But there aren't any lakes round here any more, are there? And why would he tell *you*?'

'What?'

'Why would he tell *you* about it? He hates you.'

'He said he wanted me to find out if there was a legend that might explain it...' Marco thought about this. Rosa had a way of putting her finger on things. 'No, you're right. Why would he tell me?'

He felt less worried, suddenly. Realized how much he'd missed Rosa, not seeing her for a couple of weeks.

'You fancy going up The Carrot for a soya shake?'

Rosa shrugged.

'Nothing *else* to do, I suppose.'

'Right,' Marco said.

He couldn't help watching to see if she did anything four times.

She stirred the blob of vanilla ice on her soya shake only three times, so unless her obsessive behavioural pattern had dropped down a bit, she was getting over it.

'Er...' Marco fiddled around with his own ice. 'Do you have any, um, contact, with the, er...'

'Monk?' Rosa said.

'Exactly.'

The flat in High Street where Rosa and her parents lived

backed onto the ruins of Glastonbury Abbey, which had been the oldest and one of the richest abbeys in England...until it had been trashed in the sixteenth century on the orders of Henry VIII. The Abbot, Richard Whiting, had been fitted up on false charges and dragged to the top of the Tor and then hanged, drawn and quartered.

Not a good way to go, even in those days.

Not long after they'd moved into the flat, Rosa had begun to see the shape of a cowled monk forming on her bedroom wall...although her mum and dad had claimed they couldn't see anything.

The last time she'd mentioned this to Marco – two or three weeks ago – she'd said she wasn't seeing anything in the wall any more. However...

'I don't really like talking about it,' Rosa said. 'It's kind of a private thing.'

'Oh,' Marco said. 'All right.'

Then she seemed to relax.

'Sorry. It's just...my dad. You know?'

'No better?'

'He thinks he's like...the voice of sanity in a sick town.'

'I can see how some people *might* think this was a sick town,' Marco said.

'He keeps asking if I wouldn't like to go away for a bit.'

Marco's life felt unsteady again. He stared at her.

'You can't do that...'

'You'll be leaving in a few weeks, anyway, to go back to school in London.'

'Yeah, well, I'm hoping there'll be some minor national disaster, like a great plague or something, so that all the roads and the railways have to be closed.'

He smiled to show he was only *half*-serious. Although he really didn't want to go back to London. Maybe not ever. His mum and dad had split up, and his mum was always having to go away to film stuff for the BBC...and his dad was working for Wilde-Hunt, for heaven's sake!

'All right,' Rosa said suddenly. 'What happens is...well, I sometimes see him.'

'The monk?'

'I'll be walking down the street in the evening, and I'll see him walking in front of me, just for a second, and then he'll like...fade into a wall or something.'

'Wow.'

'Or maybe I'll see his shadow amongst all the other shadows. Unmistakeable, even in a town full of people wearing robes. It's a very strange...very *still* shadow. Like the shadow of a statue.'

'Isn't that scary?'

'Just a bit. It's also kind of comforting, because...'

Rosa stopped because Rox, the waitress, was clearing the table next to theirs. Rox, like all the staff at The Cosmic Carrot, wore an apron with MEAT IS MURDER printed on it.

'...because I know who he is,' Rosa whispered, '...and that he means me no harm.'

'You really think it's him? Richard the Abbot? I mean, he was executed. And carved up. If it really was him, wouldn't he...wouldn't all his insides be hanging out and his neck stretched at a, you know, unnatural angle?'

Rosa looked up at the ceiling.

'He's *long* over that, you fool. And anyway, just because his body was mutilated doesn't mean his spirit isn't intact.'

'Wow,' Marco said. 'I can't get over how cool you've become about all this.'

'I'm not always cool. Sometimes I think I must be going bonkers. I mean, how do I *know* it's him?

'How *do* you know?'

'I just do. He lets me know.'

'He talks to you?'

'Yeah, but not in a way you can hear. You're just...aware of the words.'

'What sort of words?'

'Well, more just the *sense* of something. Like it could be, for instance...*All will be well*. Or something like that. Or it could be a warning. In which case you don't actually feel the word "warning", you just feel a *sense* of it. And you know it isn't coming from you.'

Marco remembered how Eleri had said that Rosa had developed Obsessive Compulsive Disorder because she was trying to stop herself having feelings like this, because her dad didn't like it.

The fact that she wasn't showing obvious symptoms of OCD any more...that could be linked to the way these messages were coming through. She was simply relaxing and letting them in, instead of rushing to do something an extra three times to drag her mind away from *the threshold of the unknown*.

'If you're getting warnings of bad stuff,' he said, 'I still can't understand why your dad would think that's a bad thing.'

'Because he thinks that anything paranormal that doesn't happen in church or as a direct result of praying must be evil. Because things like that aren't supposed to happen.'

'But they happen here all the time.'

'That's why he believes he's been sent here. To stop it.'

That being the case, the very last thing Big Dave would want was his own daughter going psychic. Marco could understand that.

And then another thought hit him.

'So how's he going to react when he finds out weird things've been happening to people like Jasper and Griff Daniel and Mr. Cotton.'

'What things?' Rosa said. 'Anyway he's not here.'

'Who?'

'Mr. Daniel. Dad had to go to see him about some kind of civic service the church is putting on for the council, and he wasn't at home. So Dad kept going back to his house and he was *never* at home. And so Dad rang the council and they said they didn't know where he was either.'

'Maybe he's on holiday.'

'Apparently, he never goes on holiday in case something happens in Glastonbury behind his back. He's just... disappeared.'

'As in *vanished*?'

'Well, he's not here. In fact – it's odd, but Mr. Coombes has also just...gone.'

'Jasper's dad, the estate agent?'

'We pay our rent to him, and Mum was saying that when she went in on Saturday – he always works Saturdays – they said he'd had to go away but he'd probably be back in a week. Maybe he's taken Jasper. I mean, I usually see Jasper hanging round, kind of sneering at people, but I haven't seen him for a few days.'

'Do you think that means I'm safe from getting beaten up?'

'I don't know what it means,' Rosa said. 'You said things had been happening to him and some other people. What things?'

Marco told her about the UFO and Griff Daniel's ghostly warriors. However, before they had chance to discuss any of it, the door of The Cosmic Carrot flew back, with a frantic clattering of wind chimes, and there, glaring at them, was Rosa's big, black-bearded dad in his long black cassock.

The Vanishing

If anybody ever needed throwing out of church for bad behaviour, the Reverend Dave Wilcox was obviously the man for the job.

Marco just couldn't figure how he ever managed to persuade anybody to go in there in the first place. He looked like the kind of bloke who, if you coughed during his sermon, would come bounding down from the pulpit and beat you round the head with his prayer book.

But, at least, unlike Marco's dad, he wasn't *economical with the truth*.

In fact, the word *economy* probably wasn't in Dave's dictionary. Marco remembered the first time he'd seen him – this was the first night after he'd arrived in Glasto. Woolly and a few friends had been holding an Avalonians' public meeting in High Street outside St John's Church, and Eleri had been warning the town, as she often did, of a Great Darkness about to descend.

For once, she'd been dead right. The Great Darkness had descended in a matter of minutes, in the form of Big Dave Wilcox, storming out of the church in his long black cassock, steaming with righteous rage. Accusing them of conducting *disgusting heathen rituals* outside the House of God and calling them *filthy scum*. Only Woolly had stood up to him. *Where's your sense of spirituality, man?* Woolly had said.

Marco didn't think he was as brave as Woolly. He just looked up at Big Dave with what he guessed was a really sickly smile.

'Hello, Mr. Wilcox,' he said in what sounded depressingly like a feeble little voice.

Big Dave didn't even look at him.

'Rosa,' he said. 'You need to come with me to The George and Pilgrims. The media would like to take your photograph for this week's paper, and they haven't got all day.'

Rosa blinked, looking apprehensive.

'What have I done?'

'Done?' Big Dave almost smiled. 'What you've done...is made what looks like being the most remarkable archaeological discovery in this area for many years.'

'Me?'

'Come *on*,' Dave boomed. 'No time to waste. They're pretty sure it's Iron Age.'

He still hadn't looked at Marco, and now Marco realized why.

There were two other people in the doorway of The Cosmic Carrot and one of them had a camera. Nikon digital single-lens reflex, if Marco wasn't mistaken.

The media.

Rosa looked at them nervously.

'We haven't paid for our drinks.'

'I'll handle that,' Marco said, hoping he'd still have enough for the dowsing rods.

Dave glanced at Marco with his dark, hard eyes, and then leaned over Rosa and hissed, 'We'll talk about *this* later.'

Marco counted out the money for Rox, the waitress, and watched Rosa and her dad going off with the media.

And now he'd recognized who the media were. At least, he didn't know the photographer, but he saw that the woman with him was Sonia Warbuck, deputy editor of the *Glastonbury Guardian*. A woman who, according to Woolly, was a serious, heavy-duty Glastie who hated anything weird and had refused to print some totally amazing stories about what was *really* happening in the town.

It looked like Big Dave had given the story exclusively to what Woolly called *the straight press*.

Which meant that nobody had informed the struggling alternative paper, *The Avalonian*, which was edited by Diane Daniel and Mrs. Carey, who ran the spooky bookshop.

And was printed by Sam Daniel.

Right, then.

'A sword?' Sam said. 'What kind of sword?'

'Dunno, I haven't seen it, yet.'

Marco liked hanging out at Sam's print shop. It had coloured posters on the walls, of the Tor at dawn, moonlight in the Abbey ruins, the Holy Thorn bent in a gale and significant stuff like that. It also sold printed T-shirts and these Holy Grail style beakers, with a drawing on the side of this bloke with a wispy beard, in Middle Eastern kit, and the words Joe 'Mathea's Holy Mug.

You gotter be able to laugh at yourself sometimes, Sam would say. *Else you might wake up one day and find you've turned into a Glastie.*

Meaning, Marco guessed, that Sam was afraid of waking up one day and finding he'd turned into his dad.

On Sam's desk were copies of a recent edition of *The Avalonian*, which had a major article giving the real story about Wilde-Hunt and how their plans to destroy the small shops had been defeated.

The *Glastonbury Guardian* just had the official version, about the council reluctantly having to turn down the wonderful multi-million pound plan for the amazing Avalon World which would have 'really put the town on the tourist map'.

The Avalonian had pictures of Woolly and Nancy, all smiles, with Merlin the donkey. And a blurred shot, taken by Sam, of Marco's dad leaping angrily into his car to drive back to London. Marco had sent him a copy. Maybe this had been a mistake. He hadn't heard from his dad since.

Also on Sam's desk was his wife, Diane, wearing a white T-shirt the size of a duvet cover, her feet dangling over a wastepaper bin as if she'd been bathing them.

'And you say *Rosa* found this sword?' Diane said. 'Gosh.'

Marco knew that Diane liked Rosa. It seemed she'd been

a bit like that as a girl – strange things happening to her that she couldn't explain and a father who pooh-poohed it all.

'Found it down by the river, apparently,' Marco said. 'She says it's quite a big one. Big Dave reckons it's the most remarkable archaeological discovery round here for years.'

Diane jumped down with a thunk that upset the pile of *Avalonians*.

'And it's where? Right now?'

'At The George and Pilgrims. Or at least that's where Big Dave's taken Rosa and the media.'

'Oh.' Diane bent to pick up all the *Avalonians*. 'So he's given the story to the *Guardian*. Oh well...'

'That's no big surprise,' Sam said. 'The feller hates us. Thinks we're all evil pagans. Still...public place, The Pilgrims. No reason you shouldn't wander over there for a glass of cider, is there?'

'Oh dear,' Diane said, standing up, with all the *Avalonians* spilling out of her arms. 'I hate confrontation.'

Sam always said Diane was too nice to be a journalist. 'In that case,' he said, 'we better all go. I'll shut the shop.'

Marco beamed. That was what he'd hoped Sam would say.

On their way up the street, they ran into Eleri. Marco figured it was far too hot for a long black dress and all that heavy jewellery, but he supposed she had an image to keep up.

'Have you *heard*?' Eleri said urgently.

The air in the town centre was thick and humid and the roofs of the shops were like the deep red mud you sometimes saw at the bottom of a dried-up pond. But Eleri's face was even paler than usual, and her eyes were flickering like little gas burners.

'Heard what?' Sam said.

'They've all disappeared!'

'Who?'

'The people who had the visions! Griff Daniel...Cotton... Cresswell, from the bank. And even that boy, Jasper, and his father.'

'Disappeared?' Sam snorted. 'What are you on about?'

'Vanished. And no one knows where they are!'

'Somebody *must* know where they are... My old man doesn't just disappear. Not that I haven't wished—'

'Even Mr. Cotton's wife says she doesn't know,' Eleri snapped. 'Neither does the woman at the estate agent's know where Mr. Coombes and his son have gone. They seem to have completely disappeared from the face of the earth.'

'Oh, come on, Eleri, you'll be saying they've been abducted by aliens next.'

Eleri took in a long, shuddering breath and stared into nowhere.

'Oh, hell...' Sam raised his eyes to the muddy rooftops. 'Do us a *favour*. You're a woman of learning. You used to be a *professor*, for heaven's sake!'

'No person of real learning,' Eleri said severely, 'ever entirely dismisses the idea of The Vanishing. Abduction by aliens is simply the latest explanation of a phenomenon as old as time. In past centuries, human beings who disappeared were usually said to have been taken by the fairies.'

'Taken for a ride more like.'

Sam was a true Avalonian and a believer at heart, but he reckoned you should always start out by *not* believing.

It saved a lot of disappointment later.

'And in this case,' Eleri said, 'there were portents: the ghostly army...the dark flying object over the Tor...'

'Yeah, but—'

'The sword emerging from the water like—'

'Oh gosh.' Diane turned to Marco. '*Where* did you say this sword was found?'

'Down below the town. Near the river. Rosa said her dad reckoned it had probably been underwater for years before global warming and stuff dried out the...'

Marco blinked.

'Lake?' Diane said.

'I suppose.'

'How old did you say it was, Marco?'

'I think Big Dave said it was probably Iron Age.'

'Iron Age...' Eleri breathed in like a vacuum pump. 'That means Celtic. A Celtic sword has been found on the bottom of what *was* the lake.'

Eleri raised her eyes to where the sun would be if it hadn't been smothered by oily clouds. And then, without another word, she sank slowly to her knees on the pavement, a few paces from the entrance of The George and Pilgrims, and her voice came out in a parched whisper, like the wind through dried reeds.

'*Could it be...?*'

A Dangerous Game

LONDON

'I don't get this,' Josh's father said. 'You actually *want* to go and stay with Grandma Goldman?'

Josh looked at him seriously. They were in his father's home office, with its extensive view over the Thames. He could tell his father was wondering how come Josh was sitting behind the desk.

There was an art to it.

'Well, Father,' Josh said. 'I was thinking about this a lot last night. I'm no longer a child...'

'So you keep reminding me.'

'And I have to face up to my responsibilities. Grandma Goldman has been very good to me, right?'

'She completely dotes on you, Josh.'

'And she...well, she's not getting any younger.'

'Well, none of us —'

'And people don't live for ever,' Josh said.

'Look, what are you — ?'

'And I only see her about twice a year. What if next time we go to visit her she's...gone?'

'Where?'

'You know...*gone.*'

'What?'

'It can happen, Father.'

Josh's father blinked behind his glasses. There was a gleam of sweat on his forehead.

'Josh, I realize it can – and indeed, at some stage will – happen to *all* of us. Especially me, with all the stress at work and having to deal with you as well. But I would humbly suggest that it...it's marginally *less* likely to happen, in the short term, to Granny Goldman. Who is living a very healthy life by the sea and has once again got herself elected President of the Torquay Tennis Club.'

'Tennis can be a dangerous game for the over-sixties,' Josh said.

He sat back behind his father's desk with his eyes half-closed and waited.

Obviously, he'd been studying his father's psychology for many years, so he had a good idea what was now going through his mind.

It was like this: on the one hand, he was suspicious. There was only so much of Granny Goldman that anyone could stand – in fact, there must definitely be a high level of masochism among members of the Torquay Tennis Club.

On the other hand, the possibility of getting rid of Josh for a week must be seriously tempting. It must be getting tougher for even a distinguished psychiatrist like Dr. Simon Goldman to keep up with an intellect as incisive and glittering as his son's.

'Look...' Father pushed back his chair and stood up. 'I have an appointment at eleven, so, ah...'

Josh said nothing.

'So would *you* mind ringing her and making the arrangements?'

Josh smiled thinly and nodded.

Caledfwlch

GLASTONBURY

It was the oldest inn in town. It was built of stone, and over its entrance were the heraldic arms of the medieval king, Edward IV. On its hanging sign, a knight in armour carried a shield with a red cross on it...and a big sword.

Inside, The George and Pilgrims was a bit like a church. Dark but lit by rays of red and blue and orange from stained glass in the deep windows.

Soft colours fell into the small, oak-panelled room where the ancient sword lay on a folded white tablecloth. From the doorway, Marco couldn't see it properly, but he didn't like to go in any further because of what Big Dave might say.

He was aware of a hush in the room, people standing quite stiffly.

They were posing for a photograph.

Big Dave's hands were resting on Rosa's shoulders. Rosa looked like she'd rather be anywhere but here. She was a northerner. Northerners didn't like too much fuss.

On the other hand, Big Dave, who was as northern as you could get, was beaming through his beard.

The photographer said, 'Rosa, for this one, let's have you looking down at the sword. And Mr. Wilcox, if you could be looking at Rosa – the proud father? That's it. Excellent!'

Marco peered over the shoulder of Sonia Warbuck, deputy editor of the *Glastonbury Guardian*. The table was lit up by the camera flash, and he saw a blackened and rusted blade, still thick with mud, with a knobbly lump on the end. It was longer than he'd expected. He'd seen pictures of Iron Age swords, and they weren't much bigger than carving knives.

'What did you do with it last night, Mr. Wilcox?' Sonia Warbuck asked.

'Ah...' Big Dave looked a bit embarrassed. 'Well we didn't realize quite how important it was, and my wife thought it was too dirty to bring inside so we, er...I put it in the old coal shed in the yard below the flat.'

Sonia laughed and made a note of this on her pad.

'Presumably, the museum will take it now,' Dave said.

'Oh, no,' Sonia said. 'I think it'll be going to Bristol first. Somewhere they have the facilities to clean it up and carry out various tests. It could take weeks, maybe months. Is that what you'd think, Mr. Montague?'

'Oh, at least,' an elderly bloke with a white beard said.

'I only wish we had the facilities here to examine it properly. One hardly likes to let it go.'

Marco couldn't be sure, but he thought Mr. Montague was from the local museum.

Eleri was standing next to Marco. She whispered something he couldn't make out.

'Sorry?'

'*Caledfwlch*,' Eleri breathed.

Marco was no wiser.

'The original Welsh name.'

'Huh?'

'In the Iron Age, all Britons spoke the language we now know as Welsh.'

Sonia Warbuck turned round. She had short hair and flat eyes and a smile as sweet as, er, Marmite.

'Oh,' she said. 'It's you. Did we invite you?'

'Ah...' Mr. Montague spotted Eleri. 'Dr. Cadwallader. Would you like to give us your opinion?'

Sonia Warbuck's eyebrows shot up.

'Dr. Cadwallader is a distinguished professor of ancient history, originally from the University of Wales,' Mr. Montague said to Sonia. 'And an experienced archaeologist.'

Sonia said, 'But she—' And dried up as Mr. Montague guided Eleri into the room. The face of the Rev. Dave Wilcox darkened at once.

'What's *this* woman doing here?'

'She appears to be...' Sonia Warbuck wrinkled her nose. '...some sort of professor of history. News to me.'

Sonia scowled and backed off. Big Dave stood breathing down his nose like a bull in a pen. Ignoring them both, Eleri bent over the sword but didn't touch it. Her green eyes focused on the relic with such intensity that you could almost see twin beams spearing down like lasers, pencil-thin and probing.

'It may be first century,' she said. 'Or even earlier. A similar one was found in the north-east of England. You see these circles around the hilt, Mr. Montague? These little studs?'

'Ah yes. I thought they were perhaps enamelled decorations.'

'Yes. Four on the hilt and five clustered around the hand-guard. It's in remarkable condition. It must have been very heavy.'

'Still is, Dr. Cadwallader. The sword, I would suggest, of quite a powerful chieftain.'

'Oh yes. Yes indeed. I personally am not aware of such a large sword from this period ever having been found in this country.'

'My word,' Mr. Montague said.

He and Eleri swapped excited glances.

'Er...' Sonia Warbuck turned to Eleri. 'What was that word you whispered earlier?'

'*Caledfwlch?*'

'That was it. What's it mean...Professor?'

'I am almost afraid to say what it means,' Eleri said.

And she rushed out.

That night, up in his attic bedroom, Marco took his pendulum out of its velvet case. He brought it to the window overlooking the lights of Glastonbury town and held it up and looked at it.

The pendulum, given to him by Woolly, was a stone the

size and shape of an orange boiled sweet, hanging from a slender chain. It seemed to pick up the lights from the town and glow with an inner light of its own.

Which was impossible, so Marco knew he must be imagining this – Impressionable Kid Syndrome was what Josh called it.

Josh didn't believe in anything paranormal...although maybe even *he* was coming round a bit. This evening, Marco had had an e-mail from him expressing interest in the visions of the Glasties.

Tell me about this Jasper? Do you hate him *even more* because he is now having psychic experiences?

Marco wasn't sure what Josh was getting at, but at least he was showing an interest.

Okay, back to the pendulum.

It was a way of making contact with your deeper self... bringing out information that some inner part of you already knew...or could find out. This inner self would send messages through your nervous system to your arm muscles and the tips of your fingers and make the pendulum move.

What you did, you held it up and let it dangle from the chain, held between finger and thumb. Then you relaxed and emptied your mind, and you asked it a question – usually a *yes* or *no* kind of question.

The arrangement Marco had come to with his pendulum was that when it swung backwards and forwards it meant *yes*, and when it swung from side to side, that was *no*.

But you had to be careful what kind of questions you asked. Woolly had told Marco it was best not to make them too personal or it might be affected by what you *wanted* to happen. For instance, if you asked it, *Will Man United win on Saturday?* the pendulum might say yes because it knew that was what you wanted to happen. Or it might say no because you were trying too hard to *compensate* for what you wanted to happen.

Either way, you couldn't trust the answer, so it was best to ask questions where you didn't have a personal opinion. Like...

Well, like, *Has Jasper been abducted by aliens?*

On one hand, Marco didn't think that was likely. On the other, how bad a thing would it be if he never saw Jasper again?

Right.

Marco held the end of the chain between finger and thumb, at chest height so he could look down on the pendulum. It hung motionless, waiting. Marco put the question in his head.

Has Jas—?

There was a tap on the bedroom door.

'You awake, dude?'

Marco felt an odd sense of relief.

He'd found this happening before. Sometimes when you were about to use the pendulum, something would happen to stop you. Which, he guessed, meant that this was a question you weren't supposed to ask.

Woolly came in and sat down on the bed. He didn't seem like himself.

'Don't mind me askin',' he said. 'But when you was

dowsing in the orchard earlier on, I couldn't help noticing something strange about the rods you was usin'.'

Marco blinked nervously. They were the new rods he'd bought this afternoon. They were exactly the same as the ones Woolly had given him. *Exactly.* Had Woolly dowsed the truth about them? Detected, with the help of his own pendulum, that these were not the original rods?

'Only they still had the price ticket on,' Woolly said.

Marco slumped down on the bed next to him.

'There a problem, dude?'

No getting out of this one.

'Um...sort of.' Maybe this was a sign, too, that he shouldn't try to hide anything from Woolly.

So he told him what had happened to the old rods.

Woolly nodded slowly. 'Shane Davey, eh?'

'He was one of the boys with Roger Cromwell, when he tried to make you dig up the Dark Chalice.'

Woolly nodded again. 'You should've told me about this before.'

'I didn't want to seem like a wimp.'

'I can understand that,' Woolly said. 'Only, Shane Davey, he's the younger brother of Darryl Davey, now doing eighteen months for aggravated assault.'

'Oh.'

'Bit of a social problem in that family, look.'

'How do you mean?'

'They're all scumbags,' Woolly said.

'Oh.'

They stared at one another glumly for a few seconds.

'Still,' Marco said eventually, 'at least he's not very smart, and he doesn't seem to be able to function without Jasper

Coombes to tell him what to do. And as *he* seems to have disappeared...'

'Ah...'

'What?'

'Looks like he's back,' Woolly said.

Marco's shoulders sagged.

'Looks like they're all back. The Coombes boy and his dad. Cotton. Griff Daniel. Been gone four days, but tonight they're back. Mate of mine seen Griff down The Rifleman's Arms. Cotton, too. Didn't seem normal, he said.'

'How do you mean?'

'Dead on their feet, the pair of 'em. Eyes all glazed – and, in Griff's case, that was *before* he'd had a pint. Wouldn't say where they'd been. Almost seemed like they couldn't. Weird. Real weird.'

'Eleri thought they might've been...you know...abducted by...something.'

'Well, I don't know about that.' Woolly sighed. 'But one thing I *can* tell you is things is not right. Not right at all.'

Marco was puzzled. All these exciting things were happening: UFOs around the Tor, the mysterious sword turning up – and *that* was absolutely genuine; there was nobody more honest than Rosa. But Marco didn't think he'd ever seen Woolly looking so down. 'What's wrong, Woolly? What's wrong, *really*?'

Woolly sighed. 'Maybe it's to do with the Blight, but I don't seem to have much energy no more. I feel like an old man.'

'You don't *look* like...'

But he did. For the first time, he kind of did.

'And, the worst thing of all, look...whenever I tries to

dowse...' Woolly's eyes went all wide and stricken. '...I can't do it.'

Marco leaped up from the bed in horror.

'You can't *dowse*?'

'It's never happened to me before. Not like this.' Woolly's hands hung limply down between his knees. 'I don't know what to do.'

Celeb

Rosa awoke in the night to find her bed cold and soaking. It wasn't sweat.

The undersheet was wet through. She was rolling in it. It was sticking to her back and her shoulders. The duvet on top of her seemed twice its normal weight; it was bulked out with it, and crispy at the top edge under her chin, stiffening where it had dried.

Rosa went rigid with revulsion.

Blood. It was blood.

She was instantly paralysed with fear. She lay in the blotchy darkness and began to whimper.

Ohno, ohno, ohno...

Outside, a lone car rolled by on High Street, and the TV screen opposite the bed was like a grey extra window, and her head was full of white noise like a radio between stations.

She managed to turn her head towards the wall – the wall with the stones of the Abbey built into it, where the shape of the monk...

Richard...help me...

Rosa flung out her thoughts like stones at the wall.

Help me. I'm dying.

But the stones bounced off. He wasn't there. No Richard. She was dying alone.

'You could at least have smiled for the photograph,' Mum had said over tea.

Mum worked at The George and Pilgrims as a receptionist. She'd fixed up for them to have the room to display the sword.

'If it turns out to be as important as they think, Rosie, you'll be famous, like...oh, like the man who discovered Tutankhamun's tomb.'

Not a good example, Rosa thought. The man who discovered Tutankhamun's tomb was said to have released an ancient curse.

'I don't really like it,' she said.

'Well, *I* don't like it the way it is now, all covered with gunge.' Mum was sawing off a slice of malt-loaf, the knife making Rosa think of the sword hacking through...flesh. 'But when it's cleaned up...'

'It can never be cleaned up,' Rosa said.

And didn't know where that thought had come from.

Dad had patted her hand.

'This is the best thing that could have happened, Rosa. I was getting worried that you were going to be a loner in a strange town. But now, when you go to your new school, everybody will know who you are. You'll be a celebrity.'

The thought of being a celeb made Rosa curl up inside.

'So it's silly hanging out with that boy. He'll be going home to London in a few weeks and, as I've repeatedly said, he's not the sort...'

His voice droned on, fading away like one of those loudspeaker vans in the street at election time. Rosa wasn't hearing it any more. She'd heard it all before anyway – that smart-mouthed boy and his old hippy grandparents and their pagan friends.

'...and as for that creepy-looking woman. If she was an actual professor of history, I'm the Archbishop of Canterbury! Did you see the way she ran out before she could be exposed as a fraud?'

'She ran out because she—'

Oh, what was the use? It would only make things worse. But she was sure Eleri had picked up the...what would you call it? *The emanations.* The dark history that came off that sword like chemical smoke. She hadn't really been aware of this until they'd put it on show in the pub. Because she and the sword hadn't spent last night under the same roof.

She stared at Dad.

'Why did you have to bring it back?'

'Because until it's claimed by the Crown or whoever, it's still ours, apparently.'

'Couldn't you have locked it up in the church or something?'

'Far safer here. The church was broken into last week. It's all these damned drug-sodden pagans on the streets. Besides, it's only for one night. James Montague's coming to collect it tomorrow to take it to the museum in Bristol for scientific tests.' Dad laughed. 'They were only worried that, if I took it, it might be kept in the coal shed again. As if!'

Rosa thought the coal shed would be the best place.

Well, not the *best* place.

The best place would be the bottom of another lake.

She stumbled, barefoot, out into the passage, a hand clasped to her stomach, as if she was stopping her insides from tumbling out. She felt sick and light-headed.

Faint moonlight lay like a thin dust sheet on the wooden floor of the passage and the wooden box which lay there like a small coffin.

The box had held... She didn't know what it had held originally, but it had travelled down with them from the North full of cutlery.

It was just the right size to take the sword.

She'd watched, half-fascinated, half-repelled, as Dad and the museum guy had laid the sword on an old tablecloth, folded up. But the museum guy had said that was too stiff, so Mum had found one of Rosa's old winter nighties, and they'd wrapped it in that – Rosa screaming, *No, no!* but silently, inside her head. Not saying anything aloud, because Dad had been ready, not so long ago, to take her to a child-psychiatrist, maybe have her put away.

So there it lay, wrapped in her nightie.

As they were putting it in the box, a bit of mud had flaked

off, and the museum man, Mr. Montague, had said, *Look at that...it's still sharp under there. It's odd to think of how many people this sword must have killed. Imagine that, wielded with two hands and landing on your—*

He'd realized, at this point, that Rosa was there and said, *Whoops. Mustn't give you nightmares.*

And laughed, as though nightmares were a joke.

The dream came back to her now.

She was lying on a field, and the smells around her were horrible. That was the worst of it, the smells.

Bodies, dead and not-quite-dead, were lying on either side of her and one – oh God – was across her legs, its throat slashed and gushing. She could feel hot blood on her bare legs.

Someone had lit a fire and smoke went down her throat and made her cough.

A voice rumbled from somewhere in a language she didn't know.

And yet did know.

Because she knew the voice had said, *That one coughed.*

Another voice said, *Well, finish it, then.*

And then she heard a third voice as if it was carried on the wind – as if it was *part of* the wind – and the voice whispered...

...dread. More dread.

She opened her eyes – just knew she would *have* to open her eyes – and saw the sword rise up against the sun, catching its rays, and when it came down it was like the sun itself was falling.

* * *

Rosa sucked in a big breath and snapped on the bedroom light and stared hard at the bed, closing and opening her eyes like a camera shutter.

Apart from the undersheet being all wrinkled, the bed was unmarked.

No blood.

She went down on her knees, with her head on the side of the bed and sobbed for a long time.

When she looked up, it was not yet 2.30 a.m. Another four hours before she could reasonably get up and leave the flat.

When she eventually went back to bed, she left the light on.

She got into bed four times and then laid her head on the pillow four times before she was able to fall into a snuffly sleep.

The Fabled...

Next morning, Woolly didn't get up. Marco was worried. Nancy tried to gloss over it.

'He sometimes gets like this, lovey,' she said. 'Gets these depressions, doesn't know what to do with himself. And it usually happens when there's a Blight.'

'Depression?' Josh had told him a lot about depression. 'You mean actual *clinical* depression?'

'Could be. The doctor tried to give him some pills for it once, but Woolly wouldn't take them. Said he wasn't going to put any money into the pockets of the drug companies. Woolly doesn't trust drug companies, especially the ones that experiment on animals.'

'What can we do?'

'Just wait till it's over...and pray it *will* be over.'

'How long does it last?'

'Hard to say.' Nancy shrugged. 'How long's a pendulum chain? Look, if you stay here and keep an eye on him, I'll go down the shops and get some fresh food, if it isn't all wilting in the Blight.'

Nancy put on a giant straw hat with big feathers sticking up out of its yellow band. Marco watched her wheeling her bike round the side of the cottage and then went back and sat down at the kitchen table, piled high with books and the sleeves of ancient vinyl rock albums.

Woolly suffered from depression?

What a horrible word depression was. It was...depressing.

Woolly didn't come downstairs until after ten. He looked awful. His ponytail seemed thin and sparse and his skin was the colour of the Blighted sky. He slumped down at the kitchen table with a mug of tea Marco had made.

'Sorry, dude. I just feel...useless.'

'But Woolly...' Marco was shocked. 'You're a totally crucial person. You could *never* be useless.'

'When a dowser can't dowse no more,' Woolly said, 'he might as well be dead.'

'No...' Marco went cold. 'Don't talk like that.'

'Sorry, Marco...figure of speech.'

But Marco wasn't sure it was.

And when Nancy came back from the shops it all got much, much worse.

'Just seen Griff Daniel.' She unpacked the two bags of chickpeas, some oranges, apples and grapes, wholemeal flour, a jar of vegetarian ravioli and a copy of the *Glastonbury*

Guardian. 'I thought you said he was dead on his feet.'

Woolly looked up blearily.

'That's what I was told.'

'Well, not any more he ain't. He was practically bouncing up the street. He was wearing a white suit. Griff Daniel in a *white suit*! He looked like a new man. Eleri was there, and she said it looked like he'd been...*empowered.*'

The news that the mayor of Glastonbury had been empowered just seemed to make Woolly go weaker. He lowered his head into his hands and shook it slowly.

'And then there's this,' Nancy said, and pushed a pile of psychedelic CDs on one side to spread the *Glastonbury Guardian* out on the table. 'Oh dear. This is...if it's true it's the most amazing thing ever.'

Marco had only seen three copies of the *Glastonbury Guardian*, and they'd all been so boring he hadn't bothered to read any of them. They certainly hadn't had anything like this half-page picture of Rosa, Big Dave and the ancient blackened sword under a massive headline.

'Holy Joseph,' Woolly howled. '*Holy Joseph!*'

Over Woolly's shoulder, Marco read:

Is this...
EXCALIBUR?
by SONIA WARBUCK

An ancient sword discovered this week near Glastonbury could be the fabled Excalibur, according to experts.

Legend says King Arthur's famous 'magic' sword was thrown into a lake as he lay dying of his wounds over 1,500 years ago.

Now it could have been recovered by thirteen-year-old Rosa Wilcox. Rosa was walking with her father, the Rev. David Wilcox, the new curate at St John's, when she tripped over what she thought was a rusty gate hinge.

The eminent Glastonbury-based Celtic scholar, Dr. Eleri Cadwallader, examined the sword yesterday and immediately identified it as Caledfwlch – the original Welsh name for Excalibur.

'I personally am not aware of such a large sword from this period ever having been found in this country,' said Dr. Cadwallader. 'I am almost afraid to say what it means.'

Mr. James Montague, former curator of Glastonbury Museum, said, 'Dr. Cadwallader is a very distinguished historian, and I'm sure she knows what she's talking about. Certainly, the sword looks old enough to have been used by King Arthur, if he existed, back in the Dark Ages.'

The sword is already being hailed as one of the greatest archaeological discoveries of the past century and can only add credibility to the legend of the man known as The Once and Future King, who was said to have been buried at Glastonbury Abbey.

Mr. Montague explained, 'According to the legend, when Arthur was dying of wounds inflicted by his own son, Mordred, he asked one of his most trusted knights, Sir Bedivere to throw the sword back into the lake whence it had come.

'Sir Bedivere thought it was a shame to throw away

such a beautiful thing and pretended he'd done the deed. But of course Arthur knew he hadn't, and so Bedivere was forced to actually throw it into the water... whereupon the hand and arm of the Lady of the Lake emerged from the depths and caught it.'

Marco immediately thought of Jasper and the white hand emerging from the well. He looked at Woolly.

Woolly had gone pale.

'Where's Eleri?'

'Ah,' Nancy said. 'That's what I was going to tell you next. She's in the stable with the donkey.'

'What?'

'She's in hiding. When the Glastie *Guardian* hit the streets, all the national papers and the television news people started ringing her up. And you know what Eleri's like about the straight media.'

'This is all mad.' Woolly turned to Marco. 'What do *you* know about this? The girl's your friend.'

'She just said she'd found this sword down by the river. So I told Sam and Diane and we all went to The Pilgrims, with Eleri. And Sonia Warbuck was there with a photographer.'

'Eleri said all *this*...' Woolly stabbed at the paper. '...to Sonia Warbuck?'

'I think it just kind of slipped out. Why?'

''Cause everybody knows Sonia Warbuck thinks Eleri's a mad old bat. In fact the last time she was mentioned in this rag was when she was given a GLASBO.'

Marco blinked. 'Glasbo?'

'Glastonbury's version of an Anti-Social Behaviour

Order,' Woolly said. 'They hung one on Eleri for disturbing the peace by making prophesies of doom late at night down by the Abbey gatehouse. She ain't allowed to stand there after 6 p.m. for the next year.'

Marco thought this was quite funny, but he didn't think it was a good time to laugh.

Besides, he wanted to know about Excalibur. Because, like...this was surely fantastic...mega...wasn't it?

But why was Woolly so suspicious? Was it just a symptom of his depression?

'It ain't right,' he kept saying. 'The Glastie *Guardian* don't do this kind of story. They just does stuff about the council. They don't go berserk like this over something that ain't proved. And they *never* listens to folks like Eleri.'

'Well,' Nancy said, 'there is actually a comment from Griff Daniel as well. They must've talked to him as soon as he...reappeared.'

Woolly snatched up the paper. Over his shoulder, Marco read:

> *'This is a remarkable find,' said the mayor of Glastonbury, Councillor Griffith Daniel. 'I have always maintained that King Arthur was a real person who is buried in our town. I think this proves it beyond a doubt.'*

'Aaaargh!' Woolly looked close to beating his head on the table. 'The hypocritical old— It was only last year he made a speech saying it was time we got rid of these old legends for good and all and brought Glasto into the third millennium.'

114

'Perhaps he's reformed after his vision,' Nancy said.

'There's something funny going down,' Woolly said grimly. 'I can't get a handle on it and it's doing my head in. I better go down the stable, talk to Eleri.'

Riff-raff

When Woolly had gone, Marco couldn't keep still. He wanted to find out everything there was to know about Excalibur. He wanted to get down into the town and find Rosa. He wanted to—

'Sit down, Marco,' Nancy said. 'I want to try and tell you about this.'

She made some more tea.

'It's hard for me to explain what's happening to Woolly. I suppose a lot of the Avalonians will be feeling like this, but it's probably worse for Woolly 'cause he's a local boy, and it hasn't been easy for him over the years. If you're local born and bred you're expected to be more...normal.'

'Like have short hair and drive a Renault Megane?'

'And have the *right* attitude towards all the young people with tattoos and nose-studs,' Nancy said.

'Like your, er, tattoos and nose, er...?'

Nancy pulled down the sleeve of her red dress to hide a tattoo with the same design as the cover of the Chalice Well, where the water flowed red.

'I'm afraid you don't see many truly local people like me and Woolly. Not our age, anyway. And we've taken a fair bit of stick from the folks we went to school with who all hate the pilgrims and the Avalonians and see them as intruders who are ruining the town.'

'So how did you and Woolly come to be...you know?'

'Well, I went to art college, and...everybody at art college was a bit mad in those days. And when I came back to start work as a teacher—'

'You were a *teacher*?'

'Didn't you know?'

'No, Mum never...'

Marco tailed off. This was a seriously taboo subject. Mum seemed to be ashamed of Woolly and Nancy.

Nancy handed Marco his tea in a Joe 'Mathea's Holy Mug and sat down opposite him.

'She was a lovely little girl, Marco. We used to put flowers in her hair.'

Marco tried to imagine his mum with flowers in her hair. They were unlikely to go with her business suits and her briefcase. He realized that when he'd tried to picture Mum as a child he'd always seen a little girl in a dark business suit taking her briefcase to primary school.

'Anyway,' Nancy said, 'I was a teacher and Woolly was

lead guitarist in Janice's Pimples.'

'Huh?'

'They were the biggest band round here in those days. They were so wild and deranged that they were banned from the first Glastonbury Festival.'

'Wow!'

'Then the band got a recording contract and the others wanted to move to London. But Woolly wouldn't go. He said the real scene was here.'

'What happened?'

'They dumped him and found a new lead guitarist, and then I found out I was expecting your mum, so we got married.'

'Wow,' Marco said. 'You were a rock chick. Like Sharon Osbourne.'

'Yes,' Nancy said sadly. 'I suppose I was. Suppose I still am, really. More of an old rock hen, now, though. I never went back to teaching and tried to make some money by painting, but never sold many pictures. Woolly did all sorts of jobs – sometimes three jobs at once – before he got recognized as a dowser. Hard times, but we were always happy in our strange way.'

'And now Woolly says he can't,' Marco said. 'Can't dowse.'

'Yes,' Nancy said. 'That *is* worrying.'

'Isn't there a doctor he could go to?'

'No shortage of healers in this town, lovey. Reflexologists, acupuncturists, hypnotherapists, sound-therapists. Problem is, they'll all be feeling a bit depressed, too.'

'I don't...' Marco stared at her, baffled. 'I don't get it.'

'They feel *betrayed*, Marco,' Nancy said. 'All these years, the pilgrims and the Avalonians and the alternative folk have thrown themselves into the revival of the old magic. Into making this a town that can change people's lives for the better...and what happens? Now the magic finally seems to be happening, it's happening to *them*. The Glasties wanted their town back, and now they've got it...including the legends and the magic...and Arthur's sword.'

Marco thought about this.

'But didn't Eleri think this was a good thing? You know, that the Glasties would finally agree that there *must* be magic here?'

'Try telling that to Woolly. The way *he* sees it is that the Glasties have been given the magic for nothing. While those of us who've worked hard for it and endured all the abuse over the years have...just lost it. Been sidelined. Shown up at last as the worthless riff-raff they always said we were.' Nancy sniffed and brought out a handkerchief with blue pentacles on it. 'Worthless riff-raff. Oh dear.'

'Nancy?'

'That was what *she* said...before she walked out for ever,' Nancy said.

'Who?'

He knew, of course.

His mother.

'She said she couldn't bear to be associated any more with...worthless riff-raff.'

Nancy burst into tears, as the back door opened and Woolly came in with Eleri wearing her black cloak, like one of those women she was always dreaming about in the barge.

* * *

'So...*is it?*' Marco said. 'You actually think this old... thing... could be...King Arthur's fabled magic sword?'

'It is a possibility,' Eleri said. 'Yes.'

Marco felt a tingle that seemed to rise up from the floor, through his spine all the way to his head.

'I have studied the Arthurian legends,' Eleri said, 'for many, many years, and have long felt that the lake into which the sword was thrown as Arthur lay dying was here in Avalon. It makes sense to me in all kinds of ways.'

'But there's no proof that Arthur even existed,' Marco said.

'*I* believe he existed,' Eleri said. 'I believe he is still here...closer than we think.'

Eleri looked up, and Marco saw her black eye-make-up running with tears. All this was obviously very close to Eleri's deepest dreams. But something clearly wasn't happening the way she'd always hoped it would.

'He might be close,' Woolly said, putting it all into words. 'But he ain't close to *us*, is he?'

Eleri sniffed.

Marco said, 'How *do* you know this was where the lake was?'

'We don't.' Eleri clasped her thin hands together. 'But we know that, on the following day, after throwing back the sword, Sir Bedivere went to a hermitage here in the town, while King Arthur was borne to the Isle in a black barge. So it must all have happened within quite a small area. Yes, I realize we will perhaps never know the true origins of this sword...but there is a strange poetic coherence about all this.'

'Huh?' Marco said.

'That it should be found *now*. When the visions are coming to the unbelievers. Something is happening. Or is... *about* to happen...'

'But is that *good*?' Woolly said. 'It don't make me feel good. I feel...not good.'

'It's probably the Blight,' Eleri said. 'It makes us feel tired and heavy and dulls our perceptions.'

'You mean...' Woolly stared at her. 'You mean *you* can't feel anything, either?'

'It will come,' Eleri said. Perhaps the tears in her eyes were tears of longing. 'I'm sure it will come.'

Marco looked round at Eleri and Woolly and Nancy. They were looking at each other, as if there was something each of them wanted to say but they couldn't bring themselves to come out with it.

Marco said, 'If this *is* King Arthur's sword...what could that mean?'

'It could mean anything,' Eleri said.

'Such as?'

Eleri sat with both hands around her Joe 'Mathea mug.

'Arthur is known as The Once and Future King. It has always been said that he will return when Britain has need of him.'

Marco felt like something was exploding in his head.

'You mean Arthur's...Arthur could be *coming back*?'

Another Glastonbury Story

Eleri stayed the whole day at the cottage, just a few fields away from the Tor. She said she was afraid to go back into town in case she was accosted by the media and they put more words into her mouth. Despite the humid heat, she never took off her cloak, and Marco sensed she was feeling cold...in some strange, *inner* way.

He wanted to go and find Rosa, but Woolly said this wouldn't be a good time – she'd be having her picture taken, Woolly said, by a bunch of papers over from London.

Marco didn't think Rosa would enjoy that. He wondered if she knew the full significance of what she'd found. *Arthur coming back?* He just couldn't get his head round that. How was it possible?

Around teatime, Diane rang to say the local TV news would be screening the Excalibur story and perhaps they all ought to watch it together at Bowermead Hall.

'No, I think we're better watching it on our own,' Nancy said down the phone. 'Woolly's been a bit...you know...'

It was a big old phone, and Marco could hear both sides of the conversation. He heard Diane say exactly what he'd been thinking.

'But, Nancy, you haven't got a TV.'

'Oh I'm sure we've got one somewhere,' Nancy said.

Which was news to Marco. There was no sign of a TV anywhere in the house. All Woolly and Nancy seemed to do at night was listen to ancient rock albums.

Then, not long before six o'clock, Nancy came in carrying this primeval portable with a big, thick, grey screen.

'It was in the back of Merlin's stable,' Nancy said, and then Woolly came on like some primitive tribesperson who'd just been shown his own reflection in a mirror – backing out of the kitchen, waving his arms.

'No way, no way, I don't wanner see it! Take it away!'

'That's silly.' Nancy brushed about a centimetre of dust off the set and polished the screen with her elbow. 'We can't bury our heads in the sand, look.'

She set the TV up on the kitchen table, plugged it in and switched on.

'There, you see,' Woolly said, happier for a moment than Marco had seen him all day. 'It don't work.'

'It needs to *warm up*,' Nancy said.

And she was right.

So they all sat at the kitchen table and watched the West Country news.

'This is not gonner be good,' Woolly said, for about the eighteenth time.

The report began in the Abbey grounds, with the TV reporter standing by the sign on which was written:

SITE OF KING ARTHUR'S TOMB
IN THE YEAR 1191, THE BODIES OF
KING ARTHUR AND HIS QUEEN WERE
SAID TO HAVE BEEN FOUND ON THE
SOUTH SIDE OF THE LADY CHAPEL.
ON THE 19TH APRIL, 1278, THEIR REMAINS
WERE REMOVED IN THE PRESENCE OF
KING EDWARD I AND QUEEN ELEANOR
TO A BLACK MARBLE TOMB ON THIS SITE.
THIS TOMB SURVIVED UNTIL THE
DISSOLUTION OF THE ABBEY IN 1539.

Marco could have recited it by heart because this was where Woolly had brought him for his first lesson in pendulum dowsing. The reporter pointed to the piece of ground marked out by kerb-type stones.

'Most historians today say the so-called discovery of Arthur's body was just a hoax by the monks of Glastonbury who wanted to make the Abbey seem even more important than it already was.'

There were some general shots of the Abbey ruins looking golden and soaring, with medieval-sounding music.

'But some local people,' the reporter said in voice-over, 'have always been convinced that their town *was* the last resting place of the legendary king.'

The picture switched to a view of Griff Daniel wearing his white suit. He looked unusually smooth. Even his ratty beard had been trimmed.

Woolly growled far back in his throat, like a guard dog.

On the screen, Griff Daniel nodded.

'I've always felt real close to King Arthur. I feels as if him and me has the same priorities. He wanted to keep Britain from being trashed by invaders, and I feel much the same about Glastonbury today, and all the riff-raff we got coming in with their weird ideas.'

Nancy put her hands on Woolly's shoulders to hold him back.

'And you know,' the mayor said, 'it's real strange, but I been dreaming about him lately. King Arthur coming back, leading his army of decent British knights with short hair and no tattoos. So, way I sees it, now this old sword's turned up, I reckons it's a sign that things is gonner change big time.'

Cut to a close-up of the sword, some dramatic music, and then Rosa's voice was heard. Through the tinny little speaker on the old portable, it sounded thin and sort of isolated.

'Well, it was no big deal, I just caught my foot in it.' She was standing by the river on her own, looking embarrassed. Near the bottom of the screen, it said: *Rosa Wilcox, schoolgirl.* 'We thought it was just an old hinge at first.'

'And how will you feel if it does turn out to be Excalibur?' the reporter's voice asked.

Rosa thought about this.

'I don't know,' she said.

Which was, Marco thought, *very* Rosa, not coming out with the usual *Oh, it's totally awesome, I'll be the envy of my friends* kind of drivel that kids were always quoted as saying in the newspapers but you knew the reporter had made up.

'Well...' The camera had cut back to the TV reporter. 'We may never know if it is or if it isn't...unless of course...' He chuckled. '...King Arthur himself comes back to claim it.'

Back in the studio, the two programme presenters smiled at one another.

'I wonder if we can get him on the programme, if he does come back,' the man said.

'Wooo...exciting!' the woman said.

And they both giggled.

They weren't taking it remotely seriously.

It was just another *Glastonbury story*.

Half an hour later, Diane and Sam turned up in their old Land Rover.

They both looked worried.

'Don't trust that old beggar an inch,' Sam said. 'You see the gleam in his eye?'

'Your old man?' Woolly said.

'"I've always felt real close to King Arthur."' Sam hunched himself up and put his head on one side and made his eyes bulge like Griff's. '"Best mates, him and me." As Dad would say...*gah*!'

'He never liked King Arthur,' Nancy said. 'He never liked

any of it. He only likes modern stuff.'

'*This* is more like Dad.' Sam dug a ball of paper out of his jeans, opened it out on the table. 'I found this snagged in a fence on the top field, where the dogs found the old man the other night. Must've fallen out of his pocket when they were mobbing him.'

Marco leaned over the table. The paper was a printed sheet. It said:

SELECTION GUIDELINES FOR SISTER CITIES OF SANTA CRUZ

Then there was a shortlist with hand-scribblings in fibre-tip next to each.

- Size of city – *can't be that much different*
- Coastal community – *well it USED to be*
- Economy: industry, tourism, agriculture – *got that lot no problem*
- Higher Institutions of Learning: colleges, universities – *we'll think of something*

Marco looked up.

'Santa Cruz? That's in America, isn't it?'

'That would figure,' Sam said. '*Sister city* – that sounds like their version of a twin town. The old man's obviously trying to organize a twinning arrangement between Glastonbury and Santa Cruz. What's that all about?'

'Money,' Woolly said. 'With your old man, it's always about money. Expect we'll be reading about it soon enough in the Glastie *Guardian*.'

'Oh...have you heard about Mr. Cotton?' Diane asked suddenly.

'I don't wanner know,' Woolly moaned.

'Yes, he does,' Nancy said. 'What's Mr. Cotton done?'

'Well...' Diane said. 'Rox at The Carrot...her sister's a secretary at Quentin Cotton's office. She says Mr. Cotton was absolutely shattered when he saw the photograph of the sword.'

'Recognized it as the missing blade off his lawn mower, did he?' Woolly said.

'I'm afraid what he recognized was its shape. There are little cavities in the handle of the sword where jewels or enamel discs may once have been set. Mr. Cotton said they... well, that they occurred at exactly the same intervals as the coloured lights in the UFO he saw over the Tor.'

Nancy gasped. Woolly sat up. Eleri drew a long, slow breath, her green eyes shining with wonder.

'He is saying that the sword corresponded exactly to the shape of the UFO?'

'Apparently.'

'So the UFO was like Excalibur itself, cleaving the clouds above the sacred hill,' Eleri said.

'Ah, but don't...' Woolly's eyes were fogged and desperate-looking. 'Don't forget he's a lawyer...'

'We can no longer dismiss these things,' Eleri said. 'I was afraid to say it earlier, but—'

'No,' Woolly said. '*Don't* say it.'

'He is on his way. *King Arthur is indeed returning to Avalon!*'

'Eleri, man, listen... That's just a legend. It's not meant

to be taken literally. It means that, in times of trouble, Britain will find the...you know, the spirit of Arthur. I mean, Arthur himself, he's...he's *dead*.'

Eleri rose to her feet. Her black hair hung straight down like the curtains at a funeral parlour.

'There is dead,' she said. 'And *dead*.'

The Bright Lights of Torquay

LONDON

When Josh read the e-mail, he had to hold on to the arms of his chair.

Two patients now. Mega!

...and Nancy says he's had them before, but never this bad. It's even affected his dowsing. He won't go to a doctor because he doesn't believe in making drug companies even richer.

So what I was wondering...can you or your dad drop me a few hints about curing depression? Something quick.

'Ha!' Josh said contemptuously, although there was

nobody else in the room. 'Quick-fix psychiatry? How naive can you get?'

But it was clear that Marco had anticipated this reaction.

...yeah, I know you guys like to drag it out for years so you can collect thousands of pounds worth of fees...

'Hmmph. Cynical swine.'

But this is really urgent. As I explained earlier, things are going wrong in Glasto. Only it's more serious than I thought. Much more serious...

There was a lot more from Marco about the discovery of what some misguided idiots seemed to think was King Arthur's sword. Some *even more* misguided idiots saw this as a sign that King Arthur was about to return.

Like, *come on.* A guy who, if he'd existed at all, had been dead for over 1,500 years? Where was he going to return *from*?

This gave Josh a passing shivery feeling, and Josh didn't do shivery feelings, so he turned back to his computer.

King Arthur... Right. Josh googled him to see if there were any new theories that hadn't been around when he'd read about the Knights of the Round Table as a kid.

There were about ten million links. Josh tried a couple at random and found that not much had changed at all. The legends still showed Arthur as a medieval king in the Age of Chivalry – all jousting tournaments and striped tents. Now for the history. Or *possible* history.

If there'd been a real Arthur, he'd probably been around

in the Dark Ages, the period between Roman Britain and the Norman Conquest. It was said he'd been a Celtic king, fighting off invasions by the Saxons. Hmmm... Glastonbury was in the West Country, the Celtic side of Britain, so that would fit.

But why had King Arthur – a man who might never have existed – become such a crucial figure to people today?

Answer: because he'd come to represent a mythical Golden Age of Britain – an era when exciting things were happening all the time and it felt good to be alive.

And, of course, King Arthur was surrounded by ancient mysteries, like the story of the quest for the Holy Grail, the most searched-for treasure in history.

Which also might never have existed.

Josh clicked on something called *Arturus Rex* and found himself on a website which was inviting him to download something that was promising him

THE MOST AWESOME EXPERIENCE YOU WILL EVER HAVE.

Josh smirked. It was hardly the first time he'd been promised *that*.

He clicked some more and a picture came up of an ancient iron-studded door in the side of a hill. Just the door. Nothing else. No menu or anything.

And then the letters appeared, written in the grassy hillside.

IF YOU ENTER...THERE CAN BE NO GOING BACK.

Josh's hand hovered over the mouse.

BUT IF YOU ARE THE LEAST AFRAID,
PRESS CANCEL. NO ONE WILL THINK
THE WORSE OF YOU.

Huh. Josh was faintly annoyed by the implication that he might be afraid to enter some two-bit crank website. He'd go back to it...in his own time. When he felt like it.

He started to make some notes on his laptop.

King Arthur, in other words, represents what we psychiatrists call a Utopian Fantasy.

Which translated as a load of feel-good rubbish which gullible people like Marco and his bonkers grandparents swallowed whole.

Right. Time to take some real action.

Josh switched off his computer, steeled himself and picked up the phone on his desk.

'Joshua! What an exceptional delight to hear your voice!'

'Hello, Grandma,' Josh said tightly.

'Give me a kiss!'

There was a noise like the phone at the other end had been dunked in blancmange. Josh winced.

'There's nothing wrong, is there?' Grandma Goldman shrieked. 'Your father is well?'

'Everything's fine, Grandma. Er...you know you said that if I ever wanted to experience the bright lights of Torquay...'

'Joshua! Let me just confirm once again that your room – indeed, your *suite* – is always ready, the bedding aired, the air-freshener replaced weekly...'

'Well, my diary tells me I do have a window in the coming week. However—'

There was an explosion of uncontainable joy.

'However,' Josh said, 'if it's all right with you, I *would* need to call in somewhere on the way. It's just I need to talk to a friend of mine who's having some personal problems.'

'Where?'

'It's a place called Glastonbury,' Josh mumbled. 'I've never actually been there before, but apparently you just get off the train at somewhere called Castle Cary.'

'Joshua! Glastonbury is so—'

'Yes, I know, tacky and full of—'

'I *love* Glastonbury!' Grandma Goldman screamed. 'It's a New Age wonderland!'

Josh was horrified.

'I didn't know you believed in all that—'

This time the noise was like a new universe being created.

'Who needs to believe? Just enjoy! Get your chakras recharged! Have photographs taken of your aura! Be hypnotized and find out what you did in previous lives...'

Josh had no idea what Grandma Goldman was talking about, but the thought that *she* did made him go cold with dread.

'Joshua, I shall *meet* you there!'

'No, look, that's not necessary—'

'You don't want your grandma with you? Or her chequebook?'

'No, it's just—' Josh began to sweat. 'That is...my friend... it's a private consultation. He won't be expecting anybody else.'

'No problem. You go to see your friend, I shall amuse myself practising my Buddhist chant.'

'Buddhist chant? Grandma, you're *Jewish*!'

'That means I have to close my mind to other people's belief-systems? I don't think so. And then, when you've sorted out your friend we can spend the whole weekend having fun, fun, fun in the Capital of Weird!'

Josh thought of all the insulting stuff he'd come out with about Marco's long-lost hippy grandparents. At least *they* lived in a place where there were scores of other people just as insane, so it wasn't a question of Marco spending all his time being embarrassed for them.

The kid didn't know how fortunate he was.

Knight of the Round Table

GLASTONBURY

Marco slipped outside. He still hadn't quite got used to living in a place where stuff like the idea of King Arthur coming back from the dead was openly discussed by grown-up people as part of real life.

He tried to imagine his mum coming out of the gym with one of her BBC friends and going, *So the UFO was like Excalibur itself, cleaving the clouds above the sacred hill... how interesting.*

The only way *that* would happen was if she was making a TV documentary about the weird people of Glastonbury ...which, of course, she wouldn't, because she wouldn't be seen dead in Glastonbury.

Under a sky like thick yogurt with trickles of marmalade in it, Marco wandered out towards the orchard, Merlin the donkey following him, doing his Clint Eastwood walk on his shiny hooves.

'I can't,' Marco said. 'I'm not allowed to let you in the orchard.'

The apples were ripening early this year. Avalon, Eleri had told Marco, was from the Welsh *afal*, meaning an apple. Avalon was the Place of Apples.

Donkey heaven.

He was getting quite friendly with Merlin. He'd never been allowed to have pets – too much hassle, his mum used to say, and who'd look after it in the daytime? He'd taken to cleaning out Merlin's stable first thing in the morning. All the donkey poop went into compost tubs for Nancy's veg garden. So, in a way, Merlin grew his own carrots.

Marco slipped through the gate into the orchard where it was safe to take out his mobile without having it snatched by Merlin on the off chance it had a fruity centre.

He didn't check his new mobile very often. No need, really. Josh preferred to communicate via e-mail, Mum was in America producing some documentary for the BBC and therefore far too busy. And Dad...well, Dad would only ring at times he knew the phone would be switched off so he could just leave a message and didn't have to speak to his son. In these messages Dad called him 'mate' a lot and apologized over and over for having to leave him with Woolly and Nancy, but, you know, work pressure and everything...

Knowing what he now knew about his dad and his iffy clients, Marco kind of wished he wouldn't leave messages at all. He just didn't know what to think about his dad, so it was better *not* to think. Which was terrible really, he thought, standing in Woolly's little orchard, clicking the mobile into life.

Merlin dumped his big head on Marco's shoulder, over the fence, and stared at him through one eye.

You have one new message, the phone said. *To receive your message...*

Marco did the necessary. The voice that came back was full of urgency.

'*I have to see you, but you can't call me back in case my dad's there.*'

Rosa...for the first time ever.

'*If you get this, I'll be on the corner of Silver Street at 8 p.m.*'

'Wow, Merlin, that doesn't give me much time.'

Merlin nodded, his snooker-ball eyes saying, *In that case, maybe you'll forget to close the gate.*

'No chance,' Marco said.

When he walked back in on Woolly and Nancy and Eleri and Diane and Sam, they were still talking about it, Woolly staring at Diane.

'...so you're saying it was King Arthur and his knights that Griff Daniel seen in his vision? With the dark smoky faces. King Arthur and his knights coming back from the dead. And this was the sword they was gonner use to chop his head off?'

'I don't know,' Diane said. 'And, in fact...well, suppose it wasn't about chopping his head off at all? Think back to what he said. He was told to kneel. And he saw the great sword rising...and he *thought* they were going to chop his head off. And the last thing he saw was the sword shining all golden in the sun...and that was when he started crying. What does that mean?'

'Means his past has finally caught up with him,' Woolly said. 'And he was gonner be executed for his massive catalogue of crimes against Glastonbury.'

'Woolly, what if the sword was coming down to...not to kill him, but to...you know?'

'What?'

'*You* know.'

'No, I don't.'

'When the queen...or the king...brings a sword down on one of your shoulders...and then the other shoulder?'

'*Holy Joseph.*'

Woolly had slumped over the table.

'Sorry,' Diane said.

Eleri was on her feet. 'You mean he was being *knighted*?'

Marco thought of Griff Daniel on TV in his new white suit, with his beard neatly trimmed, talking about how close he felt to King Arthur.

Councillor Griffith Daniel, Mayor of Glastonbury.

And *Knight of the Round Table*?

Woolly and Sam looked at one another, and they both went, '*Aaaaargh!*'

'I've got to go,' Marco said.

Silver Street was off High Street and bordered the wall around the Abbey ruins. There was a tall gate through which you could you see into the Abbey grounds.

He didn't see Rosa at first. She was in the deep shadows with her shoulders hunched, her hands sunk deep into the pockets of her red hoody. When he came round the corner, she jumped, as if he might have been someone about to mug her. Then she fumbled out a smile.

'Sorry. It's been a totally bad day. There've been reporters everywhere. I've had my picture taken about fifty times. I *hate* it.'

Marco wondered if *he'd* hate all the attention if he'd been in the same position. Like being a rock star. He thought he could *probably* handle it.

'Couldn't your dad keep them away? He's usually good at keeping people away.'

'You're kidding,' Rosa said. 'He thinks it's the best thing ever. He thinks it'll make me more outgoing and get me in with the local kids. Also, he gets *his* picture in the paper, too, so it makes him look like "part of the community".'

A couple of tourists came past, and Rosa shot back into the shadows.

Big Dave wasn't exactly hot on psychology, was he?

'We need to find somewhere to talk,' Rosa said. 'If Dad sees me with you—'

'Do you want to go into the Abbey?'

'It's closed.'

'Not a problem.' Marco did his Avalonian's smile. 'Woolly's got this friend, Stan, whose garden backs on to the ruins, and he lets Woolly go in and out anytime.'

'Why does he need to?'

'It's a dowsers' thing. There's a lot of interesting energy patterns around the Abbey. And it's like...it's a calming influence. The Tor can blow your mind, but the Abbey...

if something's done your head in, it'll *un*do it. If you see what I mean.'

'Let's do it, then,' Rosa said. 'I think *my* head's totally coming apart.'

'The price of fame.'

'No, you don't understand, that sword's...'

She mumbled something and began to walk in tense circles in the street, like the OCD was coming back or something.

'Sorry, Rosa.' Marco blocked her path. 'I didn't get that.'

'I said if it's Excalibur then Excalibur's full of evil.'

Deep Red

Rosa said that what had happened to her in the night... well, it wasn't like seeing the monk.

'That was just scary, until I found out who he was. That he was – you know – a force for good?'

Marco nodded warily. Had she *really* found out who he was? Or had some part of her simply decided it would be better all round if this spooky figure was someone decent and kind, like the last abbot? Her way of coming to terms with something terrifying.

They were sitting under some trees on the edge of Glastonbury's brilliant secret. Right in the centre of the town and yet hidden away behind walls and the shops on High

Street. You could probably live in the town all your life and never need to see it.

Marco looked across at the Abbey ruins and felt, for a moment, choked up with a sensation he'd had before, often at this time of day. That feeling of being totally and completely here. And yet *more than here.* As if some part of him was standing back and *watching him being here.*

And was Rosa's abbot here, too, gliding through the remains? He saw that the falling sun had left a sky-river of liquid gold, and a great broken archway was kind of reaching up for it, like two hands cupped to receive...something.

It was funny how, when you got into dowsing, you started to see *other* things in the *same* things. He thought of the Holy Grail catching the blood of Jesus as he hung on the cross, and then Jesus' uncle, Joe 'Mathea, stowing the sacred cup away on his boat and bringing it across to Britain. Landing here, founding the Abbey.

So ancient that only legend can record its origin, it said in the Abbey guidebook. People like Marco's mum would say this legend had been just a way of explaining to primitive peasants how Christianity had come to Britain. But sitting here you just knew there had to be more to it than that.

He looked at Rosa, who had changed so much since coming to live here. Just a few weeks ago she'd been badly affected by Obsessive Compulsive Disorder.

But what had come through last night sounded far worse than OCD. Waking up to find your bed was drenched with blood? Marco felt his hands going clammy at the thought of it.

'It could be some kind of delusion, though, couldn't it? A dream that lingered after you'd woken up?'

'No,' Rosa said. 'It was separate from the dream.'

Walking down into the ruins, she'd told him about the dream of lying on a battlefield, and these guys going round finishing off all the wounded people. And then the sword raised over her, like with Griff Daniel.

Only this time there was not the slightest possibility, even if girls were eligible, that Rosa was going to be knighted.

'But afterwards,' Marco said, 'your bed was dry, right? So it didn't really happen.'

'But it might just as *well* have happened. All the feelings were the same, weren't they?'

'Except that if it had really happened you'd be dead.'

Rosa said, 'I thought I was going to be dead, it was that realistic.'

'And you really think it was connected with having the sword in the flat?'

Rosa nodded, eyes closed, lips tight.

'Okay,' Marco said. 'You need to talk to Eleri. You want me to fix it up?'

'That's why I rang you. It has to be somewhere where Dad won't find out. If it got back to him that I'd gone to a...'

'Goddess-worshipping pagan priestess. Right, leave it to me. I think she'll really want to talk to you. Like, you seem to be having the kind of visions she isn't getting right now.'

'Yeah,' Rosa said. 'I get all the breaks, don't I?'

Marco looked up at the sky. The rivers of gold had melted into a pool of deep red. Woolly and Nancy were fairly okay about him wandering around the town and going to and from the cottage in the hills. But they did like to know where he was after dark.

'I suppose I'll have to be off in a bit. Your dad won't still be out looking for you or anything, will he?'

'If it's after half-past eight, I'm safe. He's got a meeting of his team-ministry – all the local vicars and curates. And Mum's working late at The George and Pilgrims because of a party or something.'

They came to the site of King Arthur's grave, as seen on TV. Marco thought it was pretty shabby that this was all there was – a rectangle marked out by stones and a metal sign. It looked kind of temporary.

And perhaps it was. He looked at Rosa.

'Do *you* think he's coming back? Maybe to...collect his sword? Like, where is it now?'

'That man with the white beard, Mr. Montague, came for it this afternoon. I think he's going to take it to some museum in Bristol, or a laboratory or something where all these experts can examine it.' Rosa looked down at the grave. 'If Arthur does come back, it's hard to think of him coming from...here.'

'Maybe he'll come out of the Tor. That's supposed to be the entrance to the Celtic Land of the Dead. Actually, Eleri says there are a bunch of different hills all over the country which are said to be the ones where Arthur and his knights lie sleeping, waiting for the big day.'

Marco glanced from side to side, at the sawn-off walls and the old rubble. He would never have admitted this in a million years, but talking about ghosts and sleeping warriors in the twilight, just the two of them in the Abbey ruins, made him...

Rosa twisted round.

'You hear that?'

'What?'

'Someone's coming.'

She grabbed his arm and pulled him down a grass bank, behind a broken wall.

'I didn't hear anything.'

'Shush...'

Marco looked up at the sky, a murky tide washing in under clouds like sandbags. The sun was a blood blister. It would soon be night, earlier than normal. He should be getting back to Woolly's.

He lifted his head above the wall. He still couldn't hear anything. But this time he saw a procession of shadowed, hooded figures, moving through the swirling crimson dusk.

A Patch of Midnight

In the gathering twilight, they looked like a circle of stones around the empty grave of King Arthur. Seven of them, where Marco and Rosa had been standing just a few minutes ago.

And they were mumbling, not much more than a hollow whisper, the voices mingling, male and female, going *shsshshsssshssshssss* in a rhythmic, hip-hop way that was kind of menacing.

This went on for a long time. Then one of them would whisper what seemed to be a name. At first it sounded like Latin or something, and then Marco thought he heard some names from the Bible – Old Testament kind of names.

As each name was said, the others would repeat it. Name after name, like a list, the voices growing stronger and more rhythmic and...intense.

Marco peered over a section of ruined wall.

'I wonder if there's anybody I kn—'

Rosa pulled him back.

'Sorry.' He tried to be cool with this, telling himself that whatever was happening here was probably quite normal. This was, after all, Glastonbury, where loads of people belonged to strange religious sects and all kinds of weird rituals were carried out. Best to keep quiet until it was over; they'd only get annoyed if they were interrupted.

Anyway, nothing at all to worry about. Except that it was getting dark, and he needed to get back to Woolly and Nancy's.

'*Pray...us...let.*'

Marco sank down, as the single voice rose up.

'*Amen...ever...*'

The voice was flat and toneless, tossing out the words. Marco peered between two stones projecting from the wall and saw that one of the figures was holding up a piece of paper to the last of the light and reading from it.

'*...and...ever...for...glory...the...and...power...the...kingdom ...the...is...thine...for...*'

It probably wasn't something you could easily memorize.

The Lord's Prayer.

Backwards.

A thin chill slid like a cold wire through Marco's insides and Rosa stared at him, her eyes full of horror.

'*...bread...daily...our...us...give...*'

Marco had had discussions with Woolly and Nancy about

the difference between satanism and paganism, learning that paganism was a form of religion which existed before Christianity, and its gods were nature gods. But satanism only existed *because of* Christianity. It was an *anti*-religion which deliberately set out to corrupt and damage the Church by worshipping the Christian devil and reversing the prayers and rituals of the Christian Church.

Satanists liked to use old churches for their rituals.

So a bunch of masked and hooded worshippers saying the Lord's Prayer backwards in an ancient abbey...how much proof did you need of what this was?

But who were they?

That was the thing about hoodies. Useful for muggers and drug dealers...and also for satanists who could walk through the streets – especially the streets of Glastonbury – in their ritual costume without anybody getting wise to it.

All the hooded tops were black, and all seven of the group were in black jeans. Two or three of them, Marco thought, were girls. One of them was carrying something, like a small cage.

There was something moving inside it.

Marco felt a little sick and more than a little afraid.

Where was Big Dave when you needed him? Sitting in a cosy meeting with all these other vicars and curates from central Somerset, probably drinking tea, eating chocolate biscuits and discussing the riff-raff flooding into Glastonbury and taking over the town like they owned it.

Discussing probably everything except the problem of real heavy-duty satanism.

Marco was sure it had gone much darker very quickly, as if a patch of midnight had formed around the Abbey. He looked at Rosa, brought up in a strongly Christian family. Felt her disgust.

He peered between the stones. The leader – or high priest, whatever he was – lifted up his arms and spoke in a low hiss.

'*Lord of the Labyrinth, O Prince of Shadows...*'

The voice was kind of intimate now, as if he was addressing one of his mates.

'*...we call upon you to come amongst us.*'

Rosa's body jerked and Marco knew she'd recognized the voice at the same moment he had.

When you knew who it was, that ought to make it less frightening, taking away the fear of the unknown. But this was a side of Jasper Coombes neither of them had seen before...not *quite.*

Jasper let something fall to Arthur's grave. Like paper, or card. He looked down at where it lay.

'*Give us power over this person that he may, through us, do YOUR bidding.*'

Which person? King Arthur? They wanted power over King Arthur? King Arthur who was...

...dead.

'*And in return,*' Jasper said, '*we give you...a gift.*'

Who was he talking to? Was Jasper Coombes actually calling on Satan to come amongst them? Like Satan was his mate and he was inviting him round for a game of pool, have a few beers together, talk about the footie...

Maybe that was how you did it. *Everything* in reverse. Like Christians addressed God with respect, but satanists could talk to the other guy like they knew him really well.

Jasper held up something which glimmered dully against the last of the light in the sky. Marco actually trembled. One of the others just had to be Shane Davey. Maybe he also had a...

...a blade?

It was. It was a long knife. Like a carving knife. Marco was aware of Rosa breathing hard and trying to stifle it. There was more mumbling, low chanting, and then the person holding the cage put it down at Jasper's feet. On Arthur's grave.

The cage went:

Miaaaaaow!

Marco nearly cried out and clutched at Rosa's arm. He was aware of sweat springing out on his face and going instantly cold.

They had a cat in that cage.

And they were going to...

They couldn't be...

People just did not *do* things like that.

Not even Jasper Coombes.

The afterglow of the red sun gleamed in Jasper's knife as if it was already coated in warm blood.

'Prepare the sacrifice,' Jasper said.

Arturus Rex.

LONDON

Josh gazed across the green landscape through which a path led to a silver-studded door in a hillside.

This was the third door.

After the iron-studded door had come a copper-studded door.

Only an idiot would walk right in through a door in a hillside, so Josh opted to wait, concealed in the trees.

It was only a matter of time. The sacred cup, the world's most sought-after treasure, was as good as his.

Right.

Well...big deal.

In fact, he wondered if it was even *worth* finding the

Grail, as there was a programme about Multiple Personality Disorder coming up on Sky TV's new Mental Health Channel. It would probably be basic stuff, but just occasionally these pop documentaries threw up something vaguely new.

All right, perhaps he'd give the Grail five more minutes. As computer games went, *Arturus Rex* wasn't *too* juvenile.

Not that Josh liked it known that he played computer games. People would only get the wrong idea and assume he was a secret geek, when playing the more intelligent games was actually a psychological exercise. Ordinary kids might play the game simply to try and win through. But Josh, as a psychiatrist, saw winning as irrelevant. The real quest was probing the mind of the guy who had devised the game.

Which was why he'd downloaded *Arturus Rex*. It was a free download, so there had to be a catch somewhere, but at least it had a title in Latin.

Arturus Rex: Latin for King Arthur. The angle was that you, the player, took on the role of the young king, and your task was to kill all these bad knights and demonic entities and fire-breathing dragons to claim your kingdom.

Josh wasn't aware that King Arthur (if he'd existed, which, of course, he hadn't) had gone in much for slaying dragons or indeed, demonic entities. But then, the game *was* American. The hero started out in California as a kid called Rex Arturus. If he made it, he would become Arturus Rex. (Geddit?)

So the player, as Rex Arturus, got to come over to Britain and, if he got through the first stages – like anybody with half a brain could fail to – he was entitled to choose the location for his royal court. His Camelot. He could have, for instance, Tintagel Castle in Cornwall, which was universally known as King Arthur's Castle. Or he could occupy Arthur's Seat, a high rock in the city of Edinburgh. Or he could go for...

Well, well...

He could, if he so chose, take The Isle of Avalon, also known as Glastonbury.

Josh had so chosen, for obvious reasons.

And this had immediately opened up a new quest...for the Holy Grail, which was supposed to have been brought to Glastonbury by Joseph of Arimathea, this international wheeler-dealer who just happened to be an uncle of Jesus.

Anyway, Josh had accepted the quest on the basis that the *real* quest was for Marco's state of mind.

He'd clicked on: *Yes, I am pure of heart and strong in valour. I shall fight for the holiest of the holy, even unto death.*

Yeah, yeah, whatever.

A few clicks later, Josh had found himself in this mellow old town with red-tiled roofs, old stone houses and a ruined abbey in the middle. Dominating the town, even though it was just outside its boundary, was this pointed hill with a church tower on top and a dark, threatening sky around it.

Josh figured the quest might well lead to the pointed hill. Meanwhile, there were other, less striking hills below it, including this one...where he'd found The Third Door.

He just knew that this particular portal would have a fearsome guardian on the other side, half formed and grey and spooky, because they always did and they always were.

And he knew he'd have to outsmart the guardian to get the Grail, because that was how it worked.

And he knew that he *would* outsmart the guardian because the psychology of these guardians was always so feeble, and he was, after all, a trained psychiatrist, and psychiatrists could outsmart *anyone*.

Josh smiled grimly, hit the mouse and went in...

Cursed

GLASTONBURY

Rosa came quietly to her feet.

Marco reached to stop her because he was thinking frantically, trying to formulate a plan of his own, but she shook him off. She stood in silence at the edge of the low wall.

Oh no. If any of the group around Arthur's grave looked up they'd be able to see her clearly.

But they were all looking down at what seemed to be a flat stone they'd carried to the grave.

A sacrificial stone?

It was now almost dark.

Something writhed.

A girl amongst them screamed.

'Ow! It scratched me!'

Marco thought, *Oh no, what if that's somebody I know?*

What if it was, like for instance, Rox from The Cosmic Carrot? What if all these people he thought were basically okay were actually satanists getting ready to sacrifice a little cat to the Devil?

There was a hush. Marco thought he could hear the not-so-distant rumble of a lorry on High Street. He only wished it would come crashing through the Abbey wall.

Jasper said, 'Lay it upon the grass and hold it down.'

The cat was squealing in terror. Marco was almost in tears that were full of pity and rage and helplessness. He just had to stop this even if all he did was go running out screaming and hitting people and getting himself beaten up, as usual.

He had to. At least somebody might hear the noise.

Jasper held the knife over his head in both hands. He'd thrown back his hood, and you could see his grin, a slash of white.

Marco stood up, took a long breath, tensed...but Rosa shook her head at him, violently.

In the complete silence, he saw that she was holding her right arm to her left side, across her body. As he watched, baffled and impatient, she brought it up in a smooth diagonal, as if she was drawing a sword from a scabbard and holding the sword high.

What are you—?

She brought the imaginary sword down again, the movement forming a triangle in the air.

Marco knew what she was doing now.

The pentagram.

Rosa had been taught this by a guy called Teddy at the crystal shop, when she'd been scared by things happening in her bedroom at night. The very first time Marco had seen her, she'd been standing in a secluded part of the car park at The George and Pilgrims trying to get the pentagram right and messing it all up because of the OCD that made her keep doing it four times.

She had it right now, though. Marco could almost see it taking shape like thin streams of light in the air. Up came the arm again, and then across and then down in another diagonal, as if she was replacing the sword in its scabbard.

It was an upwards-pointing pentagram, used for protection against evil.

As it had turned out, what had been happening in her bedroom had not been evil. Not then, anyway.

But, no question, the darkness here was thick with it, the air itself like a dark, disgusting soup and, for a moment, Marco was convinced he saw a vast and smoky silhouette against the once-golden ruined arches of the Abbey.

Rosa glanced at him.

'I said hold it still,' Jasped rasped.

The knife went up.

It was no good. Drawing a symbol in the air wasn't going to protect any of them...certainly not this poor cat.

Marco looked hard at Rosa.

'All right, let's go,' Rosa said.

Her voice was all strange and ragged.

* * *

LONDON

What?

Josh stared at the screen.

Of all the computer games he'd played over the years, none had ever done *this* to him.

The door had vanished, the screen had gone white and then this parchment-type thing had come up.

It said:

True seekers should answer this simple questionnaire from the Melcato Corporation, creators of Arturus Rex.

Huh. He should've realized it would be a scam, with that free download. A *simple questionnaire.* Josh knew all about *that* scam. Usually they came through the door in an envelope with your name on it but no stamp. They offered you a free gift if you just answered a *simple questionnaire.* Josh's father had explained this was just a trick to find out where you lived and how old you were and stuff like that so they could sell your details to other junk-mail guys, and you'd be buried under mountains of garbage.

Josh scrolled down, just to make sure.

Please tell me why you chose Glastonbury. Was it
a. because you just like the sound of the name?
b. because you believe the Holy Grail is truly to be
found here.
If b, please explain.

Hmm. Subtler than usual, but it had to be a scam.

Under b, Josh typed in:

Nothing so trivial or simplistic, you moron.

And sent this message back to whoever.

He realized at once that this was a mistake – he'd fallen into the trap. Now they'd have his e-mail address and would probably try to send him some evil virus.

Josh typed again.

And don't try and send me an evil virus, it'll just bounce off my sophisticated firewall.

He sat back with his arms crossed. After a few moments, the screen said:

If you are not a true seeker but simply in search of amusement, click on the icon to continue the game.

Oh, *very* smart. If you didn't choose to answer the questions then you must be shallow and childish.

Josh took offence at this. He was really annoyed now. He decided he wasn't going to answer the questions *or* continue the game. He would go for the Third Way.

He switched off.

GLASTONBURY

Marco blinked and pulled at the skin around his eyes. They were definitely open, so why couldn't he see properly?

He kept on running towards Arthur's grave. Or he thought he was running. It seemed a long way. He thought that maybe he'd closed his eyes when he and Rosa had gone over the top of the wall and forgotten to open them.

His hands felt numb against his face. Like sometimes you woke up in the night when you'd been lying on your hand and it felt like a lump of plaster at the end of your arm?

Concentrate. It wasn't about stopping the satanic ritual – they could worship who they liked, it was *their* immortal souls on the line, as Big Dave would say. It was about saving the cat. Distracting them so the cat could get away. Once the cat got free, they'd never catch it again. That was all that mattered.

It would just be easier if he could see what was happening. Must be later than he'd thought. And colder.

He'd forgotten how cold it could get after dark. Only it wasn't after dark yet, surely, there was still plenty of red in the...

Where was the sky?

He shook his hands, trying to feel them.

You're cold, someone said.

He nodded. He was too cold to speak. Had he stopped? He'd thought he was still running, but now he couldn't feel his feet, and he couldn't see where he was. All he could see was the cold...which wasn't something you could normally see at all, but he could definitely see this cold, like a thickening blue-black fog, and the voices he could hear...the voices were outside and distant now. Except for one.

Hey, Marco.

'What?'

Marco, you're okay. Chill out, man.

'How chilled do you *want*?'

Nothing's going to happen to you.

'It *is* happening—'

You're with friends.

'Huh?'

Just take it easy, right? Be cool. Ha ha – sorry.

'Who's that?'

He could hear his own voice, like from far away, going, 'Who's that, who's that...at...at?'

But the other voice was very close and warm and friendly.

I understand you've always wanted to see a UFO, Marco...

'Who told you that?'

Would you like to see one?

'Now?'

His own voice came echoing back from wherever his voice was.

'Now...ow...ow.'

Come with me and I'll show you a UFO.

'Where?'

I'll take you inside *a UFO. I can take you to some cool places, Marco.*

'It's just...I don't feel well,' Marco said nervously. 'I'm cold.'

No problem, the voice said smoothly. *Drink this. This'll warm you up...*

Two hands came out of the blue-blackness holding a cup that was steaming. Marco reached out, bent his head, looking down into the liquid in the cup. It smelled sweet. He was reminded of one time he'd been taken to church, early in the morning...by his mum? Had it been his mum who'd taken him to church? Anyway, it was a communion service and people were taking small sips of wine from a chalice held out by the vicar.

Only that had been a bright chalice. Silver. Softly gleaming.

Not dark grey, going on black, and lumpy.

He looked up, uncertain. He thought he saw...Rosa? Hadn't Rosa been here?

Drink, Marco. You'll feel...so much better.

The smell from the liquid was sweet and warm. He watched it swirling in the cup. He needed that warm drink; he deserved it after all he'd gone through tonight.

Okay. He lowered his head to drink. Into the steam.

Or the fog. He wondered if the fog was real or if it was just in his mind, as Josh would say...

Josh would say...

...who was Josh?

Drink, Marco...

There was a slow clumping sound.

Where?

Somewhere. Through the fog, as the liquid touched his lips, he saw pinpoints of light.

Come on, Marco...so much better...

In the distance, he heard:

Ergh...erhh...ergh...

Like, *don't, don't, don't.*

He looked up and saw the tiny lights were in the centre of these softly glowing shiny balls, coming slowly towards him. Not rolling; they were in the air.

UFOs?

He looked up at the lights and then down at the liquid in the cup, and the cup itself. The cup was heavy and had two holes where you could insert your fingers to...

From below the lights came:

Haaaaa...haaah...

HaaaaaAAAAAAAAAAAAAAAAAAAAAAAAAAAW!

The noise went into him like a punch, full of alarm and a...an ancient pain.

Marco howled and thrust the cup away and then spun round and sank his hands into...

...warm, rough fur?

It was like a kind of lightning was rushing jaggedly up both his arms.

And then he was running. Running like he'd never run before, cold sweat defrosting on him. Running towards the glimmerings of light.

To his left, he heard a hiss like red-hot metal plunged into a pool of freezing water and then the voice rising out of it, dripping with cold rage.

You're cursed. You're cursed until you die.

He half-turned, but he didn't stop running. He saw a finger, rigid, pointing straight at him, or maybe it was the knife.

And you won't have long to wait, the voice said.

He thought it was Jasper's voice, only it sounded deeper and stronger, like it knew what it was saying, knew the truth of it.

Lost to Us

The night air was tainted with the acrid smell of burning. The figure came towards him through the smoke. It was grey and it was bending over him, and Marco shrank into the ground.

'No...get away.'

'Marco?'

'Get away from me...*Satan.*'

'Close,' the voice said.

'*No...please...*'

Marco made the sign of the cross in the air, like he'd seen in some old film. He was aware of a low, growling noise very close and a heavy heat on his chest.

'Just the one letter missing,' the voice said.

'What?'

'Stan.'

'Huh?'

'It's Stan. Woolly's pal. You came through my garden.'

'Oh God...'

Marco shut his eyes tight and fell back into the cool grass, relief washing over him. Then he tensed again. It *sounded* like Stan, but the Devil was supposed to have many voices. And only one letter different. *Stan*. That was exactly the kind of joke you'd get from the Devil.

'I've phoned Woolly, son. He's on his way.'

Marco opened his eyes slowly. He was lying on the grass in a pool of yellow light from a window.

He saw a garden incinerator burning low on a concrete patio.

He saw Stan.

Looking exactly like he had when Marco had first met him the day Woolly had taken him into the Abbey early one morning. Stan looked like a real, authentic granddad. Maybe even a great-granddad. He wore a grey cardigan and wide khaki trousers with turn-ups.

Wasn't his fault his name was only one letter away from...

Marco looked around and struggled to get up, but his chest was still weighted down.

'Where's — ?'

'I'm here,' Rosa said. 'We're all here.'

She was staring down at him. She looked pale but okay, basically. She put a finger to her lips, obviously telling him to say nothing about what had happened. Rosa was a very surprising kind of person. Nervous, easily worried, but in the middle of a really terrible situation something seemed to take over and she was suddenly calmer than he could ever be. Maybe what Eleri said about her was true.

Marco looked down at his chest and wondered why he was clutching a giant hot-water bottle.

In a velvet case with a motor inside, rumbling softly.

'Huh?'

'Is that *your* cat?' Stan said. ''Cause he sure ain't mine.'

Nancy had lit the oil lamp in the window. You could see it from quite a distance. Just an old oil lamp, its glow wavering through the trees on a quiet hillside but, at that moment, it was brighter for Marco than all the lights in London.

Woolly poured small glasses of home-made apple wine and Nancy cut into a new fruit cake, and the four of them sat around the kitchen table in the nest of light made by the oil lamp and watched the big black cat shovelling up a dish of salmon like a JCB on overdrive.

Marco said, 'I still can't believe—'

'When you've lived here as long as me,' Woolly said, 'you won't have much trouble believing anything. Trust me.'

Marco looked at Rosa. Had it been the same for her? Had *she* gone into some kind of weird mental state as soon as they'd come close to whatever was happening around Arthur's grave? Whenever he thought about it, he felt close to panic. He focused on what was real, looked down to make sure the cat was still there.

'Nancy can we—?'

'Course we can,' Nancy said. 'If we can't find out who

owns him. We ain't had a cat for a few years since poor old Lancelot died.'

'Tell me about this cup,' Woolly said.

Marco took a sip of the sweet apple wine. The sweetness of the drink he'd been offered was of another kind altogether. More thick and kind of...cloying? Was that the word? He recalled the cold and the steaming, dark cup with the two holes.

'It was a skull.' Marco shuddered. 'The holes were...they were the eyeholes. They wanted me to drink out of a...'

Woolly nodded. His arms were folded and his eyes were focused and glittering.

'I got to tell you, Marco, there might not have been a cup there at all. Nor anything to drink.'

'Don't!' Nancy cried. 'He don't need to know that stuff.'

'I reckon he does, Nance. Boy's a dowser.'

'It was...' Marco swallowed. '...the Dark Chalice, right? Only, not really. Like a *vision*...of the Dark Chalice.'

Woolly nodded slowly.

'And if I'd taken a drink from it...?'

'You'd've been lost to us,' Woolly said. 'You'd have said yes to something dark. And when you've said yes once, it gets easier and easier. And that's how they get you. Like a drug.'

'No!' Nancy's eyes filled up. 'Don't say that!'

'It's true, Nance.' Woolly stared seriously at Marco. 'He'd have come in, gone to bed as normal...but in the morning, a different person would've woke up in his bed. Likely looked around this place and seen...a...well, a bit of a hovel and a couple of clapped-out old hippies. Folks who was no use to him, basically.'

'*No...*'

Marco jerked in his chair.

'And then there'd be arguments over why he couldn't have a proper breakfast with red meat. And how long before he could go back to the city. And then...' Woolly looked at Marco. 'Then you'd meet Jasper down the town, and he'd seem, for the first time, like a real cool dude, and maybe you'd ask could you have a go with his air gun...'

'Stop it!' Nancy's face was white. 'It didn't happen... did it?'

She also stared hard at Marco, as if to check that the whites of his eyes hadn't gone red.

'Or if you want to look at it another way,' Woolly said. 'Psychologically, sort of thing...boy just got a bit confused and his mind slipped out of synch and put two and two together and got seven.'

'You mean it could have been a delusion,' Marco said. Thinking of Josh and the way *he* would see it: *all* delusion, a severe case of Impressionable Kid Syndrome.

'In this town,' Woolly said, 'it's hard to tell where delusion hands over to a warped kind of reality. That's why it's a real hard place to live. A ritual carried out in a holy place generates a force field around it. Once you get absorbed in that, it plays with your mind. I just...I'm just not entirely sure how you got away from it.'

He glanced at Rosa.

'What did you do, lovey?' Nancy asked.

'Oh...' Rosa looked vague. 'I was...I suppose I was just watching, Mrs. Woolaston.'

'Nancy.'

'Nancy. Sorry. It was dead weird. It was like I was outside it. As if they couldn't see me...only Marco.'

'Before we went in, she made the sign of the pentagram,' Marco said. 'In the air.'

'It was all I could think of.'

'It was *good* thinking, lovey,' Nancy said. 'Long as you did it the right way up. What happened next?'

'They just...well, nobody seemed to notice me. Or if they did they just...kept away. And I was watching Marco. But I didn't see any of that stuff with the cup.'

Woolly nodded. 'That figures.'

'I just saw Marco go rushing in, and they were all round him, like they were going to...do something to him. And I thought, what am I going *do*? And then they started backing away from him. Hanging back, you know? Then Marco grabbed the cat. It all happened really quickly. And then it was all over, except that Jasper—'

'Merlin!' Marco said. 'Some of it must have been delusion, because at one point I...I thought Merlin was there.'

For the first time, Woolly smiled.

'I saw what I thought were Merlin's eyes,' Marco said. 'And then he did this massive bray. But obviously Merlin *wasn't* there, he was still here in his stable. And then I...I thought I was sinking my fingers into his hair. And it felt good. Like I had a friend nobody could...'

'Corrupt,' Woolly said. 'A friend nobody could corrupt.' He seemed to have relaxed. 'That's what I was looking for. Maybe I'll explain it to you later.'

'I must've been picking up the cat at the time,' Marco said. 'But it all took...ages.'

'It happened really quickly,' Rosa said. 'Honestly.'

Marco felt bewildered, out of control. Woolly leaned over and laid a hand on his shoulder.

'Time,' Woolly said, 'is relative, dude.'

'What?'

'And sometimes things do seem to happen *out* of time.'

'What didn't happen out of time,' Rosa said, 'is that Jasper cursed him.'

Woolly sat up. Nancy breathed in hard.

'Jasper screamed at him that he was cursed for ever. Until he died. And he said...'

Woolly had gone kind of grey.

'...and he said that wouldn't be long off,' Rosa said.

'Oh dear God,' Nancy said.

Woolly stood up. The oil lamp gave a little gasp and flickered.

'Don't nobody move,' Woolly said. 'I'm phoning Eleri.'

Powers of Light
and Darkness

Rosa was having second thoughts.

They stood at the very top of the Tor – she and Marco and Woolly and Nancy.

And Eleri in her long black cloak, with her back to the dark stone tower which thrust itself into the mist. No moon, no stars, only the mist and the weight of the night. And yes, Rosa *had* wanted to see Eleri...but not like this.

They'd walked up slowly and silently, by candlelight, a little procession, led by Eleri, holding up her light. There was nobody else up here, and yet Rosa had the scary feeling that there *were*...others. Others you couldn't see. She shivered. Never been to the top of the Tor before, not even in daylight.

Her dad would be horrified.

The candles were in little glass lanterns, marking out a sort of circle – five of them. Eleri had put them down very carefully, in particular positions.

In fact, Rosa was sure she'd seen her pacing out a pentagram, placing a light at each point.

'We have come to the source of it all,' Eleri said softly. 'This is the *oldest* place of worship in Avalon.'

Yes, Rosa thought, but what kind of worship? She knew what her dad would say.

'And so we call upon the powers of light!'

Eleri had stepped into the centre of the circle and was looking up to where the tower vanished into the mist and lifting up her arms, her cloak falling back over her shoulders.

Rosa felt her eyes narrowing. Who *were* the powers of light, *exactly*?

'Don't worry too much about it, lovey.'

Marco's granny, Nancy, was standing next to her.

Nancy with the tattoos and the weird, coloured hair full of pins and braids and bits of stick.

'It's only another way of saying *God*,' Nancy whispered. 'And also Allah. And it's the Great Mother and a whole bunch of other forces for good. Way I see it, the powers out there are far above all these different religions. It's just that humans aren't developed enough to know it – they all want to be part of *the big important faith*, see? So they goes on all the time about the differences between them rather than what they could have in common if they made the effort.'

'How did you know what I was thinking?' Rosa said.

'I *didn't* know, lovey. But there are some places where *the veil is thin*, as they say. And it don't get thinner than up here.'

'And that means we can see one another's thoughts?'

'Maybe not, but we can sense each other's feelings better.'

Rosa looked up at the church tower with no church and down at the lights of Glastonbury and felt the *in-betweenness* of the place and thought of all the times Marco had said that, since coming to Glastonbury, he'd often felt he was not just *here*, but *more* than here.

And then she gasped and clapped a hand to her mouth, remembering what had happened up here in the year 1539.

Richard.

They'd hanged Richard here.

She looked up, between her fingers, terrified that the *sensitive* side of her would show her his body swinging slowly from side to side, the wooden scaffold softly creaking.

All she saw was Eleri. The candles were glowing on the ground like mini airport-landing-lights, and Eleri was now standing outside the circle, with a cloth bag at her feet, and... oh God, what was that white floaty thing?

Marco. Wearing a plain white T-shirt that looked too big for him.

'We had to burn all the clothes he was wearing,' Nancy explained. 'And he had to have a good bath. With salt in the water.'

All this must have happened while Rosa was explaining to Eleri about the black magic in the Abbey. She remembered noticing at the time that the others had all disappeared. But nobody had suggested burning *her* clothes.

'You were protected, look.' Nancy said. 'You knew what to do. But Marco was likely exposed to the full force of it...and the curse.'

'Could...' Rosa shook herself. 'Could someone like Jasper Coombes really curse you? And make it work?'

'Anyone who could sacrifice a poor cat has opened himself up to the deepest evil,' Nancy said. 'He'll be a lost cause, soon, that boy. Mixing with the wrong people for too long.'

She meant Roger Cromwell, who owned the old shop under the flat in High Street. The shop with the trapdoor that let you into the Glastonbury labyrinth, at the centre of which was the ancient temple of the Dark Chalice, the anti-Grail. Cromwell had been like some kind of uncle to Jasper. An uncle who'd taught him things no kid should ever learn. And Jasper and Shane Davey had been with Cromwell when he'd tried to make Woolly show him where the Dark Chalice was hidden.

A hush had fallen.

Eleri guided Marco to each of the lights around the circle, calling out significant-sounding words in what Rosa reckoned must be Welsh because she didn't understand any of it.

'In order to dispel a curse,' Nancy said to Rosa, 'you have to raise a greater power, look. It's all about degrees of light and darkness.'

When Eleri beckoned to them, Rosa's mind flashed up a picture of her dad and the rage in his eyes.

'I can't decide for you, lovey,' Nancy said.

Rosa sighed and bit her lip and followed Nancy into the circle, where the air was...was it her imagination or was the air different in here? Quieter, somehow and yet sharper, like sea air.

'Just relax, lovey,' Nancy whispered.

Rosa took up a position opposite Marco, and they exchanged feeble, hesitant waves. And then she found herself just...letting go.

All the lights she thought she saw over the next few minutes must surely have been in her mind, like the low, electrical hum that seemed to be under her feet. She felt connected to something big and...not *kind* exactly, but she was sure it didn't mean her any harm.

At least, it didn't seem to mean *her* any harm but...

Suddenly Marco was throwing back his head like a dog about to howl at the moon. Woolly whispered something to him, urgently, and he stood there with his eyes tightly closed, clenching his fists.

Later she was aware that he'd been guided out of the circle. She saw his white T-shirt fluttering some way down the Tor and then she heard him vomiting.

Embarrassed? Too right he was embarrassed. This was just *awful.* He didn't remember ever feeling as helpless and totally useless.

Yes, he did. He remembered the school Christmas party when he was about seven, and he'd drunk four cans of fizz, one after the other, and there was a feeling like a landslide inside him and then...*eeergh* – all over the floor in the school hall, everybody backing off in disgust, somebody sending for a mop and bucket. There had been kids he couldn't look in the eye for weeks afterwards.

Woolly had gone back to Eleri's bag of tricks and returned with a trowel, and he'd dug a hole and buried all the sick.

Oh...gross. Marco turned away.

Eleri bent over where Woolly had buried the sick and made some signs with her hands. 'The curse is buried,' she said. 'For now.'

Marco lay back in the grass. He was too tired to move, and his guts were aching. He felt empty and hollow inside but the mist had cleared and he could see actual stars. Hundreds of them, like jewellery on velvet. His eyes filled with tears.

This was what you had to go through to get rid of a curse? He saw Woolly looking up at Eleri.

'What do you mean "for now"?' Woolly said.

'We can't be sure it won't return.' Eleri looked through the night towards some distant horizon. 'But this was obviously the place for us to deal with it. The Abbey is disused, so its energy levels are low, but the Tor is a live site.'

Marco said, 'But it—'

'What?' Woolly said.

'It's a pagan site.'

Eleri nodded. 'Indeed it is. However...' She moved aside to reveal the church tower, looking like some stone space-rocket on its launching pad. 'What is *that*?'

'I'm confused,' Marco said weakly.

'Of course you are.' Eleri turned to Woolly. 'He will need watching closely for at least a week. He may still be vulnerable to psychic attack.'

When they went back to join the others, Marco didn't, for once, have much to say. He just sat on the damp grass with his back to the tower, feeling totally done in, just listening.

'It's no good,' Woolly was saying. 'We *got* to find out

what's going down. Kids raising Satan? All the good visions going to the wrong people?'

'What about...' Rosa's voice was doleful. 'What about the bad visions?'

'Ah.' Eleri came to sit next to Rosa. 'Yes, I've been thinking about what you told me, and it is puzzling. Yes, the sword Excalibur would certainly carry psychic memories of violent death. And someone *sensitive* who was exposed to it would obviously pick some of that up. And yet...with something as mystical as Excalibur, violent death is just not enough. There should be something that *transcends* all that.'

'So what about the ritual?' Woolly said. 'Black magic on Arthur's grave.'

'They are evidently trying to possess him. To claim King Arthur of the Britons for Satan, with a blood sacrifice. This is not a joke.'

Marco remembered: *Lord of the Labyrinth...Prince of Shadows... Give us power over this person that he may, through us, do YOUR bidding.*

'Satanism is at its most powerful when it corrupts a Christian site,' Eleri said. 'Though ruined, the Abbey is the oldest Christian church in England. *And* the site of Arthur's grave.'

'The old pendulum reckons it was a grave of some importance,' Woolly said. 'But we don't know it was *Arthur's* grave, do we? Most historians reckon it was just a money-making scam by medieval monks.'

'That doesn't matter, Woolly. The *belief* is there – the belief that Arthur and Guinevere lay in this sacred soil. It doesn't even matter whether he really existed as a person or not.'

'But, he...' Marco felt disappointed. 'He *might* have existed...'

'Oh, he *might* have existed. He might simply have been a Celtic warlord, neither particularly good nor particularly bad, for the times. But the later stories have made him into a symbol of all that is courageous and right-thinking...the spirit of the golden age of Britain. Generations of Avalonians have *created* a force for good...and called it Arthur.'

'Right.' Marco was trying hard to understand this. 'You're saying Arthur could be like...'

'An idea,' Eleri said. 'But an idea powered by centuries of meditation and magic can take on a reality of its own. So, in a sense, Arthur definitely *does* exist. But a force for good can be twisted...corrupted. These people are taking the energy generated by all those centuries of belief and corrupting it for their own purposes – to make *themselves* powerful.'

'*These people?*' Woolly said. 'Eleri, they're just kids.'

'*Just kids?*' Not for the first time this summer Marco was staggered at how innocent adults could be. 'Look, speaking as a kid, I reckon saying they're "just kids" is like...well...'

He looked at Eleri. She nodded.

'We must not underestimate them. Children can be more dangerous than adults. They seldom consider the full consequences of their actions.'

She meant they didn't know when to stop, Marco thought.

And she was dead right there.

Hellhole

Woolly had called up Sam on Marco's mobile to explain the situation. He and Diane were waiting by the stile near the bottom of the Tor to take Rosa home to High Street in the Land Rover that smelled of dogs.

At the flat, Sam put on all the lights and Diane kept offering to make her a drink, get her something to eat. But Rosa said, No, no, honestly, she'd be fine. Wanting to get them out before Dad arrived home from his clergy meeting.

She almost made it.

They'd been gone less than two minutes before he came striding in with a face like a stormy night in November.

'What were *they* doing here?'

'Diane and Sam?' Rosa tried for a shrug. 'They just dropped in to see if I was okay.'

Dad's eyes narrowed and his mouth went tight and disappeared into his beard.

'Dad, they're friends, okay?'

'You ought to have friends your own age.'

'What, like Marco, who you hate?'

'I don't *hate* the boy, I just think he's not the kind—'

'What *is* the kind?' Rosa said hopelessly. 'Diane's like... she's a Lady, isn't she? She lives in a stately home.'

'Hah.'

'What's that mean?'

'Bowermead Hall? They're just about clinging on to it, from what I hear. They'll have to sell it soon, before it starts falling down around them. *If* they can find anybody who wants to buy it. People say her father, the late Lord Pennard, would turn in his grave if he knew she'd married a long-haired troublemaker who runs a little print shop. It's said she could have had a millionaire – or at least someone who could afford to look after the place.'

'It's not just a print shop. They publish *The Avalonian*.'

'A two-bit alternative magazine bought by cranks and pagans?' A sneer appeared in Dad's beard. 'You know what they call her, don't you?'

Rosa said nothing. She knew exactly what they called Diane, and it just showed the kind of people *they* were.

'*Lady Loony.* Forsaken her heritage to mix with the dropouts and the pagans.'

'Well, I think...' Rosa didn't look at him. 'I think she's nice.'

'I don't suppose you're going to tell me why they *really* came here, are you?'

'I've told you. They just came to see if I was...'

She gave up. He stood stiffly in the living-room doorway, and his dog collar was like the white line across a no-entry sign.

Marco wasn't sleepy, and Woolly seemed to sense this.

When they got back to the cottage, he said, 'All right, then. I'll show you something,' and led Marco through the orchard.

Merlin obviously wasn't sleepy, either. He was standing at the door of his stable, which had been rebuilt after a nasty fire a few weeks ago. His big brown eyes were like those glass globes you shook and then stars floated around.

Woolly switched on the electric light he'd had installed so there'd be no need for oil lamps, which might be a fire risk. The electric light was less atmospheric, but at least Marco could clearly make out what Woolly was showing him, as he parted the hair near the top of Merlin's back, just below his tufted mane.

'See that, dude?'

Wow. 'It's...' Marco looked up at Woolly.

There was a dark cross in the hair. Very distinct once you became aware of it.

'Do all donkeys have one of those?'

'More or less,' Woolly said. 'Part of the legend of the donkey, look. Donkey carried Mary to the stable where Jesus was born. Donkey carried Jesus into Jerusalem in triumph. A donkey's the most sacred animal there is.' He fondled one of Merlin's giant ears. 'As well as the most stubborn, ornery, unmanageable, greedy...'

Marco felt strange.

'So he really did save me from...?' He couldn't say it.

Woolly thought hard. For a moment, the old Woolly was back, his eyes full of light again, his big, white moustache bristling.

'Two ways of looking at that,' Woolly said. 'You was out here talking to Merlin earlier this evening, right?'

'Right.'

'In which case, it could be that a part of your mind stored him away and brought him out when he was most needed. As a symbol of the forces of light, kind of thing.'

Which was close to the sort of psychological explanation you might get from Josh.

'But I didn't know about the cross, did I?' Marco said.

'Ah, well,' Woolly said, nodding as if this proved something. 'When you've been in Glasto as long as me, you'll realize there's never an explanation that *fully* explains the things that goes on here.'

'Right.'

'And there never will be,' Woolly said. 'And that's the way it should be.'

An hour later, deep in the night, Marco stood in his bedroom window looking out towards the Tor.

A live site. He had an idea what that meant, and it was scary.

Everything had been scary tonight, reminding him that Glastonbury wasn't just about making exciting discoveries. Some of the discoveries were seriously shocking. For every mind-blowing thing that happened (yeah, he knew he was starting to pick up Woolly's expressions, but he didn't really care any more) there was always going to be something else that would scare you stiff.

This was not an easy town to live in.

And yet he couldn't bear the thought of leaving it at the end of the holidays. He just wished there was somebody he could talk to about all this – somebody who didn't have an opinion either way. Josh was no use at all. *His* opinions were set in concrete.

Marco went to the bedside table and picked up Marvin, the little stuffed rabbit. His oldest possession. The only cuddly toy that hadn't been thrown away by his mum and dad, or washed and passed on to some little kid.

He'd only discovered, since coming here, that Marvin had been made by Nancy, who had secretly placed in his stuffing a small pebble taken from the Tor.

Marvin was an Avalonian rabbit, the only present he'd ever been allowed to receive from his grandparents – although he didn't remember ever knowing that. He imagined that if Mum had known about the stone, she'd have got rid of Marvin before the baby Marco had even seen him.

For some reason, Mum hated the town where she'd been born and would never go back. Never talked about her parents, except to say they were weird and should be avoided...and Marco had only been brought here this summer because she was on this BBC assignment in America and his dad wanted a reason to spy on Woolly and Nancy... because Dad was working for Wilde-Hunt, who had wanted their land – *this* land – for Avalon World.

He guessed it wouldn't be long before Mum and Dad were officially divorced. Which would be a relief, in a way.

But now he'd discovered Woolly and Nancy and Glastonbury...

He'd promised his dad that when Mum rang him on his mobile from the States, he'd always pretend he was at home in London. And even though he now knew the truth about Dad, he'd kept to his promise.

It's rubbish here in London, he'd told her in one of their very few, short transatlantic conversations. *It's all hot and overcrowded. I keep thinking how great it would be to live somewhere where there was...you know, hills. Maybe a small town with historic buildings? And legends and things.*

Legends? she'd snapped, and he knew he'd gone too far. If he was going to keep on seeing Woolly and Nancy, he'd have to take it slowly, play his cards right, and maybe...

There was a noise outside the bedroom door, which made Marco feel a momentary panic because of the first time he'd heard it, earlier tonight.

And then he smiled and went to open the door.

The big black cat strolled in and jumped on the bed.

'Oh,' Marco said.

No animal had ever been on his bed before.

The big cat curled up at the foot of the bed and looked across at Marco. The room was softly lit by a small electric lantern on the bedside table, and the cat's eyes were golden in its light.

Marco said, 'Arthur?'

It was a pretty obvious name for a cat rescued from a horrible death on King Arthur's grave, but sometimes the obvious thing was the right thing.

Marco went and sat on the bed next to Arthur and stroked him, lightly at first and then harder because Arthur seemed to like that. His purr was like the electric pump at the bottom of one of the fountains in their forecourt at home in London.

It seemed to put a new strength in Marco, and he thought about Jasper Coombes and Shane Davey and he no longer felt afraid of them and whatever evil was working through them.

They don't know when to stop.

He picked up his mobile and decided to ring Josh, who always stayed up late watching Open University programmes on psychiatry-related subjects. Obviously, Josh was going to totally trash everything he had to say, but what the hell, he needed to discuss this with somebody before he could sleep, and if it had to be Josh...whatever.

As soon as he switched on, the phone jumped in his hand, telling him somebody had called, and the answering service voice went:

You have five new messages. To listen to your messages...

Marco pressed *one*.

'*Marco this is Mum, in America.*'

Marco froze. He'd only just been thinking about her. This was *so* weird.

Mum had a nice voice. It tugged at something inside him.

'*Call me back, huh? It won't cost much, and I'll call you straight back, okay?*'

He could hardly call back at this time, could he? Although it would probably be afternoon in California.

Marco waited for the second message.

'*Marco, this is Mum again. You still haven't called me back.*'

Well, for goodness' sake, he'd been busy, risking his immortal soul to save...Arthur.

Third message.

'*Marco, this your mother. Call me back AT ONCE!*'

Marco breathed in, the air hissing through his teeth. Arthur rolled over and stretched himself into the duvet. Its cover had been made by Nancy and had big orange suns on it.

'MARCO. YOU'RE GOING THE RIGHT WAY TO HAVING YOUR PHONE TAKEN AWAY FOR GOOD AS SOON AS I RETURN. NOW CALL...ME...BACK IMMEDIATELY!'

Oh well, no getting out of it. On the one hand, she'd be working out the time and wondering why he was still up, but on the other hand...

He was about to call her when the fifth message came through. He'd forgotten there were five of them.

Mum again, of course, but this time her voice had gone quiet.

As quiet as slowly cracking ice on a pond in January.

'*Marco. I have spoken to your father.*'

Uh-oh.

'*I have finally got the truth out of your father.*'

Marco gripped the phone tightly.

'*I know where you are.*'

Marco froze.

Oh *no*...

'*I told your father to drive over there without delay and bring...you...back...at once.*'

A thin cry escaped from Marco's lips.

'*However, he refused.*'

Yes, it wouldn't be a good time for Dad to show his face in Glastonbury.

'He said he was "too busy". He did, however, say he would send you enough money for the train fare. You should have it in the morning.'

'Noooo...'

Marco started running his spare hand through Arthur's fur in panic.

'*I want you on the afternoon train for Paddington, from where you can call your father and he'll collect you. Are you listening to me, Marco...? Do you understand?*'

'Nooooooooooooooooooooooo!'

'*I WANT YOU OUT OF THAT HELLHOLE NOW!*'

Part Three

'Glastonbury has ever been the
home of men and women who
have seen visions. The veil is thin here,
and the Unseen comes very near to earth.'
DION FORTUNE
Avalon of the Heart

A Mild Form of
Mental Illness

'Your eyes!' Granny Goldman reeled back in horror. 'What happened to your eyes?'

'Oh.' Josh took off his rimless glasses. 'My eyes are actually fine. These are...er...plain glass.'

She stared at him across the platform at Castle Cary train station. Although it was a dull morning, she herself was wearing sunglasses, big round ones, and her hair was pushed back under what he understood was known as an Alice band. She was wearing a long, loose, oriental kind of frock with a design of giant peacock feathers.

People kept staring at Granny Goldman, but Granny Goldman stared only at Josh.

'You're wearing spectacles with plain glass?'

'Yes, it's, er...'

How was he going to explain that *all* top psychiatrists wore rimless glasses? Why did Granny Goldman always have to *know* things?

'You want to become blind before your time, Joshua?'

'Blind?'

'Wearing glasses when you don't need them is tempting fate.' She picked up one of his bags and made for the exit. 'You must *never* tempt fate!'

'Fate?' Josh said. 'You're not actually telling *me* that you believe in *fate*?'

'Joshua.' Granny Goldman stopped on the pavement outside the station. 'When you've been on this earth as long as I have, you'll learn that *not* believing in fate is the best way of *tempting* fate.'

Josh put his glasses back on so he'd have something to blink behind. Mustn't overreact. So his grandmother was superstitious. It was only a *mild* form of mental illness.

But it got worse. Within minutes, it had got *much* worse.

They didn't have far to carry the cases, because Granny Goldman's ice-blue Porsche was very conveniently parked.

'You're on double yellow lines,' Josh said.

Granny Goldman shrugged and threw Josh's bag onto the small rear seat.

'Yellow's my lucky colour. Two yellow lines – twice as lucky.'

'Right,' Josh said numbly. He climbed in and fastened his seat belt. Granny Goldman always came up to London on the train and he didn't recall her having wheels this flash the last time they'd visited her in Torquay.

He was reluctantly impressed. This was one cool car.

Of course, he didn't show it. He leaned back in his seat like he'd travelled in loads of Porsches.

'Look, er, you do know how to get to Glastonbury from here?'

'How to get to Glastonbury. Aaaah...' Granny Goldman put on this blissful smile.

'I mean you have got satnav, haven't you?'

'Of course.' Granny Goldman switched on the engine and flipped the Porsche into gear. 'But I never use it. It invariably gives you the boring routes. Besides, that woman's voice, I just want to slap her.'

'You want to slap a computer?'

'Doesn't everybody slap computers? Anyway, I'll know when we get close to Glastonbury. I'll be able to pick up the vibe.'

Pick up the vibe?

Josh shut his eyes in anguish. He should have called this off. He should have called Grandma Goldman and told her he'd come down with something...well, something not so serious that she'd be ringing up every hour to make sure he was still alive.

This whole venture was a grave mistake. He was about to expose an already-damaged woman to the town which had turned Marco into a kid so disturbed that his condition could only be explained by the creation of a new syndrome.

Through a long and mainly sleepless night, Marco had given his situation a lot of thought. He didn't want to get Woolly and Nancy in any more trouble with his mum than they had been for the past thirteen years or more. No, he didn't want to do that.

And yet...

He'd finally fallen asleep around dawn and hadn't woken up until ten o'clock. Looked up into Arthur's golden eyes. Arthur had been balanced on the headboard. The prospects of taking Arthur back to London to stay with either Mum or Dad were too remote even to consider.

'That cat sleep in your room?' Nancy said, making Marco breakfast.

'Er...' At home, this alone would have been enough to have Arthur packed into a basket and delivered to the Cats Protection League for immediate rehoming.

'Nice to have a bit of company,' Nancy said. 'Especially after what you both went through last night.'

'Oh... Right.'

Breakfast was an omelette, with tomato and onions and potato and a big stack of toast. Marco's plate was a lot more colourful than the view from the window. The Blight had set in again. The sky looked like dirty washing.

'Where's Woolly?'

'Down the Abbey,' Nancy said. 'With his rods and his pendulum. Carrying out some tests. Well, that's where he said he was going. Seeing if any damage has been done. Him and Eleri been wondering how to protect Arthur's grave against any more interference.'

'Why don't they just go to the police?'

'Satanism's not against the law any more,' Nancy said. 'Religious tolerance is the big thing now. You wanner worship a fiend from hell who only wants to destroy, you got every right to. Worst they could get them for would be trespassing.'

'What about cruelty to—?'

'We've been over that, lovey. They'd just deny it. Mr. Coombes would likely go to Mr. Cotton and take legal action against us for damaging the good name of his son.'

'I suppose Jasper's dad's part of it...whatever it is.'

'He turns a blind eye,' Nancy said. 'He's a mate of Roger Cromwell's and acts as the agent for the property deals Cromwell does. He knows what's going on.'

'But Cromwell disappeared after we stopped him getting the Dark Chalice.'

'He won't be far away. We was talking about this last night in bed. What if the Coombes boy was still in touch with Roger Cromwell, and Cromwell was continuing to initiate him into the black arts? Grooming him for the service of Satan.'

'He knew all that weird stuff about reciting the Lord's Prayer backwards.'

'Well, anybody can do that, if they want to put their immortal soul on the line.'

'And he came out with these long words. Old Testament kind of long words.'

'Hebrew?' Nancy said. 'Greek?'

'Dunno. I can't speak Hebrew.'

'Me neither. But I know about Words of Power.'

'Words can actually have power?'

'Course they can...in the right situation. The human voice is a very powerful tool, and saying words out loud sets up a vibration. Certain words can call down forces of light... others can command the forces of darkness. Words can strike fear.'

'Er...' Marco finished his breakfast and brought his plate over to the sink. 'Talking about words striking fear.'

He got out his phone and held it out to Nancy. She wiped her hands on her apron.

'What's this?'

'If I press this, you can listen to the messages on the answering service,' Marco said.

He had to do this. There was no way out, and he couldn't put it off any longer.

He pressed. She listened. He prayed.

Josh knew he was in trouble here. And he had plenty of time to work out just how much trouble he was in, because getting to Glastonbury took for ever.

This was because Grandma Goldman drove way, *way* below the speed limit. No matter what kind of road they were on, impatient guys blew their horns from behind. In villages she had to speed up to get past people on bicycles.

You wouldn't credit it. Granny Goldman was driving way below the speed limit *in a Porsche*?

Josh turned the question over and over in his head before he managed to get it out.

Granny Goldman smiled.

'Why do I drive so slowly in a Porsche? It's because most people can't *afford* a Porsche. This way, they feel so much better about it.'

'Right,' Josh said, blinking nervously as they were overtaken by a caravan.

'Also, I know I'm a lousy driver,' Granny Goldman said, 'and I wouldn't want my only grandson to get hurt.'

'Right,' Josh said. 'Er...in which case, why do you actually *have* a Porsche?'

He winced as they were overtaken by a tractor – so ancient it had a funnel; did that mean it was steam-powered? – pulling a long trailerload of straw. Granny Goldman slowed to about 10 mph so she could look at him in even more safety.

'Joshua,' she said. 'You do ask the strangest questions.'

Josh sank down in his bucket seat, with his briefcase on his knees, looking out of the side window.

Never in his life had he travelled through countryside so slowly.

So slowly that he was forced to look at it and consider what it meant...if it meant anything. These green fields and the hills and the cows. Obviously, not his natural environment. He should've thought about this before he arranged the trip.

Face it: out here, even the great Sigmund Freud would've been truly stuffed.

The point being that the countryside wasn't something you could understand. You couldn't psychoanalyse *cows*. You couldn't plug your laptop into a *hill*.

Josh clutched the sides of the seat in a sudden, terrible panic.

He snapped open his case, plunged into it.

Oh no!

His Blackberry!

He'd forgotten his Blackberry!

He'd be technologically disadvantaged from the outset.

He stared at Granny Goldman driving through the stupid, meaningless countryside at 20 mph with that crazy, vacant smile on her face.

Turn the car round! Josh howled inside his head. *Take me back to the station. Get me out of this time warp!*

Not a Total Lie

He watched the tears forming in her eyes.

He would've preferred anger, but it was a start. He beamed crucial thoughts at Nancy: *You can stop this. You can tell her you're just not sending me back.*

'Oh, Marco...' Nancy handed the mobile back to him. 'She sounds exactly the same.'

'What?'

'Alison. I haven't heard her voice since she stopped appearing on the telly.'

'I can't go back,' Marco said firmly. 'You do realize that.'

Nancy was staring over his head, her eyes all glazed.

'She thinks the world of you, Marco. You can tell that.'

'She's just mad at Dad for lying to her. Though I can't think why, the number of times she's told me that lying's a way of life for lawyers.'

'I should talk to her.'

'Yes, I think you should. Because—'

'You don't know how much I've wanted to talk to her all these years, but Woolly keeps saying, "No you wait for her to come round – she's the one walked out."'

'Erm...' Marco took a long breath. 'Nancy...why did she do it? Why did she leave Glastonbury and not come back?'

It wasn't the first time he'd asked that, but he'd never thought he was getting a totally straight answer. Yeah, yeah, Mum had left Glasto because she wanted to work in television, and the nearest TV centre was Bristol. But that didn't really answer the question – Bristol was close enough to commute, or at least come home at weekends.

But Mum had *never* come home. She'd gone to London, started a whole new life, lost all contact with her parents. And made sure her only child never met them.

'I mean, I think I'm old enough to know the truth,' Marco said. 'Don't you?'

'The truth?' Nancy slumped down at the kitchen table. Her hair was like a collapsed haystack. 'That's just it...*we* don't know the truth. We've thought and thought and agonized all these years. I tell you, Marco, it's a dark cloud over our whole lives. Has been ever since.'

'So why didn't you just—'

'But when you arrived...that was like a sudden silver lining.'

'But now Mum wants me to go back.'

'Hellhole,' Nancy said, crying openly now. 'She's still calling it a hellhole.'

'She was just...'

'No she wasn't. She hates it. And us.'

Marco said, 'I love it here. Totally. I...just seem to belong. And I *don't want to go back.*'

Nancy reached over and took one of his hands in both of hers, a tear landing like a small jewel in the middle of the tattoo of a robin on her wrist.

'She's your mother, lovey. She has first call. If she wants you back, there's nothing we can do.'

Now it was Marco who was close to tears. 'She doesn't understand.'

'Understand what, lovey?'

He looked down at the table for a moment and then he played his best card. 'About the curse.'

'Don't talk about that. Put it behind you.'

'No, look, we can't. Eleri said I had to have like... aftercare. She said she had to keep an eye on me. In case it...'

'Oh God,' Nancy said. 'I'd forgotten about that.'

'Anything could happen, Nancy.' Marco gave it the heavy breathing and staring eyes approach. 'What if I went crazy on the train to London? Like, I once saw this old film where this guy's in a train compartment and this horrifically gross demonic entity appears, sitting opposite him. And, he's the only passenger who can see it and he's clawing at the windows to get out and everybody's screaming – they think he's gone bonkers – and in the end somebody pulls the communication cord. Only it's too late – this guy's jumped off the speeding train and his body's lying—'

'No!' Nancy was on her feet. 'Stop it!' She clapped her hands to her face.

Marco cooled it and looked at Nancy. Her fingers slid down her face, revealing seriously anxious eyes.

'What are we going to do, Marco?'

Marco stood up. 'Do nothing,' he said. 'I'll handle it.'

'Marco, your mother doesn't like—'

'Being messed around. I know, but she's in America.'

'Marco, you can't—'

'Look,' Marco said. 'Something weird's happening here, right? You're worried, Woolly's worried. Woolly was in a terrible state yesterday. It was like the old Woolly only came back when Rosa and me came out of the Abbey. It gave him like...a sense of purpose?'

Nancy looked at him, smiled kind of ruefully.

'Truth is, Marco, you turning up's given Woolly a new lease of life. Since your mother left...well, he idolized her, look. She could do anything with him. Anything she wanted, it was hers. After she left, he wasn't even doing much dowsing.'

'What?'

'Until he started to teach you. It revived his interest in everything. Don't tell him I told you.'

'I...no. Okay.'

Marco was shocked. He'd thought Woolly and Nancy lived this idyllic life in the hills above Glasto, feeling the magic, *living* it.

'Passing it all on to you made it seem worthwhile again,' Nancy said. 'The feeling that there were things we could do in Glastonbury that nobody else can do anywhere. He'd thought your mother would carry it on, and when she rejected us he was a broken man. Until you...'

Nancy lowered her head into her arms and wept quietly.

And now Marco saw it all so clearly – how it must have felt like being stabbed in the back when, just as Woolly had thought it was all coming right again, the Avalonians' role as the guardians of the town's secret history was suddenly taken over by the Glasties.

There was no way he could leave Woolly and Nancy at a time like this. No way at all. Totally out of the question. If the Holy Grail was just a symbol of what you most wanted, to make things right in the world, then making things right again for Woolly and Nancy...this was *his* Grail.

Right.

He looked at the clock. In America, Mum would almost certainly be still in bed.

He found her number in the index on his phone, hit 'call' and waited...and then nearly cut it off when he heard Mum's voice.

'Hi, this is Alison Woolaston's answering service. I'm not available right now, but please leave a message.'

Huh? Alison *Woolaston*? Mum had reverted to her maiden name? The name of the parents she'd rejected? Was this *just* because she and Dad had split up, or was there some kind of lingering regret?

Don't think about that now.

'Hi, Mum,' Marco said. 'I was just wondering why you hadn't called in ages. Or maybe there's something wrong with my phone.'

Cool. Mobile phones were a law unto themselves. There was surely no way you could prove, from a distance, whether one was actually still working or not.

'Anyway, I'll get it checked out,' Marco said. 'No probs this end, though. Everything's totally fine here. Er, there's a couple of CDs you might be able to get for me over there, but I'll talk to you again about that. Really missing you, Mum...'

'*Marco!*' When he came off the phone, Nancy was sitting up, looking startled, like she hadn't realized he could be so devious. 'What have you *done*?'

'It's not a *total* lie,' Marco said. 'And when I eventually explain it to her...'

And then he felt suddenly sad, wondering if he ever could.

The Real Thing

Granny Goldman said, 'Joshua, isn't it just so... magnetic?'

Approaching the town, she'd caught a glimpse of this famous Tor that Marco was always rambling on about and carefully slammed on the brakes.

She'd drawn in a long breath. Appeared to be in a state of total elation.

Elation: *in pathological terms, the emotion accompanying mania,* it said in Josh's dictionary of psychoanalysis.

All this over a small hill with the remains of a church on top.

'It's not very big, is it?' Josh said.

And the same went for the town. It had been morning when they'd left Castle Cary, and it was late afternoon by the time the Porsche crawled into Glastonbury. They'd actually had to stop for lunch. And then Granny Goldman had stopped four more times, in different places, to photograph the views which, to Josh, all looked like the same view. Green bits, brown bits and a dull sky. And then a small hill with a church on top. Big deal.

They booked into this stone inn. It had St George on the sign – a knight with a red cross – along with a bunch of nobodies.

The Holiday Inn it wasn't. There was unlikely to be a swimming pool in the basement.

'Joshua, it's *ancient*.' Granny Goldman stood in the reception area, sniffing the air. 'It has to be just *drenched* in history.'

Josh gave a different kind of sniff. He was indifferent to periods of history pre-dating the development of psychiatry.

A fairly friendly woman with a northern accent took them upstairs, telling them about mealtimes and stuff like that, and then wisely left them to it.

Fortunately their rooms were widely separated. Josh's had leaded windows with orange and blue stained glass. Looking out, he could see a close-up of the inn sign and a view up the main street. It looked normal enough, although he didn't recognize any of the shops: no Comet, no PC World.

All the same, he kept on staring out of the window because he really didn't want to contemplate the room itself.

This was because the room, the place he was supposed to try and sleep for two or three nights, was...

'Look at that, Joshua! A four-poster bed! And it looks like a *real* four-poster, not one of those phoney repro jobs with curtains that don't draw. I bet it really creaks when you sit on it.'

Creepy, Josh thought. Dark and horribly creepy. It was probably supposed to be haunted. Not, of course, that *that* kind of superstitious drivel...

'Isn't it wonderful?' Granny Goldman screeched. 'When I was your age, I *longed* to have a room like this. A real Guinevere's boudoir kind of room.'

'It's very nice,' Josh said miserably.

'We'll get our bags, unpack, take a nap and then see about some dinner,' Granny Goldman said. 'Do you want to invite your friend to eat with us?'

'Er...no, I...I thought I'd see him tomorrow. Make it a proper...surprise.'

'Seeing *you* here, he'll think it's his birthday!'

'Yes,' Josh said uncertainly. 'I'm sure he will.'

While Granny Goldman took her nap, he stayed in his creepy room with this month's *Psychiatry Today,* put on all the lights, even though it was still daytime, and began to draft his article on Goldman's Syndrome.

Perhaps, to illustrate it, he should take a picture of Marco standing by the Tor, his eyes burning with madness.

After dinner, they went for a walk up the main street.

There were still quite a few people about, although most of the shops were closed. In fact, in Josh's view, it would be no bad thing if most of these shops were *permanently* closed. What a load of junk! Candles and crystals and pagan Celtic jewellery and picture cards for people who wanted to pretend to tell fortunes. Who in their right minds would ever want to buy this kind of garbage?

Answer: some of the people they encountered on their way up the street.

'Isn't this all so wonderfully atmospheric?' Granny Goldman burbled as they passed a guy dressed like an old-fashioned gypsy, with earrings you could get your fist through. 'It's like being in...oh, Middle Earth, or somewhere.'

'Or somewhere,' Josh said.

One of the few shops that was actually open was a DVD rental store which seemed to sell bits of electronic kit as well. Josh stopped outside, wondering if they might actually stock Blackberrys and whether he could persuade Grandma Goldman she needed to own one.

There was a big display of video games in the window, and Josh blinked as he took in the titles.

ARTURUS REX - THE BEGINNING
ARTURUS REX 2 - THE QUEST CONTINUES
ARTURUS REX 3 - THE SECRET OF THE GRAIL

Hmm. Yes. He supposed there *would* be a big demand for fantasy games in a place like Glastonbury. Especially this game.

But Granny Goldman shook her head, mystified.

'Who could possibly want to play King Arthur video games in Glastonbury when they're so close to the Real Thing?'

Josh sighed.

'The real thing?'

'Arthur came here to die, Joshua. In the beautiful Vale of Avalon. Except, according to the legend, he didn't really die at all. He's just sleeping in a cave somewhere and will return when Britain has need of a man of true valour and vision. That's why he's known as "The Once and Future King".'

'Some people will believe anything,' Josh said, as the shop door opened and two men came out.

He gave them a second glance because they were the first totally normal-looking people he'd seen since he and Granny Goldman had left the inn. One was tall and balding and wearing a business suit and the other was stocky with a grey beard and baggy tweeds.

'Hang on,' a man's voice shouted from inside the shop. '*When* did you say he was coming?'

'*Not so loud!*' the bearded, baggy guy hissed. He stepped back inside the doorway. 'We don't *know* when he's coming, we just know he's coming *sometime*. And soon. So we need to make sure we're fully prepared for his arrival. Like that window display – you need to double the size of that, for a start.'

'It's cost me enough already!' the voice inside protested. 'This is not Bristol, you know.'

The bearded guy laughed and nudged his companion. 'One day, my friend, it'll be *bigger* than Bristol.'

'I just hope you're right about this, Mr. Daniel, that's all,' the guy inside said.

'Course I'm right. I got my *contacts*. Top-level.'

'Well, all I know is, we're all going to look pretty stupid if it doesn't happen.'

'*Gah!*' Mr. Daniel said and walked out.

Granny Goldman watched the two men walking down the street towards The George and Pilgrims.

'You'd almost think they were talking about the return of King Arthur himself,' she said wistfully. 'Wouldn't that be just *so* exciting?'

Josh raised his eyes to the dreary Glastonbury sky.

'*Gah,*' he said.

Respect

Nancy decided it would be better, at this stage, if they didn't tell Woolly about Marco's mum. Not just yet, anyway. He had, after all, been a lot less depressed the past day or so. Nancy suspected he'd secretly seen someone – some kind of therapist or healer – and she didn't want him having a relapse.

Which, frankly, he looked seriously close to when he came in. His white ponytail had come apart, his eyes were full of hopelessness and his voice was hoarse.

'Look at this.'

A splat on the kitchen table as Woolly flung down a copy of the local evening paper, *The Evening Post*. There was a big photo on the front page of a lone figure in white looking up at one of the sawn-off arches of Glastonbury Abbey.

The headline – it wasn't the main headline but it was fairly prominent – said:

THE VISIONARY

Reading the story underneath, Marco knew just how Woolly felt.

A shy public schoolboy has been hailed as a prophet after predicting the discovery of King Arthur's sword, Excalibur, in Glastonbury.

Jasper Coombes, 15, says he saw the sword in a vision which recalled the famous legend of The Lady of the Lake.

The following day, an ancient sword which top experts say could well be Excalibur was found near the town.

Jasper's father, leading Glastonbury estate agent Mervyn Coombes, said today, 'We just can't explain it. We are a normal family who have nothing to do with the so-called alternative community in this town. Some people in Glastonbury are always claiming to have dreams and visions, but my son is well-educated and has always been a very down-to-earth boy.'

The sword, which was discovered by the teenage daughter of a local church minister, has been described as the most exciting find of its kind in the West for over a century.

Mr. Coombes insists that Jasper told him about his

vision before the ancient weapon came to light.

Jasper says he saw the sword, held up by a pure white arm, when he happened to look down an ancient well behind the Glastonbury Tribunal, one of the town's oldest buildings.

He said today, 'I was actually quite embarrassed about it. At first, I told people a friend was claiming to have seen it, because I didn't want to be called a crank.' But there seemed no danger of that in the town today, as civic leaders rallied to support Jasper's story.

The mayor of Glastonbury, Councillor Griffith Daniel, said, 'This is something we have to take seriously. I have known this boy all his life, and I have great respect for his father.'

The mayor added, 'Something is happening in this town that we cannot ignore. And it's not happening to hippies and dropouts – the sword itself was discovered by the daughter of a man of God out walking with her father. Things are changing here at last, make no mistake.'

The implications of the discovery of 'Excalibur' will be discussed tonight at a special public meeting in Glastonbury Town Hall.

Marco looked up from the paper. If *he'd* had a ponytail he'd have pulled it apart in anguish, too.

'I know,' Woolly said. 'I know.'

'But he... *Look at him!*'

Marco held up the paper with the photo of Jasper in his white shirt and white cricket trousers. And his hair neatly trimmed and that innocent, soulful look in his eyes. He was like a...like some kind of *holy person*...like a...

Like a prophet.

'But you should've...' He felt furious tears springing into his eyes. 'You should've seen him last night, just...just oozing evil.'

'Nobody's gonner believe that now, are they?' Woolly said. 'You tell anybody what he was doing last night, it'll just look like sour grapes.'

'It's not f—' Marco clenched his fists. '*It's not fair!*'

'No coincidence he's all in white, is it?' Woolly said. 'It's a counter-strike by the Glastie spin doctors. Give the boy a whiter-than-white image, just in case any of it gets out from you and Rosa. And he's a local boy and you're both strangers. Who's gonner get believed?'

'Why are they doing this, Woolly? How *can* they—?'

'I don't know,' Woolly said grimly. 'But I think we better go to this public meeting tonight.'

'Me, too?'

'Why not?'

'Right,' Marco said.

Normally, he'd rather have a tooth filled than go to some dreary public meeting, but if Jasper Coombes was going to be there, looking all pure and innocent and holy, he wanted to be there to heckle or something. Accuse him of lying.

There was only one problem. Marco stared bleakly at Woolly.

'I actually don't think he's lying. He really did see the sword in the well. I think he was genuinely puzzled about it.'

Woolly folded up the paper so they wouldn't have to look at the local hero. Sorrowfully, he gathered together his ponytail and snapped a rubber band around it.

'I just don't understand it. The bad guys are winning...and we *still* don't have the faintest idea how they're doing it.'

Along with the paper, Woolly had brought back a whole boxful of assorted cat food for Arthur, who seemed to be the only one of them enjoying his evening meal tonight. Even Marco left half his nut roast, as Nancy asked Woolly about his day's dowsing around King Arthur's grave.

'Oh, er...it's bad,' Woolly said. 'Bad energy.'

'Well, you knew *that*,' Nancy said. 'These are dark people.'

Dark. Marco thought of all the fantasy books and comics he used to read, the films he used to watch. There was always a *dark lord* somewhere, who just did evil for its own sake, because he was a *dark lord* and that was what *dark lords* did.

But you weren't supposed to *believe* in any of it. That was why it was called *fantasy.* He put this to Woolly, who sighed.

'This sword and sorcery stuff – all the monsters with red eyes and horns – that *is* fantasy. You wanner teach kids about evil, you gotter spell it out for them. How they gonner know which is the bad guys if they ain't got horns and red eyes and a big black shield with a human skull on it?'

'And that's not Jasper Coombes, is it?'

'No. I'm afraid, in real life, the bad guys just look like the rest of us. You're playing on the grown-up pitch, now, dude. And so's the Coombes boy. He's being groomed.'

'By Roger Cromwell.' Nancy nodded. 'That's what I said. But he's not here any more. He's left the area.'

'I think he's still around,' Woolly said. 'And he's seen a

bit of bad in that boy, and he's been feedin' it. Trouble is, everybody thinks Jasper's a charming, polite young feller from a good family. That's the problem today, look. Nobody's allowed to call anybody evil, no more. You gotter respect 'em all, right?'

Marco nodded. It was true. The only times he'd ever heard the word *evil* used by teachers at his school were in connection with cigarettes and junk food.

It was getting complicated. He felt as if his brain was about to freeze up like a computer when you threw too many commands into the hard drive. How could you learn to spot evil if it didn't have red eyes and horns and a shield with a skull on it...just a white shirt and cricket trousers and a saintly expression?

'Question is,' Woolly said, 'how deep is Griff Daniel involved with all this? He's always been a crook, but I never quite saw him as actually *satanic*. But I'll be watching the old beggar real closely tonight, at that meeting.'

'You all right?' Nancy was looking at Woolly. 'You still look a bit...not yourself. You sure you're fit to go to the meeting?'

'Wouldn't miss it,' Woolly said grimly.

The Coming

At first, Marco thought Diane was wearing some kind of glowing make-up, but then it occurred to him that she'd been crying.

She and Sam had been waiting for them outside the town hall, this grey building in Magdalene Street, next to the Abbey gatehouse, although nowhere near as old.

Eleri was not there. Maybe this was something to do with the Glasbo that prevented her from loitering at this end of town making prophesies of doom after 6 p.m. Whatever, doom was certainly not on the agenda for most people tonight. Even before they went in, Marco saw Griff Daniel beaming through his beard and shaking people's hands really hard, as though he was pumping up their enthusiasm like water from a deep well.

It was a big crowd and although some people were looking a bit confused a lot were looking happy.

Not Diane, though.

'Something's happened,' Sam told Woolly, as they hung around by the Abbey gates, watching the townsfolk go into the town hall under the yellowy-grey evening sky.

Nancy went over to Diane, put a hand on her arm.

'What is it, lovey?'

'It's...' Diane's face crumpled. 'We've had an approach.'

'About the Hall,' Sam said.

'Nancy, it—' Diane dabbed her eyes with a tissue. 'Someone wants to buy it!'

'I never even knew it was on the market,' Woolly said, and Sam smiled thinly.

'It isn't.'

'You just had someone come to you and make an offer?'

'Coombes senior, it was. Acting on behalf of a client whose identity is being kept under wraps. Someone with piles of money.'

'Well...I suppose that's the kind of owner it needs,' Woolly said. 'And with the money, you'd be able to buy a smaller place you could manage. Bit of land, nice big kennels for the hounds. Ain't that what you want?'

'I don't—' Diane shook herself as if she didn't know *what* she wanted. 'I don't know *what* to do. It's ever such a frightful old place in many ways, but it's the family home, and I feel I'd be...betraying something.'

'*Used* to be a frightful old place,' Nancy said, 'till you and Sam took over. Atmosphere's a whole lot better now. Used

217

to be a symbol of wealth and greed and the power of the Dark Chalice, but you turned it around.'

'You really think so?'

'A house takes on the personality of the folks living there,' Nancy said. 'It's a slow process, but you're getting there. Be a terrible shame to lose it now, that's how I feel.'

Marco felt sad, too. There was always something exciting about going to Bowermead, even if meditation and fasting were sometimes part of the package.

Diane looked at Nancy, tearful but grateful.

'That's what I thought. But...Woolly's right. We have no hopes of ever getting enough money to maintain it. We may never get an offer like this again. We'll probably have to take it.'

'Funny this offer should've come through Coombes,' Woolly said. 'And funny it should've come now. What's your gut feeling, Sammy?'

'I don't like it,' Sam said. 'Not one bit.'

The town hall's big meeting room held a lot of people, and it was already well packed when they all went in. There was a stage with a table on it and, when everybody was seated, Griff Daniel bounded up in his white suit and stood at the front of the stage and a big cheer went up.

'Must've brought all his mates in from the pub,' Sam muttered.

At first, Marco didn't recognize anyone he knew, but then he spotted Rosa's dad, Big Dave, in his gleaming dog collar, and Sonia Warbuck of the *Glastonbury Guardian*, with a photographer.

'Welcome!' The mayor spread his arms wide and beamed lavishly at everybody. 'Welcome to a new era in the history of this ancient town! An era of wealth and prosperity. An era not seen since the days of...King Arthur himself!'

Other people had taken their places at the table behind Griff Daniel: Mr. Cotton in his grey suit and Mr. Coombes with his slicked-down black hair and his moustache and...

Jasper.

Jasper in his white shirt and his cricket trousers.

Marco growled.

'Reason I mentions King Arthur,' the mayor said, 'is he's a feller we don't, in my view, talk about enough. Least, we haven't in recent years. Fact is...he's become a bit of a dirty word.'

'Here we go,' Sam murmured.

'That's on account of how he's been taken up by all these New Age loonies...these half-baked hippies who comes here from all over the place 'cause they reckons there's something *magic* about it. Taking over what used to be normal shops to sell tat and rubbish. Marching up and down the Tor to "feel the vibes". Treating it like it's their town. And the worst thing is, they made King Arthur into one of *their* heroes. Well, I'm here tonight to tell you that all that's about to end!'

A roar of support rose up from the audience. Marco looked at Woolly. Woolly was silent. So were Nancy and Sam and Diane. But they were definitely in the minority tonight.

This was a gathering of the Glasties.

'See, I never had much interest in old King Arthur,' the mayor said. 'I'm a practical man. I got no time for airy-fairy rubbish. And I got no time for the airy-fairy rabble that prattles on about restoring the Golden Age on the back of a load of old legends that nobody was ever gonner prove one way or the other.'

'Well said, Griff,' someone shouted, but the mayor held up a hand for silence.

'However – much as it pains me to admit it – *I may have been wrong, look.*'

There was a slightly shocked silence this time. The mayor wagged a finger.

'These legends are *important.* They're a crucial part of this town. A part that we gave away!'

The hall stayed quiet. This wasn't what the Glasties were expecting to hear.

'We allowed our history – our legacy – to get hijacked by all these loonies from outside, who told a lot of lies about Arthur. Think about it for a minute – was King Arthur some little wimp playing feeble music on his guitar and pretending to heal folk with bits of crystal? *Was he?* No way!'

There was a buzz of anticipation.

'King Arthur was a warrior!' Griff roared. 'He was a man's man, swinging his big sword, going out there to get what he wanted. Oh, yes, it's time we faced the facts. King Arthur was *one of us.* And just like *he* went out there with his mighty sword to claim his kingdom from the invaders, that's what we gotter do. We gotter take back our town... *by the power of the sword!*'

Woolly and Sam exchanged glances. They were starting to look worried. Griff Daniel's eyes gleamed.

'And, as it happens, King Arthur's sword has returned. Has come back to us as a sign. Come to *us*, look – not *them.* Brought in by my good friend the Reverend Dave. And I...'

The mayor looked down at his feet and then lifted his eyes to the ceiling.

'...I have had a dream,' he said.

'Oh no,' Sam said. 'Spare us.'

People glared at Sam, *shush*ing.

'Yes, I personally have had a dream of King Arthur. I have seen Arthur's men marching in glory back to Glastonbury. And, at first, I was afraid. Thought I must be going a bit soft in the head, to be quite honest. And then I found that I was not alone. Several of my friends, pillars of this community, were also realizing, through strange experiences of their own, that *the time has come*. And then it emerged that a young man – a local boy, Glastonbury born and bred, educated at one of our most prestigious schools, but a modest, unassuming kind of lad – had foretold the coming of the sword.'

'*Modest, unass—*' Marco was halfway to his feet when Woolly pulled him down.

'Let's hear the worst, dude.'

The mayor turned towards Jasper Coombes, who was staring directly in front of him, above the audience, his face aglow in the lights. He looked like an angelic choirboy.

'This boy...' the mayor said. 'I have to tell you all that I believe this boy is our John the Baptist.'

There was a sudden hush.

'Gone too far this time,' Sam said under his breath. 'Surely he's gone too far...'

The mayor extended an open hand towards Jasper.

'I don't say that lightly, look. For I believes that, after him, will come a greater figure. Someone who will rescue this town from years of being a laughing stock and not having no

massive department stores and leisure complexes. Perhaps –
and all the signs are there – perhaps King Arthur himself—'

'I knew it!'

A woman was on her feet. A woman Marco had never
seen before. She had purply kind of hair and long earrings
and big sunglasses which she snatched off to reveal eyes wide
with awe. And she had a voice even bigger than Griff's.

'Mr. Mayor, I want to say to you... Well, I'm just here as
a tourist, I suppose, but I could tell, as soon as I was exposed
to the atmosphere of this wonderful old town, that
something was happening here. I could *feel it in the air*!'

'Course you could, madam.' Griff Daniel beamed at her.
'Course you could.'

'And I just want to say how honoured I feel to be here at
such a time!'

The woman's voice had risen into a kind of joyful shriek.

'And we are honoured to welcome you,' the mayor said
graciously.

Marco saw a boy sitting next to the woman – for a
moment, he looked almost like Josh – slowly sinking his
head into his hands.

'I can't stand much more of this,' Sam said, as the woman,
mercifully, sat down again.

And then...

'*It's all lies!*'

All heads swivelled. Midway down the room, this kid had
come to his feet. He looked about Marco's age and he had
on a red T-shirt with two big white words across the chest.

'He's lying!' the kid shouted.

A man sitting next to him tried to pull him back down,
but the kid shook him off. His face was red with rage.

'Can't you see he's making it all up? It's just a lousy scam!'

At first, Marco had thought the boy had a local accent, but then he noticed it was a bit different. By now, people were getting annoyed, telling him to sit down or get out, and a couple of a big security-looking blokes were advancing on him. The boy put his hands up.

'All right...all right...I'm going. I wouldn't spend another minute listening to this rubbish.'

As he stumbled down the aisle towards the door, Marco saw that the words on his T-shirt were MEBYON KERNOW.

Huh?

'Probably on drugs,' the mayor said. 'Now, if I may return to what I was saying... We needs to be prepared for The Coming. And that's why I've called this meeting. For too long, we – the true, loyal, long-suffering citizens of Glastonbury – have been afraid to embrace our destiny. But, my fellow Glastonburians, I tell you now...*we must be afraid no longer!*'

Through the billowing applause, the boy walked out, one of the security guys holding the door open for him. Marco caught another movement and spotted two other figures creeping towards the exit from the other side of the hall.

One of them was Shane Davey.

Uh-oh.

He glanced at Sam and Woolly. Sam was watching Mr. Cotton and Mr. Coombes patting the mayor on the back while the disgusting Jasper just gazed over the whole scene, all saintly and smug.

Woolly was just sitting there, very still, blinking fast. He looked as if something had hit him on the head, very hard.

Anyway, neither of them noticed Marco who, after a moment, slipped away and followed Shane Davey. He didn't feel good about this, but he knew he had to do it.

Blip

Violence...

Well, obviously violence could be exciting: car chases ending in a major smash, shoot-outs, explosions. Really exciting, on the other side of a screen.

Funny, though, how, when you were on the *same* side of the screen, just one, ordinary smack of a fist and a spurt of blood could actually stop you with the shock of it, make your heart go bang inside your chest. *Not* exciting.

They were beating up the kid in the red T-shirt.

Shane Davey, his eyes like slits, had the kid up against the town-hall wall.

As Marco came around the corner of the building, Shane

punched the kid in the mouth, and it started bleeding. The kid sank slowly down the wall, and Shane's mate caught him and hauled him back to his feet.

Shane's mate – Marco recognized him, though he didn't know his name – was a gangling boy with a shaven head, taller and older than Shane, maybe sixteen.

'You tell us who you are,' Shane said to the kid in the red T-shirt, 'or we're *really* gonner take you apart.'

'Can't you...?' The kid's voice sounded snuffly; his mouth was starting to puff up in one corner. 'Can't you read?'

Not a good thing to say to Shane.

In fact, this reference to his famously limited literacy skills probably touched a major nerve, because Shane hit him again.

This time, the boy yelped, and Shane's mate clapped a hand over his mouth, ramming his head back into the wall, and Marco looked over his shoulder, hoping maybe Sam or somebody had spotted he was missing and followed him out.

But there was nobody. This was it with adults. When you *didn't* need them they were hovering over you the whole time.

'Let him speak, Jezza,' Shane said, and his mate took his hand away, revealing a smudge of crimson blood across the cheek of the boy in the red T-shirt.

'Let's start again,' Shane said. 'Where you from? You ain't from round here. We never seen you before.' He jabbed a finger at the red T-shirt. 'Wassat mean?'

The boy sniffed and then started to cough. There was a great roar from inside the hall as Griff Daniel told people more of what they wanted to hear.

Shane raised his fist. 'Wassat *mean*?'

'Let him go,' Marco said.

Or least that was what he meant to say.

Pity it came out like dribble.

Shane Davey stopped hitting the kid and turned round and saw Marco for the first time.

Shane smiled, which was like a new crack opening up in a concrete wall.

'Well, well. Hippy scum to the rescue.'

'And I'm...I'm not on my own.'

The crack widened in the cement.

'I suppose you got armed police round the block.'

'Just a few mates,' Marco said, standing his ground, although the muscles at the back of his legs felt like wet sponges.

'You ain't *got* no mates,' Shane said.

'Look,' Marco said. 'Just let this guy go, eh? What's he ever done to you?'

Without taking his eyes off Marco, Shane hit the kid in the stomach. The kid doubled up, retching, and sank down the wall and this time Shane's mate let him fall.

'Come on, then, hippy trash. Go for it.' Shane strolled casually towards Marco, his fists going up in this automated kind of way, like it was part of his mechanism. 'Been waiting for this for a long time. Gonner beat you to a pulp, and then I'm gonner trample the pulp into something you could flush down a lavatory.'

The thing about Shane, he was no taller than Marco, but he was built like...well, like a public toilet block. It didn't take long for Marco to decide the best thing would be to go back into the hall and fetch Woolly and Sam.

Which was what he ought to have done in the first place, basically. He turned towards the corner of the building, and found himself looking up into the grinning teeth of the gangly kid, Jezza. How did *he* get *there*?

Marco froze.

Jezza grabbed hold of Marco's shoulders, almost tenderly, looked down at him for quite a while with what seemed at first like a kind of affection, and then...

'*Aaaaaaaagh!*'

Marco lurched away in total, blinding agony.

Oh God!

It was only the second time in his life that he'd been headbutted, but he should've seen it coming. Seen it happen on TV enough times.

And now, in the middle of the pain, all the special effects had started happening to him like this *was* TV. It felt as if his forehead had been split open and his brains were slurping out into the exploding night.

He felt himself tripping backwards, losing control of his legs, the buildings across Magdalene Street tilting away at a weird angle until all he could see was the muddy sky.

Then he was sitting on the ground, stunned and dizzy, for several seconds, with his eyes closing. Just wanting to lie back and black out until it was all over.

But it wasn't over.

Through half-shut eyes, he saw a big trainer, in the instant before it slammed into his shoulder with the force of a boot with a steel toecap, and he went flat, his head clunking on concrete. And now he knew he was going to finish up in hospital, connected to all these tubes and drips and a monitor beside his bed going *blip, blip, blip...*

A bit later, when he finally managed to open his eyes, he'd already started hallucinating. Seeing things that couldn't be happening involving someone who couldn't be there.

He hallucinated the gangly kid, Jezza, sitting on the ground in front of him, moaning and swaying, and someone standing over him with a black, metal-framed briefcase held up over his head with both hands.

The monitor in his head went *blip, blip, blip...*

Brain damage. When it went *wheeeeeeeee*, he'd be flatlining.

All over.

The hallucination developed a soundtrack.

'*Look!* Look at that! You maladjusted *moron*! Look at what you've done to my best case! Look at the size of that crack. *Look at it!*'

Marco's eyes flipped open, and he saw the case coming down, aiming for Jezza's head, but Jezza squirmed aside and it landed on one shoulder with a major thunk that still had Jezza crying out, and Marco could see Shane rushing in, with his pistoning fists, and then Shane toppled forward, and Marco saw the kid in the red T-shirt had pushed him hard from behind, and the kid was howling, '*Run! Run!*' and Marco somehow found his feet and ran.

Watching Over...

Rosa switched off the plasma TV, lay back on the bed and called out for the ghost.

Well, not actually *called out*; she didn't say a word. She just felt the words inside. And then she felt them go out of her into the soft evening air.

Abbot Richard...

Sometimes this worked.

In the late autumn of 1539 Abbot Richard Whiting, a kind man, well-liked in Glastonbury, had been dragged through the town on a hurdle pulled by a horse, which was then driven up to the top of the Tor.

And it was here that Richard was executed – one of the

victims of King Henry VIII's hatchet man, Thomas Cromwell, who was in charge of closing down the abbeys and taking all their treasures for the king, who'd declared himself head of the Church.

Fat Henry had wanted to divorce the first of his six wives and the Church wouldn't give him the nod, so Fat Henry had taken over the Church.

Thomas Cromwell, cunning and ruthless, was the adviser who'd backed Henry all the way and did most of his dirty work. And it was said that Roger Cromwell, owner of the old black magic supplies shop under this very flat, had often claimed to be a descendant of Thomas.

Rosa couldn't think of that without shivering. As Marco had said once, the thing about Glastonbury was that history and legend were always *so close.*

As close, in this case, as the bedroom wall.

A wall probably built, originally, from stones from the Abbey when it was trashed by Cromwell's men. In a couple of months' time, when the trees were losing their leaves, she'd be able to look out of the back windows of the flat and probably see into the Abbey grounds.

The actual grounds which, back in the sixteenth century, had been walked every day by Abbot Richard when the Abbey had been soaring and golden.

Abbot Richard had objected to Henry getting divorced and paid the price. Stitched up by Cromwell, accused of lying and hiding a gold chalice.

Tried and convicted and executed.

Horribly.

Richard had been hanged on top of the Tor – a place where everyone believed that the dark gods still ruled – and then been drawn and quartered: his body cut into four sections and taken away to four different places.

At least when he appeared to Rosa, Richard seemed to be in one piece. Maybe you couldn't cut up a spirit.

Rosa lay on her side and stared at the wall by the door where the shape of a cowled monk had appeared.

Nothing there. Completely blank.

Not that she'd *ever* seen him very clearly. Sometimes, when her eyes were closed – usually when she was on the very brink of sleep – she'd be aware of a hazy figure standing by the bed.

Which should have been seriously scary. Ghosts were supposed to be cold, bringing a chill into the room. Yet this one put out a kind of warmth and the feeling that Rosa was being...not watched, exactly, but *watched over*.

The way he'd watched over her when she'd been trapped in the labyrinth under the streets of Glastonbury.

Most nights since then, when the light went out, she'd been aware of this *watched over* feeling, and whatever was there, whatever Richard was now, no longer frightened her.

But since the sword had been stored here and she'd had the blood dream, there'd been no feeling of Richard being around. As if the sword had cut the connection.

And then she'd confirmed that she didn't want him any more, in the worst way possible. She'd taken part in a pagan ritual on the Tor where he'd been put to death.

Rosa started to breathe hard, the guilt setting around her like quick-drying cement. Yes, they were nice, kind people, especially Nancy and Diane. But they had strange beliefs and she'd gone along with them. Gone to the top of the Tor that night without a second thought – too upset about the satanism in the Abbey. Too concerned that something evil might have entered Marco.

Never thinking that something *good* might be leaving *her.*

Never thinking about the lonely death of Abbot Richard at the hands of Cromwell's men. The crowd – rent-a-mob, Tudor-style – jeering at him as he hung there, the last Abbot of Glastonbury dying in a place of pagan darkness.

Maybe Dad was right and people like Nancy and Diane and Eleri were worshipping that darkness.

But then...

...Dad was a minister in the Church of England – the Protestant Church set up by Henry VIII and Thomas Cromwell in 1539.

Like, the very beginning of the Church of England...how dark was *that*?

And if Dad had been around in 1539, which side would he have been on?

All this was so deeply, totally confusing.

Rosa wrapped a pillow around her head in anguish.

No one could help her, and no one was watching over her.

Tribe

Marco was halfway across Magdalene Street when he saw that he was not alone.

Josh – was this really, actually *Josh*, in *Glastonbury*? – was on one side and the boy in the red T-shirt with blood on his face was on the other.

And they were both looking at him, like, *Where are we going? You're the one who's supposed to know this place.*

Two fully loaded tour coaches came swishing into town and slowed in front of the Abbey gates, separating them from Shane and Jezza, who must still be at the kerbside, near the Abbey.

It was the only chance they'd have to get away. Marco

tried to ignore the pain in his head and thought fast.

'This way!'

He ran into a narrow alleyway by the side of Sam Daniel's print shop.

There was a line of high wooden gates. One...two...three... ...four. This had to be Sam's. *Please, please God, don't let it be locked.*

The latch went down, the gate swung open and Marco stumbled into Sam's yard, holding the gate open for the other two and then shutting it quietly, leaning back against it, breathing hard.

Josh looked up at a window with its blind down over a sign which said, *THE AVALONIAN – READ THE TRUTH BEYOND THE NEWS.*

'Belongs to friends of mine,' Marco said. 'There's nobody here. They're in the meeting.'

There was a wooden table in the yard, with chairs, where Sam and Diane had their lunch when the weather was okay. Marco pulled out one of the chairs and slumped down.

'And the red-haired psycho?' Josh said.

'Not what you'd call *a friend*, exactly.' Marco propped his elbows on the table and let his head fall into his hands. 'Wow, I can't tell you how much this hurts.'

'Never mind your head. Look at my case!'

'What's in it?'

'Fifteen copies of *Psychiatry Today*. I didn't expect to be able to buy anything worth reading in this town, so I came prepared.'

'It must weigh—'

'Enough,' Josh said with some satisfaction.

Marco grinned, in spite of everything. This *was* Josh. Josh had actually arrived in Glastonbury. Just in time to...save Marco's life?

Marco looked down at Josh's ruptured briefcase.

'Thanks, mate. You always said you could crush anybody with the power of psychiatry. I never quite realized what you meant.'

'You guys know each other, then.'

The kid in the red T-shirt was touching his split lip, experimentally, with one finger.

'Yep...' Marco said.

Okay, he'd find out later what on earth Josh was doing here. First things first. He turned to the kid in the red T-shirt.

'So what *does* it mean?'

'This?' The kid plucked at his shirt. 'Mebyon Kernow? It means the Sons of Cornwall. It's the Cornish nationalist party.'

'What?'

'Cornwall used to be a separate nation at the western tip of England. Some of us think it should be one again. Independent.'

Marco stared at him. He'd heard of Welsh nationalists and Scottish nationalists, but...

'*Cornwall?*'

'Why not? We get a lousy deal out of being part of England. We're the poorest county of the lot. There used to be loads of tin mines and a big fishing industry and stuff, but all we've got now is tourism. Letting foreigners trample all over us for money.'

Josh seemed intrigued. He leaned back and folded his arms.

'Yes, the psychology of nationalism is very interesting,

especially when it's a truly hopeless cause. It's quite often adopted by people who feel inadequate as individuals and seek to acquire a stronger identity by being part of an oppressed tribe.'

The kid looked at him. 'You trying to start another fight?'

Josh cleared his throat and put on his glasses. 'They also tend to acquire a surface aggression which can sometimes lead to mob violence and minor terrorism. For instance—'

'Josh?' Marco said.

'Yes?'

'Shut up, eh?'

Josh shrugged. Marco turned to the Cornish kid. 'What's your name?'

'Jethro Trelawney, by any chance?' Josh said.

The Cornish kid sighed. 'Brian Brown.'

Josh caught Marco's eye and turned quickly away. His shoulders were shaking. Marco controlled his own laughter by tapping his bruised forehead and biting down on a cry of extreme pain.

'So, Brian, what brings you to Glastonbury?'

'Not your problem.' Brian had one of those dark, glowering faces that could kind of shut down under his heavy black hair. 'But thanks for...you know...helping with those...'

'No problem,' Marco said. 'Er, back in the town hall, you shouted out that the mayor was pulling some kind of scam. What did you mean?'

'Look,' Brian said. 'I just got mad, all right? Couldn't stop myself. My brother's gonner kill me when he gets out of that meeting.'

'Your brother's in the meeting?'

'He was sitting next me. My brother's grown-up. He's...
My brother's Ted Brown.'

'Not *the* Ted Brown?' Josh said, and Marco flashed him
a look that said, *Can it, smart-arse*.

'Ted's the President of Mebyon Kernow.'

'Oh,' Marco said. '*That* Ted Brown.'

A stifled squeak came out of Josh. Marco thought, *We
have got to stop this*. Brian Brown got to his feet.

'Right, well, if you guys've finished taking the—'

'Look,' Marco said. 'We're sorry. Honest to God. We're
just glad to have got out of that situation without getting our
heads totally kicked in, and so we're a bit... And anyway, if
you want to talk about, like, oppressed minorities... I'm a...'
He swallowed. '...an Avalonian.'

Brian stayed on his feet but didn't go anywhere.

'What's that?'

'It's somebody who really believes in the old magic of
Glastonbury. That is, not like the mayor. You know?'

Brian peered at Marco. 'You don't even sound like you're
from Glastonbury.'

'I'm not. But my granddad is. I suppose I'm what you'd
call...'

'Ah,' Brian said. 'You're a third-generation *hippy*.'

'Well, no...not *exactly*...'

'In fact,' Josh said, 'he's simply a deluded, rather
disoriented boy from a broken home, who—'

'Look,' Marco said, halfway out of his seat, 'I know you
saved my life and everything—'

'Look,' Brian said, 'what did you mean by *not like
the mayor.*'

Marco sat down. 'Same as you, probably. We all thought

238

Griff Daniel was lying, too, about this vision of Arthur and stuff. We thought they were *all* lying. Jasper Coombes – that's the smug guy in the white shirt – is a total scumbag and a...a practising satanist.'

Brian sat down, too. 'You're having me on, right?'

'No, I'm not.' Marco felt his smile fading. 'He was going to sacrifice a cat.'

'The guy in the white—?'

'There was going to be a blood sacrifice in the Abbey grounds. Last night. Over Arthur's grave.'

'Arthur's grave?' Brian shook his head. 'That's just another Glastonbury scam.'

'It *doesn't matter*,' Marco said, passing on what he'd learned from Woolly and Eleri. 'It doesn't actually matter whether Arthur was buried there or not. A lot of people've believed in it for centuries, so it's got *power*.'

Brian Brown looked unconvinced. Marco leaned forward.

'Listen, I'm serious. This Jasper Coombes is a really bad guy. And the red-haired kid who was hitting you – Shane? – that's his mate, all right? He's not too bright, but he's seriously vicious. Looks like Jasper must've given them a signal to follow you out, find out where you were coming from.'

'How do you know that?' Brian said.

'Because...because my granddad and the Watchers of Avalon – that's an even *more* oppressed minority – are pretty sure that the mayor and those guys are trying to pull some stroke, and they think there could be, you know...evil behind it.'

'Evil?'

'Evil.' Josh raised his eyes to the darkening sky. 'Give me strength.'

'What d'you mean?' Brian stared hard at Marco. 'What kind of evil?'

'Probably a dark lord,' Josh said in his bored voice.

Marco turned on him.

'Bog off!' Okay, Josh was his best friend, but sometimes he was seriously irritating. 'Listen, we don't *know*. That's what we—'

Brian put both hands flat on the wooden table.

'You mean you really don't know what all this is about? All this building Glastonbury up as the most important Arthurian centre in the country? You actually *don't know* what that's about?'

'You mean you *do*?'

Brian said, 'You're telling me you don't know about Rex Arturus?'

'No,' Marco said. 'Except that's a bit like what it said on the original grave.'

Josh said, 'Did you say *Rex Arturus*?'

Marco saw that Josh had taken off his phoney glasses and was sitting up looking kind of gobsmacked.

Really Heavy Vibe

When they dared to venture out of the yard, Magdalene Street was full of people, some of them walking away in groups, one of them landing on Josh like a vulture out of the heavy evening sky.

'*There* you are, Joshua. I was beginning to think you'd vanished into the ether!'

'Ah...' Josh looked uncomfortable. 'Grandma, this is my patien— er, friend, Marco. Marco, this is my grandmother, Mrs. Gloria Goldman.'

Yes, it *was* the woman who'd interrupted Griff Daniel to tell him she could feel something in the air.

There was a peacock in the middle of her dress, in full flash.

'Er...hello,' Marco said. Josh's gran, too? What was *happening* here? He'd find out later. What he needed now was to get hold of Woolly and the other guys, because what he had to tell them was going to *totally blow them away.*

He saw that Brian Brown had met up with his brother, who'd come out of the town hall looking like a guy who'd just heard his team had gone down six-nil. Marco was about to go over to them when his hand was grabbed by Mrs. Goldman. It was like being arrested.

'Marco! I'm delighted to discover Josh has such a *good friend* in this truly remarkable, *happening* place. And how *great* it is when the town mayor is a man who understands about its *elemental magic.*'

'Er, yes,' Marco said. 'The mayor's a really, er, cool person.'

Mrs. Goldman swung round to her grandson. 'And you know what, Joshua? He's just asked me to dinner!'

Josh stared at her in serious horror. 'That old bloke with the ratty beard?'

'I haven't yet been here a day and already I have a date with the First Citizen! What *about* that? I am just so glad we followed all those people into that meeting. I feel we're truly at the centre of things now and, as you know, the centre is *my kind of place.*'

'Uh, Grandma...' Josh hesitated, obviously thinking about what he'd just learned from Marco and Brian Brown and what all this said about Councillor Griffith Daniel. He took a breath. 'Look...before you go to dinner with the mayor, there are some things you need to know.'

Mrs. Goldman zapped him with a hard look. 'Things?'

'Um, for instance, from what I've learned about the mayor's psychological profile...and given that he doesn't know you from Adam, my guess is that he, uh...'

'Did a quick valuation of your jewellery,' a man's voice said. 'And thought, *This is a woman I obviously need to get to know better.*'

Sam.

Marco turned to find, with some relief, that they'd all arrived – Woolly, Nancy and Diane – who frowned at Sam, well-bred, upper-class people being generally more tactful and diplomatic.

As you'd expect, Grandma Goldman was looking more than slightly affronted.

'And what led you to *that* conclusion, young man?'

'I learned the hard way,' Sam said. 'I'm his son.'

'I see,' Grandma Goldman said. 'And there are family...'

'Differences,' Sam said. 'Or so I've always hoped.'

'You're wrong,' Woolly said. 'You couldn't be more wrong about Mr. Daniel.'

He stood there with his arms held kind of stiffly by his sides. Sam looked at him.

'You all right, Woolly?'

'You're wrong,' Woolly said again. 'We've all been wrong. We've been afraid.'

'What?'

'Afraid to admit it,' Woolly said. 'Afraid to admit that the mayor of Glastonbury might've seen the light. That he might be a truly good man with the interests of this town close to his heart. We jumped to conclusions, and we were wrong.'

'Woolly,' Sam said. 'This *is* my old man we're talking about?'

'You should respect him more,' Woolly said. 'We all should.'

'Huh?'

'For he has been blessed with vision,' Woolly said.

Sam stared at him. Marco smiled, waiting for Woolly to come out with some smart remark and then they'd all have a good laugh.

But it didn't happen. He just stood there, his white ponytail hanging limp, a strange sad expression in his eyes.

He was *serious*?

Sam looked at Nancy. 'He all right, Nance?'

'Well, he...' Nancy's face went all furrowed and anxious. 'I don't know. I don't know, Sam. He had one of his depressions, and then he was fine again. He was—'

'None of you will admit it, will you?' Woolly said. 'None of you'll admit that the mayor is a decent, honourable man and we have to listen to what he's saying.'

'Take him home, Nancy,' Sam said. 'He needs to relax.'

Marco must have looked scared – he certainly *felt* scared – because Nancy put a hand on his arm.

'You stay with Sam and Diane and your friend, Marco. I'll get Woolly home. He don't know what he's saying. He needs a good night's sleep, that's all.'

'Nancy—'

'It's all *right*,' Nancy said. 'He'll be fine in the morning.'

Marco could see Josh watching Woolly intently, with a glow in his eyes that Marco had seen before. It meant Josh was now entirely convinced that Marco's granddad was mentally ill.

And, of course, he was totally, totally wrong.

Well, he was.

Wasn't he?

Marco watched Nancy taking Woolly back to the van, holding onto his arm. Woolly was walking slowly, occasionally stopping to shake his head, as if he knew there was something wrong with him. At one point, he tried to turn back but Nancy pulled him around.

Josh was nodding.

'I don't like to make a snap diagnosis, but there are a couple of conditions that could be. One of them requires a fairly long-term course of treatment, but—'

'Shut up,' Marco said. 'Just shut up, all right?'

'No point going into denial about it,' Josh said. 'You've just got to face up to the fact that when someone gets to his age— All right! All right!'

Josh backed off with his hands up, as Sam said, 'Nancy's right, Marco. He's been getting himself in a fret. We all have. It can take you funny ways when you get to—'

'He's *not* old!'

'Course he's not,' Sam said. 'Look, we'll give Nancy half an hour to get him to bed, then I'll drive you home.'

'No,' Marco said.

'You don't wanner go back to Woolly's?'

'I...' Marco turned and beckoned to Brian Brown and his brother. 'These guys are from Cornwall. There's some stuff you need to know.'

'Cornwall?'

'It's important, Sam. You need to hear what they have to say.'

'Fair enough.' Sam shrugged. 'Bowermead?'

Marco nodded.

* * *

Josh went with them.

Well, he had to be there because he knew about the Arturus Rex situation. And, of course, if Josh was going to be there, no way was his grandma going to potter off back to The George and Pilgrims for an early night.

So the Cornish guys followed Sam and Diane's old Land Rover, and Marco and Josh went in Grandma Goldman's...

...*Porsche?*

If he hadn't been so worried about Woolly, Marco might have been seriously impressed. Especially as he got to sit in the front, to give Grandma Goldman the directions, while Josh was squeezed into the small rear seat, nursing his injured briefcase and looking resentful whenever Marco turned round.

At 20 mph, max, it took a while – well, obviously, she didn't know these country roads. But when they drew up in the courtyard behind Sam's Land Rover, Mrs. Goldman flopped back in her seat as if she'd just come roaring and steaming to a halt after overtaking Jensen Button on the difficult final bend.

She was staring up at Bowermead, with a look in her eyes as if she'd found a massive parcel under the Christmas tree. Then she looked at Marco.

'*This* is it? Your friends live *here?*'

Marco nodded, as Sam and Diane got out of the Land Rover and went over to Ted Brown's van.

'You mean they rent an apartment here, right?' Grandma Goldman said. 'The house is divided into apartments.'

'No, Diane inherited the house from her father, Lord...something or other.'

'The *entire mansion?*'

Grandma Goldman did some blinking.

'Lord Pennard,' Marco said. 'That's the name.'

'Give me time,' Granny Goldman said, 'I'll've heard of him.' She gazed at the house. 'Marco, it's...rather magnificent.'

'Only, it looks like they might have to sell it. They say it costs a fortune just to keep it from falling down.'

'I can imagine. So your friend's wife is...a titled person herself?'

'Lady...something. Sort of.'

'I *see*,' Grandma Goldman said. She climbed slowly out of the car, as if she was floating into a dream, leaving Marco and Josh behind.

'I don't like this,' Josh said. 'I don't like the way she's behaving.'

'Then why did you come?' Marco swung round in the front seat. 'I mean why *did* you come?'

'Because, I...' It was too dim now to make out Josh's expression. 'Because it sounded...moderately interesting. In a mental-health context, that is.'

'You were bored, weren't you? You were bored in London, on your own.'

'Absolutely *not*. No one with an intellect like—'

'Yes, you were.'

'That is absolutely ludicrous.' Josh hugged his briefcase. 'I just realized, after reading your e-mails, that if there was anywhere I could widen my experience of totally bonkers people this was it.'

'But now you know that what's actually going on here is a really heavy vibe—'

'*A really heavy vibe*? Who taught you all this stupid,

Jurassic jargon? Is that your bonkers granddad?'

'He's not as bonkers as your—'

The passenger door of the Porsche was pulled open.

'Look, you two might be happy enough sitting there slagging each other off all night,' Brian Brown said, 'but some of us here are trying to save Cornwall.'

Sam carried a big, grey computer monitor into the banqueting hall and set it down on what looked like an old school desk. Then he went off again and came back with a tower unit about the size of a small dishwasher.

Josh inspected this pile of ancient kit in disbelief and then he looked at Sam, and Marco didn't know which of them he felt most embarrassed for.

'All right, it's old-tech.' Sam plugged the computer's thick wire into an extension lead which snaked across the dusty oak floorboards to a socket in one of the panelled walls. 'It still works, don't it?'

Josh hung back, like the computer might overheat and explode and shower him with battery acid or something.

'It's got...*knobs*.'

Sam sighed, looking around for a phone socket.

'Look, if I boot it up, and get you online...'

'Okay, I'll do what I can,' Josh said in his long-suffering way, and Marco rolled his eyes.

The others were sitting in a circle in the centre of the vast room. Where the Watchers sat to meditate or, in certain cases, think about food.

It was growing dark, and there was a tension in the air. Most of these people didn't know one another. They were bound to be a bit suspicious. In fact, only Marco really knew who everybody was.

Sam said, 'I'm still not getting this. You say Arthur's actually returning to Avalon? Through a computer?'

'Not exactly,' Ted Brown said. 'It's complicated.'

Ted was a big bloke with a shaven head and a small gold earring.

'But he *is* returning?' Sam said.

After a few minutes, the huge, shadowy room was lit by white flashes from the computer screen and *WINDOWS 93* came up and Josh kneeled down and started mousing something up on the screen.

The computer coughed, and then an image came up of a black door, partly open, to reveal a pale glow and the quivering words:

ARTURUS REX

'Mr. Daniel,' Ted Brown said, 'trust me when I tell you that, for all we know, *he could be here right now.*'

A Kingdom...

'As you can see...' Josh was in lecturer mode. '...*Arturus Rex* is a computer game. A quest game in which the player takes the role of the young King Arthur, as he goes in search of his heritage...his mystical kingdom. He has to deal with monsters and evil entities and a lot of stuff that wasn't in the original stories.'

'I thought computer games came in boxes and cost an arm and a leg,' Sam said.

Josh smiled. 'That's very true but, in this case, the early phases of the game can be downloaded free. Players soon get hooked. They become addicted...absorbed into the fantasy. They want more. And that's when they have to start paying out. Big time.'

'*Arturus Rex* has become a worldwide phenomenon,' Brian Brown said. 'Millions of people from as far away as Russia and China have become obsessed with it.'

'Making millions of pounds,' Ted Brown said, 'for the games company, the Melcato Corporation, of California. They've never looked back. Become one of the richest firms in the business.'

Sam was shaking his head, and Marco could guess what was going through it: why would people pay out millions of pounds to get into some electronic quest when they could be involved in the real thing, in places like Glastonbury? Why spend money on phoney magic when the world was full of *real* magic?

Answer: because it was easier sitting in front of your computer than going out in the fields and hills to find the secret places.

Face it, Marco thought. *I was like that, too, till I came here.*

'Of course,' Josh said, 'I downloaded Arturus Rex purely for research purposes.'

Marco grinned. 'That's what they all say.'

'I *did*—'

'Let's get to the point,' Ted Brown said. 'The Melcato Corporation has hit on a hugely successful formula, and the founder of the company, Mr. Bradford Kavanagh, puts it all down to his son, Rendall Kavanagh. Or, as he's come to be known...Rex.'

Marco sat back, far more interested than he'd ever been sitting here meditating with the Watchers of Avalon.

Ted Brown nodded at the computer. 'Why don't you google up the Melcato Corporation, see what you get?'

Josh went back to the computer and, after a few mutterings about people who hadn't even got Broadband, came up with the Melcato Corporation's website.

There was a big photo of a man and a boy. Josh snorted. 'This kit's so old you can't even see their faces.'

'Reason you can't see their faces,' Ted Brown said, 'is because they've been deliberately blacked out. Melcato are very secretive. Especially about the boy. Read what it says.'

They all leaned forward to read a special message to Melcato shareholders from the president of the Corporation, Brad Kavanagh.

I owe everything to my son, Rendall and his fascination, from an early age, with the stories of the famous King Arthur and the Knights of the Round Table.

Well, we'd all read about this stuff as kids, but we grew out of it. Moved on to *Superman* and *Star Wars*.

But with Rendall, this didn't happen. His interest just grew and grew and, after a while, we all realized that it was more than just an interest, more than a mere childish fad...and it was kinda scary.

Also, from the age of about three, Rendall had insisted on being called Rex, just refusing to answer to any other name. In the end his mother and I just had to bow to that, and so he became Rex – although none of us knew at the time that this was the Latin for 'king'.

By the time he was six years old, Rex was having regular vivid dreams, all of which took him to a wild, green country far away from our home in...

'...Santa Cruz?' Sam was on his feet.

252

'It's where the Melcato Corporation's based,' Ted Brown said. 'By the sea in California.'

'Also the place my old man's trying to set up as Glastonbury's twin town.'

'Figures,' Ted said.

'Why?'

'Keep reading...'

Marco already was, as Josh scrolled down to the second page of the message. Brad Kavanagh was explaining how, by the age of eleven, his son, now known to everybody as Rex, had read scores of books on King Arthur and Merlin the magician and Lancelot and the world of the ancient Britons. And his dreams were becoming so vivid and disturbing that his parents were getting worried and eventually took him to a child-psychiatrist.

'Very wise,' Josh said. 'Obsessions can be hard to break. The fantasies we have as children can often destroy our mental health in later life.'

But the psychiatrist had been unable to explain it.

'Ha,' Marco said.

'More likely his parents refused to accept the diagnosis,' Josh said. 'The kid was probably schizophrenic. And where's the money in *that*?'

'Shush, Joshua,' Grandma Goldman snapped. 'This is getting interesting.'

By now, Rex – and also we, his parents – had become convinced that this was no mere obsession. We began – with, I might say, some trepidation – to consider the possibility that our son, in some way, was Arthur. And – I know this is gonna sound a little off the wall, but bear with me – that his dreams were recollections of some past life, way, way back in history, when he ruled his kingdom of the Britons from the mystical court of Camelot.

During this period, I was developing my company, devising and constructing computer games – the usual stuff, based on themes similar to *Star Wars* and *The Lord of the Rings*. And then one day, Rex came into my workroom with a drawing he'd done of a hill. A hill with a door in it. 'Dad,' he said, 'this is what I dreamed about last night. But I guess the dream ended before I could go through the door. What do you suppose that means?'

I will always remember that morning, and the way Rex and I looked at one another above the banks of computer screens.

'I don't know, son,' I said, 'but maybe, with the help of the virtual world, we can find out.'

And that was the beginning of Arturus Rex.

'Oh, *very* smart,' Sam said. 'You launch a new computer game about King Arthur, and then you devise a myth of your own to publicize it. They'll believe anything in California.'

'It's not just California,' Ted Brown said. 'Hundreds of thousands of people in this country are into it, too.'

'Still sounds to me like he made the whole thing up to add a bit of mystery. Computer geeks love codes and secrets.'

'Whatever,' Ted said, 'it's big business. Brad Kavanagh's worth billions – and he wants to bring a few of them over here.'

Sam went still. 'What?'

'That's what this is all about. The boy's still having his dreams. Only, now he's a teenager, dreams are not enough. He wants the reality. He wants his kingdom. And he's a kid who's been getting just about everything he wants for some years now. You see where this is going?'

'Er...no.'

'His dad's going to give him what he wants. What he feels he's entitled to as the inspiration for *Arturus Rex*. A kingdom of his own.'

All eyes were on Ted Brown now, his earring glinting in the light from the computer screen.

'King Arthur's kingdom was obviously in Britain – but nobody knows quite where, right? It could have been around here, but it could also have been at Tintagel, in Cornwall, where we live. Where there's a big ruined castle right at the sea's edge where it's said King Arthur was born.'

'It's not old enough, that castle,' Sam said.

'Who knows what was there before?'

'Okay, that's a point.'

'There are other places, too, with a claim on Arthur,' Ted said.

'Like Arthur's Seat above the city of Edinburgh,' Josh said.

'Spot on, son. What made you say that?'

'Because in the game – the one you can download – you get a choice of where you want your court to be. It's either Tintagel, Glastonbury or Edinburgh. And then, when you make your choice, you get asked why you've chosen that particular place and not one of the others.'

Sam was shaking his head. 'I'm lost. Where's this going?'

'Exactly,' Ted said. 'Where's it *going*?'

'What?'

Ted leaned forward, looking from face to face to see if anybody had got it yet.

'The new factory,' he said. 'Brad Kavanagh's planning to bring Rex to the land of his so-called birth, yeah? That is, to whichever place Rex decides is the home of the real Arthur. And *that*...is where Brad Kavanagh plans to build a new Melcato plant to produce the next series of Arturus Rex. Wherever Rex chooses will become famous worldwide...and make loads of money.'

There was a silence. Then Sam let out his breath in a long, slow *whoosh*.

'So the return of Arthur...we're not talking about the *actual* Arthur...just a boy who *thinks* he's Arthur.'

'With a dad willing to spend millions to keep the spoiled brat sweet,' Ted said. 'Not that it wouldn't be worth it, anyway – if Arturus Rex is produced in the real land of Arthur it's only gonner make it seem more credible and millions more people will buy into it.'

'And for the town that gets the factory?' Sam said.

'Whichever place Rex goes for, he'll just *pour* money into it – can't have his son's kingdom looking like a bit of a dump. Bottom line is, whichever town Rex picks, a lot of people will get rich real quick.'

'Like, say...the mayor,' Sam said.

'And various business people. And lawyers. And estate agents.'

This time the silence was *vast*.

Spirit of Arthur

It was weird the way things turned around.

The very last time they'd been in this room, Eleri, in her robe and her snake headband, had been going, *Something is beginning to happen! Something that we, as the Watchers, should be aware of.*

And they'd gone without food all day and sat here in deep meditation, trying to tune into mystic forces, to get a feeling of what was happening in the town.

And failed.

Now, except for Eleri, they were here again, and it was all becoming clear.

Fortunately this time, fasting was off.

Sam and Diane had lit some candles and planted them all around the room and brought in egg and tomato chutney sandwiches and the last of Sam's home-made cider.

The computer was still switched on. They'd downloaded the message to the shareholders from Brad Kavanagh, and the company logo was frozen on the screen.

MELCATO

Marco was looking at it over his sandwich, through half-closed eyes, thinking what an odd name it was. What did it mean? Was it a foreign language word? Was it two names put together – Mel and Cato? If so, who were they?

'So how did you find out about this, Ted?' Sam was saying to the big Cornish guy.

'There was a meeting,' Ted said. 'In London. Couple of our councillors from Tintagel went along. They'd been invited to meet a bloke from Melcato to explain why they thought their areas ought to get Arturus Rex – why they were most connected to King Arthur. A few of us had spent a lot of time putting together a special presentation document putting the case for Tintagel. Cornwall needs all the new jobs it can get.'

'But you'd be letting yourselves get taken over,' Sam said. 'This fat cat from America, he'd be putting so much money in that you'd have to do whatever they wanted. Whole town'd be taken over by his kid!'

Ted shook his head, wearing this tight smile.

'Nobody takes the Cornish over. They'll learn that in time. But by then we'll have the factory and the jobs.'

'Except we won't,' Brian said. 'It'll all come to Glastonbury.'

'And *we'll* get taken over, big time,' Sam said, 'because that's what they want, Griff and his cronies. Within a year, this place'll look like Las Vegas, and it'll be full of businessmen in suits. All the little shops gone, all the magic. It'll be like Avalon World coming in by the back door. So this meeting – when *was* it?'

'Last weekend,' Ted said.

'Ah!' Sam turned to the others. 'You hear that? That was where they must've gone. My dad, Cotton, Coombes and Jasper. They went to try and sell Glastonbury to this Melcato outfit. And Eleri thought they'd been...spirited away.'

'Spirited away all right,' Ted said. 'Seems there was a big dinner laid on and loads of free booze, and they all got loaded on their last night.'

'Flaming typical!' Sam scowled. 'No wonder the old man looked knackered when he got back. Knackered but happy.'

'Our fellers were pretty miserable when *they* got back. Brian's right, they reckoned your team had 'em beat hollow with all this stuff about visions and UFOs and the sword, Excalibur...we just couldn't compete.'

'I *knew* all that had to be a scam,' Sam said. 'Just couldn't figure out why they'd done it.'

'Or how,' Diane said. 'How did they make it so *convincing*? Your dad breaking down like that? That's still ever so puzzling.'

'No, he couldn't dream that up,' Sam said. 'He's got no imagination at all.'

'Amazing how well some people can put on an act, mind, when there's a few million in it,' Ted said.

'It's all so *sordid*, isn't it?' Diane put down her sandwich, looking sick. 'It's not about magic. It's just about money.'

'What did you expect?' Sam said gently. He turned to Ted. 'So Kavanagh and boy – *they* weren't at this meeting?'

'No chance, man. They keep their heads down. Nobody even knows what the boy looks like – Brad Kavanagh's probably scared of him getting kidnapped. Son of one of the richest men in the USA? However...' Ted helped himself to a glass of cider. '...the feller from Melcato did reveal that the boy would be paying a secret visit to each of the possible locations – Edinburgh, Tintagel and Glastonbury – to see which felt most right.'

'That's what you meant when you said he might be here now?'

'Ah.' Josh looked at Grandma Goldman. 'That's obviously what the mayor meant when he was in that computer shop. You remember, Grandma? They had a big stack of *Arturus Rex* in the window, and the mayor said he ought to get lots more. He also said that one day Glastonbury would be...bigger than Bristol.'

'Bigger than—?' Sam reared up like he'd been stung in the bum. 'The scumbag! He just wants to get rich and destroy everything this town stands for!' He turned to Josh. 'When was this?'

'An hour or so before the meeting. The guy in the shop asked the mayor if he knew when...whoever it was...would be coming, and the mayor said he didn't know but it was definitely going to happen.'

'You see any likely-looking strangers in town?' Ted said.

'Only...' Marco grinned. '...Josh.'

Josh scowled at him, kind of, *Do I* look *like an American computer geek?* Marco turned away to hide his amusement and viewed the computer screen out of the corner of an eye, and...

Suddenly saw what it *was* about that word.

All you had to do was switch the letters around and M E L C A T O became...

Wow. All the time the firm's name had been concealing a *secret* name...

C A M E L O T

He wondered if he was the first to spot this. Probably not. It was probably a talking point all over the net.

But meanwhile there was another puzzle – a mystery that nobody had talked about yet. 'Where does the bad stuff come into it?' Marco said.

People looked at him.

'The black magic ritual over Arthur's grave,' Marco said. 'How does that help to attract Arturus Rex to Glastonbury?'

Josh and Granny Goldman and Brian and Ted looked blank. They didn't know anything about this.

Diane said, 'If they had power over the spirit of Arthur, they could use it in a magical way to attract the Melcato millions. Couldn't they?'

Somewhere in the vast house, a phone began to ring. Sam nodded.

'She's right. That might well be how they're thinking. And that would give them power over this Melcato itself...and Melcato would never know.'

'But your dad wouldn't think like that,' Diane said. 'He doesn't believe in magic of any kind, he just believes in... money, I suppose. But then, his love of money leaves him wide open... Excuse me, I'll have to get the phone.'

As she moved away through the candlelight, Marco tried to work this out.

'Wide open to what?'

'We all know what,' Sam said. 'And who. Cromwell? Could be Cromwell's back.'

'You can't mean...' Grandma Goldman sat up. '...*Oliver* Cromwell?'

'Far worse than that, Mrs. Goldman,' Sam said. 'This is *Roger* Cromwell, who reckons he's a descendant of *Thomas* Cromwell...feller who destroyed the Abbey for Henry VIII? Roger Cromwell likes destroying, too, and he's good at it.'

'Just so much history here,' Grandma Goldman said, sounding kind of vague and out of it. 'Just *so* much history. All these people...in the air.'

And then Diane was back. 'It was Eleri. She said she's been on edge all night, a feeling of something coming.'

Sam sighed, accidentally blowing out one of the candles. 'So what's new?'

'What's new,' Diane said, 'is that there's an awfully serious fire broken out at a house on the edge of town.'

Sam put his head on one side. 'And?'

'It's Mr. Montague's house. Eleri's friend, who used to run the museum? He's still in the house. It's full of smoke, and he won't come out. That's if he...if he's still alive.'

'That's terrible,' Sam said. 'Poor guy. But what can *we* do?'

'Eleri doesn't think it's...accidental. It seems he...' Diane bit her lip. 'Eleri thinks he's got the sword in there. *Excalibur.*'

All the Fireworks in the Box

The burning house was near the foot of Wearyall Hill. It was dusk now, and a great filthy, swirling quilt of smoke was covering the lower part of the hill and the main road out of town.

Traffic was being filtered into a single lane and there were blue emergency lights and vehicle headlights making tunnels in the gloom.

Sam parked the Land Rover in a side road some distance away and they got out into stinging, polluted air full of distant shouts and clanging.

It was just Marco and Sam now. The Cornish guys had had to get back to Cornwall, and Josh had been dragged back to The George and Pilgrims by his gran, who'd said there could be no possible use for a psychiatrist in the middle of a fire and they'd just be in the way.

Diane stayed at Bowermead, by the phone. She'd wanted Marco to stay, too, but, like, *no way.* He wasn't sure what was going to happen but he wasn't going to miss it...even though he felt guilty at getting excited over what could turn out to be a tragedy.

A longish drive led up to Mr. Montague's house, but it was blocked by two fire engines. There were police cars there, too, and a policeman stood at the entrance.

'He ain't gonner let the likes of *us* go up there, is he?' Sam said. 'What're we supposed to say? Let us through, we're the Watchers of Avalon and we have reason to believe dark forces are at work?'

As he'd said *dark forces*, Marco had seen a cloaked figure fading from the murk, raising a pale and skeletal hand. Sam strode towards it through the stinking air.

'Eleri!'

Her hair was ragged and tangled and there were black smuts on her narrow face. She reached out for Sam. 'Thank the gods. We have to get it...'

'What?'

'The sword. We have to get the sword. Oh, Sam, this is all my fault. *All my—*'

'The hell with the sword!' Sam yelled. 'What about old Jim Montague?'

'You don't understand.' Eleri seized Sam's arm. 'If we don't get it out of there, he'll *definitely* die. It brings only death.'

There was a kind of knowing sigh from the policeman at the gate.

'All right, Professor Cadwallader. I know he's a friend of yours, but I think you can leave this to the rescue services. Best thing would be to go home, look.'

'You don't *understand...*'

'Oh yes, I think I do,' the policeman said, in pretty much the way Josh would have said it. 'Off you go, now.'

Eleri spun away with a frustrated sob, dragging Sam after her, and Marco followed them back to the main road where Sam caught a mouthful of smoke and went into a coughing fit. Marco was keeping his own mouth shut, but the fumes were making his eyes water.

'Listen,' Eleri said. 'There's a footpath that will bring us out on the other side of the house.'

'You—' Sam looked up at the hill, slapping his chest. 'You *sure* Mr. Montague's in there? He could be out somewhere, couldn't he?'

'I think not. I saw him this afternoon, in the Post Office. He was looking awful – grey-faced and older than his years. He said he'd lain awake most of last night because whenever he fell asleep he had terrible dreams of blood and violence and—'

Eleri started coughing, too, and went to lean against a wall. Marco saw another dark figure – Rosa's dad, Big Dave – striding across the road towards the policeman. 'James Montague's one of my parishioners,' Big Dave was shouting. 'I'm not going to get in the way. I know the problems you've got in a situation like this – used to be in the job myself.'

'—*and fire*,' Eleri gasped. 'He dreamed of burning. Houses burning and dead bodies burning in heaps. And, thanks to me, he had *the sword* in the house.'

'I thought it'd been taken to some museum in Bristol,' Sam said.

'It was supposed to be. James was going to take it to the museum today, but I asked him to hold on to it so we could examine it – I knew Wilcox would not let *me* near it and I...I had begun to suspect that it was not what we all thought it was. James, of course, was happy to keep it at his home. What historian could resist the opportunity to examine it at leisure? Unfortunately, he lives alone. No one to hear his cries in the night. Oh, it's my fault. This is *all my fault!* Only the girl saw the truth!' Eleri gathered up her cloak and led them along the pavement as an ambulance warbled to a halt and went on warbling so Marco could hardly hear. '*Rosa.* She too had the dreams of blood and slaughter.'

'And what *is* the truth?' Sam caught up with Eleri as she stopped at a wooden stile on the edge of a field sloping up towards Wearyall and the Holy Thorn. 'I'm not even sure *I* believe any of this, specially after what we've just been hearing about this Glastie scam to—'

'*Listen!*' Eleri turned to face them, her eyes burning like torch bulbs in the blackness of her face. 'I realized that if this was Excalibur, it was *not* the Excalibur we know from legend. And if this was Arthur's sword, and its phantasm was used to confer a psychic knighthood upon Griff Daniel, then Arthur was...' Her voice sagged. '...not the man of integrity and valour of which the legends speak.'

'You're saying Arthur was—' Marco tripped on a crack in the pavement and fell forward against the wooden stile. It was like his Avalonian world was crumbling around him. 'You're saying Arthur was...*evil*?'

'I didn't know what to think any more.' Eleri's voice was raw and roughened by the smoke. 'I didn't know what to believe. There was a new madness in this town, and we had become separated from the light and could only flounder on its fringes.'

She tried to climb the stile and fell back, and Sam leaped over and helped her from the other side and then waited for Marco.

'You stay well away from the house, Marco, you got that?'

Like he was going to dive into the flames? Marco followed. The footpath was narrow enough for them to have to walk in single file, and it wasn't until Sam stopped that Marco was aware of the hot glow at the core of the smoke.

It was obviously quite an old cottage and the flames were leaping through what was left of its roof, with this gas-jet kind of noise, or maybe that was the sound of the hoses of firefighters blasting the front.

They couldn't see the firefighters. They'd come out at the back, behind a wall around the cottage. There was a gate, but they didn't go through it to the path cutting across a lawn to a darkened doorway. The door was shut, but all the windows were like blazing lanterns. As they watched, there was a *whump* behind one of the upstairs ones, and it exploded, and Sam pulled Marco down behind the garden wall as a hot hail of glass splinters flew out. Then there was an awful crunching sound and a whoosh of fizzing flames like all the fireworks in the box going off at once.

'Roof's fallen in,' Sam said. 'Even the firemen daren't go in now.'

Marco felt the horror behind Eleri's indrawn breath.

He said, 'Does that mean he...he won't be able to get out?'

'Doesn't look likely,' Sam said quietly. 'We oughter leave. Nothing any of us can do.'

'He'll be...burned alive?'

'No, that's...not what happens. He'll be overcome by the smoke before the flames get to him. But I'm afraid he—'

Two firefighters came round the side of the house. One was wearing a mask and breathing apparatus.

'They can't get in the front way,' Sam whispered, 'so they're trying the back. Still be hopeless, I reckon. Place'll be like an oven inside.'

The firefighters were followed by a third figure. A black silhouette outlined against the flames: Big Dave Wilcox in his cassock. He stopped a few metres behind the firefighters, putting his hands together and calling aloud to the smoke-filled sky.

'Dear Father... We pray for Your servant, James. We pray that he may be delivered from this inferno...'

His big, deep voice battling against the roaring, spitting fire.

'Yes,' Eleri said. 'We must pray. There's nothing else we can do.' She rose up, above the wall with her arms flung out into the smoke and the sparks. 'O Holy Mother! O Goddess of the Sacred Moon! Please help us this night. Bestow your favours upon James Montague that he may be delivered from the flames and this all-pervading evil!'

For a moment, apart from the hissing of the blaze, there was a massive silence. At the words *all pervading evil*, Marco could have sworn he could see shadows hunching in the bushes either side of the door. Then Big Dave's voice came blasting out of the smoke.

'How dare you! Get out of here, you foul witch!'

He came lumbering towards them across the back lawn, his dog collar gleaming white.

Sam rose up. 'Back off, Dave! You need all the help you can get, situation like this.'

'When I need help from a pagan, I'll know the world has finally gone mad. There is but *one God,* and your heathen hordes know him not!'

'A prayer's a prayer, Dave!'

'That's not a prayer, that's a filthy incantation!'

'*Look!*'

One of the firefighters, his voice muffled by his oxygen mask, was backing away from the blazing cottage. Eleri screamed, her cloak flapping like a crow's wings.

Marco saw that the back door had been flung open and a great wedge of flame was thrust out.

And it didn't stop. It came rushing along the short path through the grass and, although there was a wall between them, Marco instinctively backed away.

And that was when he realized, with a spasm of shock, that it was a man.

A man on fire all down one side...one hand raised to the sky and, clutched in it, the great sword, black and jagged, stabbing up into the smoke as the hunching shadows uncurled from the bushes.

Jolly Good Night

'I don't know *why* we had to leave,' Josh said. 'It was just getting interesting, and the prospect of studying the behaviour of already unbalanced people under severe stress...'

In the entrance of The George and Pilgrims, Granny Goldman gave him an unusually hard look.

'You think they *want* to be studied at a time like that, Joshua? Fighting to save some poor man from being burned to death?'

Josh shook his head at the stupidity of this woman. People who didn't *want* to be studied were *far* more interesting than the ones who simply arrived in your office and said, *Okay, analyse me.* The real insanity was *out there.*

And this town had insanity like McDonald's had burgers. This town could be a *world centre* for insanity.

Josh sighed. 'Grandma, I keep telling you...I need to take every opportunity to widen my working knowledge of the human condition.'

'In that case...' Granny Goldman pointed a forefinger glittering with diamonds into the bar, where a tweedy figure sat hunched over a brandy glass. 'You can study *him*.'

And then she advanced into the bar like she was about to make a citizen's arrest.

'Good evening again, Mr. Mayor.'

The mayor looked blearily up from his brandy glass, squinted and then beamed.

'Ah! Good evening again, madam. Been for a pleasant evening walk in our lovely streets?'

Grandma Goldman peered at him. More frostily, Josh noted, than when she'd stood up in the hall to spout all that senile drivel about feeling stuff in the air in this wonderful old town.

Wonderful old town? Somebody ought to warn these Melcato people what they were getting into. If they had any idea what Glastonbury was really like, they'd be signing on the dotted line to take their factory to Tintagel, Edinburgh, Milton Keynes...anywhere at all but the so-called Isle of Avalon.

Josh watched as the mayor's wet little eyes travelled over Granny Goldman, from the diamonds on her hands to the diamonds in her ears. That bloke Sam had been right about *that*. The old guy was definitely on the make.

'You've remembered our dinner date, I hope,' the mayor said.

'Well, Mr. Mayor,' Grandma Goldman said. 'After what I've been hearing tonight... Well, of course, that was hugely inspiring, but one can't help being a little puzzled.'

'Then I am the man who can enlighten you. Let me buy you a drink.' The mayor called across to the barmaid, 'Lorraine...a drink for my friend, Mrs...'

'Goldman.'

'Mrs. Goldman. And something fizzy for the boy. Your son?'

'Grandson.'

'Never! You're not old enough to have a grandson!'

Granny Goldman actually giggled.

Josh thought he was going to be sick.

'Now then,' the mayor said. 'You sit down here and tell me exactly what's bothering you.'

'Well...' Granny Goldman took the bar stool next to the mayor. 'It's just... Well, for instance...when you say that Arthur is about to return to Glastonbury, how can this *be*? I mean, in what *form* will he return? A man who's been dead for well over a thousand years?'

'Ha!' The mayor took a slurp of brandy. 'I'm glad you asked that. Because what we're talking about here, look, is not Arthur himself – well, obviously not, 'cause he's dead – but the *spirit* of Arthur. The spirit of a man with a bit of go in him. A man with the guts to claim back his town— kingdom, that is...from the rabble.'

'What particular rabble would that *be*?' Granny Goldman asked innocently.

'Oh, well...' The mayor blew out his lips. 'I mean, back in them days there was a *lot* of rabble around, all over the streets, with their nose rings and their daft clothes. Just like today, in fact. And Arthur, he knew how to deal with them, that's all I'm saying.'

'But how will you *know* when he returns?'

'Well, er...' The mayor thought for a moment and then beamed through his beard. 'Well, it's obvious, innit? We'll know when *things start to improve*. When the hippies clear out and we get some decent shops and, er, factories. When we start to *seize the future*...like what King Arthur did. And then...' The mayor rose up on his bar stool, puffing out his chest. 'Then will we know that his spirit is amongst us.'

Josh looked at Griff Daniel and started to lose patience with him. How could the town expect to have any future worth seizing if it was run by this drunken old windbag?

He was also miffed that the mayor was all over Granny Goldman but dismissed *him* – that is, Joshua Goldman, the person with probably the biggest intellect between here and...oh America, at least – as *the boy*.

Thinking of America, a scene from earlier in the evening replayed itself in his head: that bloke Ted, from Cornwall, saying, *You see any likely-looking strangers in town?* And smart-mouth Marco replying, *Only Josh.*

Only Josh.

Hmm...

'And let me say,' the mayor said, 'that anybody with any sense and some money to invest is pretty soon gonner want a bit of a stake in this town.'

'*Invest? Stake?*' Granny Goldman looked blank. 'You mean *money*, Mr. Mayor?'

'Well, for instance, property prices hereabouts are about to take off as never before. So if y— that is, if anyone wanted to become part of The New Glastonbury, seems to me they could do worse than to have theirselves a classy new house built on a prime site here before the prices goes through the roof.'

Josh remembered Marco, or someone, saying that the mayor was in the building trade. Well, honestly, how could anyone be so *blatant*?

He figured it was time for drastic action.

'I *see*.' Grandma Goldman was already looking thoughtful. 'Well, I myself, as it happens, *am* looking to acquire a second home. The town I live in is very pleasant, and by the sea, of course, but—'

'*Grammaw!*'

Josh had stepped between Grandma Goldman and the mayor, pointing at his watch and keeping his voice low, but not so low the mayor wouldn't be able to hear.

'Grammaw, you know what the hell time it is?'

'Joshua, *please*—'

'More to the point, you know what the time is *back home*? Grammaw, you just *gotta* be *jet-lagged*.'

Grandma Goldman stared at Josh. '*Jet-lagged?* Joshua, what are you—?'

'Way I see it,' Josh said, 'you gotta get some shut-eye, else come morning, you're gonna be, like, *wrecked*?'

Grandma Goldman blinked.

The mayor's head swivelled.

The mayor's eyes bulged.

The mayor was gripping his glass so hard that Josh was expecting it to splinter any second now.

Grandma Goldman said, 'Joshua, why are you talking in that silly accent?'

'Accent?' Josh thought fast. In fact he was often amazed

at just how fast he *could* think when he was in a tight spot. He let some dismay drop into his voice. 'Aw, hell, Grammaw, I guess I just clean forgot...'

And then – how cool was this? – he reverted to *English*. And not just any old English but the kind of English he guessed Americans spoke when they thought they were talking *like real English people.* Having once gone along when his dad had been attending a psychiatrists' conference in Chicago, he knew from experience that a surprising number of Americans were convinced that all Englishmen wore bowler hats and pinstripe suits, played croquet and greeted one another with expressions like 'pip pip, old top'.

He straightened up, stiffened his spine. Went into the persona of an American kid working undercover.

'Golly, you're absolutely right, Grandmother! I simply don't know *what* came over me.'

Now the mayor had gone deathly pale. He was backing away from Grandma Goldman and then looking at Josh with something approaching naked fear. He cleared his throat.

'Er, look, I'm...I'm terrible sorry, look, I didn't realize you'd had such a...a *long* trip. Of *course* you should get some sleep. Don't let me...that is...'

Grandma Goldman peered at him. 'Are you all right, Mr. Mayor?'

'Never better,' the mayor gasped. 'Never better.'

'Well, as my grandson...' Grandma Goldman gave Josh a dark, suspicious glance. '...is obviously dead on his feet, perhaps we *should* call it a night.'

'Oh, absolutely, Mrs...I'm sorry...'

'Goldman.'

'Of course,' the mayor said. 'Of course.'

Josh gave the mayor a lopsided, knowing grin and raised an eyebrow.

'Good name, huh, Mayor? *Gold?* Geddit?'

'Yes.' The mayor swallowed. 'Oh, yes, indeed, a very good name. And...let me say...let me just say, don't worry. Your secret's safe with me, R—, R—' He swallowed. '*Rex.*'

Josh looked around.

'Rex? I don't see a *dawg* in here.' He laughed.

The mayor laughed, too, only his was forced and you could tell how dry his mouth was. 'Ha ha,' the mayor said. 'Very good!'

'Yeah,' Josh said. 'Well, like the old lady says, gotta hit the sack. Guess we'll see ya around, Mayor... *Whoops!*' He clapped a hand self-consciously to his mouth. 'I mean...have a jolly good night, First Citizen. Pip pip!'

As he rushed out of the bar ahead of Granny Goldman, he was feeling it all building up inside him, his cheeks puffed out to bursting point. Just about making it to the stairs before he collapsed and all the laughter just totally *erupted* out of him.

Suddenly, he was loving it here.

In fact, he couldn't remember when he'd last enjoyed himself so much.

It Kills...

You couldn't see everything from behind the wall, but it looked like the firefighters had been hosing Mr. Montague down, and now the paramedics were trying to get him into the ambulance, but he was resisting.

And they couldn't get him to let go of the sword.

'David!' he cried out. '*Where's David!*'

'Where *is* Mr. Wilcox?' one of the paramedics shouted against the rushing and crackling of the fire and the hissing of hoses. One of the firefighters lifted up the shield on his helmet and pointed to the bushes.

'Went to chase off some sightseers – kids. He's good at that. Used to be a copper.'

'*Sightseers?* They...' Mr. Montague must have been in terrible pain; his beard was blackened, you could see steam coming off him. '...weren't *sightseers*. Don't you realize? They were...they wanted... Oh, thank God...'

Big Dave had come back, pushing through the emergency guys.

'Little beggars! Vultures!'

'David...' Mr. Montague, half-crippled with coughing, was still managing to hold on to the sword. 'Listen to me. You have to—'

'How is he?' Dave said to the paramedic.

'Been very lucky, Reverend, but he's got some nasty burns. Tell him we *have* to get him to hospital, okay?'

'Trying to steal it...' Mr. Montague was pushing Excalibur at Big Dave. 'Trying to—'

'Those kids?' Dave said.

'I don't *know*. Faces...concealed. Caught them trying to break in, and they...ran off... Came *back*...more of them this time...throwing stones at the windows...trying to get me to...come out. They—' Mr. Montague turned his head towards the smoke. 'My house! Oh my God, my *books*...'

'You mean *they* did this?' Big Dave reeled back. 'They *started* the fire?'

'Rag pushed through...letter box. Petrol...'

'Where are the police?' Big Dave swung round. 'James, you have to let them get you in the ambul—'

'Knew what...they were after...wouldn't come out. Tried to put out the fire with...jugs of water...rang...fire brigade then...hid in the cupboard under the stairs. Couldn't bring it out until...knew it was safe...'

Now the ambulance had backed right up from the front

drive, across the grass, where it waited with its engine running and the back doors flung wide, blocking Marco's view. But they must have got Mr. Montague in because he saw the sword dropping into the grass and Big Dave picking it up.

'Okay, James, don't worry, I'll take care of it for y— *What*? No, no, don't *worry...*'

The doors clanged shut.

'Oh my goddess,' Eleri breathed. 'The fool. He doesn't understand.'

And before Sam could stop her, she was through the gate and running at Dave as the ambulance pulled away down the main drive.

'Take it to your church!' Eleri shouted. 'Take it to your—'

'Get out of here, you insane woman!'

'You don't underst—'

Eleri tried to grab the sword, but he wrenched it away.

'He wants me to look after it, don't you—'

'He wants you to *destroy*—'

'You lunatic, it's a valuable artefact!'

'It's full of evil. He wants you to... Get your hands off me, you—'

Two policemen had moved either side of Eleri, taking an arm each, as Dave walked away with the sword, looking, with his cassock and beard, like one of those dark lords from the fantasy games. He was well away by the time the cops let Eleri go, leaving her standing there wringing her bony hands and then stumbling back towards the wall, where Sam was waiting, shaking his head.

'Leave it, Eleri. Nothing you can do with a feller like Wilcox.'

'He didn't understand. He thought James was asking him to take care of the wretched thing. He should be praying all night over it and drowning the evil in holy water. What if he takes it home again? The girl...Rosa...'

'He wouldn't take it home again. He'll probably take it to the police station for safe keeping.'

'Sam, it *kills.*'

'Look,' Sam said, 'the old boy's in a bad way – his house is half burned down, lucky to escape with his life. You can't blame that on an old sword.'

'*Can't you?*' By now Eleri was looking positively deranged. 'Why was James not letting it out of his sight. Why was he staying in a blazing house until he knew it was safe to bring it out...without *them* getting it...'

'Who?'

'The Coombes boy and his friends is my guess.'

'Why?'

'Perhaps because of its true origins. I have spent most of the day in research, phoning old colleagues in the world of academe and archaeology. And I believe I now know what this sword is.'

'Hang on,' Sam said. 'You're now saying it's *not* Excalibur?'

'Sam, if I tell you it corresponds to Excalibur in the same way that the Dark Chalice corresponds to the Holy Grail, would that make it any clearer?'

'Holy Joseph, Eleri—'

'I have reason to believe...that this sword is a relic which has been missing for many years and which was once known to scholars of the ancient world as...the Blade of Mordred... or the Blade of Night.'

The cottage creaked and crackled and hissed.

Sam said, 'This isn't another of your dreams, is it?'

'I only wish that it was,' Eleri said.

Old Metal

Rosa awoke, as she always did, when the front door opened with a squealy kind of scraping that sent harsh echoes along the uncarpeted passage and up the stairs.

She hadn't been *very* asleep, because of all the extra noise from the street and the competing warblings of police cars and fire engines and ambulances.

Quietly, she got out of bed and went to the top of the stairs and heard Mum's voice, pitched low but urgent.

'Dave, what's happened?'

'It was James Montague,' Dad said. 'His house has burned...well more or less burned down.'

'Oh no—'

'Badly burned, but amazingly, he got out. He's been taken to hospital, and meanwhile, he's asked me to...look after something for him.'

There was silence, and then...

'Oh *no*,' Mum said. 'Oh, Dave, what have you brought *that* thing back for? I really thought we'd seen the last of it.'

'It's an old sword, that's all. A rusty lump of old metal.'

Rosa gripped the post at the top of the stairs, a chill suddenly rolling like a snowball around her insides.

Oh please...*please*...

'You know Rosa didn't like it in the house,' Mum said.

'Yes, yes,' Dad said wearily, 'we both know that Rosa's an impressionable child. Who unfortunately has been allowed to mix with the wrong type of people – not that the *right* type of people are easy to find in this town. However, what she doesn't know can't harm her. Anyway, it'll only be for one night. I promise I'll phone the museum first thing in the morning.'

Rosa shut her eyes and hugged the post even though, like everything else in this flat, it felt cold and hard and hostile.

'I'll put it in the cupboard in the passage,' Dad said. 'In the old tennis bag.'

Up here?

Rosa shook.

Practically opposite the bedroom door?

This just could *not* be happening. She felt her chest heaving and thought she was going to choke on her own breath, her mind silently screaming, *Tell him no. Tell him you won't have it. Tell him to take it away right now!*

'Well, do it quietly, Dave,' Mum said. 'Take your shoes off.'

Rosa heard Mum's soft footsteps on the bottom stairs and crept to her bedroom.

Back in bed, she lay staring into the grey and pulsing darkness, her whole body as stiff as if she'd been deep-frozen, old whispers hanging like brittle cobwebs in the air.

In the End

'**M**ordred,' Eleri said. 'Nobody is quite sure who he was. Some legends say he was Arthur's son, some his nephew. Only one thing is sure: it was Mordred who killed Arthur.'

It was close to midnight. The candles at Bowermead were burning low and shadows rose mistily to the carved ceiling. The light through a high, circular window was deep blue and purple, and Eleri's voice was heavy with sorrow.

'It is a story of tragedy and betrayal. Of darkness and desertion. Of lost love and spoiled friendship.'

Sam Daniel sighed. Eleri, sitting in the tall chair with her back to the dead fireplace, looked at Sam and then at Diane and gathered her dark cloak in folds over her lap.

'I know,' Eleri said. 'Get to the point, Eleri.'

And, for once, she did.

She told the story with none of her usual dramatic stuff. Which, Marco supposed, was why it left him close to tears.

He was sure he must have known at least some of this before. He remembered once reading a whole book about King Arthur and the Knights of the Round Table, but...well, when you were young you just enjoyed the fight scenes and the spooky stuff. You skipped over the girly bits – like about who fancied Queen Guinevere and who got her in the end.

Actually it had been Sir Lancelot, Arthur's top knight, who had fallen in love with the king's wife. And she liked him a bit, too, and so they went off together.

Well, these things happened – look at Mum and Dad. True, it was Dad who'd got himself a girlfriend, but suppose it had been Mum who'd got a boyfriend, say in America?

In that situation, would Dad have got all the lawyers from his office to go over to the States to beat up the other guy and his mates and get Mum back?

Frankly, Marco did not see Dad doing this.

But then this wasn't the Dark Ages and Dad wasn't King Arthur.

Who took it badly.

It was his half-sister, Morgan le Fay, who tipped him off that Guinevere was playing away. Morgan was a bit like Eleri, seriously psychic, and she didn't like Guinevere or Lancelot. Anyway, she proved to Arthur that they had this thing going. And before you knew it, it was all in ruins.

Not just the marriage, the whole Round Table thing. The chivalry and the comradeship and the knights going in search of the Holy Grail. All over.

What happened was the Round Table was split down the middle, with some knights siding with Lancelot and others supporting Arthur. Old friendships went down the toilet. Traps were laid and fights broke out and some of the guys were killed and the atmosphere was getting really bad.

At one stage, there was even pressure on Arthur to have Guinevere burned for treachery. You imagine that?

Anyway, Arthur and his men went out after Lancelot. They pursued him to France, where he had a castle of his own. And Arthur left Mordred – who was either his son or his nephew – in charge of the British kingdom.

And in charge of guarding Guinevere.

A bad move, basically. But Mordred had volunteered, and the state Arthur was in by now – feeling totally let down – he was just like, *Sure, whatever...*

Of course Mordred totally fancied Guinevere, too (she wasn't his mother; he wasn't *that* weird) and he arranged for a forged letter to arrive from Arthur in France saying he'd been mortally wounded by Lancelot and the whole deal had gone down and the best thing now would be for Guinevere to marry Mordred.

Which told you what kind of person Mordred was.

There was *no way* Lancelot was *ever* going to deliberately harm Arthur or any of Arthur's knights. He *liked* those guys. He *respected* Arthur. He didn't want *any* of this. He hadn't wanted to fall in love with the queen, it just happened, the way these things still did.

Eleri put it into perspective. Her long face was solemn;

she was staring into space, as if she could see it all being played out before her in some parallel time frame.

'All we need to understand,' she said, 'is that both Arthur and Lancelot were decent, honourable men.'

Another honourable man, Eleri said, had been mortally wounded in a hand-to-hand fight with Lancelot. This was Arthur's faithful knight Sir Gawaine. His brother had been an accidental casualty of the war with Lancelot, and Gawaine had decided he and Lancelot should sort it out between them...with a couple of heavy swords.

Lancelot, who knew he could take Gawaine, was like, *No way, man, forget it, you're an old mate, and I'm younger than you and I'm better at this*. But Gawaine persisted and they fought all day, and eventually Gawaine was beaten to his knees and he was going, *Okay just kill me, get it over*, and Lancelot said, *Why don't you just give up, it doesn't have to end like this*.

But Gawaine wouldn't give up and Lancelot couldn't kill him and, in the end, just walked off and you could tell he was in a terrible state.

Meanwhile, Guinevere, who was also basically okay, had managed to get a message to Arthur telling him about the scam Mordred had tried to pull to get her and the kingdom.

Arthur went ballistic.

He came straight back across the Channel to Britain, where Mordred had put together a major army to make sure he kept the kingdom for good.

Normally this wouldn't have been too much of a problem for Arthur, with all his knights behind him.

But they weren't, were they? Most of them had been killed, and he'd only just patched things up – kind of – with

Lancelot, so he wasn't going to ask *him* to help...although Marco knew there was nothing Lancelot would have wanted more than to be playing on Arthur's team again, to make up for all the good guys he hadn't meant to kill. But there was just too much history, and Arthur couldn't ask.

So Arthur and Mordred lined up for the big one.

'And then Arthur had a dream,' Eleri said, and Sam moaned.

'I wondered when that was coming.'

Eleri ignored him. 'He dreamed of Sir Gawaine, who had now died. Gawaine told him he should not take on Mordred yet, but wait for Lancelot, who was coming at last to help. And Arthur – unlike *some* people – had respect for dreams.'

'Didn't help him in the end, though, did it?' Sam said. 'Everybody in his right mind knows you *never* trust a dream.'

To try and buy some time, Arthur had cut a deal with Mordred, giving him Cornwall (Marco could hear fifth-century versions of Ted and Brian going, *Yeah, typical... we're always the first to get traded in*) and they arranged to meet up, with just fourteen men each, to seal the agreement.

So you had these two groups of guys facing each other across a field, and it was really tense because they were seriously suspicious of each other, Arthur's guys thinking Mordred's guys were going to pull a fast one at any moment.

Whether Mordred *did* have another scam planned, well, nobody ever knew because fate – proving that Sam had a point – intervened in the form of a poisonous snake appearing and biting one of the knights in the foot.

'Hang on,' Marco said. 'Didn't knights have these iron boots? How could a sn—'

'Not in the fifth century,' Eleri said through her teeth. 'Anyway, the knight drew his sword to kill the snake...and that was it. The other side got the wrong idea and thought it was an ambush. Instantly, *all* the swords were drawn, and...'

It was like one of those bar fights in the old movies, where one guy throws a punch and within a couple of minutes people are smashing bottles and breaking chairs over each other's heads.

Only this was worse.

'Even though there were fewer than thirty knights altogether,' Eleri said, 'it lasted all day, and all but two of Arthur's knights were cut down. It was, Arthur said, "a *doleful* day".'

Doleful was a heavy word. It suggested the hand of fate.

And the hand of fate was Mordred's hand and it was holding a sword.

Strangely, at this point, Marco stopped hearing Eleri.

He found himself looking into the air the way she was, and somehow, in the cloudy vastness of the massive room, he was seeing...

...an empty, treeless landscape under a sky like a Glasto sky during the Blight.

The grass was all trampled down and soggy with blood, and there were dead bodies.

Mordred was a lot younger than you'd have imagined. He didn't have a beard, and his hair was quite short and tightly curled.

When Marco spotted him, Mordred was just leaning on his sword, looking a bit tired, with these dead guys at his feet, and Marco realized how small-time all this was, and he knew how the king must be feeling: totally gutted at having all his best knights cut down because of this jerk getting greedy.

He could hear talking now: low, harsh voices speaking a language he couldn't understand, and yet he knew what they were saying.

Right. Arthur eyeballing Mordred from some distance. *That's it.* Holding out his hand. *Spear.*

And Marco thought, *Spear?* Why the spear? Why not Excalibur? Excalibur never failed.

One of the remaining knights handed Arthur a spear, shaking his head. Arthur gripped the wooden shaft in both hands. It was like a rake, maybe a bit thicker, and Marco could feel how cold it was and sticky with what could only be blood.

Marco was thinking, *No, this is totally stupid...*

But Arthur's head was down and he was running across the slippery grass, straight at Mordred, with all his weight behind the sticky spear.

Uuuuuurgh...

The blood spraying all over him as the spear went in.

Through Mordred and out the other side.

Mordred must've known that this was *it* for him, because he didn't even try to back away, just pushed himself further into the spear, right up to Arthur and you could see his eyes bulging and smell his sweat.

On his way out.

But just before he died, with both hands, he brought his sword down on Arthur's head.

The Blade of Mordred.

Marco shut his eyes. It was like...

It was like both of them *knew*.

There was no explanation for this other than Arthur realizing, somehow, that this was going to be his last battle and that he couldn't use Excalibur because Excalibur *never failed*.

So Arthur actually *knew* he was supposed to fail this time? That this was his destiny?

Marco felt angry and deeply sad and, worst of all, he didn't understand.

It didn't have to happen.

'Marco!' Diane was on the floor in front of him, hands on Marco's shoulders. 'Are you all right?'

The room was full of shadows, swirling like the smoke around Mr. Montague's cottage.

'I don't get it,' Marco said. '*Why?*'

He realized he was in the middle of the room, on his own on the cold floor, actually in tears and he didn't care. Because Arthur...

Despite what Griff Daniel had said at the meeting, Arthur had been an Avalonian who believed in a kingdom that stood for helping people and trying to do the right thing, whereas Mordred was just after personal power and wealth, like, like...

'Just a story, Marco,' Sam said.

But, as the candles burned down until they were just tiny flecks of flame in pools of liquid wax, they both knew that it wasn't.

Marco was aware of Eleri, on her feet.

Eleri, black-cloaked, just like the weeping women who

had borne Arthur's body by barge. The last, sad journey to Glastonbury.

Marco just knew Arthur *had* been buried in the Abbey. There could be nowhere else. He looked up at Eleri.

'It didn't have to end, Eleri.'

Eleri laid a bony hand on Marco's shoulder. 'It *doesn't* end,' she said.

A Weapon of Destruction

With her heart banging away, Rosa rolled over to face the darkest part of the bedroom, and he was there.

It was always a shock, even though she'd known, as soon as she'd awoken, all scrunched up and sweaty, from another foul-smelling nightmare, that it was going to happen.

When you opened your eyes quickly in the dark, you could see different *kinds* of dark: grey-blue clouds and floating mauvish blobs, like a pattern forming in a kaleidoscope.

But it was a gloomy kaleidoscope, because these were colours that were not quite colours, not strong enough to be colours, just patches of night, and tonight they looked like old clothes hanging in a dark and dusty open wardrobe, and out of the old clothes she could see him watching her, his eyes far back under the cowl.

The Abbot was back.

She'd been afraid that he'd abandoned her because she'd taken part in a pagan rite on the Tor. She'd called out for him and...nothing.

But now he'd come.

And it was so cold.

So cold – in August – that Rosa was hugging the duvet to her chest.

She understood this, of course. It was always cold, at first, when he was manifesting. She remembered what Eleri had told her: *Don't be afraid of the cold. Understand that he needs to take heat from the room to build up enough energy to become visible to you.*

Knowing that, she'd always sensed a warmth within the cold.

But it had never been cold like this. This was a dank and wintry cold, and she was thinking, as she shuddered, that for the first time she understood the meaning of *cold as the grave.*

Had he ever had a grave?

She was aware of his eyes, sad and deep and desperate, peering from the dullness of the not-quite-colours. Peering at her from the other side of death. His body had been brutally carved up and bits of him sent to different places and hung on things. Perhaps none of the bits had ever had a resting place. His spirit must be exhausted.

And it must be so hard for him to come through under those circumstances, especially with *that*...in the flat.

No, it wasn't her role in the pagan ritual that had driven him away. It was the presence of the sword...*Excalibur.*

When the word appeared in her mind, it brought a sudden *throb* in the darkness. He was leaning forward now, against a thin, steep black shadow – his staff, perhaps. Both his hands tight around it. She knew this even though she couldn't see any hands: she was feeling the pressure of the grip and knowing he was leaning towards her, sending out a kind of urgency that made the dull colours vibrate and the temperature in the room drop way beyond goosebump point.

I can't, Rosa said without speaking. More sweat was breaking out, cold, on her face. Because she could sense what he wanted.

What he wanted had been forming in her mind from the first moment she'd been aware of him in the dark, the way your conscience sometimes spoke to you, telling you what you really ought to be doing. Which was always something you already knew you should be doing but really didn't want to, and...

'I just *can't.*'

This time she'd actually said it, but this only seemed to make him more desperate, and now it was like being locked inside a deep freeze.

He was her conscience – conscience was such a cold thing – and he was telling her what she must do.

'I can't—'

There was a flaring in the room, and suddenly it was far more than a bedroom, more like a kind of cloister that went far back, further than the wall, further than the whole building. The distance shimmered, glow-worms of light on old stones, for just a moment and then disappeared.

Afraid that she would be sucked into it, Rosa sank back into the headboard, holding the duvet right around her as there came a second flaring, like the light through a stained-glass window.

And she saw the Abbot, all black in silhouette, in his robes, with his arms raised over his head, and felt the ages of his pain.

'How do you know this *is* the Blade of Mordred?' Sam asked, always sceptical.

Sam did, basically, believe. He just thought that Eleri needed *grounding* – that was the word he and Woolly used. Another dowsing word. When strange energies made the rods twitch, dowsers had to keep their feet on the ground.

'We don't,' Eleri said. 'We never *know*, we only feel the truth.'

'And when did *you* feel the truth?' Sam said.

'When the girl, Rosa, told me of the dreams she had while the sword was lying nearby, she spoke of words which she recalled as "more dread". It was then that the idea began to germinate in my consciousness.'

'But you knew the Blade of Mordred existed?' Sam said.

'Only in legends. By which I mean the legends spoken of in the occult fraternity. This was a story not recorded by Sir Thomas Malory or Geoffrey of Monmouth or the other Arthurian chroniclers. This was something preserved only by those who would benefit from it. The story of the Blade of Mordred has been handed down – like the sword itself – through the black lodges.'

'You mean guys like Roger Cromwell?'

'Exactly.'

Sam punched a fist into a palm. 'They should've let Woolly have a go at it with his pendulum. If he'd been able to dowse it before they brought it back he'd've been able to tell you how long it'd been down there by the river.'

'Not very long is my guess,' Eleri said. 'I would suggest that it was found by the people who were supposed to find it.'

Sam sat up. 'You're saying it was planted?'

'Of course it was planted. The discovery of what seemed to be Excalibur would be the final element confirming Glastonbury's status as the Arthurian capital of Britain. Even if the sword was discredited after a few months of tests, it would have served its purpose.'

'Because by then Melcato would've signed on the dotted line,' Sam said, 'and the Glasties would be in the money.'

'What better secret emblem of lies and treachery than the Blade of Mordred, disguised as Excalibur? And who better to find it than the no-nonsense northern curate from St John's, whose word no one could dispute.'

'Smart,' Sam said. 'But we still got no proof. If we had an old picture of it or something – even a drawing – we could compare it with—'

'It doesn't matter what it *looks* like,' Eleri snapped. 'It may be recognized only by its *aura*.'

'Ah.' Sam nodded, half smiling. 'Should've guessed.'

'What needs to be understood,' Eleri said, 'is that, just as the Dark Chalice is merely part of a skull invested, through centuries of ritual, with the power of the Antichrist, thus the Blade of Mordred could be *any* blade. In fact, James Montague suspected that the blade itself and the hilt appear to be from different swords. Bitterly disappointed, he was, when he rang to tell me that.'

'It's been cobbled together?' Sam said. 'From bits of old relics?'

'It may have been "cobbled together", as you put it, many centuries ago. Its original handle, for instance, may have rusted away and been replaced. You see, it is said that, for the sword of Mordred to retain its energy, it must always be a...a weapon of destruction.'

The room became dimmer as one of the candle flames drowned in the remains of its own molten wax, and Sam's voice sounded like it was drowning, too.

'What are you *saying*, Eleri? What do you mean by *its energy*? And what do you mean by *destruct*—'

'It is said...' Eleri sat down, as if she was suddenly too weak to stand. 'It is said that the sword continues to kill. That when it is exposed to the light it *must* kill.'

'What?'

'The bodies that Rosa saw in her dream are the bodies of the dead of many centuries. The blood which has flowed through the years over the Blade of Mordred.'

Somewhere in the house, the phone rang again. Eleri looked up.

'Now it has been exposed to the air and the light. It...it longs for blood.'

'Honestly, Eleri...' You could tell Sam was trying to smile. And failing. 'Nobody would ever think you used to be a professor of history.'

The phone didn't stop. Diane rose to her feet. 'I'd better get it.'

As she went out, moving so lightly for such a big lady,

Marco was thinking that the last time the phone had rung was when they'd learned about the fire. *More dread,* he thought. *More dread.*

Rosa, Marco thought, *Rosa's in there with the sword,* just as Diane came back holding an antique cordless phone – one of those with an aerial you pulled out.

Diane looked worried sick. She held out the phone to Eleri. 'It's Rosa. She's in the street. She doesn't know what to do.'

Eleri came to her feet, taking the phone. 'Which street?'

'She doesn't know,' Diane said. 'Any street. And she's got the sword with her.'

Collecting It

'Listen to me, Rosa.'

'Yes.'

The mobile was slippery in her hand. She was sitting on the step in the darkened doorway of the crystal shop on High Street. The street was empty and the lights were out in the shop windows full of weird things. No cars were on the road.

'Where exactly are you?'

'In the doorway of Teddy's shop.' She was whispering.

'Good,' Eleri said. 'Teddy's a good man. His crystals are always full of healing light. Tell me quickly – why did you do this?'

'The...the Abbot...'

'Told you to?'

'I think it was what he wanted. He...manifested.' Rosa trembled suddenly in the shadows. She hated that word.

'You thought the Abbot was telling you to take it out of your flat?' Eleri said.

'It was in an old tennis bag on the landing, where Dad had left it. It was hard to lift at first, very heavy. I carried it down the stairs and out of the front door, and by the time I got it outside, it somehow felt...it felt light.'

She heard Eleri's intake of breath. 'Don't touch it!'

'But I—'

'We're coming,' Eleri said. 'Stay where you are, Rosa. Stay in Teddy's doorway. We're coming. We're coming to collect it.'

Eleri cut the signal.

In fact, Rosa's feet were on the sword.

She tried to pull them away but they didn't want to move. When she looked down her feet seemed a long way away and out of her control, somehow. The hilt of the sword was sticking out from under the sole of her left trainer. It felt knobbly. It felt warm.

She looked down. There was a sharp flash of light from the sword, as if it was responding to her glance. It was a reflection from one of the street lamps. That was all.

The last time she'd seen it, it had been too blackened with age and grime to reflect anything. Perhaps Mr. Montague had cleaned it up. She didn't think you were supposed to do that, not so quickly, anyway. In the archaeological programmes she'd seen on TV, people spent weeks peeling the dirt off ancient finds so as not to risk damaging them.

Dad had told Mum about a fire at this Mr. Montague's house, where the sword had been.

...more or less burned down.

Perhaps that was why the sword still felt warm.

Ridiculous. That was hours ago. And it hadn't felt warm when she'd opened the cupboard on the landing. It had felt like she was opening an old tomb to expose decaying bones. When she'd unbuckled the canvas bag, she was sure cold air had come wafting out, and she'd looked over her shoulder to see if the Abbot had followed her, but she'd been alone.

Now the temperature had dropped and a low mist prowled the street, making haloes around the street lamps. Did the Abbot walk the street?

Nothing was impossible in this town. Dad must have been mad to bring them here. All that rubbish he talked about being summoned to bring some decent, solid faith to a pagan place. Dad saw everything in black and white. He didn't see the layers of things. He was just not the sort of guy who should *be* here.

But what about me?

Oh yeah, she knew she'd changed and, in some ways, for the better. If she'd been faced with taking the sword out of the cupboard a few weeks ago she'd have had to take it out *four times* and keep putting it back before the OCD would have let her carry it downstairs.

Rosa hugged herself in the darkness. She was sure she could feel the heat from the sword rising up her legs.

Excalibur. A magic sword. Arthur had pulled it out of a stone to prove he was the king.

Or something.

She squirmed back into the doorway, and the sword...

Don't touch it! Eleri had hissed.

...was dragged along with her, scraping the step. She wrapped her arms around herself and squeezed into a corner of the doorway. She wished they'd come.

To collect it.

'*Pssst.*'

Rosa shot to her feet. 'Who's that?'

It had come down the street like a dead leaf rustling along the pavement. Rosa stood stiffly, holding her breath. 'Eleri? Is that you?'

'*Pssst. Rosa...*'

'Marco?' Was it Marco's voice?

'*Come on. Quick.*'

She bent and picked up the sword and came out of the doorway. She saw a figure moving ahead of her in the shadows between the street lamps.

'Who's that?'

There was laughter from behind her.

'Your friend.'

She turned, and there was Jasper Coombes lolling against a lamp post.

'Nice sword, Rosa,' Jasper said.

'What do you want?'

'You know what I want.'

Rosa gripped the sword in her right hand. Under the street lamp, Jasper, in white shirt and white trousers, seemed to be aglow. He smiled at her.

'Hey...thanks. Thanks for saving my guys the trouble of having to go in and get it.'

Rosa didn't reply, just backed away from him.

'We need it back more than ever,' Jasper said. 'There've been developments. So I'm collecting it.'

'What for?' Rosa playing for time. They'd be here soon, surely, Eleri...and Sam. 'What do you want it for?'

Jasper grinned his wide, easy grin, curly hair glistening in the street light. He was good-looking and his family was rich. He had everything. It was impossible to understand why he couldn't just enjoy being what he was instead of having to *destroy*. Were some people just born evil?

'If you take it,' Rosa said, 'I'll just tell everybody you stole it.'

'Oh, sure.' Jasper nodded, still doing his wide grin. 'And they'll believe every word you say, won't they? With your reputation for being...shall we say emotionally fragile? I'm *sure* your old man will believe you for a start.'

'You scumbag,' Rosa said.

She turned away from him – no way was she going to be intimidated – and began to walk up the street, dragging the sword behind her so that the blunt point skittered along the pavement.

There was no sound of him following her which meant – Rosa's insides began to shrivel – that the shadow she'd seen up ahead had been one of his mates.

Get out, get out, get out...

Rosa began to run and then, without breaking step, spun off to the right, into a side street – Silver Street, which was tucked just behind High Street. It was dark and had a wall which backed directly onto the Abbey grounds, with a gate. Somewhere to hide, somewhere to hide, somewhere to—

She almost bumped into him.

She screamed.

'Easy, sweetheart,' Shane Davey said.

Blocking her path. Totally. He seemed very wide and dense, like a thick, stunted tree.

And now there *were* footsteps behind her, two sets of footsteps, walking slowly, almost lazily, from different directions.

'Give us the sword, Rosa,' Jasper said. 'Give us back the sword and nobody will get hurt. Not yet, anyway.'

Rosa stepped back.

She stood panting, holding tight to the handle of the sword. It took both her hands and there was room for two more, and it felt warm, and the night was warm, too, now, and it was all around her, just the night, pulsing with energy. All around her and inside her, and it felt good, and Rosa's breath came faster.

And suddenly she understood why Jasper was like he was. It was a kind of power. The power of evil.

When the sword swung back, she thought it was Jasper snatching it from behind, and she spun round and the blade went swishing through the air, slow and even, like the rotor on a helicopter starting up, going round and round and round, gathering speed, and Rosa spun with it, in what seemed like slow motion, the shadowy buildings blurring.

There was a cry.

'*Aaaah...no!*'

She spun slowly into stillness to find Shane Davey, down on his knees in the roadway; she'd heard both his knees go cracking on the tarmac. She saw his eyes, shocked, looking up.

'She's insane, she...' Shane began to scuttle backwards, like a crab. 'She nearly *took my head off!*'

The power of evil.

The heat from the sword made Rosa's wrists tingle. Someone, Jasper or the third guy, had a torch, and it threw a white pool around Shane, as he cowered, hands up in front of his face.

'*No!*' Shane said faintly, falling over onto his back, squirming away. 'Please, no...'

Rosa had the sword already raised, both hands tight around its throbbing heat, high, high, *higher* over Shane's head. *Directly* over his head.

The voice of the night said, *Finish it...finish it...*

She felt something huge and yawning inside her.

...more dread...

'Die, scum,' Rosa screamed. '*Die!*'

Part Four

'Then came Arthur, and the
sword leaped forth in his hand.'
DION FORTUNE
Avalon of the Heart

Small Pale Glow

The morning was dull but the sun was trying to squeeze through, prising itself between the tight clouds, pretty much the way Marco was trying to open his eyes. Sticky sleep kept sucking him back, but he knew there was so much he had to think about.

When, eventually, he stumbled down the narrow wooden stairs from his attic, he had no idea what time it was, but it had to be late. He remembered streaks of pink light in the sky when he was throwing himself on the bed, still half-dressed and...and there was nothing after that.

But there'd been an awful lot before it. Now, in the daylight, the memories were crowding into his head and it wasn't big enough for all the scenes of fighting and fire, sirens and screaming, and a computer screen flickering out MELCATO...

And Josh? Really Josh? Was Josh really here, or was that a dream? Was it *all* a dream?

And then there was Rosa.

Rosa's face twisted with hate.

Oh God.

Nancy looked up from the stove as he staggered into the kitchen.

'You look terrible pale, Marco.'

But not as pale, surely, as she looked. He was shocked. For the first time, her face was washed totally clean of make-up and her hair was straight, with the grey showing through. It was like he'd awoken in a different house in a different, sadder time.

Time...

The clock said 10.15. Not as late as he'd expected.

'What time did I...?'

'Sam brought you back... You was jabbering on, and I said we'll...talk about it in the morning.'

But now it *was* morning, and Nancy looked too upset to talk. She was buttering toast and the knife kept slipping between her fingers. He wanted Nancy to say, it's okay, Marco, everything's fine, but...

He looked all around the kitchen and out of the window. 'Where's Woolly?'

'He's...down the stable, with Merlin.' Nancy's face had totally clouded over. 'And his pendulums.'

He remembered: Woolly going funny after they came out of the meeting at the town hall. Not himself. Saying they'd

310

got it all wrong and Griff Daniel was a decent, honourable man. Not himself at all. Walking away with Nancy, like his mind had gone off course.

Looking like...like an old man.

Woolly.

They'd all said he'd be okay after a good night's sleep.

'He ain't right, Marco,' Nancy said. 'I been trying to get him to go to the doctor's. The real doctors, not one of the alternative healers. It's like he's had...had a stroke or something. Oh, Marco—'

Nancy just crumpled, sinking down with her hands over her eyes and one elbow in the butter dish. 'I never, *ever* thought, Marco. We puts on all our fancy clothes and plays loud music late into the night, like it's still the 1960s, and nothing's gonner change. I never...I never thought we was gonner get old...old and sick.'

'Nancy, you're *not*, you're—'

'It's all over, Marco. All over for us now. The future belongs to the Glasties. Griff Daniel's a hero, and the bad kids've got their precious sword. Sam told us all about it. He sat us down here when you'd gone to bed and he told us all about the Americans coming to take over and make Griff and Mr. Cotton and Coombes and all those fellers rich. And he told us about the fire and the Blade of Mordred. But Woolly...he didn't seem to be taking any of it in, look. It was like he'd given up, and he was saying, "The gods've spoken and they ain't spoken to us. We should let the Glasties have their town the way they want it. They're not bad people really and they deserve it." Oh, Marco, he's *terrible sick...*'

'*No!*'

'And he won't get no help...'

'*We* have to help,' Marco said.

But what could they do?

Rosa stared at the wall.

The wall was blank. For the moment.

Her mind was blank.

For the moment.

She didn't want to get up.

It wasn't safe.

She had no control.

They controlled her.

Forces.

This was what it was all about, being psychic. You were open to any discarnate forces that wanted to take you over.

And some were evil.

Tears spurted into her eyes.

She'd come *so close* to killing that boy.

All right, yes, he was nasty, vicious, all that stuff. The voice had been telling her that. Telling her he didn't deserve to live.

Finish it, the voice had said. Whose voice?

The voice of the sword, burning in her hands.

Telling her to kill.

But that was rubbish, wasn't it? It was just a lump of metal. What had been speaking was just some crazy, psychotic part of her own mind.

Dad was right. She was ill. She was a danger to others. Not safe to be on the streets. Certainly not in a town like this where so many people believed in weird stuff. She needed to be kept in a psychiatric hospital, in a white room with padded walls where she couldn't harm anybody or even herself.

She remembered saying something like this to Eleri and Diane as they brought her home. She remembered Eleri's cool hands on her hot forehead, Eleri's murmurings. Not words she'd understood, but they'd calmed her. She remembered feeling very tired and thankful she'd left the front door unlocked. She remembered Eleri quietly seeing her up the stairs and padding softly away, while Mum and Dad slept on. Eleri was scary-looking, but she was kind. They all were.

Rosa remembered looking out of her window before she'd fallen into bed, and seeing Sam Daniel in the street outside, pacing and looking up at her.

Making sure she didn't come out again to try and kill somebody.

As if even just handling the sword could turn you into a killer.

The sword that was *not* Excalibur.

The sword that was, apparently, the very opposite of Excalibur – delivered into this world not by the alabaster arm of the Lady of the Lake but, you could imagine, by some scabby claw from the dark waters under the earth.

(And she thought of the underground stream in the Glastonbury labyrinth, the maze of damp tunnels enclosing the forgotten temple of the Dark Chalice.)

Tonight, when her mind had seemed to explode and she'd hurled down the sword in horror and disgust, the kid, Shane, had leaped up and snatched it and run, and she'd heard him sniggering from the shadows in Silver Street.

She hadn't seen the others who were waiting for Shane.

Only heard Sam shouting after them as he and Diane and Eleri and Marco had come dashing in from High Street to find her still staring at the locked metal-barred gate into the Abbey from where she'd seen a pale, desperate glow in the seconds before her mind had exploded and she'd hurled the sword away.

The memory of that small, pale glow was the only hope she had.

She stared at the wall.

Mum would have gone to work at The George and Pilgrims, and it was probably Dad's day for taking the early communion service at St John's Church.

He'd be back soon.

And then he'd find out that the sword was missing, and he'd be furious.

But, worse than that, the sword was out there and this sword was all about killing. All it had ever done was kill and kill and kill, and it carried the psychic stain of violent death.

A stain too deep ever to be wiped away.

The Real Controller

It was altogether better than Josh could have imagined.

The minute he and Grandma Goldman had hit High Street, he'd become aware of people looking at him.

First, there was a tall, middle-aged guy in a suit – possibly the one they'd seen with the mayor last night in the video shop. And then some kids, glancing at him sideways and finally following him, staying a respectful distance behind.

Oh, yes, it was clear what had happened. The mayor must've sobered up in a hurry last night and gone round telling everybody to get their acts together...

...because Rex Arturus was in town!

The mayor had obviously described Rex: good-looking young guy. Intellectual-looking.

Grandma Goldman, of course, didn't get it. Breezing up the street smiling at everybody. Probably thinking people in this town were just naturally friendly. She still seemed a little annoyed with Josh, however.

'I only hope,' she'd said over breakfast at the inn, 'that the mayor was drunk enough last night to have forgotten all that rubbish you came out with, Joshua. Taking advantage of an inebriated man!'

'Oh, he's *bound* to have forgotten,' Josh had said, noticing the way the waitress was staring at him.

Now, looking up and down the street, smiling distantly, like he already owned the place, he spotted a guy with a moustache sandwiched between two carousels of houses for sale in an estate agent's. The guy was watching them intently.

Grandma Goldman still didn't notice. She'd seen something in a shop window.

'Oh, just look at that! I just *have* to have one of those in my conservatory.' Peering at this giant chunk of crystal, the size of a round of Swiss cheese, only with more holes.

'Tell you what, Grandma,' Josh said. 'If you want to go in and drool over those rocks, I'll just carry on strolling up the road, maybe check out some of the eateries, see where we can get some lunch.'

Anything to avoid faking interest in all this alternative tourist tat. He noticed he was already slipping into his American voice; luckily Grandma Goldman was too absorbed in the crystals to notice.

'Good idea, Joshua.' She didn't even turn round. 'Give me half an hour?'

'You got it, Grammaw. Er, I mean, no problem.'

So she went into the shop and he strolled across the road, noting that the kids were still behind him. Actually, these kids could become annoying. Why couldn't celebs be left alone to get on with their amazing lives?

Josh slipped into a café called – oh *dear* – The Cosmic Carrot and wandered over to the counter.

'Cawfee,' he snapped. 'Black.'

Well, he didn't have to actually drink the foul stuff. It was just that 'chocolate milk shake' didn't sound very cool. Not for someone like Rex Arturus, anyway.

The woman behind the counter was wearing an apron with MEAT IS MURDER printed on it in blood-red.

'We only got decaff,' she said.

Josh shrugged.

'Whatever. Just make it strong, lady, and make it fast. I got some major stuff to take care of.'

He carried his coffee over to a table by the window and examined all the dysfunctional misfits around him, with their tattoos and lip rings and flared jeans and rainbow hair. It was like a playgroup whose mothers had abandoned them about twenty years ago and never come back, and *none of them had realized.*

Josh found this concept so amusing that he didn't notice the seat next to him had been taken.

'So what do you *think* of the place?' a smooth voice murmured. 'Dreadful, isn't it?'

Josh spun round. The boy sitting next to him looked very relaxed, even in the presence of someone who was about to more or less buy the town.

'Not what you're used to, huh...Rex?'

'Oh.' Josh got himself together. 'I think you're mistaken, buddy. My name's—'

'I don't think so. I think you're Rex Arturus.'

Josh shrugged. Might as well see where this was leading. He recognized this guy now. He'd been introduced at the meeting last night as the John the Baptist figure who'd had a vision foretelling the coming of Arthur.

'So what was it blew my cover?' Josh said.

'People say you keep putting on a ridiculous English accent.' The boy held out a hand. Josh reckoned he was a year or two older than him. 'My name's Jasper Coombes.'

'Hi, Coombes.' Josh shook hands. 'You live in these parts?'

'For my sins. It's rather pitiful, isn't it? These people are so...utterly dysfunctional.'

'Hey,' Josh said. 'That was precisely *my* word for it.'

In fact he wondered if he'd maybe spoken it aloud when he was sitting here just now. No matter. This guy was certainly the first sign of intelligent life in Glastonbury.

Jasper Coombes was still wearing the white kit he'd had on last night. He put his head on one side. 'So you'd actually agree that these...alternative types are detrimental to the town's image?'

'Are you kidding?' Josh took a tentative sip of his strong black, decaffeinated coffee and winced. 'Listen, when me and my old man start to sink some serious dough into this joint, all these jerks gonna be out on their asses.'

'Cool,' Jasper Coombes said.

'One thing bothers me, though.' Josh put his cup down – never again. 'The mayor? Mayor Daniel? Our millions really gonna be safe with that guy?'

'Ah.' Coombes leaned back, pushing long fingers through

his tight curls. 'You went to the mayor's meeting last night, correct?'

Josh narrowed his eyes, playing cautious.

'*Could* be I was there.'

'Well...' Coombes leaned closer to Josh. 'There's something you need to know about the mayor. He might *think* he runs this town...but he doesn't. The mayor's just a front for the *real* power.'

'Oh?' Josh was getting almost interested. 'Who we talking about?'

'I think you know.'

'I do?'

Josh didn't.

'Think about your exciting range of computer games,' Coombes said silkily. 'Think about Arturus Rex. Think about the secret door in the hillside.'

Josh nodded seriously, like he really *was* thinking about this rubbish.

'So the power comes from..?'

'The power comes from *Arthur* himself, of course.' Coombes said. 'The Once and Future King.'

Oh, no. Just when you thought you were speaking to a person of intellect he came out with some Marco-like drivel. However, as Rex was obviously sold on this rubbish, Josh figured he'd better go along with it.

'The power lies here? In, uh...?'

'The Isle of Avalon,' Coombes said. 'The ancient power is here to be tapped. The mayor, of course, is too stupid to know just what he's dealing with.'

'I thought he'd had a vision,' Josh said. 'And you too. You saw Excalibur, right?'

'Yes.' Coombes's eyes went still. 'I saw a hand holding the sword out of the water. And then the sword was found close to the river.'

'You sure you saw it? I mean, I'd hate to think this was some kinda scam.'

Coombes stared into space, his eyes glazed.

'The arm was white. As white as alabaster. And a light shone from the blade like the light of the full moon. It was...' He stopped and looked hard at Josh for a long moment. 'We, too, would hate to think this was, as you put it, some kind of scam. We are the guardians of an ancient magic. We have been waiting for Arthur for many centuries. We would hate to be taken in by...an imposter.'

Uh oh. Josh thought fast. He was, of course, an imposter.

Also, there was no doubt in his mind that this kid Rex was, too.

The only difference being that Rex didn't realize *he* was an imposter. Rex had, from the start, been a victim of chronic self-delusion. A delusion turned into some form of reality by the fact that he'd become the hero of the world's biggest-selling range of computer games.

It was clear that this Rex now totally believed he was an incarnation of King Arthur.

Oh yes, he was obviously one very mentally sick kid.

And if anyone could think himself into the mind of a very mentally sick kid it was Joshua Goldman, psychoanalyst.

Right. Okay. This could be a useful exercise.

Josh let his own gaze go out of focus, the way Coombes had, guessing his eyes would be looking all glazed and weird. He rose up in his rickety chair, let his voice go deeper.

'You *doubt* me?'

Slipping a steely slice of Englishness into his voice – *real* Englishness, none of the phoney stuff he'd put on for the mayor.

He was so good he almost shivered. It was as if something was taking him over.

Or – as he and his father and the psychiatric profession in general would put it – as if he'd become schizophrenic.

'You *dare* to doubt me?'

Jasper Coombes's chair slid back. He looked immediately fazed by the sudden power of the presence of King Arthur.

Role-playing was a very potent psychiatric tool.

'Just...testing,' Coombes said. 'Look...forget about the mayor. There's someone here who can help you. The follower of an ancient tradition. Obviously, I don't mean...' He waved a dismissive hand at the rabble in the café. '...any of these idiots. I mean a real *adept*.'

'A magician?' Josh said. 'Like my old associate, Merlin?'

'You could say that.'

'Do I get to meet him?'

'It could be arranged.'

'When?'

'What about now?'

'Oh.' Josh was thrown and slipped back into his American accent. 'Uh, well, my...the old lady who takes care of my personal arrangements...I told her I'd meet with her in, uh, a half-hour?'

Coombes smiled. 'Oh, yes, sorry. I suppose your father wouldn't want you wandering about on your own in a strange town. So the old lady's in charge of you, is she?'

'The hell she is!'

Josh felt his back stiffen.

Coombes's smile went thin, his eyes like slits. 'You do *want* to seize your destiny, don't you, Rex? I mean as the new Arthur. The heir to the kingdom. You have travelled through many lives to reach this point. Do you remember?'

Many lives? Was this guy real?

'Sure,' Josh said uncertainly. 'Many lives. A whole bunch of lives.'

'If you *don't* remember, I should tell you that we have someone who can take you back, through those lives – through the very gates of death – to your glorious incarnation as Arthur.'

'Yeah?'

Josh began to feel uneasy. It had been fun at first, but he didn't like the way this was going. Knew he really ought to end it now, admit it was a scam. On the other hand, if he could somehow solve the mystery that was obsessing Marco and his cranky friends – and solve it with his superior knowledge of human psychology – that would be rather cool, wouldn't it?

Also, there was no way he could walk away from it at this stage without seriously losing face. Josh really hated to lose face. To buy some time, he wound up just nodding in a thoughtful kind of way, aware of this Coombes guy watching his every expression.

After a moment, Coombes said, 'I understand from my...that is, from a contact of mine in the property business...that your father's planning to buy Bowermead Hall – once we persuade Lady Loony and her lower-class husband to sell.'

Wow. *They* were the people who'd put in a bid for Marco's

mates' crumbling mansion? Josh supposed it made sense, if Melcato were to take over this town, for the boss to have the nearest thing in the area to a stately home.

See...one mystery solved already.

'Oh,' he said, trying not to show much interest. 'You mean the old house back of town? Well, you know, it's a tad *small*, but I guess if we extended the place, installed a couple pools, it'd be *okay*...'

He was getting more wary now. Didn't like the penetrating way Coombes was looking at him. But if this was going to be a battle of wills, no way was Joshua Goldman going to be outclassed. It was a matter of principle.

'Meanwhile...' Coombes was still staring at him, without blinking. 'How would you like to see your sword?'

Josh blinked.

'My sword?'

'*Excalibur.*'

'Oh, *that* sword.'

'You want to see it? It may bring back lost memories. And you don't even have to pull it from a stone.'

'What?' Josh went into Arthur mode again, feeling his spine extend. 'You're saying *I* am too weak to pull the sword from a stone? Is this a challenge?'

'Sorry,' Coombes said. 'No offence intended.'

'Anyway, I figured it'd be in some museum by now.'

'We have access to museums,' Coombes said.

'We?'

'The adepts. The real controllers of Avalon. That is...until *you* take over your rightful place, of course.'

'Right.'

'Well?'

Josh fumbled the coffee cup to his mouth, if only to moisten his dry lips.

'So, where is it? The sword.'

'It's safe. I can take you there.'

'What...now?'

'Now.' Coombes rose from his chair. 'That is, unless you're afraid that your old servant woman will be *too put out.*'

'No. Not at all.' Josh was thinking hard. A battle of wills over lousy coffee in a crowded café was one thing, but he wasn't sure he wanted to go anywhere else with this guy. 'Er...how do I know it really is Excalibur?'

'You'll know as soon as you pick it up,' Coombes said, 'by the way it handles.'

'Uh...right.'

'Ah...' Coombes scrutinized him through those slitted eyes. 'You're not just a bit *afraid,* are you, Rex?'

'Me?' Josh put both hands on the table and stared back. 'You forgotten who I am, buddy?'

'Absolutely not, sire,' Coombes said.

'Okay, then.' Josh stood up. 'Let's do it.'

Course of Treatment

In Woolly's half of the stable, the divining rods were hanging on the walls like medieval weapons and the pendulums glittered from a revolving carousel that Woolly had bought from a Glastonbury jeweller's shop which had closed down.

It was a mysterious, exotic place, Woolly's half of the stable.

Merlin's straw was also kept in Woolly's side, and Woolly was sitting on a stack of bales, his short legs dangling. His face had a peaceful, faraway look, and his head was nodding, as if to the rhythm of some music only he could hear.

He didn't speak, he just smiled like some kind of guru.

'See?' Nancy howled. 'Look at him! He's so sick he can't even admit it.'

Sam inspected Woolly from the doorway, as if whatever Woolly had might be catching. Nancy had phoned for Sam to come. Sam had said he was coming anyway because things were looking bad and they needed to talk, without delay.

Dead right, Nancy had said.

Only Woolly didn't seem to appreciate the urgency. He just sat there, nodding.

'He *looks* all right,' Sam said. 'And yet...'

'He's *not* all right.' Nancy was wringing her hands, knuckles cracking. 'I've been with him for more years than I'm ever going to admit to, and I'm telling you, Sam Daniel, that Woolly Woolaston is *not all right.*'

'Well, I realize he was a bit depressed the other day, Nancy, but he does get that from time to time, don't he? Especially during the Blight.'

'This is more than just depression,' Nancy said.

'Not any more.'

This was Woolly mumbling into his T-shirt. It was an ancient Rolling Stones T-shirt with big, squashy lips on the front. Woolly's own lips, however, had hardly moved.

Sam said, 'What did he say?'

'He said "Not any more",' Marco said.

'See?' Nancy threw up her arms. 'He keeps coming out with rubbish like that!'

'It's sorted,' Woolly said, and Sam stared at him.

'What's sorted?'

Woolly stopped nodding and looked up at Sam. His eyes were blank.

'I ain't *got* depression no more. I'm fine.'

'Only he ain't,' Nancy said. 'It's like he's got somebody else inside him.'

'He *looks* like himself.'

'The truth of it is,' Nancy said, 'is he's as mad as your old man.' She turned to Woolly. '*As mad as Griff Daniel!*'

Woolly sighed.

'You don't get it, do you, Nance?' He shook his head, smiling sadly. 'Griff Daniel ain't what you think. He's a fine man. An honest and decent human being. We should be proud to have him as our mayor.'

Nancy looked at Sam.

'Look, Woolly,' Sam said. 'A joke's a joke, but this one's gone on for too long. We got serious business to discuss. The Blade of Mordred's fallen into the wrong hands. And I know it's just a knackered old sword, but if you'd seen that girl's expression when she was holding it last night, you'd want to move heaven and earth to get it buried as deep as the Dark Chalice.'

Woolly rolled his eyes. 'You need to chill out, boy. Life's too short to get uptight about things you can't do nothing about.'

'Who says we can't?'

'Why *bother*, Sammy? Why bother when the town's in such capable hands? Be thankful for your father, that's what I say. Be thankful.'

'*Now* will you believe me?' Nancy said.

Marco stared hard at Woolly. Still waiting for him to say. *Had you all fooled there, didn't I? Now let's* deal *with this.*

Woolly smiled at him. 'Don't look so scared, Marco. Everything's changed. *We must be afraid no longer!*'

'That's what *he* said.' Sam stepped fully into the stable

and shut the door behind him. 'The old man. At the meeting. He said, *We must be afraid no longer.*'

'Words of wisdom, Sammy.'

'Do something!' Nancy grabbed Sam's arm. 'Make him go to the hospital. Get him some treatment!'

'Oh,' Woolly said. 'I had that. I realized I was making life hard for you, Nance, moping round the place, so I got some treatment.'

'Treatment?' Sam's eyes narrowed. 'What kind of treatment?'

'He never did!' Nancy yelled. 'He's just trying to—'

'Nancy, man, I'm telling you I got it seen to. No more depression. I'm a contented man now, look.'

'He never went to the docs, Sammy,' Nancy said, ''cause I checked with the receptionist.'

'Course I didn't go to the docs. What do docs know?'

'Who was it then?' Sam said. 'Where'd you go, Woolly?'

'Way I sees it...' Woolly sniffed. '...a man's mental health is his own business.'

Then he cracked up laughing, but it was scary laughter. It was unnatural. Everything was out of control, going to pieces. Marco tried to think of the last time Woolly had seemed normal. Last night, before the meeting? It was. It was when they'd talked about Roger Cromwell and satanism and Woolly had said, *I just don't understand it. The bad guys are winning...and we still don't have the faintest idea how they're doing it.*

And now he didn't seem to care.

'Woolly Woolaston...' Nancy reached up to the carousel. 'If you don't wanner become the first dowser strangled by his own pendulum chain—'

'Stay cool, Nance,' Woolly said. 'I didn't wanner say anything because it was...well, it was a bit expensive, to be honest.'

'Expensive?'

Woolly looked at the floor. 'Two hundred quid, the whole course of treatment. I'm sorry. I done it for *you*, Nance. I don't normally like that kind of stuff. I don't like surrendering my will...'

Nancy and Sam moved closer to Woolly.

'Just tell us,' Sam said.

Woolly sighed so hard his breath made the pendulums shiver on their carousel.

'I went to that new feller in the Glasto Experience Arcade. Randolf Murchison?'

There was another silence.

'The hypnotherapist?' Sam said. 'You went and got yourself hypnotized?'

'Seemed like a good idea. He helps people give up bad habits. He gets rid of anxiety problems. Least...that's what it says on his advertising poster in The Carrot.'

'I can't believe this,' Nancy said. 'You went to a hypnotist without even telling me?'

'I done it for you,' Woolly said miserably.

Sam said, 'When was your last session with this feller, Woolly?'

'It'd be...yesterday afternoon?'

That fitted. Woolly had told them he'd spent the entire afternoon dowsing at King Arthur's grave to try and find out what was wrong. So he was actually in the Glastonbury Experience Arcade getting that 'look into my eyes' stuff. And yet...

'But he was *okay* afterwards,' Marco said. 'Wasn't he, Nancy? He was totally rational...until we all went to the meeting at the town hall.'

'It's true,' Nancy said, 'that's when he first went funny.'

'Right,' Sam said. 'In that case, I reckon it's time to have a chat with Mr. Randolf Murchison.'

'Look,' Woolly said. 'He didn't do nothing I hadn't paid him to do.'

'How do you know that? You were in a hypnotic trance, you daft old—'

'I don't understand, Sammy.'

'Nor do I.' Sam opened the stable door. 'Not *yet...*'

Gone

The Glastonbury Experience Arcade was down the bottom of High Street. It had spooky shops and glittery shops and grotto-type shops and mysterious doors through which you could go to consult mystics and seers, have your fortune told and your aura read.

A fascinating place with secret doors and hidden corners. When you looked up you'd see more doors, at the top of wooden steps, and when you looked down you'd sometimes find yourself walking on coloured crystals sunk into the concrete.

But today there was no time to take in the atmosphere.

'Gotter be here somewhere,' Sam said, his head swivelling

amongst the crowd of shoppers and sightseers. 'Gotter be.'

Sam's plan was to find out exactly what Murchison had done to Woolly and then get him over to Woolly's place to hypnotize him again and reverse it.

But did Sam really know what they were taking on?

'How do you know he won't get inside *your* mind?' Marco had said on the way here.

''Cause you can't be hypnotized against your will. You got to cooperate with the hypnotist or it doesn't work. However...if Woolly's *agreed* to be hypnotized to try and get rid of his depression, become a happier person, it might be possible for a hypnotist to plant something *else* in his head.'

'You mean...while Woolly's in a hypnotic trance, the hypnotist could, like, plant the idea that the mayor's a nice man?'

'Exactly. And then he tells Woolly to forget where he got it and when Woolly wakes up it's like my old man's been his best friend for years.'

'Why would he want to do that?'

'Because somebody's paying him to, Marco. Somebody who saw an opportunity to gag Woolly. And it worked.'

Now Sam was standing in the middle of the arcade looking round.

'It's our job to make Murchison reverse whatever he did. Give us the real Woolly back. Only problem is...I can't see his sign. Why can't I see his sign?'

The arcade was full of tourists, people who'd come to check out whether Glastonbury really was as weird as they'd been told. Sam looked between them and over their heads, and Marco looked too and couldn't see any sign that said anything about hypnotism.

'I thought it was here.' Sam pointed to a plain black door. 'I'm sure that was it.'

'He can't just have disappeared, can he?'

'You're kidding.' Sam said. 'People come and go all the time in Glasto. *Damn...*'

'But if he was here yesterday...'

'Hang on, I'll ask Sadie.'

Sam turned the iron ring on the next door along, which was orange and pink. This one did have a sign:

The Scented Cauldron...
Balm for the body, serenity for the spirit.

Only, the door didn't open. Sam rattled the handle, but it wouldn't turn. He banged on the panels with the flat of his hand.

'Sadie? You in there? Open up!'

'Huh!' A passing woman in a long dress glared at Sam over her sunglasses. 'That's *true* serenity of the spirit.'

'Yeah.' Sam went on banging. 'I've come for my money back. Come on, Sadie!'

'Who's that?' a voice said from inside.

'It's Sam Daniel. From the print shop. Come on, Sadie, we ain't gonner keep you a minute.'

There was the sound of a big key turning in a big lock and then the door opened and a woman stuck her head out.

'Sam?'

She was wearing a black kimono with golden birds on it. Her hair was the colour of a ripe tomato. Her eyes were swollen and her make-up was blotched all over her face like a paint chart.

Sam put his head on one side. 'What's wrong Sadie?'

'Everything,' Sadie said.

She stepped back and they went into a small room lit by an orange oriental lantern. Its light glistened off rows of coloured bottles on rickety shelves. There was a long, low couch in the middle of the room and Sadie heaved herself onto it.

'My life is over, Sam. Shattered! Destroyed!'

She waved a hand, dabbing at her eyes with a handkerchief in the other. The air was full of a horrible sickly pong.

'Sorry to hear that, Sadie,' Sam said. 'Only, we need a bit of help, look.'

'I've taken the day off.'

'I don't mean treatment,' Sam said. 'Randolf Murchison – his shop seems to have disappeared.'

'*Oooooooooo!*' Sadie dumped her head into her hands and her shoulders began to heave. 'You think I don't know that?'

'When did he go?'

'I don't *know*. I came in this morning, just after ten, and his sign had been taken down and his curtains were drawn. He's just gone, Sam. *Gone, gone, gone!*'

'He'd done a bunk overnight?'

'He was going to take me with him! He was the best thing that ever happened to me, Sam.'

'This week, anyway,' Sam murmured.

Marco suddenly felt sick, and it wasn't only the smell. If this Murchison had hypnotized Woolly and planted all kinds of weird stuff in his head and then disappeared, who was going to take it away? Did this mean Woolly would be damaged for life?

'You don't understand!' Sadie sobbed. 'It was the real thing this time! He was so handsome and generous. And he was doing so *well*...'

'So well he obviously couldn't afford to pay his rent,' Sam said.

'That's not true!' Sadie's head came out of her hands. Her eyes were completely dry. 'He was making a lot of money. Hypnotherapy is a very lucrative business, and he was brilliant at it. He could stop people smoking, he could give them more confidence, make them more relaxed. He had a whole string of clients...important people.'

'Football stars?' Sam said. 'TV cooks?'

'I mean *really* important people. Your father, the mayor... Mr. Cotton, the solicitor...Mr. Coombes, the estate agent. The sort of people who would never normally come to a place like this. People who—'

'Say that again.' Sam's whole body had gone rigid. Sadie looked at him, blinking.

'The mayor..?'

'And Cotton? And Coombes? They all came to see Murchison? When was this?'

'Last week...the week before...I don't know. Time goes haywire when you're in love.'

'Who else? Who else came to see him?'

'Oh...lots of people you'd never expect. Mr. Coombes even brought his son.'

Sam and Marco stood there in silence, staring at one another.

'Holy Joseph,' Sam said quietly. 'This could explain everything. Thanks, Sadie.'

'What have I said?' Sadie scrambled off the couch. 'What's *happening*?'

'I don't know. But I think we're on the verge of finding out. Come on, Marco...'

'Where are we going?'

'We're calling an emergency meeting of the Watchers of Avalon. Right now.'

His long hair streaming behind him, Sam stormed out of the door of The Scented Cauldron, through the tourist crowds in the Glastonbury Experience Arcade and back on to High Street.

The sun was out, bouncing off the red-tiled roofs, softening the old stone in the walls of The Pilgrims. There was a yellow haze over the town and Marco was tossed into that wobbly state of mind where you were here, but *more* than here. Like you'd become part of the town, all its colours glowing in the centre of your head.

Maybe Sam was the same. He was moving as if he was in a trance, almost knocking over a bloke dressed as a Russian priest with a tall hat, going, 'Sorry, sorry,' as he ran up the street, pushing between people, with Marco rushing after him, trying to put the pieces together: *the mayor...Mr. Cotton, the solicitor...Mr. Coombes...even brought his son...*

'Sam...does this mean...? *Ooooof!*'

He hadn't been looking where he was going and he'd gone smack into a giant brown carrier bag in the arms of a woman hurrying down High Street. The bag felt like it was full of bricks and Marco stopped, winded, and the colours faded.

'I'm sorry,' the woman said, 'but if you must go dashing around like— Marcus? *Marcus!* It *is* Marcus, isn't it?'

'Marco.' Clutching his chest, Marco looked up into a pair of giant sunglasses. 'Mrs. Goldman?'

'Have you seen Joshua?'

'No. Not since last night, anyway.'

Josh. With all the worry about Woolly and Rosa and the Blade of Mordred, he'd forgotten all about Josh. Josh was going to be seriously hacked off with him by now, but that was hardly important compared with—

'He's vanished,' Mrs. Goldman said.

'Vanished? Josh doesn't *vanish*.'

'I'm telling you he's gone. He told me he was going to find somewhere for us to have lunch, and that was an hour ago.'

'Well, I'm sure...' Marco could see Sam further up the street, motioning to him to get his ass in gear. 'I mean, he's probably...'

'Marcus, this is *Glastonbury*. Anything can happen here! He could have been kidnapped by some weird *cult*!'

Offhand, it was hard to think of a cult weird enough to want Josh. So, unless he'd gone off with Randolf Murchison to discuss the use of hypnotism in practical psychiatry, Marco didn't see any immediate cause for panic.

'Look, Mrs. Goldman, I'm sorry, but I have to split. We've got a really heavy scene here.'

'*Heavy scene?*'

Mrs. Goldman dropped her carrier bag.

The bag just missed Marco's left foot. It hit the pavement with a crunch. Mrs. Goldman grabbed both Marco's shoulders with hands which, for an old lady, were surprisingly strong and sinewy.

He felt his feet almost leaving the ground; it was like being snatched up by a giant bird of prey.

'As far as *I'm* concerned...' Mrs. Goldman put her face close up to Marco's. '...the only *heavy scene* is the disappearance of my grandson. And *you*, sonny – as his so-called *best friend* and the sole reason he decided he had to come here – are going to help me find him.'

Coiled Serpent

Once outside the café, Jasper Coombes whizzed Josh into the crowd of shoppers and up the street, across the main road and down an alleyway.

It took about thirty seconds, and when they were out of the crowd Josh noticed there were now two other guys with Coombes: a tall, thin kid with a shaven head and the squat, red-haired kid with dull, hostile eyes and a face with more craters than the dark side of the moon.

'This is Shane,' Coombes said, 'and Jezza. Consider them your minders.'

The two boys just stared at him and didn't speak.

Minders? What did he need minders for?

'Oh, I'm sorry,' Coombes said. 'The term is probably unfamiliar to you, as an American. It means bodyguard. This can be a dangerous town.'

While he was talking, he'd opened a door at the rear of a derelict-looking building, and now they were inside and looking at stone steps.

Steps leading down into what looked like absolute darkness.

Josh was aware of being sandwiched between Coombes and the two heavies right behind him. There was no way he could turn back, much as he wanted to, seeing there was no light down here and the air smelled thick and dusty.

He followed Coombes down, and the dust went into his nose and he sneezed.

'Bless you, Rex.' Coombes giggled, almost shrilly. 'In a manner of speaking.'

The two guys behind him also giggled, as Josh stumbled on the steps. Oh, this was totally ridiculous. Less than five minutes ago they'd been sitting in the stupid café, and now he had absolutely no idea where he was, and...

...and neither had anyone else.

Grandma Goldman would have left the shop by now, with her bags full of useless crystals. She'd be looking for him.

And Grandma Goldman was a woman not known for her patience. And she—

'*Aaaah!*'

The steps had ended unexpectedly, and Josh's feet had landed on solid ground with a jarring sensation he could feel all the way to the top of his head.

What was he doing here? Why in the name of all that was

psychologically acceptable had he gone along with this? Okay, back in The Cosmic Carrot, it had seemed worth a shot, but now it seemed like...madness.

Madness. The worst fear a psychiatrist could ever experience was the fear that he himself might be going mad. Losing control of his well-oiled, precision-tooled mind.

In those ridiculous e-mails, Marco had suggested that this town could have strange effects on people's minds.

Which was rubbish, of course. Utter, superstitious nonsense. It was just that when you couldn't see a millimetre in front of your face...

'Where are w—?' Josh was disgusted at how weak his voice sounded. He cleared his throat. 'Where exactly are we, Coombes?'

It was pitch-black. He could feel hot breath on the back of his neck. The appalling Shane and Jezza. Why didn't they just back off? Josh hated being crowded.

'Coombes?'

'Stay cool, sire. All will be revealed.'

'What is this place?'

'This? This is part of the Glastonbury labyrinth. The easy part, you'll be glad to know. No crawling on your hands and knees through damp tunnels.'

'*What?*'

Josh stumbled after Coombes. Of course, he knew all about the Glastonbury labyrinth from Marco's e-mails. Marco had done the crawling on the hands and knees bit, and he'd said it had nearly killed him, although Josh had been convinced Marco had been totally exaggerating, may even have made it all up.

Evidently not.

Whatever, Rex Arturus wouldn't know any of this. It was safest to sound ignorant.

'The real power is down here,' Coombes said. 'The secret energy of Avalon was long ago diverted underground. It lies under the streets – under the Abbey, under the Tor – like a great, coiled serpent, waiting to be awoken.'

'A serpent,' Josh said. 'Right.' Wasn't the serpent a symbol that religious people associated with, um, the Devil?

'The dark serpent could be your servant,' Coombes said.

'Cool,' Josh said.

Dark serpent?

Behind him there was a snigger from Shane or Jezza. He walked on in total darkness, stretching out his arms to feel for a wall on either side, but he felt nothing but cold air.

And the air *was* cold now. Josh felt goosebumps rising below the short sleeves of his *Sigmund Freud Rocks* T-shirt. He pulled in his arms and hugged himself instead.

'Don't suppose any of you guys thought to bring a flashlight?'

'We know our way,' Coomes said. 'Besides, darkness is an important part of the initiation ceremony. It's about sensory deprivation. Your mind must cast off all associations with the outside world.'

Initiation ceremony?

'Makes sense,' Josh said nervously. 'Certainly in some primitive cultures—'

'Only then can you reclaim your kingdom,' Coombes said. 'But you knew that, surely?'

The hell he did. This time Josh said nothing. Ignorant was safe, right?

'I just assumed you'd know,' Coombes said, 'as, of course, a degree of sensory deprivation is what's recommended for someone advanced enough to reach Level 29 in the Arturus Rex cycle.'

'Right,' Josh said.

Uh oh. He'd only had time to reach Level 22 before he'd had to abandon the game. Naturally, he *would* have made Level 29, no problem, if he'd just had one more day before having to leave for Glastonbury.

There was silence. In total darkness, silence was totally unnerving. Josh clenched both fists, feeling his nails piercing his palms. He could almost feel the dark serpents uncoiling around his feet.

Coombes laughed.

'Glad you haven't forgotten your own game. So you'll realize why, in a couple of minutes, we're going to have to blindfold you.'

Cold panic streaked through Josh's insides.

'How about if I just close my eyes?'

Jasper and Shane and Jezza all laughed, for quite a long time.

Making it pretty clear that Josh wasn't going to get away with just closing his eyes.

Despite the cold, he began to sweat.

Take Away the Evil

'**R**osa. Come in here, would you?'
Oh no.

Dad was waiting for her in the kitchen. White dog collar, black cassock, no sign of a smile behind the black beard.

'I want to talk to you.'

She'd been hoping against all hope that he wouldn't come back after his Holy Communion service. If he didn't come back until tonight, maybe, just maybe, Sam and Eleri would have found the sword and she wouldn't have to explain why it was missing from the tennis bag in the cupboard on the landing.

Her only fallback idea had been to say she'd gone out

early for a walk and must've left the front door unlocked –
so somebody could have slipped in and stolen the sword.
That way, in his eyes she'd only be guilty of carelessness,
rather than something that would throw him into one of his
rages.

She had no idea what she was going to do now. From the
doorway, she could see that he'd cleared the kitchen table
apart from some of his religious kit – a leather-bound Bible
and a black case, like a doctor's bag.

'Rosa...' Dad's eyes had softened. 'Don't look like that.'

'Like what?'

'As if you're half-terrified. *I'd* never do anything to
frighten you. You do know that. I'm your dad.'

His voice had softened, too. The old northern accent was
back. He'd gone a bit posh lately, especially when he was
preaching in the church.

'Come and sit down,' Dad said. 'Look, *I'm* sorry if I seem
to be angry all the time. I don't want to be. That's not what
Christianity's about at all, is it? What it's about – what it
should be about – is love. And healing.'

'Healing,' Rosa said.

'A word that's become devalued in this town, I'm afraid.
All these pagans who think they can heal the sick by banging
a giant gong or spreading folks' bodies with smelly liquid
and surrounding them with bits of crystal.'

Rosa didn't say anything. She rather liked the idea of
people being healed by giant gongs and crystals. Not as scary
as being pumped full of drugs and connected to tubes,
was it?

'Anything but prayer, eh?' Dad said. 'So many people in
this town would rather do something exotic than go into

church and kneel down and ask for God's help.'

'Maybe that's just their *way* of asking for God's—'

Rosa shut her mouth, seeing his eyes hardening up again. She sat down at the kitchen table.

'The sword,' Dad said. 'I want to talk to you about the sword.'

Rosa froze.

'For some reason, whether it's Excalibur or not, people have started to become afraid of that sword. Are *you* afraid of it?'

Rosa shrugged.

'*Are* you?'

'Yes,' Rosa said.

'Why?'

'I don't know.'

Dad shook his head sadly.

'Well, if you don't mind me saying so, that's just typical, of you lately. *I don't know.*'

'Well, you know, it's not something I can—'

'The truth of the matter is, Rosa, that it's *pure superstition.* An ancient sword gets discovered and daft people start talking about old legends.'

Rosa said nothing.

'Now, I don't actually know how the fire in Mr. Montague's house was really started, but it wasn't started by a sword, was it?'

Rosa said nothing.

'However, I've come to realize that me simply standing up and rubbishing superstition is not enough. I'm an ordained priest, and my job is to deal not only with evil but with what people *think of* as evil.'

'So you don't really believe—'

'Not for one minute, girl. But I'm also a father, and my job as a father is to make sure my child feels secure.'

Oh no... She stared at him. *What was he going to do?*

'Fetch the sword, Rosa.'

'What?'

'It'll be going to a museum before the day's out, but I realize that just letting it go and washing my hands of the situation is not good enough. So you go and fetch it, while I prepare things in here. It's in the old tennis racquet case in the cupboard on the landing. It's not all that heavy, as you know.'

Rosa didn't move. She *couldn't* move.

'Why...why do you want it?'

Dad folded his arms and smiled at last.

'I'm going to ask God to take away the evil.'

'Dad—'

'I have a Bible here and, in this case, I have two flasks of holy water, fresh from the church. It's my intention, right here on this table, to perform a cleansing of the sword followed by a blessing.'

Dad beamed.

'That ought to sort it, don't you think? I can guarantee that by the time we've finished, me and God, you won't have a thing to worry about. How's that?'

'But—'

'Come on!' Dad clapped his big hands together. 'Chop chop. Let's get this show on the road.'

He came at her, waving his arms in the funny way he used to do when she was little, and she had to get up and back out of the door.

'Give me two minutes to compose myself and say a little prayer,' Dad said.

Rosa went up the stairs and stood on the landing, eyes squeezed shut in anguish.

Oh God. Help me.

'In the cupboard!' Dad shouted. 'Bottom shelf.'

Numbly, Rosa opened the door of the big cupboard. There was the tennis bag, as she'd known it would be, on the bottom shelf.

She reached out and touched it, half expecting the sword to have come back by itself, which would be horrible, but at least it would get her out of this mess.

But the bag lay exactly where she'd left it, soft and floppy and unzipped and entirely...

...empty.

Rosa tried to cry out, 'Da—'

Dad! It's gone! The sword's not here! Somebody must've got in and taken—

She heard the words in her head and how feeble and unconvincing they sounded.

She pulled the long, canvas bag out of the cupboard.

'Okay, Rosa,' Dad called out cheerfully. 'I'm ready now.'

Rosa clutched the bag to her chest for a moment and then, choking back a bitter sob, stumbled down the stairs with it.

When she reached the bottom, the sob broke through from somewhere, and Rosa carried the empty bag along the passage and then, fumbling open the front door, ran out into the crowded street and kept on running.

Stupid Game

Sam had run out of patience.

'All right, look, Marco. You stay and help Mrs. Goldman find her grandson.'

'But, Sam...what about Woolly?'

'I'll do what I can to help Woolly. Not sure how, seeing as we're not likely to find Murchison, but— Anyway, you got more of a chance of finding this boy, so—'

'We'd *better*,' Granny Goldman said, still gripping Marco's arm.

'And then you can walk back up to Woolly's, all right? Gotter go, Marco. I'm beginning to see what's been happening in this town...'

Marco watched Sam walking away up the street. How come, whenever Josh was on the scene, everything went pear-shaped? He was probably in some second-hand bookshop, in the section marked Psychiatry, where nobody else had been in years.

Marco looked up at Mrs. Goldman, sighing.

'Where did Josh *say* he was going?'

'He *said* he was going to find us somewhere to have lunch.'

That figured. Lunch was Josh's other specialist subject. Granny Goldman pointed across the road at The Cosmic Carrot.

'What about that place?'

'Not a chance,' Marco said. 'It's all vegetarian. And it's full of...people Josh wouldn't get on with.'

'We'll check it out anyway.'

Mrs. Goldman steered Marco between a tour coach and a purple hearse waiting at the traffic lights and propelled him into The Cosmic Carrot...where they were spotted at once by Woolly's mate, Orf, who was named after a sheep disease and had a tree tattooed across his chest.

'Yo, Marco!' Orf forked up some green slush from his plate. 'What's happening, man?'

'Hey, Orf.' Marco wandered over. 'We're looking for this guy about my age, wearing glasses.'

'Which he doesn't need to wear at all,' Mrs. Goldman snapped, 'because his eyes are perfect.'

'I'm with you.' Orf pondered, chewing. 'Hey, Rox, was there a four-eyed kid about Marco's age in here? I don't remember.'

Rox wiped her fingers on her MEAT IS MURDER apron.

'American, right?'

American? Josh? Marco's heart sank.

'Hmm,' Mrs. Goldman said. 'What did this boy do?'

'Just ordered a coffee,' Rox said. 'Black. And then he went to sit down at that table by the window, and he was looking at everybody and kind of smirking.'

Marco was relieved. It *was* Josh.

'And then Jasper Coombes came in. Which was a bit odd because Jasper Coombes never comes in here. Anyway, he went to sit with this boy, and they were talking for a long time and then they got up and left.'

'Where did they go?'

'No idea, but the kids were following them.'

'Which kids?' Granny Goldman snapped.

'Queenie's kids. They're over there.'

Three kids, aged about eight or nine, were sitting at a table excavating king-sized, carob-flavoured, soya ice-cream specials. Rox called across to the oldest-looking one.

'Bilbo, were you following the boy with the glasses in the clean T-shirt?'

'You mean Rex Arturus?'

Rex Arturus? Marco stared at Bilbo, who had a carob-cream moustache and a London accent. Mrs. Goldman immediately moved in on him.

'Where'd he go, kid?' Her accent had changed. 'I need to know. I'm his...I'm his grammaw.'

Bilbo put down his spoon.

'You're actually Rex Arturus's gran?'

'Call me Gloria. And tell me where you last saw him.' Mrs. Goldman dumped her bag of rocks on the table, making all the dishes wobble. 'And make it the truth.'

'Or what?' Bilbo said.

'Or you and your associates don't get another double-helping of that disgusting slush.'

Bilbo considered the offer.

'How about Rex Arturus's autograph,' he said. 'As well.'

'You drive a hard bargain, kid.' Mrs. Goldman snatched up her bag of rocks. 'But why didn't you just *ask* him for his autograph?'

'Well, because he...didn't look all that friendly,' Bilbo said. 'Know what I mean?'

Marco nodded. It was *definitely* Josh. But why would they think he was—?

'Kid,' Mrs. Goldman said in the same excruciating American accent, 'you show me where my boy went and I'll get you a signed photo.'

'Cool.' Bilbo sniffed and wiped some carob ice off his nose ring. 'I'll show you where we last saw them, okay? We cleared off quick, though, 'cause Shane Davey was with them, and, like, you just don't hang around if Shane's there. Everybody knows that.'

Marco tensed.

'Plus, where they went,' Bilbo said, 'it looked a bit scary down there. Know what I mean?'

Rosa was standing opposite the Post Office, at the distinct point where the weird High Street became the normal High Street, with ordinary shops taking over from the ones that sold ritual candles and pagan fridge-magnets.

The people seemed to change, too, at this end of the street. More men in suits and farmer-types in tweeds and mums with prams and only one guy with long hair and an earring and—

'Sam!'

'Rosa.' He stopped, panting. 'I was hoping to see you. You all right, girl?'

'Not really.'

She saw him looking down at the tennis bag, his eyes widening.

'Oh hell, Rosa, you haven't found—'

'No. That's the trouble. Dad was going to bless it, with holy water and stuff, and he asked me to go and get it, and...and of course I knew it wasn't there, so I just grabbed the empty bag and ran out.'

Rosa looked up at Sam, felt her bottom lip starting to quiver.

'When was this, Rosa?'

'Just now. About twenty minutes ago. I don't know what to do, Sam. I don't know where to go. Now, he'll think I've just taken the sword. He'll think I took it away because I didn't want it to have a Christian blessing.'

'That's a difficult situation,' Sam admitted. 'Because he's—'

'Difficult? I'm *dead*, Sam. I can't go home. He'll think I wanted to stop him taking away the evil. He'll think I've sold my soul to...to... Oh, why couldn't he still be a policeman?'

'One of us needs to have a word with him,' Sam said. 'Only there's no time right now. Maybe you should just go back and—'

'I *can't* go back. Please—'

'All right.' Sam dropped a hand on her shoulder. 'You better come with me.'

'Where are we going?'

Sam didn't answer. He stood for a moment, looking down the hill into the town centre, which looked so normal, scores of people criss-crossing and their thoughts...their thoughts were spraying out in all directions; Rosa imagined she could see the thoughts like multicoloured ribbons, most of them not very long, soon dissolving. She shook herself: what was happening to her these days?

Sam said, 'The thing is, he's right.'

'My dad?'

'Something does need doing with that sword before it takes a life. I saw your face when you were holding it over that boy.'

Rosa shuddered. 'Don't!'

'It wasn't you.'

'Who...who was it?'

Sam turned away. 'Come on, Rosa.'

Marco and Granny Goldman followed the kid up through the streets, Granny Goldman still carrying the bag of rock crystals, Marco looking at her, puzzled.

'Why does he think Josh is Rex Arturus?'

'It was a game, Marco. A silly scam he was pulling on the mayor. Trying to be clever. I don't know what came over him – he isn't *always* like that.'

'No.' Marco grinned. 'Sometimes he has to sleep.'

'What?'

'Nothing.'

'This is it, Gloria,' Bilbo said. 'That building at the bottom.'

They were up above the town centre, not far from the

Chalice Well gardens, where it was said the Holy Grail had been taken and the water ran red. The backstreet they were in had a few garages and what looked like some kind of derelict industrial building with concrete walls, half hidden by untamed trees and bushes.

'They took him in there?' Grandma Goldman said. 'Are you telling us the truth, Bilbo?'

She'd forgotten to put on her American accent, but Bilbo didn't seem to notice. He kept looking nervously around – he really *did* know Shane Davey, didn't he?

'Can I go now?'

'Yes, all right.' Granny Goldman gave him a five pound note. 'And you'd better be—'

But Bilbo had gone.

There was only one door in the building. Its wooden panels had rotted at the bottom. Marco pushed at it, and it opened with a grinding crunch and stood shivering on its hinges.

Granny Goldman made no immediate move to go in.

'Marco, this boy Joshua was with...you know him?'

Marco nodded.

'And?'

'He's bad news, Mrs. Goldman.'

'Gloria. Call me Gloria.'

'He's *very* bad news, Gloria, and he gets away with it because he's smooth and good-looking. And his friend Shane's a psycho.'

Gloria Goldman leaned back against the concrete wall. It was thick with dust and cobwebs, and some gunge came off on her frock. She didn't seem to notice. Eventually, she went to stand in the doorway, looking inside, into darkness.

'What's really going on in this town, Marco?'

Marco rolled his eyes. How long had she *got*?

He followed her inside, telling her what he could about Jasper's satanic leanings and what had happened to Woolly. They were in what looked like a storeroom. It had no windows, but with the door open there was enough light to see a flight of stone steps, with an iron rail, heading down into a cellar.

Oh no.

'This isn't good,' Marco said. 'A lot of these cellars used to lead into the labyrinth.'

'What's that?'

'It's this maze of old passageways under the streets. You don't want to go down there, Gloria, trust me. Some of the passages are so low and so narrow only little kids can get through.'

Grandma Goldman moved to the stairs.

'Joshua's not such a little kid.'

'No. That could be a problem. See, it's hard to get out once you're in. There are so many different ways you can turn that you just get lost in no time. And the roof's not safe, it can all come down on you – like, tons and tons of earth and rocks. And it's dark.'

Gloria pointed to the steps.

'Which of us goes first?'

'But there's no *light.*'

'Not a problem.' Gloria shoved the bag of crystals at Marco. 'Hold these.' She dived into her handbag and brought out car keys. 'Used to have a Porsche key ring, but it seemed like showing off, so I swapped it for something more practical.'

It was one of those key rings with a tiny torch bulb, about the size of a mouse's eye. It would probably light an area of less than half a metre in front of your face. If the tiny battery was new.

Marco's claustrophobia, his long-time fear of confined spaces, came out in a sudden cold sweat. He stared with desperation, past Granny Goldman, at the rectangle of pale daylight outside the door frame.

'Okay, let's go down,' the old lady said.

The Final Stage

The echoes were back, and they were bigger.

For a while, there had been no echo at all, and Josh had felt the warmth of the sun on his arms and the softness of grass under his feet.

He'd trodden extra carefully. He'd never trusted grass, unless it was well-mown. This grass was long and scratchy, and the ground sloped up, and he could hear birdsong and the comforting sound of distant traffic, but it didn't last long.

Because now they were inside again, only inside something bigger.

Vast, even. The echoes had told him that.

'Could you take this off now, please?' Josh said. 'The...
blindfold?'

Except it was more than a blindfold.

It had been close to the end of the tunnel, when the first
light began to show, that they'd made him put on the black
fleece hoody.

Put it on back to front, so that he was staring blindly into
the hood.

And then they'd tied it behind his neck, so it felt like his
head was inside a thick bag. And they'd zipped it up, so that
his arms were trapped. And knotted the sleeves tightly
behind his back like...like one of those...

...straitjackets!

As worn by unstable psychiatric patients, in the old days
before proper mental health procedures were introduced...

...back in the days when psychiatric patients were known
as *lunatics* and kept in *asylums.*

And they'd done this to *him*...Joshua Goldman,
psychoanalyst. What kind of sick joke *was* this?

He was furious. Totally, *totally* furious.

Furious rather than scared. No question about that. He
was definitely *not scared, okay?*

'I said, can't you get me out of this?'

'Not yet, Rex.'

Josh stiffened. It was a different voice. A man's voice.
A deep voice, low and even, laid-back and sure of itself.

Wherever they were, this man had been waiting here for
them.

'Who are you?' Josh said.

The only answer was a deeper silence. Josh sucked in
wool from the back-to-front hood and started to gag. His

glasses had come off and were trapped under his chin. He felt smothered, stifled. He could suffocate.

'Who are you?' He was almost screaming now. 'Just tell me who you are.'

The voice rang from above, like an old bell in a stone tower.

'Think of me as your magical mentor. Your teacher. Can you put a name to me, Rex?'

Josh shook his head, spitting out wool.

'I can't think at all with this... Just let me out...*please...*'

'Try. A name. The name of your earliest tutor.'

'I don't *know*.'

Josh clenched and unclenched his fists. This was just claustrophobia. It *definitely* wasn't fear. He could control it, right?

'You *do* know. Say it.'

It was ridiculous, but he said it. 'Merlin?'

Hands began to clap around him.

Josh spun round, helpless. He was encircled by clapping hands, and it wasn't pleasant. It was kind of mocking, and he was glad when it stopped.

'Long ago,' the man's voice said, as the echoes died, 'before you were born – before you were born the *first time* – there was a castle on the Tor which, in those days, was a high place of the old religion. This was long before they tried to build a church on it and the church fell down, leaving only the tower – the dark finger that once more proclaims its origins. You learned of this...do you remember?'

Josh said nothing. Maybe he was handling this all wrong. He tried to work out how Rex Arturus would react to being kidnapped and kept in the dark.

A degree of sensory deprivation is what's recommended for someone advanced enough to reach Level 29 in the Arturus Rex cycle.

Maybe, knowing this, Rex would be less suspicious and therefore less perturbed about the situation than Joshua Goldman. Maybe Rex would even enjoy it, flattered that someone had taken the trouble to recreate his own computer game in the real world.

Josh tried to take a deep breath without swallowing any more wool.

'Glad to meet ya, Merlin,' he said, knowing it was coming out as muffled mumble. 'Been a long time.'

'A very long time, Rex. We were always gratified to see how you absorbed the messages you were sent.'

Huh?

Messages? Messages from Merlin? Messages from some guy who thought he was Merlin? How crazy was this?

'You were one of the few who understood that the Internet had become a fourth dimension, allowing the distant past to enter what the less enlightened ones think of as the present.'

Josh had heard this before, and it was total garbage. There was nothing other-worldly about the internet. It was just a predictable development in computer science.

'And because you were open to the etheric nature of magic, thus were you able to learn of your true heritage. You have travelled far to discover your kingdom.'

'All the way from Santa Cruz, California,' Josh said.

It sounded ridiculous.

'Yes. To finally become transformed from Rex Arturus into Arturus Rex. And now comes the final stage.'

'Good,' Josh said. 'Does it just happen inside my head or do I get to watch?'

A low rumbling had started up somewhere. Like a motor.

'Rex, you get to participate. Do you know where you are?'

'No.'

'Guess.'

'It sounds like...a theatre or something.'

'Try again.'

'A...a cave? A big cave?'

That figured. They'd come in directly off the grass. On a hillside. It *had* to be a...

Josh went tight inside. The images came up in his head. The images from the computer screen: the iron-studded door, the copper-studded door, the silver-studded door... The end of the quest.

Yes, I am pure of heart and strong in valour. I shall fight for the holiest of the holy, even unto death.

'The door in the hillside,' Josh said. 'We came through the door in the hillside?'

The circle of clapping began again, all around him.

'We're inside the hill? Inside the Tor?'

'Close,' the man's voice said. 'Very close.'

'So, like...where are we... *Where are we, Merlin?*'

'I taught you about the Lord of the Dead. This is his chamber. A place of transition. A place where the living may come to meet the dead. And where the dead may prepare to rejoin the living.'

Josh said nothing. This was total insanity. And yet, as Merlin spoke, his mind was already creating a huge, shadowed temple with shapes flitting within the shadows.

'A place of death,' Merlin whispered. 'Welcome, sire.

Welcome to your final challenge. Give him wine.'

Josh almost sobbed with relief. They were going to release him from his straitjacket. Thank God, thank—

'*Uuuuuuurgh!*'

His head was rocked back by the force of it.

It must have been a whole bucketful and it was cold. It soaked through the hood, into his eyes and up his nose and into his open mouth, sweet and sticky. It was disgusting, and it left Josh retching and sinking down on his knees, snuffling and smarting and blinded.

Meanwhile, the clapping resumed, rhythmic and muted, and the background motor rumbled on, overlaid with the deep tolling bell that was the voice of Merlin.

'Arthur died. Arthur died fighting, his head cleft by the blade, his lifeblood soaking into the field of battle. And his body was brought to Avalon, where it was said he would rise again. Are *you* the king that would rise again?'

Even if there was anything he could say to this, Josh couldn't speak. His face was soaked by wine and tears. And the voice boomed on.

'Speak, Rex! Your people cry out to you! Can't you hear them? A whole community has grown around your myth. Thousands have travelled here – pilgrims, drawn by the legend of The Once and Future King. A town built on legends. Will you give them the reality they crave after all these years of fantasy? Will you fight for your heritage?'

Josh's nose was running and his sightless eyes were full of the sticky, stinging wine.

'Will you fight, boy? *Will you?*'

'*Yeeeeeeees!*' Josh rolled on the hard floor, over and over, squirming and snuffling. '*Whatever! Just get me out of this...*'

The voice rose in triumph. 'He will fight!'

Hands seized Josh. He was dragged to his feet. The sodden cloth was ripped from his face, and he heard his glasses tinkling to the ground, as he opened his smarting eyes...

...into a savage blast of searing white light.

The voice bellowing out of it like a voice from the sun.

'Arturus!'

Josh tried to shield his eyes, but strong hands held his arms behind his back, and his head was held painfully by the hair.

It just...never ended. What were they trying to *do* to him?

'What?' he screamed. '*What?*'

'*Death...*' The voice had gone low, almost a hiss, like steam rising from the heat of the light. 'Death came to you last time from the Blade of Mordred. Do you remember, Arturus?'

'I don't—'

His head was wrenched back by the hair.

Agony.

'Do you remember the blade that split your skull?'

Josh sobbed. His skull felt like it was being split right now.

'Can you win back your life, Arturus?'

'I don't even understand what y—'

'Can you relive the last battle...and survive?'

'*I...*' His head was full of pain and his eyes were full of blinding light. '*All right! Yeeees!*'

They let him go.

Whoever was holding his hair let go and – wet, cold, shivering – he was able at last to look down, out of the brutal light.

At what someone had pressed into his right hand.

'No...look...' Josh's voice rose in panic. 'I don't *do* this!'

Bent Twigs

No sooner had Sam said, 'I wish we could find Eleri', than she was there. They were on their way to Woolly's cottage, in Sam's Land Rover, when Rosa spotted her walking briskly up Wellhouse Lane.

Sam had told Rosa about this Rex Arturus and the Melcato Corporation, and her mind was humming – on overload. Eleri also looked full of nervous energy, her eyes burning, her cheeks flushed. She'd even taken off her cloak and was carrying it over her arm.

'I am needed, I think.' Eleri climbed into the Land Rover as if it was a bus she'd been expecting. She was wearing a flimsy white dress and lots of jewellery. 'I had a feeling of Woolly...in a grey mist.'

'You're on the money there, all right, Eleri,' Sam said. 'You know much about hypnotism?'

'Ah, *mesmerism.*'

'No, *hypno*—'

'It's the same thing. When I was studying it, we preferred to call it mesmerism, after its greatest exponent, Anton Mesmer.'

'When you say studying it...?' Sam turned into the track that led to Woolly and Nancy's isolated cottage. 'Does that mean...?'

'It was a long time ago, Sam. I'm probably not as good at it as I used to be.'

Sam's face lit up. 'You can *do* it?'

'Anyone can do it,' Eleri said. 'If they're prepared to work at it. Why...what exactly is the problem?'

The problem was sitting astride one of the kitchen chairs, turned the wrong way round, his chin on his arms over the backrest. He kept nodding his head like one of those plastic bulldogs on a car shelf and smiling like there was nothing at all wrong.

Eleri pulled up a chair opposite him and looked into his eyes.

'How long has he been like this?'

'Since last night.' Nancy's voice was uneven. 'Only it's getting worse all the time. Oh, Eleri, everything's falling to pieces...*look* at him. I'm so *afraid.*'

Woolly looked up at her sharply.

'We have been afraid too long,' he said. He looked down

at his Rolling Stones T-shirt as if he couldn't work out why he was wearing such a thing. '*Too long.*'

'Oh God,' Nancy said.

Rosa felt so sorry for Nancy. Her eyes were hot-looking and tired. She was a really nice, homely sort of person and, underneath all that wild hair and make-up, she was an *ordinary* person.

Dad didn't seem to understand that the *alternative* people were not alternative at all underneath. He thought anybody who didn't look like his idea of normal must be either high on drugs or on their way to some pagan sabbath.

Rosa looked around. The kitchen was like some kind of sickroom. Diane was here, too, trying to pour tea into all sorts of weird-shaped mugs on the table in between piles of books and old vinyl LPs.

'Throw them old records in the bin if they're in your way,' Woolly said. 'Don't know how I could ever listen to that racket.'

He looked like an elderly baby in a high chair, but it was Nancy who began to whimper. Even Rosa, who'd only been here a few minutes, could tell Woolly was getting worse.

Sam had told them how Randolf Murchison, the hypnotherapist, had cleared off, leaving Woolly still under his influence. All the time Sam was talking, Woolly just sat there shaking his head and smiling faintly as if he wasn't really hearing any of it.

'That is *so* irresponsible,' Diane said. 'Surely there's a code of practice for hypnotists? It's people like Murchison who make me afraid for this town.'

'We been afraid too long, that's the trouble.' Woolly looked across at Diane. 'Here, don't you go doing them menial jobs, Your Ladyship. Leave it to the peasants.'

'You need help, Woolly,' Sam said. 'Just admit it, that's all it needs for Eleri to get started.'

Woolly looked at Diane again and then back at Sam.

'*You* landed on your feet, didn't you, Sammy? Big house, titled wife. But you'll never be the man your dad is.'

'Woolly,' Sam said patiently, 'you went to Murchison. You let him into your mind.'

'Rubbish, boy. Plain daft. If I was being fed bad stuff, I'd've known, wouldn't I?'

'No, Woolly, you agreed to it, look.'

'Load of old rubbish, anyway. No such thing as hypnotism.'

'You need help, Woolly. You been got at.'

'Got at? You're all daft. Plain bonkers, the lot of you. You should listen to the mayor. *He* ain't got no time for—'

'Stop it!' Nancy screamed. 'Somebody stop him! This ain't the man I married!'

Woolly looked solemnly at Nancy. 'Let me explain something, Nancy. The man you married was daft. He believed all kinds of stuff as nobody in their right mind would give house room to. I mean, look at that dowsing rubbish. I ask you! Bent twigs and a dangly thing, and folks believe that *works*? Load of old codswallop. Just wishful thinking.'

'Stone me,' Sam said quietly. 'He really thinks he means it, doesn't he? Woolly...listen to me. You got to let Eleri help you. Hypnotize you again.'

'What?' Woolly said. 'That daft old bat? *No* chance!'

Rosa glanced at Eleri, who didn't even blink at being called a daft old bat. Underneath all the weirdness, Eleri was a really good person, too. Someone who devoted her whole life to helping people and wasn't at all concerned about what anyone thought of her.

Rosa looked at Sam, who was a bit hot-headed and never totally convinced about the other-worldly things Eleri took for granted. He plainly thought the world of the plump, posh, slightly dizzy Diane, who seemed to have suffered – like Rosa herself – for being psychic. And Sam...well, all of them, really...

...these were just brilliant people and she hated to see them brought down like this.

She looked at Woolly, who Marco had said was the best granddad you could ever hope to have because there was something inside him that had never totally grown up and never would.

Rosa was quite glad Marco wasn't here to listen to Woolly now. In fact, she wasn't sure how *she* felt about being here. She'd not only run away from her dad, she'd joined up with people he saw as his enemies.

Woolly had his hand round the back of his neck, where he found his white ponytail. He seemed irritated.

'And another thing,' he said, and Rosa saw that his eyes were all pale and glassy. 'It's about time I had a proper haircut.'

This was when Nancy broke down.

A Door

At least it was high enough for them not to have to crawl. But the passage was narrow, and they had to walk one behind the other, and Grandma Goldman's key-ring torch put out about as much light as a single candle on a birthday cake.

'You don't understand,' Marco kept saying. 'The labyrinth goes on for ever, and that little torch battery's going to last about twenty minutes, max. What are we going to do when it goes out?'

'We'll think about that when it happens, Marco.'

'Yeah, but by then we'll be deep in the bowels of the earth with no hope of finding our way out. I've been down here before. It is not fun.'

'Hmm...' Granny Goldman held up the tiny light to examine a chunk of stonework. 'That could be part of a Norman arch. No, it's not *fun*, exactly, but it's *interesting*.'

'It's even more interesting if you don't die,' Marco said.

'Oh, we're not going to *die*, Marco. If Joshua can survive this, anybody can. We both know that boy's had what you might call an extremely sheltered life. Just like his father was at that age – too clever by half and totally impractical. They think the mind has all the answers.'

'You mean it doesn't?'

'Of course not. Luckily, my side of the family specializes in *native cunning*. Which can be far more important than brains. Unfortunately, it only seems to be handed out to the girls. Did you see a speck of light just then?'

'It's just an illusion,' Marco said gloomily. 'Down here, you start imagining things.'

'You have no faith, Marco. Look!'

Wow. It was, too. There was a faint grey sheen on the stone wall ahead of them, suggesting daylight. And they couldn't have walked more than a couple of hundred metres. Maybe this passage didn't lead into the labyrinth at all.

'Ow!'

Marco had kicked something hard.

'Steps,' Grandma Goldman said. 'Going up. Go on...go and find out what's at the top.'

Marco didn't need telling twice. He stumbled up the steps, about fourteen of them. At the top, there was a rusty metal grille full of blinding daylight. A padlock was supposed to be holding it down, but it had been broken and was hanging off. It was easy to push the grille aside and haul yourself out into...

'Holy Joseph!'

Marco stood there blinking and shading his eyes. It was your average Glasto blight-yellowed sky, but when you were emerging from the underworld it was still seriously painful.

And the enormous mound directly in front was awesome.

'What is it?' Grandma Goldman demanded from below. 'Where are we?'

'It's a kind of overgrown yard, with a broken-down wall around it and...'

An unbelievable view of Glastonbury Tor as Marco had never seen it before: massive and dominant. It was like looking up at the walls of a huge, forbidding fortress. And yet it was still some way away...a good five or ten minute walk.

Grandma Goldman scrambled out and looked around.

'Looks like this used to be some sort of depot. I think whoever owns it just sealed off that passage because they had no use for it. The passage and the cellars are obviously much older than the buildings. Those kids must just use this as a short cut to...what, exactly? The Tor?'

Marco thought about it. He supposed if you had to get out of town quickly, this would put you right into the countryside without anyone seeing you go.

'Must've been a terrible shock for poor Joshua,' Grandma Goldman said. 'He hates the countryside. He had a panic attack in my garden, once.'

'Josh has panic attacks?'

'Used to, poor child. The question now is...where have they taken him? And why?'

'Could be anywhere.' Marco climbed on the broken-down

concrete wall. 'He could be on top of the Tor... anywhere, really.'

'Right,' Grandma Goldman said. 'These kids – you weren't kidding when you said they were bad? *How* bad?'

'Gloria,' Marco said, 'let me put it to you like this: who was that guy...Hannibal Lecter, right? Imagine when Hannibal Lecter was a kid?'

'Hannibal Lecter's a fictional character, Marco.'

'But you see where I'm going with this.'

'In that case...' Grandma Goldman plunged into her handbag and pulled out her mobile phone. '...I know where *I'm* going.'

'The police?'

'You said it, buster – damn that Joshua, he's turning me into an American.'

Grandma Goldman prodded at the phone. Marco felt uneasy. Things here were complicated enough without the police being involved. Besides, the Glasto cops weren't too quick to respond, according to Woolly, having seen too much over the years.

'Hell's teeth!' Granny Goldman shook the phone. 'Why can't I get a signal? There's nowhere in *Torquay* I can't get a signal.'

'This is Glastonbury, Gloria. It's amazing how many modern bits of kit don't function here. I had a problem with my laptop for ages. It's the earth-energy. Being so close to the Tor can't help.'

'So how far do I have to go before I get a signal?'

'Hard to say. Shepton Mallet?'

Grandma Goldman made a hissing sound through her teeth.

'Okay. How do I get back to the town centre?'

'Well...' Marco climbed back on the wall. 'I can see St John's church tower, and I can hear the traffic on High Street so I reckon if you follow this wall, you're bound to get there within a few minutes.'

'Right.' She thrust the carrier bag of crystals at him. 'Hold onto these for me. You'd better stay here, because at least you know what these kids look like. And if you do see any of them...'

'Follow them but stay out of sight?'

'Correct. And don't do anything you think might be clever – kids are always wrong. And anyway I'll have this place flooded with police within half an hour. And tracker dogs.'

'Gloria, I wouldn't be too sure the police will—'

Grandma Goldman held up a hand to shut him up.

'If they don't cooperate, I shall suggest they contact Torquay Division.' She hitched up her peacock frock and climbed over the wall. 'In Torquay, the police have learned the hard way not to get up my nose.'

Marco watched her walk away through the scrubby grass.

She was basically okay, was Gloria. It was strange how sometimes you could connect better with adults if you skipped a generation. Grandma Goldman wasn't at all like Woolly and Nancy, and yet...

Okay. Where would they *really* have taken Josh, if they thought he was the kid who thought he was Arthur?

He looked up at Glastonbury Tor. From this particular side, you felt you were almost *under* the Tor. Directly above the church tower – short and stubby from here – there was a gash of violent yellow sunlight in a slab of grey cloud. Like the tower had ripped at the sky, leaving an open wound.

Like nature was saying, *Stay back. Kids can also get ripped.*

It had to be the Tor. Between Marco and *that hill*, there was part of another hill and, at its base, the remains of a footpath.

Listening hard for any voices, any other movement, Marco followed the path as it wound between small, spiky trees, bushes and brambles which rolled out like coils of old barbed wire, snagging his trainers. As he walked, the tower on the Tor grew shorter, as if it was being smoothly retracted like a stubby aerial.

The trees started getting taller and the bushes bushier. But on the ground, Marco noticed how the grass had been flattened, twigs snapped. You didn't have to be an experienced tracker to know that people had passed this way, and not too long ago.

He glanced behind and couldn't see the wall or the yard or anything of the town. The greenery had come together behind him. Already he was in another place and, no, it didn't feel friendly.

Ahead of him, the path widened where two trees met overhead. You could see how some of their branches had been bent back and snapped, so that they formed a kind of archway, leading to...

...*what?*

Marco saw grass and more grass. A hillside. A hillside with...

...with a door in it?

Die Again

Josh looked up in something close to horror.

'*I don't do this,*' he said again, and this time he couldn't hold back the desperation. 'Don't you realize, this is not the kind of thing I do?'

He held it up to the hard light in total disbelief.

'What am I supposed to *do* with this?' he shouted. 'What it's *for*?'

They'd given him a sword. An old-fashioned, medieval sort of sword.

Well, old-fashioned but not actually *old*. He'd seen swords like this on people's walls. Its blade was thin and shiny, and it was fairly light...and new. In other words, it wasn't a real sword. It was like a stage-prop sword. A fake.

And Josh was standing there in the spotlight, like he was about to...

...perform.

Perform?

A sudden thought came to him. A thought that, at first, was a serious relief and then became seriously shaming.

Just suppose that this whole situation was as phoney as the sword?

A set-up.

A joke.

Okay, a sick joke, but a joke nonetheless. All that rubbish about Arthur and fighting for his new life. It was symptomatic of the kind of madness that surrounded this town...a town that was totally polluted by ridiculous legends which people desperately wanted to believe in because there was nothing else in their lives.

Because these were the kind of people who hated science and psychology and everything that someone like Joshua Goldman stood for.

Well, okay.

Right, then.

Enough already!

Josh looked down at the pool of light he was standing in. The powerful spotlight was obviously powered by a generator, which explained the motor.

It was like a stage light. Or a TV light.

A TV light...*of course.*

The light was here because somebody was *videoing* the whole thing.

He was going to be a video star.

Oh no.

The total shame of it...

By this time next week, it could be on the net. His family and his so-called friends could all log on to pictures of Joshua Goldman weeping and flailing about and putting on his phoney American accent and then losing it and generally coming across like a total dweeb. Like the *Star Wars* boy.

Josh gripped the handle of the sword. He wasn't sure whether he was squirming in embarrassment or trembling with rage as he realized there could be only one person behind this scam.

Somebody who wanted to get back at him for sneering about magic and earth-powers and dowsing.

Oh yes, it all made sense now.

He looked up to where he'd last heard The Voice.

'Do you think I'm stupid? *Do* you?'

Nobody replied.

'Do you know who I *am*?'

Somebody laughed.

'Yeah,' Josh said bitterly, wiping away the wine and the tears. 'Very funny. Now where is he? Where's *Marco*?'

The whole idea of a door in a hill...this was a bit scary. Marco remembered what Woolly had told him about the Tor, the first time they'd walked to the top. The day when Marco had had this really weird experience, the sensation of leaving his body.

The old gods were real powerful here, Woolly had said. *It was believed the Tor was hollow, look, and this was where the King of the Underworld held court. This was the actual entrance to the Celtic Land of the Dead. And some folks believes it still is.*

The Celtic Lord of the Dead was called Gwyn ap Nudd – pronounced *ap Neeth* – and, according to legend, he used to ride out from the Tor with his hounds of hell, rounding up stray souls. And one evening, just a few weeks ago, during a thunderstorm...

Stop it. Be cool, man.

Marco went right up to the door and was relieved to find that it was surrounded by concrete.

Of course, there was no reason at all why Gwyn ap Nudd shouldn't have concrete around his back door but this was, you would have to concede, unlikely.

Brushing off superstition like cobwebs, Marco tried the door. Pulled at it and pushed at it and...

...it opened.

Oh.

He stepped back into the bushes. A door like this, set into a hillside, well you'd think it would be locked or sealed or bricked up in some way to comply with all the government's health and safety regulations.

From the open crack at the edge of the thick, wooden, slightly oily and fairly modern door, Marco heard a voice.

He froze.

A voice coming from *in there.*

He waited a few seconds and then stepped out from the bushes.

And don't do anything you think might be clever, Grandma Goldman said. *Kids are always wrong.*

Marco approached the door again. The voice from inside was more like a cry.

Come on, Gloria. Give me a break. Your precious grandson might be in there. Maybe having a panic attack.

Very slowly and carefully, being as quiet as he could, he opened the door a little wider and squeezed through the gap into darkness.

Not like the darkness of the tunnel, though. This was the kind of gaspy, echoey darkness you would expect from a vast hall.

Like the hall of Gwyn ap Nudd, Celtic Lord of the Dead.

The cobwebs of superstition came down again and settled on Marco's shoulders.

He looked back at the crack of daylight down the side of the door. The daylight beckoned to him.

The daylight said, *Come out, kid, while you still can.*

At the same time, the voice from within rose into a kind of yelp.

'*Marco! Show yourself, you scumbag.*'

Josh was still shouting for Marco when the big spotlight went out.

Just like that. Pop. *Gone.*

'What's up?' Josh shouted scornfully. 'Batteries used up?'

Puzzled for a moment at still being able to see. More clearly, in fact, now that he wasn't blinded by the light. He could see that he was in a wide but not very lofty chamber with a large space in the middle surrounded by big square pillars that could almost be concrete. He could see shadows moving and small lights springing up, one by one, all around him.

When the shadows receded, Josh saw that he was standing in a circle of candles.

Big candles in iron holders. One at each point of a great black star in a circle on the hard, grey floor.

He counted five candles. At least, he thought they were candles; he couldn't actually make out the wax stems, only the little flames.

And then he could.

The reason he hadn't been able to make them out at first was that they were black. All the candles were black.

'Oh, for heaven's sake...a joke's a joke.'

Josh threw down the sword in disgust, watching it bounce tinnily inside the circle of light.

'Pick it up,' someone said from the edge of the circle.

'Get lost!' Josh shouted back.

He heard slow footsteps, and then Jasper Coombes walked into the circle of light, standing opposite Josh, so that they were four or five metres apart.

'Pick it up, Rex.'

'Pick it up yourself.'

Josh had totally had it with these guys. Up to here.

'I already *have* a sword.' Jasper walked towards him from one of the points of the star. 'See?'

The sword Jasper was holding was not new. In fact, it looked a bit twisted and corroded.

And it was black. Looked even more black against Jasper's white shirt and white trousers.

'Where's the camera?' Josh said. 'Where's Marco?'

'Get real, Rex.'

'Oh yeah,' Josh said. 'You guys know all about real, don't you? You think I don't know this is a scam? You think I'm stupid?'

Jasper walked right up to Josh and smiled at him. Then,

very lightly, he stroked his black sword down Josh's bare arm.

'You want real?' he said. '*This* is real.'

Josh looked down at his arm just as the blood welled up, almost black in the candlelight, and trickled down to his wrist.

'Pick up your sword, Rex,' Jasper said.

Be Afraid

'What are you going to do?' Rosa was trying not to cry. 'You've got to do *something*.'

Woolly had lost it completely now. He'd gone to a drawer in the Welsh dresser and pulled out a giant pair of scissors and was closing them around his ponytail by the time Sam got to him.

Sam was still holding Woolly back while Nancy, who'd grabbed the scissors, was keeping them above her head, out of his reach.

'She's right,' Eleri said. 'This is heartbreaking...and horribly sinister.'

She'd put on her cloak, as if this might make her more

powerful. She folded her arms and bent her head over them, closing her eyes, taking deep breaths and swaying.

Woolly started to shake, as Sam lowered him back into his chair. He looked up at Sam like a puppy told off for messing the carpet but not realizing what it had done wrong.

'It's all right, Woolly,' Sam said. 'Gonner be fine.' He looked at the rest of them. 'Woolly was a gift. He went to Murchison and submitted to hypnosis. Somebody saw their chance.'

'This was someone's actual idea, to do this to him?' Nancy was holding the scissors behind her back. '*Who?*'

'Could be my old man himself. Or one of the others who deliberately got themselves hypnotized.'

'What?' Eleri's arms fell to her sides. 'What are you *saying?*'

'The old man...Cotton...Jasper Coombes...all the Glasties who had so-called visions.'

'My goddess!' Eleri went pale. 'You mean—'

'Comes down to Melcato,' Sam said. 'The Glasties had a meeting arranged with Melcato – their best chance to persuade them to set up their operation in Glastonbury rather than Edinburgh or Tintagel, bringing untold wealth and brown envelopes full of money for bent councillors. Only problem being that Melcato want to buy into Glasto's ancient Arthurian scene.'

Eleri sighed in a kind of awe. 'Of *course...*'

'Melcato were looking for people as fired up as young Rex and his dad about the *reality* of Arthur,' Sam said. '*They* didn't want to talk to stuffy old councillors and tradespeople and solicitors who thought it was all a big myth.'

'Gosh,' Diane said. 'There'd be absolutely no way for Griff and Mr. Cotton to fake some sort of belief in Arthur. They just wouldn't have it in them. Unless... Oh gosh...'

'Unless they really believed they'd had personal experiences,' Sam said. 'Things they could describe in convincing detail.'

'Visions,' Eleri said. 'Arthurian visions implanted in their minds...by hypnosis.'

'Exactly.'

'Visions of events which...never happened?'

'You remember what the old man was like...' Sam put on his dad's voice, all quavery. *'I can see the glint of burnished steel and the red light glinting off their helmets...and their faces all black and smoky and ghosty!'*

'That was all put into his head?' Nancy said. 'And all that stuff about being made a knight of the Round Table?'

'Only round table my old man's ever sat at, Nancy, is in the corner at The Rifleman's Arms. And no way he's got the imagination to invent the other stuff. Just like Cotton, a dry-as-dust old solicitor claiming to've seen a UFO over the Tor – a UFO that he later realized looked like a certain sword. *He* wasn't lying, either...he really believed that that was what he'd seen.'

'They all agreed to be hypnotized,' Diane said, 'so that their stories would be absolutely convincing when they went to meet the people from Melcato?'

'Willing subjects. If you don't agree to it, it's not gonner work.'

'But who – you know – who put them on to it? Your father would never think of something like hypnosis.'

'No, but Roger Cromwell would.'

'You mean Murchison's working for Cromwell?'

'Seems likely. Cromwell's still got a lot of influence in this town – and he's got friends. It certainly explains Woolly's condition. So it gets back to Cromwell that Woolly's signed up with Murchison, in all innocence, for a course of hypnotherapy to fight his depressions...'

'Cromwell sees his chance,' Eleri said, 'to neutralize his main enemy in this town. A man he hates.'

'There you go,' Sam said.

'That's plain daft, Sammy.' Woolly had sat up. 'Mr. Murchison wouldn't do anything like that. He's a decent human being. Just like the mayor – a prince among men.'

'I rest my case,' Sam said.

Woolly looked puzzled, almost tearful. As if he knew the things he was saying weren't right but he couldn't *not* say them. It was frightening, Rosa thought. And there was something else...

'What about the sword?'

She didn't realize she'd said it until they all turned to look at her.

'Ah, Rosa,' Eleri said, 'the sword...is where the real evil lies.'

For Rosa, the details no longer needed spelling out. She was beginning to see the whole picture.

It had begun with Jasper Coombes agreeing to be the messenger – the prophet foretelling the arrival of Arthur... just to make this Rex kid feel good about coming to Glastonbury.

So Jasper Coombes had agreed to be hypnotized into believing he'd seen Excalibur lifted from the well by a supernatural hand.

'And then the actual sword gets discovered by you and your dad,' Sam said. 'A sincere man of God whose word would never be disputed. Perfect.'

'So the sword was planted where we'd find it?'

'Is that where your dad regularly goes for walks?'

'It's where he goes every week to compose his sermon.'

'Looks like someone'd been watching him.'

'Yes...and it was kind of sticking up across the path. So one of us would be bound to trip over it. Dad said he... *Yes!* Just before we found it, Dad thought he'd seen someone moving around.'

'However,' Eleri said, 'it goes deeper. This is where we are faced with another dimension of evil. Because the sword chosen to represent Excalibur was not going to be Arthur's sword but the sword which *destroyed* Arthur.'

'The Blade of Mordred,' Sam said.

'It was probably the only sword they could put their hands on that might lend itself to being identified as Excalibur. Could be the actual Blade or another relic of a similar age – infused, by magical ritual, with its bloody history.'

'*Can* you plant false history into a sword?' Sam looked doubtful. 'I mean, the same way you can hypnotize a person?'

'Of course,' Eleri said. 'Think about it. Millions of people believe that a Roman Catholic priest can supervise the transformation of a communion wafer and a chalice of wine into the body and blood of Christ. The Catholic Mass is an ancient magical ritual. That, of course, is a *positive* transformation. This, however, is...'

'Satanic?' Sam said. 'That's what we're looking at?'

'There has been a satanic element from the start. Consider the attempt to despoil the grave of Arthur with a dark, sacrificial ritual...to weaken the aura of light around it. They *might* simply have obtained an ancient blade, offering it up to Satan or one of his demons in memory of the evil perpetrated by Mordred...so wherever it goes that sword will bring violence and misfortune.'

'Poor old James Montague?'

'Indeed. And who knows what savagery it may have caused at Rosa's home, above the dark shop...' Eleri looked at Rosa, her eyes sad. 'I am thinking, I'm afraid, of your father. A good man, in his way, but a man so easily moved to anger. And when he brought the sword into the house for a second time...'

'My dad wouldn't—'

'An angry man in a house infected by *the virus of evil*...'

'Steady on, Eleri,' Sam said. 'You'll be saying Rosa's dad might've hacked his own family to d—' Sam sat down suddenly. 'Oh, come on, Eleri...'

Eleri's eyes were still. 'Why were Jasper Coombes and his friends hanging around like vultures of the night, just as they were outside James Montague's cottage? Did they simply want the sword back, or did they want to see what it might do? We shall never know, because Rosa's guardian intervened.'

'The...' Rosa's throat was dry. 'The Abbot?'

'The power of light represented by Abbot Whiting knew that if the sword stayed in your flat, with a man as dangerously volatile as your father... Who knows what might have happened?'

'But it...' Rosa went cold. '...it could have passed to me.

I could have...I could have killed Shane Davey. The feeling I had holding the sword over him...was probably the worst feeling I'd ever had in my life. I could have...'

'You *could* have...but you didn't. Why?'

'I...I suddenly felt this terrible...you know...'

'Revulsion?'

'Maybe. And I think I saw a...a glow from the gate into the Abbey grounds. It was like a small, faint...something.'

'You are protected, and you have a rare inner strength. And that is why you were entrusted with the task.'

'But they still got the sword back...in the end.'

'I am afraid,' Eleri said heavily, 'that it is not yet the end. Why did they need the sword?' She nodded at the tennis bag at Rosa's feet. 'Is that the case it was in?'

'Mmm. I had to bring it out or Dad would've known the sword was missing. Now he'll just think *I've* taken it.'

'We may have to do something about the bag,' Eleri said. 'It will have been tainted by what it contained.'

She bent and unzipped the bag and opened it wide, making a symbol with her finger in the air over it. Then she turned away and blew her nose into a tissue. Sam came to his feet.

'What's wrong?'

'There's something still in it.'

'The bag?'

Sam bent down. Eleri whispered, 'Be careful,' as he felt around inside it.

'Can't feel anything.'

'There's something...'

'Well, if it is, it's something psychic that you can feel and I can't, because... Oh...'

Sam brought his hand out, fist closed.

He opened his hand. A tiny copper-coloured circular stud lay in his palm. Eleri bent close to it, still holding the tissue over her nose.

'It's from the handle. There were three of them. I remember one was a little loose.'

'What do I do with it?' Sam stood up. 'If it's infused with whatever blood and death was surrounding that sword, we need to get it out of this house...especially with Woolly...'

'No!' Eleri was on her feet. 'We must not be afraid. That's what they want. We must not—'

'That's right,' Woolly said. 'That's the whole point, look. We must... We must be afraid no longer!'

'Besides,' Eleri said. 'A tiny piece of the sword might be able to lead us to the sword itself.'

'You reckon?' Sam said, sceptical.

'Unfortunately, the only person who could do this is... Woolly.'

Sam moaned aloud.

'With his pendulum and a map,' Eleri said. 'I have seen him do it before with a small fragment of something missing.'

'You hear that, Woolly?' Sam kneeled in front of the little guy. 'We need some help. We needs some dowsing. Get your pendulum, eh?'

'What for?'

'Eleri thinks you could point us to the sword.'

'No, it's daft.'

'What is?'

'Dowsing. It's just wishful thinking, Sammy. It don't really work.'

Sam put his hands on Woolly's shoulder.

'Woolly...please...'

'You're a good boy, Sammy,' Woolly said. 'Chip off the old block.'

'It's too late!' Nancy was in tears. 'It's gone too deep. He's never gonner be normal again.'

'Don't be afraid, Nance,' Woolly said. 'We been afraid too long.'

'Why does he—' Eleri's head twisted round. It was like a watchful hawk spotting a sudden movement. 'Why does he keep saying that?'

'Can't you do something?' Sam pleaded.

'Sam—' Eleri threw out her arms. 'He has to be a willing subject.'

Rosa said, 'Where do you think the sword could be?'

'Cromwell's got it,' Sam said. 'No question.'

'So they're definitely working together?' Diane said. 'Cromwell and the mayor?'

'Only up to a point, I reckon. Glasties like my old man don't want to do the town any actual *harm*, they just want to change it – get rid of the mystical types and make it more like what they see as normal. And make some money for themselves on the side, of course – which is why they struck what amounts to a deal with the Devil.'

'Represented, of course, by Cromwell,' Eleri said. 'Cromwell is a destroyer. He hates this town with a passion that goes back through history...absorbing the greed and hatred of Thomas Cromwell, who he sees as his ancestor. And, as we now know, a hatred even older...all the way back to Mordred. A vein of evil snaking through the history of this town.'

'So what's the bottom line, Eleri?' Sam said.

Eleri looked down for a moment and, when she looked up, Rosa saw tears in her moonlike eyes.

'The hopes of the Avalonians have always rested on the second coming of Arthur...the spirit of Arthur guiding them to a new dawn.'

'But this ain't a *real* second coming. This is just a daft kid from the States with an obsession.'

'An obsession that carries a weight of emotion,' Eleri said. 'An obsession that can be used...symbolically. Magic, black or white, is all about symbolism. Through the use of symbols, we can bring about what ordinary people think of as reality.'

'All right.' Sam sighed. 'Go on.'

'We live now in the age of the computer. Computers dominate and control the lives of billions of people. Because of the enormous sales of the game, Arturus Rex, people, young and old, the world over, are seeing this boy as the actual incarnation of Arthur. When he arrives in this place of power and ancient sanctity, their fantasy becomes reality.'

'But it's still not...I mean, at the end of the day, the kid's not a real king.'

'You are wrong.' Eleri held up a rigid forefinger. 'In the modern world – the *electronic* world – this boy *is* a king. He is the heir to a global business empire of quite staggering wealth.'

'Well yeah, but how does that—?'

'For Cromwell, a second coming of Arthur would only have meaning if it was followed by...a second death.'

There was silence in the room, as they all worked out

what Eleri was telling them. Woolly seemed far away now, his eyelids drooping like his ponytail.

'You mean he's planning...' Sam rocked back. '...to kill the kid? Kill Rex Arturus?'

'It has a dreadful poetic logic, Sam.'

'Just give us the English version, Eleri. For morons.'

Despite the heat, Eleri pulled her cloak over her knees.

'The ritual killing of a king,' she said, 'has ancient origins and can release tremendous energy. A more recent example was the sacrifice of William II – William Rufus – in the New Forest early in the last millennium.'

Rosa nodded. She'd learned about that at school. The king was shot with an arrow, but she hadn't known it was a ritual murder.

'*This* king,' Eleri said, 'is a figure who represents not only the spiritual hopes of generations of Avalonians but also the material desires of the Glasties. A figure of enormous symbolic power. His death would be a huge triumph for Cromwell...and his dark master.'

There was another silence. Behind her eyes, Rosa saw a field sodden with blood, and sour with the smell of smoke and burning flesh.

Sam stood up.

'Just as well the poor kid ain't here yet,' he said.

Psycho

Josh scowled.

If Jasper Coombes thought he could be psychologically disadvantaged by a trickle of blood from a superficial cut on the arm, he had no idea of the kind of person he was dealing with.

'You need to have a weapon in your hand,' Coombes said. 'It's important.'

He picked up the shiny sword and held it by the blade, pointing the handle at Josh. He could do this, no worries, because the blade was so blunt.

Josh ignored it.

'You know your problem, Coombes. You might be psychotic, but you're not very smart.'

He could feel his American accent slipping away, but that didn't seem important any more. He wondered where the man who'd called himself Merlin had gone.

He was probably somewhere beyond the edge of the candlelit circle, operating the video camera.

'And you're also surprisingly nervous,' Josh said. 'Never been in a movie before?'

'What?'

'You're conspicuously on edge over something. And yet there's this underlying excitement. Well, obviously, as a psychopath, you thrive on excitement. The need to live on a higher and faster level than the rest of us poor ordinary mortals.'

'Shut up,' Coombes said.

'You have an indestructible belief in your own superiority, and if something doesn't go the way you want it to go, you're liable to fly into an uncontrollable rage.'

'SHUT YOUR SMART MOUTH!'

'Yes,' Josh nodded calmly. 'Something like that.'

Jasper Coombes seized Josh's right hand and tried to prise Josh's fingers open, presumably to wrap them around the handle of the sword.

Josh didn't resist but, as soon as his fingers were closed around the handle and Coombes stepped back to grab his own blackened relic from outside the circle, Josh opened his fingers and let the sword clang to the hard, smooth floor.

'Don't you realize,' Jasper Coombes said, 'that you're going to die?'

Josh rolled his eyes.

'Of *course* I do. To deny one's own mortality is futile. Meanwhile, I'd be rather interested to ask you some questions about your early childhood, Coombes. It's well known that most psychopaths will exhibit behavioural problems from quite an early age – torturing their hamsters, that kind of thing. And, of course, when they start school, they lose no time in establishing themselves as the class bullies. Picking on smaller kids without any sense of remorse, just a sense of mounting glee at the increasing distress they're causing.'

'When you die,' Coombes snarled, 'it's going to be particularly slow and agonizing.'

'Yeah, whatever. And, you know – this is *particularly* interesting – if the psychopath is from a middle-class home – like yourself, I'd guess – and attends a private school, he would be likely to adopt the antisocial habits of the inner-city ghetto child: taking drugs, carrying knives...or swords, of course.'

Josh folded his arms, smiling. However, he was determined not to be complacent, realizing that after that early embarrassing episode with the straitjacket he still had a lot of ground to make up if he was going to emerge from this video with any credibility.

'I'll make it easier for you, Rex.' Coombes reached out and snatched off Josh's glasses. 'This way, when my blade falls and cleaves your brain, you won't see it coming.'

'Thanks, mate,' Josh said.

Jasper Coombes let the glasses fall to the floor, where they lay reflecting the light of the black candles before he brought down the heel of his trainer, twice, crunching both lenses into the concrete.

Josh shrugged. Back home, he had another four pairs of plain-glass specs, all with different metal frames.

What a jerk this Coombes was.

Way beyond the candlelight, Marco crouched behind a concrete pillar.

He didn't know whether to laugh or cry.

In the end, he decided just to get anxious, because it was clear Josh had no idea what he was taking on. He was talking like he thought he could overpower Jasper with the sheer force of his gigantic intellect. But *he* hadn't been abandoned by Jasper Coombes to die in the labyrinth. *He* hadn't been there when Jasper was about to sacrifice Arthur, the cat.

Marco could almost hear Grandma Goldman.

Just like his father was at that age – too clever by half and totally impractical. They think the mind has all the answers.

Still clutching Grandma Goldman's bag of stupid crystals, Marco looked around into the dimness of the great cavern.

Well, for a start, it obviously *wasn't* a cavern. It was certainly underground, but it was man-made. The pillars holding it up were precast concrete and the floor was concrete too.

He knew there were more people here, watching from the shadows at the opposite end of the great chamber – maybe Shane and Jezza – and he thought he'd heard a man's voice.

And, as his eyes adjusted to the half-light, he was able to make out the shape inside the black circle with the candles around it.

Five candles...a five-pointed star in a circle.

A pentagram.

He remembered how, when he was once watching Rosa inscribe the pentagram in the air, she'd told him there were two ways of doing it, and you had to make sure you didn't do the wrong one or you'd bring down the wrong kind of influences.

The good pentagram had one point at the top.

The wrong pentagram had two points at the top. Like the devil's horns.

Like the one in the circle in which Josh and Jasper Coombes were standing.

Or, at least, that was how it looked, because Jasper, having stamped on Josh's fake glasses, had stepped back and was standing with one foot in each of the two points.

Josh stared at him with his own useless sword at his feet and a sneer on his face.

'You know...people sometimes ask why psychopaths often remain undetected until they grow up and turn into serial killers,' Josh said. 'Well, the answer...'

Jasper switched his sword, the – *please, no* – Blade of Mordred, from one hand to the other and back again, like he was testing its weight. Marco bit his lip and wondered what on earth he could possibly do if it got too nasty.

'The answer, of course, is very simple,' Josh said. 'Psychos are often immensely charming – and this is something they also learn in childhood. A child who appears charming to adults can get away with almost anyth— *uuuuuugh!*'

Marco sprang to his feet.

It *had* got too nasty. Josh was reeling back, bleeding from the mouth. Jasper had the Blade of Mordred raised above him.

He'd hit Josh in the mouth not with the blade but the handle, bringing it down from his superior height.

Josh backed off, spitting out blood, and fell over.

'Get up,' Jasper said.

Josh gurgled.

Jasper kicked him.

'Don't worry, Rex, you'll still be able to scream...'

Josh tried to roll away. Jasper kicked him again, in the side.

'...but at least I won't have to listen to you spending the last minutes of your life being clever. Now...fight. Be a man.'

As Josh scrambled to his feet, Jasper pushed the shiny sword at him, and this time Josh didn't let go but grasped it and tried to swing it experimentally through the air. Excalibur it wasn't, and it was already bent.

'I am Mordred,' Jasper said. *'Fight me to the death.'*

Marco thought he'd never before seen Josh looking so utterly shocked and terrified.

'Lissen a me,' Josh said, in a swollen kind of way. 'This ish not wha' you think, awright? I'm norra...norra... *norArturus...Rex.* It wash a joke! I jush pretended to be... *wash a joke...'*

'What a shame.'

Marco tensed. It was a voice from the shadows. And a voice from his own shadows. The voice he'd last heard, in a kind of dream-state, offering him sweet wine from the upturned brainpan of a skull, whispering, *Drink this. This'll warm you up...*

Why hadn't he realized?

Cromwell.

Marco pictured him over there, this tall, thin, unsmiling man...gliding...a shadow among shadows.

Cromwell was the living shadow over Glastonbury. He believed he was part of an ancient tradition dating back to when Glastonbury was rich and powerful and holy... the spiritual capital of Britain. Henry VIII's hatchet man, Thomas Cromwell, had believed it was his mission to bring Glasto down.

Roger Cromwell seemed to believe he'd inherited that mission...even though the town wasn't rich any more and the Abbey was in ruins. Dealing in dark magic from the shop below the flat where Rosa lived...linked, through its cellars, to the labyrinth.

It didn't make any sense.

But when did evil *ever* make sense?

Marco remembered Roger Cromwell when he was trying to make Woolly dig up the Dark Chalice. Remembered him hitting Woolly. The sky full of thunder and Cromwell's eyes like stones.

Hadn't seen him since.

Only heard his voice.

'What a shame my friend Mordred has no sense of humour. Mordred...listen to me.'

'Yes,' Jasper said.

'The Dark Chalice passes from hand to hand. For here, for now, for eternity...he *is* Rex.'

'Yes.'

'*Naw!*' Josh screamed.

'The time for pleasantries is over,' Cromwell said. 'We've talked about this.'

Jasper began to pant.

'Do what you must,' the shadow that was Roger Cromwell said.

Trigger

In the hot and crowded little kitchen, Eleri arose.

'Something is wrong,' she said. 'Something is going wrong *now*.'

Well, it was hardly the first time she'd said *that*. She was, Rosa knew, famous for it. Notorious in Glastonbury for spreading despair and foreboding. Banned from the marketplace for scaring the shoppers.

For once, when so much obviously *was* wrong, she could hardly be accused of dressing it up, but Sam, stressed out, almost lost his temper.

'You wanner tell us something we don't know, Eleri?'

'Where's Marco?' Eleri said.

'He went off with his mate's gran. They went to find his mate, the know-all kid.'

'I feel a darkness,' Eleri said. 'And when I think of the Blade of Mordred, I think of Marco.'

'Dear God!' Nancy scuttled over to Woolly. 'Did you hear that?' She began to shake him. 'Marco's in terrible danger!'

'Nancy...no...' Diane pushed herself between them. 'He can't help it. It's not his fault. He's been damaged.'

'He could find Marco. He's the only one of us who could find—'

'No. Please, Nancy, don't make it worse.'

'He could at least let Eleri put him under...'

'His mind's been programmed to resist it. Like a computer. You can't alter it. I'm guessing he's been programmed to resist all of us...the Watchers.'

Nancy began to sob. Woolly looked at her and shook his head very gently, and Rosa thought, *It's getting worse. He's losing his mind completely. He can hardly speak any more. Pretty soon he'll be a vegetable.*

And she wished Diane hadn't said that about computers. It made her think of what had happened once when a virus had got into her own PC – just small things going wrong at first, but then it got worse and worse very quickly, and then everything froze and her hard disk was destroyed for ever.

Rosa jumped up. '*I'll* go and look for Marco. I'll go back into the town!'

'Rosa!' Sam shouted. 'Sit down, for heaven's sake.' He looked around the room, his eyes wild. 'Look at us! We're all over the place! It's turning into a madhouse.'

'None of us knows what to do, Sammy,' Nancy said. 'We don't know where to turn.'

Rosa shook her head and ran to the back door, leading to the garden and the orchard and...

...almost bumped into a strange woman in grey who was standing there, silent and very still, like a ghost.

Rosa stopped.

It all went unbelievably quiet.

The woman stared into the room as if someone who'd just awoken from a long sleep.

Nancy gasped and went even paler than a ghost.

The woman walked into the room like she *thought* she knew where she was but couldn't be quite sure.

'Let me talk to Dad,' the woman said.

Josh threw down the useless sword and cried out, 'I yield!'

'You can't yield,' Jasper said. 'That isn't in the legend. That didn't happen. You have to fight until you're lying twitching in a pool of your own blood and guts.'

'Stuff that! I'm yielding, and if I yield then – and I know the history, Coombes – it's against all the basic rules of chivalry to...to...'

'Chivalry...' Jasper laughed. 'You poor, deluded—'

Josh held up both hands and spat out a mouthful of pinky blood. When he spoke again, his voice was almost normal. Except that it wasn't normal at all.

Josh had been...broken.

Time for Marco to make a move. But what kind of move?

'All right!' Josh yelled out. 'I'll tell you. *I'll tell you the truth.* I'm a...I'm a student of psychiatry. I only came here because I was interested in my friend, Marco – his mental condition. Goldman's Syndrome. Goldman – that's me. I was going to call it Goldman's Syndrome.'

Goldman's Syndrome?

Marco seethed.

His head flooded with everything that Josh had ever done to him.

...like the day he'd been locked in a small, dark, stifling cupboard to help him deal with his claustrophobia.

...the night Josh had produced some cans of extra-strong lager he'd said were alcohol-free and Marco had been too drunk to find his way home, even though they only lived in the flats opposite – Josh watching gleefully from his window as Marco fell into the water feature.

...those encouraging words from Josh when he first learned his dad was dumping him for the holidays on Woolly and Nancy: *You've got to go and stay,* for the whole summer, *with some totally mad old people you have never met in your entire life before,* ever, *and who are so completely sick and weird that even your mother can't put it into words...*

All the time, all he'd been to Josh was a...a guinea pig!

Marco was so furious at this betrayal that he was hardly aware of running out from behind his pillar, across the concrete floor and into the candlelight, making the sick little flames waver as he erupted into the devilish circle.

Rosa watched in a kind of daze, as the woman in the grey suit walked across the kitchen and stood in front of Woolly.

'Hello,' she said softly. 'Hello, Mum. Hello...Dad.'

Woolly said nothing. His eyes were wide and fogged, like

the eyes of people on drugs Rosa had seen on posters. Nancy was as pale as a slice of white bread and couldn't speak either.

'Stone me,' Sam said. 'Alison?'

'Hello, Sam...Diane. I heard you two were...'

'You're supposed to be in America.'

'I came back. Came to fetch my son. And then I couldn't... I couldn't just walk in. I...went round by the orchard and into the garden.'

Nancy started to say something, and the woman put up her hands. 'Mum...later.' She looked a bag of nerves, Rosa thought. 'Please. I...'

Sam said, 'You were standing outside the door? You heard everything?'

'Yeah. Most of it.'

Rosa thought, *Wow.*

This was Marco's mum? Marco's mum who'd run away from Glastonbury to join the BBC and had never been back and had made sure Marco never came back...until Marco's dad had betrayed her trust.

'I was going to say...nothing changes, does it?' Marco's mum said. 'Same old asylum.' She looked at Eleri. 'Always some weird woman in a cloak...'

'Eleri's a good person, Alison,' Diane said.

'Yeah,' Alison said, a bit sadly. 'I don't doubt it. All right. Marco. Where is he?'

'We don't know,' Sam said. 'You probably heard that.'

'Alison...' Nancy steadied herself on the table. 'I can't—'

'Mum, please, it'll wait. We have issues and they'll *wait.* Sam...the worst-case scenario is...what?'

'All right,' Sam said, 'I'm not gonner dress it up. You remember Cromwell, don't you?'

Alison shut her eyes for a moment. She wasn't very tall, a bit like Woolly, but the way she walked and everything you'd think she was taller.

'He hasn't changed,' Sam told her. 'He was running a shop selling satanic supplies, until it was closed down – thanks mainly to Woolly. So you know what he'd like to do to Woolly. And Marco's Woolly's grandson. I don't *know* this, Alison, I'm just giving you what you asked for – worst-case scenario.'

'And there's a way Dad might be able to find him, that's what you said. With the pendulum?'

'That's right.' Sam opened his hand. He still had the tiny stud from the sword. 'Or at least he could tell us where the Blade is. If it wasn't...'

'...for what this Murchison did to him,' Alison said. 'I heard that. I don't remember Murchison.'

'He hadn't been here long. We don't know anything about him, either. Probably one of Cromwell's old clients at The Emporium of the Night.'

'We need to get Woolly to submit to hypnosis, Alison,' Diane said. 'To get him back. Maybe...Nancy always says...'

'He'd do anything for Alison.' Nancy started to cry. 'Always the same.'

Rosa saw tears in Alison's eyes, but then she straightened up and walked over to Woolly and kneeled down by the side of his chair.

'Dad, you need to help us.'

Woolly just stared into space. Alison picked up his hand.

'What are you afraid of, Dad?'

'Afraid?' Woolly smiled weakly. 'Not the time to be afraid. We have been afraid too long.'

There was a crack. Eleri had clapped her hands together.

'My Goddess! It's a trigger! It's "afraid". Who said that – "We have been afraid too long"?' Eleri's eyes swivelled from face to face. 'Anybody! Quick!'

'Well...the mayor, of course,' Nancy said. 'It was in his speech at the town hall...just before...'

'Just before Woolly first went strange?'

'Yes. I do believe—'

'It's the trigger,' Eleri said. 'Murchison planted a key phrase that would act as a signal to Woolly's subconscious mind, and the next time he heard it he'd remember the information he'd been fed while in a hypnotic trance. This way, when it kicked in, even Woolly would not connect it with Murchison. And every time he hears it...he sinks more deeply into a kind of oblivion.'

'Right.' Alison nodded. 'At least we know.'

'But does it help us?' Diane said.

'I don't know.' Alison looked into Woolly's cloudy eyes. 'We've all been afraid, Dad,' she said. 'For too long.'

By Mordred's Hand

Marco looked at Josh.

'You...you...' Josh was glaring out at him through sweat as thick as the wax dripping down the candles. 'I just knew you were part of this.'

'Me?' Marco howled. '*Me?* I spend *hours* with your grandma trying to find you because you were stupid enough to get yourself lifted...after you tell everybody I'm a mental case...and...and... You *total—*'

'*Look out!*' Josh screamed.

There was a thin, keening sound, and Marco threw himself to one side. Two candle flames went horizontal as the Blade of Mordred cut through the air, right where he'd been standing.

'You first, then, hippy trash,' Jasper said.

He swung the sword back. Behind him, on the edge of the circle, was a gangly shadow and a dumpy shadow: Shane and Jezza.

Glasto psychos.

It's well known that most psychopaths will exhibit behavioural problems from quite an early age – torturing their hamsters...

Or cats.

And now it was three kids who liked to hurt against two sheltered-life kind of kids who read books and stuff.

Marco wondered which was the best way out of here.

'You're crazy, Coombes,' he snarled. 'Satanism? Black magic? I mean, what's that *about*?'

'It's about *reality*, trash. Satan's the Lord of This World. The god of the unbelievers. He's about bringing the real world into a town that lives in a fantasy world. Grown people blabbering on about the Holy Grail, like it actually exists. When you grow up in a town infested with idiots, you just want to wreck it. You want to give them some hard reality. And this is where you get *yours*...'

The blade came at Marco again, and he automatically ducked and it went skimming over his head, slicing the air like the wings of a dark bird of prey, and he almost screamed in horror.

Knowing that if hadn't ducked in time it would have taken his head off.

Golden light danced into Jasper's eyes. He stepped back to watch Marco and Josh cowering. Marco hissed at Josh. What he meant to say was:

This is the last time you will ever set me up like this.

What he said was:

'Go. Get out of here. Between those two pillars. I left a door open.'

'I can't,' Josh said.

'Yeah, well, don't bother about me. I'll handle this.'

(*What?* He'd actually *said* that?)

'You don't understand,' Josh said. 'I can't get out of the circle.'

'What?'

'I can't get out of the damn circle, all right? When I get to the edge of...of the circumference...'

Like, who else could use a word like *circumference* at a time like this?

'Just spit it out, Josh, you—'

'My legs go weak, and I can't...'

'What?'

'I can't get out!'

'Of course you can't.' Jasper stood leaning on his sword, taller and fitter than either of them. 'Roger's spent most of the week priming this circle with ritual. Your will power isn't strong enough to break through. You're trapped, guys, and I'm gonna cut you to pieces. I slash, you duck. Until you duck the wrong way, and it's all over.'

'Yeah,' Marco said. 'You and the Blade of Mordred. And your mates back there, in case you run into problems.'

'There won't be a problem.'

'Look, *think* about this.' Marco was finally panicking. 'You'd be a...a murderer.'

'In your case, it'll be waste disposal. I cursed you once. Now the curse falls. This is destiny.'

'Aw, come on...seriously. You'd go to jail for a long time.'

'Nobody goes to jail for a long time any more. A young person, first offence? *Forget* it. But that's beside the point, because nobody's going to find your bodies. We drag them into the labyrinth – a maze of forgotten passages that nobody apart from kids can get into. We drag the bodies into some forgotten passage and then we collapse the roof. Easily done – like you found out yourself. You're as good as dead, trash.'

'Hang on,' Marco said. 'I'm not in the legend, am I?'

'What you on about?'

'In the legend, it's just Arthur and Mordred. *He's* Arthur. There's no third guy in the fight.'

'Thanks,' Josh muttered.

'Stuff your legends.' Jasper swung back the Blade. 'Including the legend of life after death. You're out of here for good, trash.'

He raised the sword like an axe. Like the sword that came down on Arthur.

Oh my God, this *was* the sword that came down on Arthur.

The candlelight didn't reflect from the sword and it didn't touch Jasper.

Marco backed off, looking around for a weapon. The phoney sword they'd given to Josh was no use. And all *he* had was...

He realized he was still holding the plastic carrier bag with Grandma Goldman's crystals inside. The crystals were quite heavy, so maybe he could swing the bag like a mace.

He swung it experimentally and there was a ripping sound and he looked down and saw half a crystal sticking out – one of those they called cathedral crystals, with lumps of quartz sticking up like towers. *Oh no.* If he swung the bag again, they'd just all drop out.

Nothing was going to go right, was it?

'*Aaaaah!*'

He jumped to one side as the Blade came hissing through the air, so close it must have taken fine hairs off his arm. *Oh my God—*

'I bet you...' Backing off, panting. If he was going to die he'd at least go out winding up this sneering scumbag. '...I bet you don't even know the legend, do you, Jasper? You wouldn't read that stuff, would you? *Hippy books.*'

'I know that Arthur died by Mordred's hand. His skull cleft by the Blade – *this* blade...'

Marco jumped into the air as Jasper swooped low and the Blade came scything at him close to ground level.

'Eeeeeeergh!'

It had only been a passing hit, slicing the sole of his left trainer, but the pain was huge and jagged, and Marco rolled away and...

...let out a scream of real agony when his rolling body came to rest inside one of the points of the black pentagram and the crystals in the bag splintered on the concrete and he gripped a black candle with his left hand, and now the hot grease was sizzling between his fingers.

He almost passed out with the pain, his eyes squeezed shut...

...and he saw a bleak and empty, treeless landscape under a sky like the Blight and the grass all trampled down and soggy with blood.

When he opened his eyes, he saw...

'*No!*'

412

...Josh holding the useless sword in both hands and rushing, suicidally, at Jasper.

Jasper waited, as if he had all the time in the world.

And then he struck.

It was like a video in slow-mo, frames clicking and jerking, Marco watching through his pain as the useless sword flew out of Josh's hand and Josh fell to his knees, clutching his wrist and looking up.

Josh, frozen, his mouth half open, looking up into the razored edge of the Blade of Night, raised high in both of Jasper's hands, trembling less than a metre above the crown of Josh's exposed head. And Marco saw in Jasper's eyes a pure physical need to cause ultimate damage.

Jasper let out a full-throated roar of wild joy and the Blade quivered and fell, as Marco shut his eyes and convulsed.

His ears shut out the shriek but he thought he'd hear its echoes for ever.

...But Not Before

He saw the truth of it now. The truth about the Dark Ages.

All that stuff about the code of chivalry and courteous knights and the rules of combat...that was all made up later to disguise the nasty, sordid, vicious, cruel truth and the cheapness of life back then.

Marco staggered wearily to his feet, the torn plastic carrier bag dangling from his right hand, his left hand smarting like hell from the hot candle grease.

There was a dull clunk as the base of the cathedral crystal landed on the concrete followed by a thick sliver of quartz. It was about ten centimetres long and had a pointed end, so he picked it up. It wasn't exactly a sword, but it would do. He was going to die soon anyway.

He heard voices from somewhere and, closer, a dull moaning.

Josh wasn't dead yet, then.

Jasper was dragging it out, just like he'd promised.

Marco gripped the shaft of crystal with both hands, ignoring the pain, and limped towards the centre of the black pentagram, where Josh was lying.

Jasper Coombes was sitting on the concrete, a bubble of blood on his forehead. Two of the candles had gone out.

'I don't know what you threw at him,' Josh whispered, 'but it hit him just above the eye, and the sword...'

Marco saw that Jasper no longer had the Blade of Mordred. He saw the sword lying half out of the circle and could have sworn it was trying to move.

He realized that when he'd convulsed in agony and despair he must have hurled the broken crystal out of the bag like a stone from a sling, half of him still somewhere else, in a blood-red field under a yellow sky. Arthur running at Mordred, clutching a spear sticky with blood.

The surge of relief that he and Josh were still alive was met by a savage surge of pain from his burned hand. He could still feel congealing wax oozing between his fingers as he squeezed the stem of the pointed quartz crystal.

He saw Jasper coming to his feet, looking around for the Blade, his fingers flexing as if it would come back to him on its own.

Marco seemed to be looking down on all this from above. Once again, he was *more than here*. He heard himself snarling at Jasper.

'You were right. Arthur *did* die by Mordred's hand...but not before Arthur had finished Mordred.'

Jasper didn't seem to have heard. He wiped blood from his forehead.

'Don't think this is over, hippy scum.'

'Too right it's not over. You don't even know the proper story, do you, Jasper? I bet you never got further than *Arturus Rex.*'

'*Shut your—*'

'You didn't even know enough to fake it. You had to be hypnotized – like the mayor and Mr. Cotton.'

'*Shut your lying mouth!*'

'Nah, you don't know anything about the real Arthur,' Marco said.

Immediately, he had an image of Arthur, the friendly black cat Jasper was going to kill on the grave of the other Arthur.

'And what you obviously really *don't* know is...that Arthur ran Mordred through with a spear like...'

Marco heard cries and a rush of footsteps. An awful white rage coursed through him and he held the pointed crystal out in front of him like a thick needle and threw himself forward.

'*...like this—*'

Goldman's Syndrome
by Proxy

'Something,' Eleri said, 'is starting to happen.'

She wasn't wearing the snake headdress, and she looked more bizarre than Marco had ever seen her.

She had on a fluffy light-blue jumper and a skirt.

Her hair had been brushed.

Scary.

The light was fading in the long windows, and the miserable-looking angels and sour-faced cherubs of Bowermead Hall looked down on the circle of ten people sitting in stiff-backed chairs with their heads bent over their knees.

Shadows were beginning to dance up and down the walls

like dark ghosts, and the air was sharp with the smell of vinegar.

'Real good chips, these, Nancy,' Sam Daniel said. 'Where'd you get them?'

'Oh...that new place up from the Assembly Rooms,' Nancy said. '*And* they knocked me a few quid off for ordering ten portions.'

'Fair enough. Sorry, Eleri, what did you say?'

'I said something is happening. I feel a new energy. Not that the war is *over*...but I feel we now have the energy to fight.'

'Not exactly my favourite word right now, if you don't mind,' Josh said. 'Fight.'

His wrist was badly bruised and he claimed he'd lost half a tooth. He also said he felt naked without his glasses.

But he'd told Marco that what worried him most was the feeling that he might have become a victim of *Goldman's Syndrome by Proxy*.

Served him right. Marco was still hacked off about being set up as the first victim of Josh's new syndrome – especially if that was the *only* reason Josh had come to Glasto.

It seemed that Goldman's Syndrome was when you lived among insane people and convinced yourself that you were also becoming insane. Or psychiatrically disadvantaged, as Josh put it.

Goldman's Syndrome *by Proxy,* apparently, was when you convinced one of your friends who was absolutely normal that *he* was becoming insane.

'What are the symptoms?' Marco had asked, hoping they were shatteringly unpleasant.

'I'd rather not talk about it at the present time,' Josh had said sniffily. 'I may have to consult my father.'

'Maybe *I* should consult your dad,' Marco said now, supporting his bag of chips with his bandaged hand. 'Be a change to talk to a proper psychiatrist.'

Josh looked shocked. 'But you're my—'

'Only patient, yeah.'

'That's not *entirely* true...'

'Yes, it is. Somebody would have to be *really* insane to consult you.'

Josh's eyes narrowed as he tried to work out whether this was a *major* insult.

Marco sighed. 'All right, tell me what happened to convince you you'd got...you know...'

'Goldman's Syndrome by Proxy?'

'Whatever. Why don't you tell us *all* what you saw.'

'No way.'

'It won't go out of this room.' Marco had noticed that everybody was listening. Including Granny Goldman and...*the Tenth Person in the room*, who had not yet spoken. 'The Watchers of Avalon are very discreet.'

'Definitely not,' Josh snapped.

'So, was it *before* you begged Jasper for mercy and tried to blame it all on me, or—?'

'I did *not*—'

'Was it before you couldn't find the will power to walk out of the circ—?'

'*All right.*' Josh crumpled up his chip paper. 'I'll tell you. It was just before all *these* guys...' Josh waved a hand around the room. '...burst in and grabbed you and took that pointed rock off you. I mean, they were going to be too late, weren't they? You'd gone completely berserk, Marco. You were determined to maim Coombes. I could give you the psychiatric term for your mental state, but—'

'Berserk's close enough,' Marco said.

'And then something stopped you. It was as if *something* had come between you and...him.'

'Oh,' Marco said.

'Didn't you see it?'

'No. I felt...I'm not sure what I felt, but it was weird. Anyway, never mind.'

Stuffed again. Marco *definitely* didn't want to talk about this.

At least, not in front of the *Tenth Person in the room.*

'You didn't see *anything*?' Josh said.

'No, suddenly, I just didn't want to go on with it, all right?' Marco looked closely at Josh and decided attack could be the best defence. 'You mean *you*...saw...something?'

'I...' Josh coughed lightly. 'No. Didn't see a thing. Absolutely nothing. That is... Look, it was a hallucination, all right? It's not uncommon during a high-stress situation. And the light was bad. You turn your head suddenly, and you think you see something like a...a...'

'What?'

'Monk,' Josh said.

Across the room, Rosa gasped.

'But I didn't,' Josh said. 'It was a hallucination, okay?'

'Right,' Marco said.

'Due to stress. And bad light.'

'Absolutely.'

'Or possible Goldman's Syndrome by Proxy,' Josh said. 'I'll need to think about it.'

* * *

Just a few hours after it was over, it could almost have been a dream.

The whole thing – the real, the bizarre and the unearthly – all fading into one another like clouds at sunset.

Could people today really be a part of something that had begun well over a thousand years ago? Was it, as Eleri kept insisting, really *still going on*? And was this, as Woolly kept saying, because of the strange magnetic powers of the place? The powers that were Avalon beneath Glastonbury, where you didn't even have to know much about it to be drawn under the spell of the past. Just like Jasper Coombes whose hatred of the Avalon side of Glastonbury had sucked him into a channel of evil that went all the way back to Mordred.

In the end, it had been Rosa's dad, Big Dave, who'd grabbed Jasper, stopping him getting away as easily as Shane and Jezza had.

Big Dave, stalking the streets in search of Rosa, had been accosted by Grandma Goldman, demanding to know where the police station was. Dave had identified himself as a former cop and asked if he could help.

'Well, there was no time to waste,' Grandma Goldman said now. 'And he looked more like a real policeman than *some* of the specimens you find in uniform these days.'

She'd left nearly half her chips because she said she needed to keep her waistline trim if she was to splatter Andrea Horowitz all over the court, in next week's finals of the Torquay Tennis Club senior ladies' singles.

'Anyway, I explained the situation as best I could, and Mr. Wilcox agreed to come with me. He said he'd been told there was a pagan temple in the vicinity, where people with tattoos met to carry out unspeakable rites. Of course we didn't find the entrance, and I was starting to feel embarrassed...just as you all arrived with Mr. Woolaston, knowing *exactly* where to go.'

Mr. Woolaston had finished *his* chips, no problem.

He was sitting next to Nancy, opposite Marco, and occasionally their eyes would meet and Marco would grin and Woolly would wink and glance at the *Tenth Person*, who never returned any of his glances, just stared and stared at the amber light through one of the long windows, as if in some kind of trance.

Marco still wasn't sure how they'd brought Woolly out of *his* hypnotic state, although he gathered Eleri had finally managed to hypnotize him with his own pendulum, letting it swing in front of his eyes, like stage-hypnotists did with a watch on a chain. It was pretty appropriate, and it had worked. She'd taken him back to his previous hypnosis and deleted it, like removing a virus from a computer.

Woolly had come round as if from a long sleep. While he was still in a trance, Eleri had told him he'd feel totally refreshed, his mind clearer than the river, clearer than Chalice Well, his dowsing skills fully restored.

Ready for action. It had taken him less than fifteen minutes to find the Blade of Mordred. Textbook stuff, apparently. He'd put the rusty stud from the sword's handle into his sampler-pendulum, which was perspex and came apart, so you could place your specimen inside.

Then they'd got out the large-scale map of the Isle of Avalon and Woolly had dangled the pendulum over it on its chain with a pencil in his other hand, sliding the pencil down the map until the pendulum had started to spin, drawing a line across the map at that point. Then he'd followed the same procedure horizontally until the pendulum again told him to stop. So where the two lines crossed...that had to be where they could find the rest of the sword.

When they'd seen what was marked by the pencilled cross, they'd all looked at one another.

'The old reservoir,' Woolly said. 'Disused for years. And as close to the base of the Tor as you can get. Not the first time the place has been used for magical purposes.'

Woolly looked at Diane and Diane shuddered. There was obviously some history here but now, it seemed, was not the time to go into it.

'So we dashed straight over,' Woolly said, 'and there was Gloria wandering about the hillside with Big Dave.'

Big Dave was probably still at the police station. He'd gone storming into the circle and ended up physically dragging Jasper Coombes out of it. Dave clearly hadn't had a problem with the magical barrier – or maybe you had to be inside the circle for a while before that kicked in.

Or maybe being a priest had given Big Dave extra *oomph*.

Whatever, he'd got in and he'd got out. And he'd said he didn't care how long it took him but, one way or another, he was going to see Jasper taken off the streets and banged up in some young offenders' slammer.

Sam didn't think this was going to be easy. Forensic scientists were examining the remains of Mr. Montague's cottage for evidence that the fire had been started deliberately. Although Mr. Montague was recovering in hospital, apparently he was very confused about what had happened to put him there.

'Always a problem in Glasto,' Sam said, 'You imagine standing up in court, telling a jury about the legend of the Blade of Mordred? And, of course, with Cromwell gone... and the sword gone, too.'

Woolly had taken the sword and buried it somewhere suggested by Eleri. And, oh yeah, Roger Cromwell had disappeared. In fact there was no proof that Roger Cromwell had ever been there at all.

Marco still wasn't sure to what extent Cromwell and the Glasties had been working together. Sam had suggested that Cromwell had simply used their greed for money and their obsession with getting rid of the Avalonians to further his own dark ambitions. Some of the Glasties might be crooks, Sam said, but they weren't killers.

Cromwell was the real would-be murderer but, once again, he'd probably escaped justice. Cromwell himself had become a misty, almost legendary figure. Marco remembered the first time he'd seen the guy, at the foot of the Tor. It had seemed as if he'd faded out of the hill, like Gwyn ap Nudd himself. And in this latest episode, none of them seemed to have seen him at all...only heard his voice.

Creepy.

Or maybe that was just how he wanted you to feel.

'He won't forget, though,' Eleri said, 'and he won't simply walk away.'

There was a growl from Woolly.

'He better not walk anywhere near me, that's all...'cause I ain't gonner forget neither.' He sighed. 'Not that I ain't been a fool, going to that Murchison and everything.' He turned to Nancy. 'First time I ever went behind your back, girl. And it'll be the last.'

Nancy blushed. At least, she *might* have blushed; it was hard to tell with all the new make-up she'd slapped on.

Sam stood up and tossed his chip paper into the vast baronial fireplace.

'And then there's Rex Arturus,' he said. 'What happens when Rex and his dad turn up for real?'

'You'll have to tell them the truth,' Grandma Goldman said. 'And if the boy does come, at least he'll be safe here.' She smiled. 'Thanks to my grandson, Joshua.'

Josh looked faintly sick with embarrassment. Marco decided Gloria was a clever person who knew a lot more about Josh's psychological make-up than Josh thought she did.

'But, imagine if the real Rex *had* come,' he said. 'And they'd kidnapped him and taken him into the temple to be ritually slaughtered?'

Sam nodded.

'Nobody would ever have known what had happened to him. His body would have been disposed of in some forgotten passage of the labyrinth, the roof collapsed to bury it. And because he was the son of one of the richest businessmen in the world, *everybody* would've suffered. The Glasties wouldn't have got their new factory...in fact nobody in their right mind would want to set up a major factory here ever again.'

And the Avalonians, with their weird beliefs, would probably have been blamed for Rex's disappearance, Marco thought. And the whole reputation of Glastonbury would have been blackened, just like it had been after the hanging of Abbot Whiting.

'If they do come,' Sam said, 'like Mrs. Goldman says,

I reckon we'll just have to tell them the truth. They won't get it from the Glastie *Guardian*.'

'Then we watch them go speeding off to Cornwall,' Woolly said, with his old smile.

Diane smiled too, a bit ruefully. 'And to think they might have bought this place.'

Gloria spun round. '*What?*'

'I didn't really *want* them to buy it, but...'

'This place? You were going to sell this magnificent house to these computer people?'

'Bits keep falling off it,' Diane said, 'and we can't afford to put them back.'

'But it's part of your heritage. And, more importantly, it's *the headquarters of the Watchers of Avalon!*'

'Oh, well I'm sure we could—'

'How much would you need to do the necessary repairs?' Gloria demanded.

'A lot.'

'In that case...' Gloria looked thoughtful. 'Have you ever thought of making it pay for itself? What I'm thinking of is a business venture based on Bowermead. Perhaps a kind of New Age hotel with a wonderful spiritual atmosphere and acres of grounds...and views of the Tor, of course. After all, there are thousands of people like me – ladies of a certain age – who would love to discover their inner selves...only they like their outer selves to be catered for, too.'

Sam looked doubtful.

'Wouldn't like it to be a fancy hotel for rich people. That's not what Glasto's about. Posh banquets and that.'

'They won't want *banquets*, Samuel,' Grandma Goldman laughed. 'These people are all *on diets*. They expect *frugal*.

They expect *vegetarian*. They would simply prefer it in a situation of some...opulence.'

'We *could* do it, Sam.' Diane had drifted over. 'If we had the money to start things off...'

Grandma Goldman smiled. 'Not *necessarily* a problem,' she said. '*I* have money. What am I going to do with it? Leave it to Joshua? And I know several other really quite nice people who also have money. And I like this town – more and more. And Joshua could come and stay during the holidays...'

Marco saw Josh sitting up in horror, catching his bruised wrist on the arm of his chair, jamming his other fist into his mouth to stifle an objection.

Marco smiled.

Later, he found himself standing with Woolly and the *Tenth Person* on the edge of the great lawn, looking down to the lights of Glasto and the Tor sitting up like a big guard-dog on the edge of the town.

'Look, Mum,' Marco said, 'I didn't *want* to tell you a bunch of lies, only...'

He dried up. There was nothing to be said.

He was as good as dead.

Outside the reservoir, Mum had hugged him more fiercely than he could ever remember her doing when he was little. He'd felt her trembling, and afterwards one side of his face had been all damp. But he'd been so hyped-up and stressed-out that he couldn't be sure, until they were back at Bowermead, that she hadn't been just another hallucination.

Well, of course he was glad to see her. But he was also

scared of what was going to happen. The way she'd just sat there, on the edge of the circle, eating about two chips and saying nothing. Just taking it all in.

It wasn't like her. Not like her *at all*. Sitting on the edge of things...Mum did not do that. Ever. Mum was an *at-the-centre-of-it* kind of person.

'Alison,' Woolly said. 'Look, I know there's a lot of issues to be resolved. Relationships don't repair that easy after fifteen years. Could take all night. All tomorrow. Maybe longer. Maybe a lot longer.'

'Shut up, Dad,' Mum said softly. 'It's not your fault.'

Woolly blinked hard.

'None of it,' Mum said.

'I don't understand,' Woolly said.

'And I can't tell you,' Mum said. 'Not yet. But I had to get away and stay away...and it's *not your fault.*'

Woolly stared at her and then he let out a big, *sobby* kind of breath and turned away and gazed at the Tor which, as usual, seemed to be holding the last of the light around it. Then he turned to Marco.

'It was your mum got me out of it, dude. Out of the 'fluence. You ready for this...' Woolly stood up straight and pulled in a big breath. *'The mayor's an old crook and I wouldn't trust him to open a school fête without nicking stuff from the bran tub.* How's that?'

Marco smiled. He looked at his mum, and there were tears in her eyes. He thought of her and Dad and how things used to be, and his smile went away.

'I don't understand either,' he said.

'I thought I could run away from it,' Mum said. 'I thought I *had* to run away from it. I thought it would all be okay if

I just stayed away from Glastonbury...from...Avalon.' She turned to Woolly. 'I should've stayed here and dealt with it. Or at least come back.'

Dealt with it? Dealt with what? Being a dowser? Being psychic? *What?*

'And now,' Mum said, 'I've just exposed my kid to...to the consequences.'

Marco was getting that old *more than here* feeling. He'd become aware of a triangle of moving lights over the Tor. They were greenish and they just kind of hovered. It could be...it actually *could* be. Not that it mattered that much at the moment.

He felt a hand on his arm and turned to find Rosa there, saw Mum smiling at her. Gratefully, Marco thought. As if they shared some secret. Something he didn't know about and Woolly didn't either...

'Your friend Rosa and I have had a chat,' Mum said. 'She's...explained a few things. About what's been happening.' Her face softened. 'Marco, love, it's okay. I'm not going to take you away.'

Marco's heart leaped.

'*Ever?*'

'I *meant* until the end of the holidays,' Mum said.

Woolly said, 'On the other hand...'

'Yeah, I know...' Mum shook her head slowly. 'I know what you're saying, Dad. There's part of him I won't ever be able to take away now, and that's a big responsibility for all of us. Because he...he's become something I never wanted him to have to be...'

Out of the corner of an eye, Marco watched the UFO hovering over the Tor.

'Rosa too, I suppose,' Mum said. And he knew she was thinking, *Heaven help her.*

'Avalonians?' he mumbled. 'Is that what you mean?'

He saw Mum shudder, like some wild electricity had suddenly bolted through her body, and he knew that all this was far from over. That maybe it had only just begun.

When he looked again, the UFO had vanished, the way UFOs did.

Discover Marco's first mystical experiences
in Glastonbury...

Marco's Pendulum

When Marco is dumped in Glastonbury for the summer
with his weird hippy grandparents – who he's never even
met before – he discovers a town steeped in myth and
legend. He thinks it's all rubbish at first, until his
granddad gives him a pendulum and teaches him the
ancient art of dowsing. Then strange, disturbing things
really start to happen...

Together with Rosa, another newcomer to Glastonbury,
Marco discovers a terrible secret that's been buried for
centuries. And as dark forces gather over the town, its
evil looks set to be unleashed.

Mysterious, scary and utterly compelling, *Marco's
Pendulum* is a powerful story about the magic found in
real places.

ISBN 9780746067604
£6.99

For more powerful and mysterious tales
log on to
www.fiction.usborne.com